BLACK LIGHT

About the author

K. A. Bedford ekes out a precarious existence in the radiation-blasted wastelands north of what's left of Perth, Western Australia. He is the author of the Aurealis Award-winning novel, *Time Machines Repaired While-U-Wait* (also shortlisted for the Philip K. Dick Award) and numerous other top, cracking reads, all of which make ideal gifts for all occasions <nodding very seriously>.

BLACK
LIGHT

K.A. BEDFORD

FREMANTLE PRESS

This book is for Georgia

1

May, 192—

The ambulance raced through the narrow city streets.

My Aunt Julia, unconscious in the back, looked fragile, even frail. I sat next to her stretcher, holding a wooden spoon in her mouth, as the driver had instructed me, to prevent her swallowing her tongue in the event of another seizure. I had not seen my aunt in years. I knew she was now only in her fifties, but lying there in the back of the speeding ambulance, she appeared withered with age, and too pale.

I sat by her side for the long drive from Maylands Airport to Perth Public Hospital. The ambulance jinked and swerved as the driver tried to get us through the afternoon traffic. There were no windows in the back of the ambulance, but I could hear the driver swearing at motorcars, buggies and carts, even people on horseback, all of them in his way, going about their tiresome business, keeping us from reaching the help Julia needed.

The driver had told me that Julia had become agitated, even panicked, during the last few legs of her flight, and that, not long before landing, she had fallen unconscious after suffering "some sort of fit" as the aircraft, a converted Vimy heavy bomber, came rattling in to land.

"A fit? Julia has no history of that sort of thing," I had said. But then, what did I know? Twelve years had passed. Anything might have happened to her in that time. The Julia I remembered from my old life in England had been lively, funny, never unwell for a single day of her life. I held her cold and clammy hand, and thought that if she was so unwell, had it been wise to undertake this epic journey — all of those consecutive flights! — to reach me?

Julia and I, before our falling out, had been close, great friends. She was the only one in my family, other than perhaps my mother, who understood me, or at least accepted me the way I was, without question. My father, by contrast, had always been formal and serious, as if he'd been memorialised into a suitably grave statue even while still alive. He had been a pillar of the English Establishment, and I, his only child, a profound disappointment.

The ambulance arrived at the hospital. Rutherford, following behind in the Bentley, pulled up nearby. He joined me in the waiting room, pulling off his leather driving gloves. "Is there any news?"

I filled him in. He nodded, rubbed at his face, but said nothing. We managed to find seats and waited. I was struck by the noise of the place. Every hospital I had ever visited had the noisiest waiting areas and wards, despite the large signs throughout urging everyone to keep quiet. We were surrounded by family members, mostly mothers and wives, worried sick about loved ones; there were a great many men injured, perhaps in the course of their work, and just as many lively young children, generally little boys, who had taken one too many foolish backyard risks. It seemed children could sense the urgency and alarm hanging thick in the air. I was sympathetic. Many of the women looked exhausted beyond words. They had done their bit: they'd managed to get their husband or child here in one piece; the rest was up to the doctors. It reminded me of the night my father died, and the long trip from the family estate to the hospital, with Father so still and grey in the back of the car, and my husband Antony driving like a demon along those winding, narrow roads, desperate to get Father to the hospital in time.

Rutherford cleared his throat; he indicated the approaching doctor, a young, tired-looking man in a white coat with bad scarring on his left hand that may have come from War service. "Mrs Black?"

I went over to him. "I'm Mrs Black. How is she?"

"Can we just move over here?"

"Of course, Doctor."

"I'm Dr Mendes."

"Good evening, Doctor." Rutherford had moved to stand behind me, offering his support.

"Are you Miss Templesmith's next-of-kin?" He had a clip-board, making notes.

"I am, yes. Julia is my aunt, on my father's side."

Mendes nodded. "I see," and made a note.

"Can you tell me anything?"

He checked his notes. "Miss Templesmith has suffered what appears to be a mild attack of epilepsy. Does she have a history of—?"

"No, not at all," I said. "Will she be all right?"

"It's possible she'll have recurring attacks," Dr Mendes said. "There are some fairly crude medicines we can prescribe…"

I knew about such drugs. The worst was bromide, now something of an old-fashioned treatment. I dreaded the thought of Julia being given that. Such medications amounted to sedating one's brain into a state of living death. "I see. Is there anything else that might help?"

"A country rest-cure couldn't hurt. Somewhere quiet and peaceful. Good food, pleasant scenery, free from upsets and disturbances. Things like that would be a start. I don't think it would eliminate the chance of further attacks, but—"

I held up a hand. "I know the perfect place, Doctor." I explained about my home in Pelican River.

"Sounds ideal," he said. "We'd like to keep Miss Templesmith in for a few days' observation before we can release her, of course."

"Very well, Doctor. Of course. When would be a good time to return?"

"Visiting hours close at eight. Perhaps after seven this evening would be best. Just ask when you arrive."

I nodded, thanked the doctor for his time, and left, Rutherford following. It was now approaching five in the afternoon. I would need a hotel.

*

Outside the hospital's Casualty department, with its noise and odours, the world looked bleak. The approaching storm front was almost upon us. Across the street loomed St Mary's Cathedral, impressive and as ancient as anything could be in this young city, all flying buttresses, towering spires and stained glass, manicured grounds, and a modest graveyard. It was not something I wanted to see at this point. Everything seemed more than a little ominous. Things happened, I believed, because they were caused. I had always been an empiricist, and did not believe in coincidences. Aunt Julia, by contrast, believed very much in them, and ascribed to them great significance.

Rutherford dropped me off at the Savoy Hotel, on Hay Street.

In my room, I could not relax. Thoughts of family and mystery plagued me. I missed my late husband Antony still, all these years later. I wore his gold signet ring on my right hand. He had worn it on the pinky finger of his left hand; on me it was so large that I had to wear it on my right middle-finger, and even then it was loose. I fidgeted with it when nervous. Sometimes I fancied I could smell him, as if he were in the room with me, and I could talk to him. It was comforting. He and I had always been able to talk. Far more than any other thing that we did or did not have in common, we had always talked. We'd been great friends as well as lovers. I had looked forward to a lifetime together with him, to having a sprawling family of unconventional children.

Soon the sweet-smelling rain came, pouring down from the dark cloud hanging over the city. I stood out on the balcony, getting wet, allowing myself time to enjoy the feel of the cool rain on my face and hands, which reminded me of better days. It had rained the day I met him, in one of Father's shooting parties in the wood behind the manor. Antony had been a dashing young man, dark and full of the world, with knowing eyes but a cheeky smile. He had taken one look at me, in my "mannish" clothes and short hair and no makeup, and he smiled with great charm, saying, "You, my lady, are destined, to be my wife." I mocked his cockiness. Father, surprised out of his wits, said, "Good God, Antony, you can tell there's a woman in amongst all that?" Antony smiled at me, saying, "Oh yes indeed, Sir Gustav. Yes indeed." Naturally, I hated him with great vigour, and continued hating him for a long, entertaining time after that.

Rutherford knocked quietly at my door at a quarter to seven, looking crisp and refreshed. It was time to go. I sent him to fetch the car. The streets were almost deserted, the entire city closed for business.

*

Aunt Julia was in a ward containing a dozen other patients, whose bedside tables were decorated with get-well messages and irregular vases that held cheerful floral arrangements. A severe matron monitored the situation from a formidable desk. Tired young nurses in heavy uniforms and large starched hat contraptions scurried about, attending to their patients' never-ending needs. The air here reeked of antiseptic, pungent flowers, and something unpleasant but nameless.

Julia was sitting up in bed, looking weak and confused. Seeing me, she brightened. "Ruth!" she said, trying not to shout. Unlike the Casualty department, this ward was aggressively quiet. No-one would dare emit anything as gauche as a noise with Matron glaring from her desk.

I had stopped at the shop downstairs and obtained some grapes and boiled sweets for Julia, which seemed to bemuse her. "Oh dear, I am an invalid, aren't I?" She smiled, saying this, and helped herself to a grape or two as we went through the greetings. She was very taken with Rutherford, who did not sit, despite being offered a chair. He stood at the end of the bed, hands crossed behind him in the "at-ease" position, gloves and hat under his left arm, looking efficient. I could tell Julia would have liked to chat with him about the sheer impossibility of looking after her wayward niece, but she was more concerned about other matters.

"I received your telegram, Julia. What's—?" I produced the crumpled telegram and showed it to her. I had received it four days earlier. Julia had sent it from Kuala Lumpur, one of the last stops on her epic series of flights out here from Britain. Julia's telegram read:

RUTH—YOUR LIFE IN DANGER STOP COMING TO SEE YOU STOP BE CAREFUL STOP WITH YOU SOON STOP LOVE JULIA

"Yes, yes, of course. I've been so confused, with all the…all this fuss. Do you know what these doctors are telling me, Ruth? They're telling me I have *epilepsy*, for goodness' sake! What rot!"

Which seemed to rule out the disturbing thought that she had a history of the condition that she'd kept secret. I felt that she would have told me, in these circumstances, if there had been such a history. The condition was too alarming to lie about it. "The doctor in Casualty told me you'd collapsed during the final part of the flight," I said.

Julia looked puzzled, and touched her forehead. "All I remember, I remember feeling anxious, and somewhat ill—nasty turbulence, they said—and I was so worried about you. I set out two months ago, and all that time this anxiety has only grown worse. It was the most frightful trip you could imagine. I couldn't keep any food down, so I've been terribly hungry—thank you so much for the grapes, I must say, just the thing!—and all I could focus on was that I simply had to tell you about my dreams—"

"What did you mean, 'Your life in danger'?"

Julia, about to eat a grape, nodded, and then stopped. "I have been having the most frightful dreams, Ruth. Frightful! Something was happening to you—or possibly someone else, I couldn't quite be sure, not at first. Something terrible. In the later dreams, which I started having *en route*, I saw someone trying to kill you, someone with the most enormous hands—"

Julia had always claimed to have "the Sight", as she called it.

"Surely, though," I said, sceptical, "this is just the sort of nonsense we all get in dreams. It doesn't mean anything."

"I entirely disagree, Ruth. I know the difference between ordinary, common or garden dreams, and these...these *experiences*, that I've been having. You see, in these dreams, I'm looking out through the eyes of this person, and he's stalking through your house, looking for you, looking through your papers, that sort of thing, and then he comes to your bedroom, and you're asleep and..." She was getting upset, and apologised. Her strength was fading, now that she'd at last unburdened herself of her message.

"How did you know it was my house? You've never seen my house."

She sniffled. "I just knew it was your house, the way you know things in dreams. It looked very nice, too. Just the way I'd always imagined it."

I glanced at Rutherford, who also looked minutely disturbed. He must be worried sick, I thought.

I said to Julia, who now was looking like she would fall asleep at any moment, "You're coming to stay with me, in Pelican River, at least for a while. I have everything laid on, an excellent cook, and the town itself is charming. Right on the sea."

She looked, despite the weariness, astonished, and further chagrined at said astonishment. "Are you sure that's a good idea, Ruth?"

"How do you mean?"

"Your house. That town." She stared at me, as if it was blindingly obvious.

"Yes. My home. Very nice, comfortable, splendid view of the water—"

"Quite. Of course. But don't you see, dear. These visions are warning me—warning *you*—about your house! The very last thing you should be thinking is returning there, let alone with me."

I was speechless for a moment. Rutherford stepped in. "If I may be so bold, Miss Templesmith, I served with distinction in the War. I still have my service revolver. Anyone wanting to enter that house with murder on his mind will first have to contend with me."

Julia stared at him for a moment. He stood there, next to me, the image of the stalwart and resolute English soldier he had once been. She looked at me, then back at Rutherford, who glanced at me now, as if worried that he'd overstepped the bounds of propriety. Julia said to me, "It would appear I have little choice."

"Of course you have a choice, Julia. But consider: your evidence for this belief, that my life is in danger from someone breaking into my house one night, is your dreams and visions. You don't know for certain that it will happen."

"My dreams often do come to pass."

"Yes, and equally often do not come to pass. You must admit that."

"Why can you not simply agree to move into a hotel for the duration?"

"Yes, and for how long? How long would I have to stay in this hotel? A week? A month? A year? You don't know, from what you saw in your dreams, exactly when this attack is meant to happen. It could be tomorrow. It could be years from now."

"Yes, there is that," Julia said, and disconsolately munched a grape.

"Moreover," I went on, pressing my point, "what's to say that the, let's say 'the killer', would not simply find me wherever I went? It could be that the location in your dreams is beside the point, and that the salient point is that it is me on the receiving end."

"That is true, I must admit," Julia allowed.

"I could go to the South Pole, and it wouldn't matter. If he wants me dead, he'll—"

"Yes, yes, your point is made, dear Ruth. No need to beat me about the head and shoulders with your argument."

"So what do you say? I have no plans to move out of my own home. And if it's good enough for me to stay there..."

"You really think it would be safe?"

"Rutherford has never failed me."

Rutherford blushed lightly on hearing this.

"I don't know. I think you're mad, but if you think it would be all right..."

"I could have a word with the local police, if you like. They could increase their patrols." It would keep them from their fishing and crabbing trips, so they would not be pleased about it, but they might possibly do it.

Julia sagged visibly. "Very well, then. I am persuaded. I have always loved the seaside."

"Then it's settled," I said.

2

In the two days of her stay at the hospital, Julia and I spoke at length each night, about home, family—and those troubling visions. Feeling foolish, I began to see that perhaps these were not dreams but something more powerful, and more focused. The more Julia described specific items and rooms of my house, the more I felt unsettled. In my hotel room those nights, it took longer than usual for sleep to come for me, and, when it did, it was neither restful nor satisfying. I woke late in the mornings and felt out of sorts. My own dreams offered no insights; indeed, I could remember nothing about them, other than a jarring sense of confusion. Rutherford, by contrast, informed me that he was sleeping very well indeed. The constant traffic outside, with its rattling engines and clopping hooves, shot through with yelling newsboys, did not bother him; he said he had slept through much worse during the War.

What was I to make of Julia's very specific visions? The more she described, the more it did indeed sound like my house. Her description of the intruder thoroughly and professionally rifling through my desk, for example, was chilling. I quizzed her as hard as I dared, considering her condition, on the specific items on the desk and in the drawers, and she was correct eight times out of ten. Her description of the intruder's attempt on my life was unnerving; so detailed, so confident, it was as though Julia was not quite herself as she described the events; it was as if she were accessing the mind of the intruder himself from some future point. I had never heard of anyone being able to recall things seen in even particularly strange or noteworthy dreams with such cool clarity of detail and intent. Not even the accounts described in volumes by Freud, whose work I did not entirely believe, matched these for sheer chilling detail. When I asked her to stop, when I could hear no more of such things, Julia blinked a few times, glanced at me as if seeing me for the first time, and would say, "Oh my goodness! Ruth! Whatever's the matter?"

What was the matter was the prospect of "seeing" one's own death described in such a detached manner, in a voice which, though it came from my Aunt Julia, held no trace of her personality. Even Rutherford looked pale on hearing these accounts. He would no doubt be wondering why he did not feature prominently, dealing with the intruder's threat long before he could reach my bedroom.

I also asked her more pointed questions about her collapse. In the daylight hours before my nightly visits to the hospital, I had taken the opportunity to consult with a number of doctors about epilepsy, as I tried to find out as much as I could about its symptoms, origins, and alternative treatments. The more Julia told me about her "fits" the less they sounded like "common or garden" *grands mal* epileptic seizures, and the more it sounded—and this will seem fanciful—like a human brain trying but failing to wrestle with some greater "force". I only considered such an unlikely notion because of Julia's well-known but oft-ridiculed psychic access to what she had always called "the other bits of reality". I was wondering if one of these "other" bits of reality was endeavouring to force its way into this world—and if it had succeeded, taking root in a quiet part of Julia's brain, away from her conscious perception. Such things, I had read, were not unknown, if one consulted the right history books.

Once we reached Pelican River, I planned to seek out my dear friend Gordon Duncombe, for his opinion on the matter. Gordon had manifold talents with electrical and mechanical engineering and had also been known to dabble a little with rather more "unorthodox" ways of influencing the world around him. One hesitated to describe him as an "amateur magician", with his precious old books and fussy manner, but perhaps that's, at least in part, what he was.

My greatest concern was for Julia herself. Was I even wise in taking her home? This question gnawed at me during the long and bumpy four-hour ride, listening to loose limestone gravel spraying up from the car's tyres and rattling across its undersides. I knew that if I were to leave Julia to look after herself with the Perth medical community, she would be consigned to a home before she knew it. The first sign of another fit or attack would guarantee her fate. And if she were to describe her visions to a doctor, and that same chilling, detached voice emerged from her mouth, she would also quickly find herself incarcerated. Equally, I did not like the thought of sending her home to England. I could afford to have the best medical minds in Australia come to Pelican River to look at Julia, if the need arose—Antony's life insurance and the modest proceeds from my previous novels saw to that; I was established as a woman of means, and I would look after Julia as best I could, and in the best, most peaceful environment I knew.

And yet, as we passed the sign for Pelican River—a sleepy little fishing town sixty or so miles south of Perth—I did wonder how whatever might be lurking in the back of Julia's brain might feel about arriving in the very house featuring so heavily in those visions. Would this bring forth the events she had foreseen? Was it Julia, or something employing her body, that would steal through the house and kill me? Or—and this was some sort of comfort—was the fact that I had been warned enough to deflect that fate? After all, I could arm myself, both with weapons and with information. It might be possible to determine, for certain, what was going on with Julia, and prevent everything happening.

If only life were that easy, that tidy.

3

Rutherford brought the great vehicle to a stop out the front of my home. He climbed down and came around to help Julia and me disembark. Doing this, he settled into the usual routine, ordering the three other staff about, getting Young Ryan to come and help with the luggage, and asking Sally Hall if she and Vicky Tool had made up a room for Miss Templesmith, as per his telephoned instructions. Sally said they had prepared the Yellow Room, next to mine, thinking that Ma'am would want her relative close by. I greeted everyone, and told them they were doing a fine job, as always. Though I did pause as Ryan went by, and said, "The new hair cream not working out?" He coloured and said, "No, ma'am, sorry, ma'am," and struggled into the house, bearing more luggage than his skinny body looked capable of carrying. I introduced Julia to everyone, and in particular to Sally and Vicky, and instructed them to take the very best care of her. "Aunt Julia's not been well, and is in need of a good pampering."

Julia was staring around her at the house — a modest red-brick two-storey Federation-style property with an extensive verandah all the way around. One of the house's most novel features was the circular windows here and there, like portholes on a ship. "It's bigger than I thought," she said, smiling weakly back at me. She was also staring at the enormous, but very strange-looking, paperbark gums looming around us, their pale, peeling trunks looking as though they had some terrible skin disease. Native birds cawed and squealed and carolled noisily; the breeze carried the salty tang of the sea, and a faint waft from the fish canning factories on the foreshore. Julia, swatting at flies, seemed all at once aware, as she looked at these alien trees and heard those unusual birds, that she was indeed somewhere very different, and very far, from home. I knew she was an inveterate traveller, but she had never come this far, as if to another world.

Rutherford looked at me, concerned, and I could see he was wondering if bringing Julia here was a wise decision. I, too, was having second thoughts about this, but resolved to adhere to my plans. I told him to take the car around to the garage and give it a clean; it was white with gravel dust. "Yes, ma'am, as you say."

At once pleased to be home after the ordeal of travelling to the "big smoke", and yet also concerned at what the future might bring, I went inside. Regardless of all other considerations, I still had a writing deadline, and I meant to beat it. I left Julia in the care of my staff.

In the quiet coolness of the house, with its high ceilings, polished jarrah floors, tasteful but unfashionably minimal furniture, I breathed in the complex aroma of home. I could never describe its exact scent. Part of it was the very air of this region of Western Australia, part was the native-plant pot pourri, part was the fresh smell of a house kept meticulously clean, part was the lingering traces of last night's fire in the big fireplace. There were many elements, and I treasured them all. No house in England would ever smell like this. I remembered the grand, stuffy, echoing manorial homes in the old country, much like my own family's house, with its thirty-two rooms, all of them cramped with too much heavy furniture, maddeningly busy wallpaper, ancient heirloom floor rugs, hunting trophies, sombre portraits of long-dead ancestors looking like they hated the artist and the fuss of having to get all dressed up when they'd much rather be out with the hounds and the horses and all their inbred chums. By contrast, I had determined, this house I bought would be full of air and light; it would never be stuffy, it would be welcoming not intimidating, and comfortable without that cloying, cramped feeling I still remembered and hated from my old life.

Post had accumulated during my absence; nothing that could not wait—mainly bills. The great mahogany clock over the mantel in the drawing room showed it was not quite noon. As if reading my mind, Murray appeared. She smiled politely. "You look starved, ma'am. Can I get you something, just to tide you over 'til lunch?"

"How is Julia doing?"

Murray sighed. "She'll manage, ma'am. Now if I—"

"A sandwich, I think, would suffice. And coffee."

"As you say, ma'am," she said warmly, and left the room. I had recruited Murray, like all my staff (other than Rutherford, who had come with me from Britain), locally. They had taken some time to settle into their roles and duties—all except Rutherford, who had displayed a natural talent for his job that had surprised me.

I joined Julia in the Yellow Room, where she was having a word with Vicky. Before entering, I heard Julia ask, "What on Earth would make a sensible young girl stay in such a place, I ask you!"

I interrupted, knocking pointedly on the door. "Now now, Julia, you mustn't harass my staff like that. Is everything under control, Vicky?"

"Yes, ma'am," she said, not stuttering too much today. I sent her to help Sally.

"Well," Julia said, sitting on the bed as if worried it might eat her. "You appear to have created a very nice little realm in the midst of all this chaos."

"Chaos? What do you mean?" I knew very well what she meant.

"Do those birds ever shut up? And what's all this…" She lacked a word for it but simply waved a hand at the view through the window, which showed extensive natural bushland: gum trees, wattles, grevilleas; it was marvellous, and I had gone to great trouble to preserve as much of it as I could. It was exotic, alien in every respect. When I first arrived, I could not stop looking at it, marvelling at how such unusual plants could possibly survive in such an arid environment. The people who sold me this house had offered to get people in to clear all this "clutter", to make it, "you know, suitable" — whatever that meant. The only concession I had agreed to was to allow a clear area around the garden's perimeter. I found out about this from the land agent when arranging the purchase of the house. He told me the perimeter was in case of bush fire, and I stupidly asked what exactly that might entail. He said, "It's the end of the world, Mrs Black." Feeling foolish, I agreed, and allowed a clear perimeter. Trying to get a lawn to grow on the cleared land, however, was another matter.

I explained to Julia about the bush, that it was something fundamental to the landscape in this country. Julia glanced at me as if to suggest that I was the one with problems in my head. "But it's just so awful! It's so wild and uncontrolled!"

Later, Julia and I sat in the drawing room. She kept looking around the great room. "How do you manage with all this...all this *space* everywhere?"

*

After lunch, I rode my purple Imperial Racer bicycle around to Gordon Duncombe's house. My staff would take care of Julia, and I felt my time could more usefully be spent consulting with Gordon about what had happened. Gordon lived on a small farm on the outskirts of town; he had converted the great barn, its old wood long turned greyish-silver, into a workshop-laboratory. Even before I arrived, his dogs — twelve of them — erupted into a deafening barking frenzy. As I opened the front gate, and wheeled the bicycle inside, the dogs, mutts all, swarmed around me, jumping, barking, wagging their assorted tails. Expecting this, I had brought a small bag of meaty offcuts which I doled out with great care. None of the dogs lunged or made as if to bite me. They accepted the idea that they would have to wait before receiving their treats. Once it was all handed out, the dogs wagged off, going about their own business on the extensive property, and I walked my bicycle up the long gravel drive to the house.

Gordon, who would have heard the dogs, stood waiting on the

front porch, under the verandah. He was in his fifties, a soft sort of man with a slight stoop, as if having trouble bearing the weight of the world. Losing his beloved wife, Alice, several years earlier had left him gutted and broken, much the way I still felt about Antony's loss. Seeing me, he stepped down onto the path and walked down the drive to meet me halfway. He shuffled along, clad as ever in clothes that looked too large for him, including one of his three oft-patched grey cardigans, which he liked to wear because they reminded him of Alice. He had his own way of doing things, and he would not be shifted. Back in the old country, eight years ago, he had cared for Alice night and day for months as she withered away from stomach cancer. After she passed, he sold everything, including his workshop and its contents, and booked himself onto a ship leaving for Western Australia. We had never spoken about what he did during those endless months at sea, but I had the impression that somehow it had been a profound experience for him. Something had happened to him during that voyage. By the time he arrived at Fremantle Harbour, bearing only a small shabby bag containing not even a week's worth of clothes and some toiletries, he had somehow learned to live without Alice, to be his own person.

I wished he would teach me how that was done. I put on a good front, and carried on like a fearless, independent and colourful woman, but I knew I was, as people here would say, "having a lend of everyone". I still wore black, and wore it like a shield, not to keep the world out, but to keep myself in. I still woke up in the mornings thinking that Antony was already up and about, in the kitchen making coffee, or reading the newspaper, or in the bathroom shaving. In bed, almost entirely asleep, I still found myself rolling toward my memory of him, wanting to hold him, to warm me and my cold hands and feet—only to find nothing but empty bed.

I still dared not look at old photographs or the bundles of letters he used to send me from overseas postings, especially during the War.

I had also never cried for him. Never. Secretly, I wondered if there was something wrong with me.

Gordon smiled, "Ruth! What a grand surprise—and here, I've just put the kettle on, too. Coffee?"

I thanked him, and he took my bicycle, as usual, and walked it up under his verandah, where it would be safe if it rained. I followed him inside, careful the dogs didn't bowl me over as they boiled around my legs. I knew they each had names, but I had not yet learned them, even though I heard him talking to these dogs all the time. They kept him busy. He, for his part, kept his home surprisingly tidy and clean. The odour of dog was rarely detected in his modest house, despite the menagerie.

In his kitchen, I watched an elaborate contraption of metal containers, levers, springs, piovoting things made of wood, and gas burners boil the water, percolate the coffee and pour it into separate carefully placed cups, without spilling too much. This was Mark VI of his continuing coffee-machine project—I suspected he would say it was a quest—which had occupied him during much of his life in Pelican River. He had other unlikely contraptions around the house, many of them failed devices that he had stripped for parts to use in newer machines. His plan for a machine that would do the laundry and hang it out to dry on a clothesline that folded out of the back of the thing had never quite worked out, despite great enthusiasm. And then he had large-scale ideas, like his plan to irrigate the vast interior deserts of this country, and thus open up all that land for development. Unfortunately, it also depended on a reliable means of influencing the weather. The idea of simply carving immense canals into the land, taking existing rivers far inland, had occurred to him, and he thought it "had some merit" but there weren't enough moving parts for his taste. He was a man who liked to see lots of things turning, going up and down, making intriguing noises, and to have lots of knobs and dials, even when such ornamentation was not required.

Then there was his Grand Project. As I sipped my black coffee, scalding hot as ever, and as Gordon adjusted a knob on the coffee machine's thermostat, he told me about his latest findings. At length, when he noticed that I was not making the right appreciative noises—and no doubt wishing I was an engineer instead of a novelist—he took me out to his barn, where the beginnings of his great work lay under tarpaulins. He pulled the tarps clear of the basic framework, which was a structure of long steel pipes, almost as large as the barn itself, and there would be a small cabin where two passengers might sit. He showed me huge and intricate drawings illustrating his latest thoughts, and went on about "chronodynamics" in a way that did not seem healthy.

"I'm still having trouble coming up with a good name for it," he said, finishing his coffee, and setting the empty cup in a rack which itself was mounted on a toy train line, and which would, once he activated it, take the cup into the house for refilling. "I feel I can't simply call it 'Time Machine Mark Four', for example. It needs something…something more, you know, catchy, that captures some aspect of how it actually works…" He was looking at me for some germ of inspiration.

I smiled helplessly and finished my coffee. "Chrono-Traveller? The Time Hopper?"

"Hmm," he said, stroking his beard. "Time Hopper isn't too bad, considering. Except the whole craft doesn't hop, as such; it largely stays fixed in one's local frame of reference. In our latest correspondence, Mr Wells said something about inertial transitions and it gave me a bit of an idea…" He peered at his drawings again, and made lots of "hmm" noises. I was looking around at everything. In amongst countless odd bits of hardware and machinery, not much of which was recognisable, were the frankly terrifying Tesla towers Gordon was assembling, and which would, he had explained previously, provide the prodigious power for his time machine. Meanwhile, up in the rafters, I saw three bird nests, a great many elaborate spiderwebs in the upper corners of the barn, and there was a smell of oil, machinery, electricity, and dirt. Gordon had large metal drums containing kerosene, different kinds of oil, a wide variety of paints and glues—and a comprehensive collection of tools, all of them pegged up on the walls of the barn where he could reach them if he needed them, and every tool had a black painted silhouette to which it belonged. No tools were missing; they all looked clean; many gleamed in the dim electric light. It had also long ago occurred to me that everything in this barn was a dreadful fire risk. Just being in there made me anxious. How it would feel once everything was running?

"Listen, Gordon, could we pop back inside? Some things have come up that I'd like to ask you about..."

He glanced up, surprised, "Oh, you should have said. I'm sorry, I didn't mean to drag you out here to show you all this nonsense when you had something on your—"

"It's quite all right, really. I'm glad you're making progress with the time machine. Just promise me this: when you finish it and take it for a test flight, do wear protective clothing of some sort!"

He smiled, a little chagrined. We both remembered the last two times, when he'd managed to get earlier time machine prototypes almost working. No actual time travel took place, but the explosions could be heard for miles around.

Back in his cozy lounge room, I took a seat on the old couch and Gordon sat across from me in his favourite overstuffed brown chair, with its very large rounded arms. No sooner had he sat than two of his dogs appeared and leapt straight into his lap. He yelled, shooing them off, "Come on, you lot, get out of here! We've got company! Yes, that's right. There's someone else in the world apart from you mongrels!" The two dogs stared for a moment, then trotted off, tails high. He looked at me, a little embarrassed. "Sorry about that. What a madhouse!"

I rather liked that it was such a madhouse, to be honest, but I didn't want to tell him that, in case it sounded somehow condescending. I liked that things were always happening here, that there was such a lot of life about. I loved my own home, for its peacefulness, for its grounds and for its view of the distant estuary, but it was a house for quiet contemplation and reflection. Gordon's house, by contrast, was a place for making things happen.

I explained the situation with Julia.

Gordon's manner changed, growing serious and thoughtful. His lounge room, as with much of the small house, was full of jammed bookcases, none of which matched, just like his dogs.

The whole collection looked like something put together over time by someone with limited funds but a great passion for books and knowledge. The shelves, bent and straining, managed to hold some wonderful old books, and not all of them were science and engineering texts. He was soon up on his feet and perusing his shelves, squinting hard because he was too proud to get spectacles, and then he would complain about fierce headaches. This was something we argued about a lot. I knew he would much rather buy a book than something as useful and practical as spectacles. He would rather buy a book than clothes. Most of the time he would rather buy a book than food, too, if it came to that. He managed on sandwiches and crackers and soup, and was generally hardly even aware of food. It was a tedious necessity. I had only seen him sit down and enjoy a good meal for its own sake when I invited him to my home for a friendly dinner; he always had to have a notebook with him, or a technical journal, or a new book open on his lap or next to his plate. And his plates often went cold if inspiration should strike mid-meal. I understood this; I had found that intriguing ideas for stories popped up at all kinds of inopportune moments, including over dinner. While I didn't have a notebook next to my plate, I did have a well-trained memory for things. Gordon and I talked a great deal about creative impulses and what they meant, how they worked. Such conversations inevitably boiled down to Gordon ruminating about the functions of the human brain and how it must work in order to produce the kinds of things it could produce.

He came back into the room, bearing a thick book. "You say she seemed to speak in a different voice, almost, describing things she had never seen, but describing them correctly..."

"Yes. And, of course, killing me."

"Hmm, yes..." Already he was off again, skimming lines of minute text. "How do you feel about hypnosis?"

Surprised, I stared at him. "Pardon?"

"Do you think she'd agree to going under?" He sat in his old chair again, book open in his lap.

"She might..." I really had no way of knowing. I did know she was deeply worried about what might be going on in her head, though I had not discussed with her my darkest, most alarming fears: that something had taken root in her brain, in a place where it would not appear to her consciousness. "I suppose it couldn't hurt," I said.

4

I invited Gordon to join us for dinner that evening.

He laid out the evening meal for his dogs before we left. As usual, he purchased the finest cuts of beef he could afford for them, meat that would grace a table for nobility, while no doubt contemplating a strawberry jam sandwich for himself and perhaps some fortifying tea. It is strange when one finds oneself envying the food of dogs.

I telephoned for Rutherford to come and fetch us, and at length, we left. Rutherford did the honours with my bicycle, gently placing it in the Bentley's immaculate boot, where it looked small in the great space. He greeted Gordon, too, with genuine respect, "Good afternoon, Mr Duncombe. I trust you are well today?"

Gordon, who came from a decidedly working-class back-ground in the English Midlands, had a difficult time dealing with the idea of servants. It never occurred to him simply to speak to them as he would to me, for example—and he had had enough trouble working out how to address me, too, in the beginning, because of the ridiculous class nonsense. He regarded them as some sort of posh automaton, to which one must speak extremely carefully for fear of the thing going on a crazed rampage of destruction. He'd been attempting to deal with this for some years now, and had, lately, decided to try a strategy of simply nodding and repeating back the main greeting. He said, "Afternoon, Rutherford," and looked relieved to have achieved this much. He climbed into the back of the Bentley, still marvelling at the space and appointments of the car, and sat a respectful distance from me. I suspected he would love to talk to Rutherford about the engineering aspects of the car, but I knew that he never would, because who knew what the Rutherford-thing might do in retaliation?

Back home, I informed Murray that there would be another guest for dinner. Gordon would not stay the night even if our discussions ran late. He needed to look after his dogs, who fretted, he said, if he was away from home too long. Murray nodded, said, "Right you are, ma'am," and went back to the kitchen, ready to terrorise poor Ryan, her apprentice, afresh.

I took Gordon inside. Rutherford asked if sir would care for a drink, and Gordon asked for a cup of tea, three teaspoons of sugar, thank you. The same as always. Rutherford disappeared to prepare the drinks. Whilst we waited, I fetched Julia, who had been napping. Waking, seeing me, she smiled. "I say, what a perfectly splendid bed!"

Ah, something that met her approval at last, I thought. "Will you be joining us for dinner, Julia?"

She perked up further. "What's on the menu tonight? Your cook would not say."

I smiled. "Murray is like that, I'm afraid. I don't know, either. Dinner is always a surprise. Murray takes these things very seriously. Dinner must be an event."

Julia looked nonplussed. "But you know how my stomach is, Ruth. There are—"

I knew, of course. One could not help but know about Julia's "delicate" internals. I explained that I had already taken the liberty of briefing Murray on Miss Templesmith's dietary concerns. "All will be well, fear not."

She looked happy for the first time since I had seen her. I thought this would be an opportune moment, and mentioned that I had invited my old friend Gordon Duncombe to dinner as well. Julia liked meeting new people—after all there might be a fortnight's stay at their estates on offer at some point—and brightened considerably. Julia, at least in the old days, spent much of the year staying at a succession of friends' and relatives' estates; she was hardly ever actually home. I explained that Mr Duncombe was out in the drawing room as we spoke, and that he might have some useful thoughts about her condition.

"Is he a medical man?" she asked, climbing out of bed and searching for decent clothing—which Vicky had left folded on the chair.

"Mr Duncombe is something of a Renaissance man, if you will."

"I see," she said, washing her face and hands. "Known him long, have you?"

"We met shortly after I settled here. And no, we're not 'like that'. Gordon is a very good friend. He's also an inventor of things, I might add, and he dabbles a little in magic."

She looked at me in the mirror. "Magic? Rabbits out of the hat stuff, then?"

"Not as such. I mean he dabbles a little in what one might call 'real' magic. As well as his inventions."

"Extraordinary," she said. "These days, I gather, most true magicians work for the government or conduct research at universities."

I was surprised to hear this. I had never known.

"So your Mr Duncombe. He builds things, and dabbles in the other as well? How remarkable! Can he fly?"

I smiled. "Not with magic, no. He *is* attempting to build a time machine, though."

"I say. He could scarcely be more colourful, could he?" she said, amused.

A few minutes later, I had made the introductions. Rutherford hovered nearby offering to fetch things as required. I asked him what time dinner would be tonight. "I believe dinner service will commence at half past six. And no, I do not know what Murray has planned. Discreet study of her shopping lists and ingredients would suggest, perhaps, a roast, but this could merely be one of her ruses."

Gordon was talking to Aunt Julia. "Ruth has told me a great deal about you, Miss Templesmith, if you'll pardon my saying so."

Julia looked amused. "Pardon me for asking, but is that a West Yorkshire accent, Mr Duncombe?"

"Fourth generation, born and bred, as they say. Whereabouts in England are you from, if I might ask?"

I rolled my eyes. Gordon had just "asked for it". Julia started in, probably unable to believe her luck. "Well, and this is a fascinating question, one on which I have spent quite a considerable sum these many years, though I must first preface my remarks by saying that the Templesmith country seat—"

I interrupted. "How's your tea, Gordon? Need a refill?" I glared at Julia, who smirked.

He glanced across at me like a man suddenly aware he is in deep waters without a life-preserver. "Yes, please. Thank you." Rutherford provided the fresh cup almost as soon as Gordon had placed the request.

Aunt Julia wisely adjusted her approach. "Ruth tells me you are building a *time machine*, Mr Duncombe?"

He looked up from his tea, face slightly flushed. "Ah, well. Yes, or rather, trying to, at any rate," he said. "There have been some technical, and possibly conceptual problems, at least so far—"

"Tell Julia how you destroyed your own barn—twice!" I said, teasing gently. Gordon did his best not to be flustered.

"It was the wrong voltage, and in any case, I had no way to know the capacitors were full, now, did I?"

Julia was quite taken by the thought of travelling through time. "I've read Mr Wells' marvellous book, many times. It's one of my favourites. I do admire those hard-working Morlocks, don't you, Mr Duncombe?"

Gordon, looking pleased to find a like-minded soul at last, leaned forward in his seat. "Speaking strictly confidentially, I can let you know that I am in occasional contact with Mr Wells, through the post. He *assures* me that the book is a carefully disguised memoir."

"You are pulling my leg!" she said, amused, watching him over her teacup.

"I should think not, Miss Templesmith," he said, a little nettled.

It was time to intercede. "Julia, I believe Gordon might be able to help with your condition, somewhat."

She looked up, blinking, surprised, at me. "Oh yes. Yes, of course. Mr Duncombe, you are also a medical man?"

Gordon looked concerned, frowning a little, and he took a long draught of his tea. "I have been something of a dilettante in my reading over time, but I could not claim to have studied medicine formally."

"My niece informs me that you are also versed in the..." She looked like she felt awkward about using the term. "In the magical arts. That you 'dabble,' as Ruth put it. Is that quite safe?"

He ran a hand through his thinning hair. "Oh, well, yes, ah, yes. Absolutely. You take all the right precautions, and do everything according to standardised procedures. It's no more dangerous than working in any of the physical sciences, I should say."

I interrupted again. "My Aunt Julia, Gordon, is neglecting to mention her own abilities beyond what one might call the strictly empirical. Isn't that right, Julia?"

She quickly smoothed over any appearance that she was miffed to have her sport spoiled, and said to Gordon, "Since I was a girl, I have been able to see *other* parts of reality, Mr Duncombe. Parts not readily apparent to other people."

"Indeed?" he said. "What do you see?"

Julia, surprised out of her wits, stopped and stared at him. All her life she had been accustomed to either lack of interest or outright scepticism or condescending comments of "Of course you do, dear..." No-one in her life had simply asked her, straight out, what she could see. At length, I saw she looked very different. She looked, for her, vulnerable. When she spoke, her voice lacked its usual brisk humorous tone. "Well," she said. "I see all sorts of things. I..."

I prompted her. "Tell Gordon about your dreams."

"Ah, yes, yes of course," she said, looking at me with relief. To Gordon she explained about how, shortly before she embarked on her epic journey out to Australia, she had begun having dreams "qualitatively different" from the colourful dreams that were her normal experience. And when Gordon gently prompted her to describe these dreams, he saw, as I had in the hospital, the change stealing over her. She sat differently. Her voice dropped into a flat, deep—and very sad—monotone. Her eyes stared at things only visible from inside her mind. Gordon listened, transfixed, to the narrative as the voice described entering my house without difficulty, without alerting either Rutherford or Young Ryan, and then the business-like search through my post, my modest collection of heirlooms, and then into my study upstairs where the voice described a thorough, professional investigation of my desk's contents without any interest in the stack of manuscript pages piled next to my faithful Imperial typewriter. At last, the intruder made his way, without hesitation or searching, to my bedroom, where he negotiated the door without effort, and then...

I interrupted, shaking Julia's shoulder vigorously. She seemed to wake as if from a deep sleep and glanced about at our horrified faces. "Oh dear," she said, upset, "it happened again, didn't it?"

"How is your head feeling now?" Gordon asked, without any of his usual politeness.

She touched her head delicately. "It's rather sore, I must say. I feel somewhat...weak, I'm dreadfully sorry. Perhaps I should go and lie down."

I did my best to reassure her that all was well, despite her insistence that things were clearly not. I asked Rutherford to fetch a stiff drink for her, and she did not, unusually for her, protest.

"Gordon, any thoughts?" I asked.

After Rutherford retreated, Gordon looked concerned, but also confused. "There are many worrying aspects, I must say. The ability of whomever it is to move through the house—and it's clearly this house, no question—without making a sound is most troubling. Particularly since the outer doors are locked, as a matter of course..."

Julia was surprised. "You lock your doors?" Back home, village life was still such that locks were rarely needed. Here, things were different.

"It's because of the elves," I began, and Gordon nodded, crossing himself discreetly.

Julia was baffled. "Elves? There aren't any elves left. They died out over a thousand years ago, everyone knows that."

"It's rather a long story, Julia. But they are a problem, sometimes breaking into houses, looking to steal food."

She was surprised—again. "You cannot be serious, Ruth!"

"If we might return to the matter at hand," I said.

Gordon said, "Miss Templesmith, I believe it might be helpful to—"

"How can you possibly have *elves* here, I ask you. You know as well as I do how far away from home this is, we're at the end of the world, for goodness' sake. We could not be further away and remain on this planet!"

"Miss Templesmith," Gordon said, resorting to a tone a shade stronger than was perhaps called for. "I would be only too pleased to discuss with you the paradoxical problem of the elves. For now, I'm trying to help you with your concerns. Is that understood?"

She had the grace to look startled at his manner. "I say…Mr Duncombe!"

"I apologise, of course, Miss Templesmith, but I feel we ought to focus—"

I said, "Julia, listen to him. He has an idea."

Gordon explained his notion of hypnosis. This wasn't a form of any kind of magic. Indeed, he had only learned about it after reading Sigmund Freud's texts on psychoanalysis; Freud employed the technique extensively in order to access areas of the mind not readily available to one's conscious perception. It was a controversial technique. The medical establishment, most particularly the neurologists, argued that Freud was a fraud, and that he was making up his findings as he went along, and quite possibly harming as many patients as he claimed to help. Nonetheless, the technique of hypnosis had been with us for many years. Julia had heard of it, but only in the carnival sideshow realm of things.

"Are you sure it's quite safe?" she asked Gordon. He said he believed so, if one went about it with the right precautions and minimised the time in which the hypnotic subject was "under".

"I must confess," he went on. "I do not have a great deal of practical experience with it. But I think, if we—"

"Ruth, dear. What do you think?" Julia asked me.

"I think it might help. But it is of course up to you."

"Will you be quite gentle, Mr Duncombe?" she said, and allowed herself the tiniest of mischievous smiles.

Gordon, noticing, blushed. He gathered himself. "I will do my very best for you, Miss Templesmith."

"Then let's have a try," she said.

5

Dinner that night was a grand construction featuring roast duck at its centre. Another triumph for Murray. Julia, who put aside her anxiety about her dreams long enough to enjoy seconds, sat after each of four courses, exclaiming that, "I could not possibly eat another bite!" while Gordon, another healthy eater if someone else was going to all the trouble, leaned back and complained, "It's that after-Christmas-dinner feeling all over again!" As Ryan and Vicky cleared away the clutter, I excused myself from the long table and nipped back to the hot and aromatic kitchen where I congratulated an exhausted, damp-faced Murray on another excellent meal. For her part, she only nodded, and pointed out how it could have been so much better, and "bloody Rutherford" had not helped by spying on her in order to find out what was on the menu. "You'll need to have a word with him, ma'am. If you don't, I will!" She was serious. She was always like this. No wonderful effort was ever good enough for her. She always apologised for various parts of the creation. It was like God apologising for cloudless sunsets.

Much later, Gordon, Julia and I sat in the drawing room, close to the fire, enjoying a brandy. Gordon took forever over his brandy, as always. He was not accustomed to such things. He wanted to make it last as long as possible, without looking impolite about it. Julia, by contrast, finished hers quickly and asked Rutherford for another. He lifted an eyebrow, but I allowed it. Julia, full of dinner and wine, was talkative, perhaps more even than usual. She was telling Gordon about her childhood in the draughty, crumbling Braethorn House, where she could escape from nannies and governesses and even her mother for hours at a time, exploring secret passages and huge, long-abandoned rooms where the furniture was draped with dusty sheets and you could still hear, when the weather was right, the ancient house settling into its foundations, even after so many centuries. She told Gordon about her encounters with ghosts ("Most of them terribly sad people,") and fey wraiths of no discernible character ("Creatures of pure feeling, one might say,") and, once, an outlaw thief hiding in an abandoned wine cellar ("He stayed three weeks, and I brought him food, but I had to be so careful, Mother and Father suspected something was not right and their kitchen staff were reporting that food was going missing...")

"Did you get caught?" Gordon asked, intrigued.

She smiled. "Yes, of course. I was only a silly girl. I was no match for a house full of suspicious relatives and servants."

"What happened?"

"As it happened, they packed me off to a boarding school for nine years."

"That seems harsh."

"The outlaw I was helping had, apparently, also murdered a family of four. He hadn't told me that part."

"Careless of him," I said.

Boarding school, for Julia, was a miserable experience. She hated the regimentation, the constant press of other students, the lack of privacy, the punishing study routines, the pecking order. Indeed, she ran away three times, but was always caught. And one time she almost set fire to her dormitory, but a nervous confederate confided to the staff before it could happen. The one thing Julia had liked about Ashling School for Girls was that it, like the old family estate, was teeming with ghosts. She got on well with them, since the great majority of the ghosts were deceased schoolgirls who had come to bad ends, some by their own hand. Julia understood how this might happen in such a hideous place.

The old clock on the mantel was chiming midnight. Gordon looked up. "Is it that late?"

I nodded, politely swallowing a yawn. Julia said, "Oh dear, I've been prattling along for hours! Ruth, dear, you should have told me to put a sock in it long ago."

"I did try," I said, smiling. There was no shutting her up, once she was rolling.

"Mr Duncombe," she said, "exactly when shall we conduct this hypnosis business? Right now would seem an opportune moment. There's nothing like midnight, if you ask me, for venturing into the hidden realms of things, wouldn't you agree?" She smiled at him, her eyes alive in the firelight.

"Gordon?" I looked at him, wondering how he felt. He would be thinking about his dogs.

He swirled the remains of his brandy. "I suppose it couldn't hurt, could it? Shouldn't take long."

Julia beamed, excited. "Right, then! What do I need to do? Am I all right sitting just here, or should I move to a more conducive chair?"

He told her she was just fine where she was. He fished out his sterling silver pocketwatch, given to him by his own family when he reached his majority, more than thirty years ago. The case was elegantly engraved; it would fetch a sizeable sum at auction, should he ever be foolish or desperate enough to sell it. "All I need you to do, Miss Templesmith, is to relax, take deep, slow breaths, and keep your eyes on my watch here." He sat on a stool before her, and dangled the watch from its fob chain; it turned this way and that, glittering like liquid gold with reflected firelight. "I want you to relax as much as you can, from the tips of your toes, all the way up to the top of your head. If you feel a need to settle back in the chair, please feel free. I just want you to relax, relax, perhaps think about some of those favourite places from your childhood, and keep watching the light on the watch here..."

I had to force myself to look away; I was feeling rather sleepy myself. Soon she had drifted away into a state somewhere between awareness and sleep, and she curled up in the large chair, looking like nothing so much as a little girl. She wore a small smile. The firelight flicked across her face.

"Now what?" I whispered, trying not to sound too impressed.

"First, we give her a subconscious trigger so that we can bring her back to consciousness immediately if anything worrying occurs. Then another trigger that can be used, in the future, should we need to induce this state again."

"Why would we want to do it again?"

"It's what Freud does, though there I suppose he's thinking about recurring weekly visits."

We decided to omit the latter trigger. Soon Julia was ready.

Gordon took her back to her home, more than three months earlier, to before she began experiencing the disturbing dreams. At the time Julia had been living at the country home of her cousin Jeremy, an earl, and his wife, Countess Mary. It was a modest holding, four hundred acres, in a picturesque valley not far from Leeds. "What do you do each day, Miss Templesmith?"

She spoke in a quiet, sleepy sort of voice, and described wonderful meals, extensive reading of newspapers and novels, visits into Leeds for afternoon tea with local friends, visits to the library each day for fresh books, evening walks through the hills with Jeremy and his dogs. It sounded like a wonderful, uncomplicated sort of life—except for the manner in which Julia was handed around between all the relatives. She did not like her own home these days, but could not bring herself to sell it and move; this was the family estate: it had to remain in the Templesmith family, even though she was the last of the direct line. If Antony and I had had any children, they would one day have inherited the old pile. As it was, though, it was far too large for one woman and a pair of servants, to say nothing of the running costs.

"All right," Gordon said, "let's go to the first night you experienced the dream."

Julia looked anxious, shifting in the chair.

Gordon said, "It will be all right. Nothing can hurt you."

She settled. He proceeded.

Julia went on to describe the first dream, which, perhaps disappointingly, consisted of no particular distinct imagery, but instead a growing sense of cold unease that built, slowly, into panic — and then something indefinable that made Julia blurt out my name, gasping, as if afraid for her own life.

"Bring her out, Gordon!"

Julia was greatly distressed, crying now, "*Oh my God, Ruth! No, not Ruth!*" She went on and on. I gathered this was how it had been, that first night. Gordon interrupted, and brought her away from the source of that fear, brought her back to a safe, quiet place. She calmed. I dabbed at her tears with my handkerchief.

"Now what?" I said.

"We need to find out where this is coming from. It seems unlikely that, in the middle of an otherwise serene sort of life, she should suddenly get upset over something to do with her niece, whom she hasn't seen in years. Makes no sense. Unless," he said, looking at the fire, "she's sensitive to things involving your life because..."

"I would not say we are close, but we always got on well, after a fashion." Which, of course, was true, right up until that day at Antony's funeral.

Gordon went back to Julia, and asked her if she could go back to the point where she first felt that anxiety. She nodded, and said, fidgeting already, "All right. I can feel it. It's cold. I'm so cold."

"Where is the cold coming from, Miss Templesmith? Is it like a wind or a breeze?"

She looked confused for a moment, then "looked" to her left. "Yes... yes, I can feel it coming from..."

I was feeling cold, too, listening to this, and wondering where Gordon was going.

"Julia, I want to see if you can move into the wind. Can you do that? Can you see where the cold wind is coming from?"

She was shivering, but looked determined. It was easy to imagine the child Julia looking like this on finding a secret passage in the old house, and intent on finding out where it went, regardless of the possible danger of exploring in a darkness lit only by candle or lamplight. "I can feel it growing stronger. It's...so cold..." I could see her chin trembling a little. She rubbed at her arms. I fetched a blanket, and Gordon used suggestion to help her feel more protected from the wind.

"Tell me what you see now, Julia?"

"I'm...I'm in a sort of tunnel, or a passageway. It's very dark. The floor creaks. Things are fluttering around my face. Moths, I think, perhaps. There's a bad smell. I'm not sure. I can just barely see."

"How is the wind?"

"Stronger. Much stronger. It's..." She frowned. "It's hard to press ahead."

"You have the strength to get there, Julia. You have the strength."

"I'm not sure I want to get there. I'm scared. It's...not just cold. There's something else. Something bad."

"Gordon? Is this wise?"

He glanced at me. "I'm not sure how many chances we'll have to do this."

"Be careful!"

He nodded. "Julia?"

"Yes?" It was a little girl's voice.

"Can you go on?"

"I want to."

"Let me know if you want to stop. Just raise a finger or use the trigger word, all right?" The trigger word was, prosaically enough, "exit".

"All right."

"What can you see now?"

"There's a light."

"What sort of light?"

"C-candles, I think. There's a room."

"Is the wind coming from this room?"

She nodded slowly, and looked very frightened. Her eyes still closed, she looked around. Whispering, she said, "It looks like a cellar. Smells dusty, and there's old bottles and casks in racks, and some steps."

"Is anybody there with you?"

She shook her head. "No. There's just...there's...a circle thing...on the floor..."

"A circle on the floor?" I did not like the sound of this. "Is it painted or drawn in chalk?"

"It looks like paint," she whispered in the tiniest voice, "but it doesn't smell like paint." She wrinkled her nose. "It's dreadfully bad..."

"Is this a room you have seen before?"

Julia shook her head again. "I've seen rooms like it. It smells."

"Can you move into the room?"

Feeling tense myself, I said to Julia, "It's all right, Julia. You're safe."

But she was shaking her head again. "It's not safe! It's cold here, it's cold! I'm freezing to death, it's, it's...like a blizzard, I want to go!"

"Gordon, bring her out!"

He wanted her to stay under a little bit longer, to learn more, but Julia's desperation was all too palpable. "All right. Julia?"

Julia suddenly gasped in fright: "Someone's coming! Footsteps!"

"*Julia — exit!*"

6

She slumped down into the chair, asleep, as Gordon had intended. I tucked the blanket tighter around her.

Gordon looked a little embarrassed. "That was not good. I'm sorry, Ruth."

I said, "What was all that?"

He frowned, deep in thought. "Difficult to say, for certain. The passageway, however, was almost certainly more metaphor than physical. I know that much."

"How do you mean?"

"You're asking me about metaphors?"

I shot him a Look. "No. I meant—"

"Ah," he said, understanding. "It's a bridge, of sorts, linking Julia to something in your own realm. In a manner of speaking. Er..."

"What about the cellar? Was that metaphorical, too?"

"Almost certainly not. Something's going on in a cellar somewhere around here. Something involving you."

"Why me?"

"How should I know? Maybe someone resents your success, or your, er, eccentric manner."

I went to respond, but Julia was stirring. She rubbed at her eyes, still looking like a little girl. "What happened?"

"Do you remember anything?" Gordon asked, worried.

She frowned. "I remember feeling very cold." She looked at the blanket, then at me. "Did you...?"

"You seemed to need it," I said.

"I do hope I didn't do anything silly..."

I put my hand on her shoulder. "You did very well. We learned a great deal."

Surprised, she looked from me to Gordon and back. "Really? Such as? Did you find out—?"

Gordon yawned, but said through the yawn, "I'm afraid I must be getting back to my dogs, if that's all right. Ruth will explain everything for you." He stood up and stretched—and looked like a man who didn't want to deliver bad news to someone who might not take it well.

Julia stared up at him. "You can't simply leave me hanging like that, Mr Duncombe! I deserve to know!"

Which she did, I thought. "I think you should tell her, Gordon."

He looked pained. "Could you please arrange a lift home for me?"

"You really ought to learn to drive, Gordon. It's not all that terribly hard."

"I can't afford a car!"

Julia was up out of the chair and attempting to get Gordon's attention; she looked nonplussed. "Mr Duncombe! If you'll pardon my interjection—could you *please* tell me what you found out?" Gordon could not escape Aunt Julia once she had that look on her face.

Fortunately, he looked at her, and realised this for himself. He slumped, shoulders seeming almost to disappear. He had wanted to spare her. "Please accept my apology, Miss Templesmith. It's simply..." He was wondering how to phrase such grim news. "It's just that we found a cellar. Most likely it's somewhere in the immediate vicinity, here in Pelican River, but possibly a little further afield."

"Mr Duncombe!"

He looked to me for assistance, but I was letting him handle it. He said, "The cellar contained a summoning and constraining circle. It appeared, from your description, that it was painted in blood. The room was accumulating a foul energy. It was building up, something like a battery, or capacitor."

Julia's eyes had never been wider. She went to say various things, but at length could say nothing. She looked at me. "What have I done?" she whispered.

"You've done nothing wrong, Julia. It's quite all right. You were a great help to me. We can start an investigation now. Get to the bottom of things. You've been indispensable."

Gordon agreed, and tried to soothe her unwinding feelings.

"I'll fetch Rutherford," I said.

By the time I returned, Julia had settled back into her chair. "I knew there was something about this place. I knew it!"

"Julia?"

She looked up. "You must leave this town, Ruth. You must leave, as soon as humanly possible!"

"It's no good running from things, Julia. This is my home. If there's something going on we have to stop it before it gets out of hand."

"But you've got a perfectly good home back in England. Everything you could ever want, it's all right there. Why did you ever want to leave?"

I did not know how I could answer that, not in only a few words.

Rutherford appeared at the drawing room doorway, fully attired, looking rested, flexing his hands in the black leather gloves, looking every inch like he'd simply been resting in his quarters, just waiting for me to call on him. He was eerie that way. "Mr Duncombe? When would it be convenient for you to depart?"

Gordon, as ever when asked questions by my servants, looked stricken and a little confused. At last he managed to indicate that he would be ready in just a few minutes. There was something he wanted to do first. He said to me, "Ruth, there's a simple protection charm that I can employ here. It's nothing big or complicated, but it will keep anything malicious distracted from looking for you. To them it would appear that you've disappeared, after a fashion, only to pop up in all sorts of odd places except where you really are."

Gordon had never offered to use any of his wizardry on me or even in my interest. It gave me a strange feeling, that we were entering a new realm. Our relationship was changing. I felt strangely disturbed at the prospect. Julia, looking on, trying not to yawn, still seemed distressed. She looked at Gordon, too, when he wasn't looking her way, as if trying to figure out what kind of a man he was: part inventor, part magician, part friend.

I agreed to his suggestion, and he quickly set about his mystical business. He said little, and did less; he moved around me, touching lightly certain points on my body—the base of my spine, the point where my skull met the top of my spine, my belly, the part of my chest where my heart lay, beating much faster than usual. It was all very quick, too fast to notice anything other than a faint tingling warm feeling that might simply have been a rush in my blood circulation. He soon finished the procedure, and said a final statement in a language I did not recognise, though it sounded rather like Latin. He said to me, "The deal is done."

"The deal?"

He explained. "All magic consists of a deal, or a bargain, with the Powers that provide the alteration to the universe. In return for their service, the magician must offer something. It's a negotiation, essentially."

Julia glanced at me, then back at Gordon, alarmed again. "You have to offer something? What...?" She could not bring herself to finish the question. I knew how she felt.

"Gordon?"

He smiled, looking embarrassed. "It's nothing. It's not. Really. Don't worry about it." He clapped his hands together, warming them. "Anyway, it's late. I must be getting back. The dogs'll be worried sick."

He refused to explain further, and extricated himself. He and Rutherford left. Soon I heard the low rumble of the Bentley's massive engine, and the crunch of its wheels on the gravel driveway.

Julia looked worried, and very tired. "I should never have come…"

"If you had not come, we would not know what we now know."

She shrugged. "I could certainly do with another brandy, if that's all right."

I agreed. A little later, we sat back in the perhaps too-comfortable chairs in front of the diminishing fire, which popped and cracked, and occasionally spat hot bits of charcoal out at us, only to be intercepted by the mesh screen. We watched the fire a long time. Julia told me stories about some of my other relatives back home. Inconsequential stories, small victories here, petty jealousies there, devious one-upmanship all around. To hear her tell it, my extended family was a nest of vipers alive with powerful emotions but much too polite to do anything straightforward and upfront with them. Everything was a scheme or a plot, wheels within bloody wheels, constant tedious intrigue. I had come out to Australia in part to escape from their endless pettiness and machinations. Life, I had learned the hard way, was far too short. People here, by stark contrast, were frank, straightforward, and blunt. What you saw was what you got. If, in the course of walking along Pelican Terrace, I ran into Fran from the bakery, I knew she was likely to tell me off about my clothes, or urge me to get a decent ladylike haircut. I rarely had the feeling that people spoke behind my back, full of bile. There had been many times, in my life here, when people like Big Phil the "milko" had yelled abuse at me, accusing me of unwholesome practices or habits. Why? I had done nothing to him, other than exist, other than make a little money for myself. Women did not do such things, of course. We (just barely) had the vote, but we did not have the right to live without a man. It was, as Phil would say, "unnatural". That was fine with me. I would far rather have such views presented to my face than be part of the bitter webs of nastiness back home. I could tell Phil, "I'm sorry you feel that way, Phil, but there's not much I want to do about it." And if I then offered to buy him a beer at the Commercial Hotel, he'd laugh, shake his head in disbelief, call me a "mad bloody cow", but be quite happy to have a drink with me.

So, I decided, I could probably rule out Big Phil as a suspect in whatever was going on. Someone in the area had such a loathing of me that he—or she, I supposed—was resorting to *demonology* as a means of attack, of all things. It seemed rather an elaborate, irrational, even a rather silly, response. Why not just have it out with me? I was susceptible to a reasoned argument. True, I would not leave this town if I could help it. Who hated me so much that the only answer was to *summon a demon*—for God's sake!—to kill me? Why not just do it themselves? The visions Julia described did not sound to me like those of an ordinary human attacker. Such an attacker would have trouble with the locks on the house; would make some sort of noise in the course of moving through the house because many of the floorboards creaked; and, unless they had a copy of the architect's drawings from the last century, they would have more trouble locating my bedroom than the figure in Julia's visions. Could it be someone who knew me and knew the house so well that such considerations might not apply? Could a knowledgeable attacker steal through the house without stepping on certain boards? Perhaps also armed with a key? But who would that include? My servants, certainly. Gordon, of course, who had been here many times over the past decade—which made little sense.

Elves? It seemed hard to imagine such twilight, fey creatures being able to put together such an efficient raid. And again, why me? Though there you could also ask, Why *not* me? It was something that gnawed at me, in the middle of the night, when I had trouble sleeping.

The elves here in Australia, gravely etiolated, more twilight than sunlight, were our fault. We British had brought them with us, a kind of supernatural, cultural shadow of our own presence: where we went across the world, they came along, smuggled in our dreams, myths, fears, and darkest imaginings, and they came despite all our best efforts to prevent it. But how do you prevent your own shadow from coming with you? This harsh land of dazzling sunlight was hostile to them. To the extent that they intersected with our plane of reality at all, they were drawn to trees and forests, but forests here in Australia lacked some essential quality found in abundance back home. Or perhaps there was too much supernatural competition from the Aboriginal Dreamtime beings said to fill the land. This land was killing them. They barely existed as refugees, creatures stranded, washed ashore and unwelcome. But they were our fault. And they were waiting for us to leave and go home, so they could go home with us. I feared this would never happen, and, quietly, late at night in my more disturbing dreams, I grieved for them.

It was hard to entirely rule out a band of hostile elves. They were known to employ an ancient form of magic, drawn across the endless oceans from home, so it was possible that they might feel so aggrieved that resorting to some kind of demonology seemed to them like a good idea. But it was hard to believe that creatures so orthogonal to this reality could be so offended by the likes of me, a widowed writer of scientific romances living in a small country town, that they would mount such a campaign against me. Then again, I thought, maybe it was not about me, as such. Could the remaining elven population, barely connected to this world but determined to hold on to what they had, be intent on destroying more than merely myself? Could they be out to destroy the entire town? Could they be so desperate to return to Britain that they would drive us out of Australia? Certainly, I knew, Aboriginal people, when asked, reported that the elves' presence in the world made them sick, and scared. They wanted the elves dispatched even more than we "whitefellas". It was only too easy to imagine the elves feeling so cornered that they would resort to desperate measures.

All things considered, the real question one would have to ask would be: *What had taken them so long?*

7

I lay awake all night; at one point, while pacing in front of the bed, I heard movement in the hall outside. I jumped, startled, and could not suppress the thought, *Already?*

Then I heard floorboards creak, a muttering, and then someone bumped into a wall next to my bedroom door, and I heard Julia's voice, "Oh bother!"

I let her in. She looked me up and down, then looked over at the tangled bedclothes. "You, too?"

We went downstairs to the kitchen. I made hot cocoa. The kitchen was full of the aromas of the evening meal; it was comforting, in a way, like a reminder of the simple, ordinary things going on in the world.

We sat and sipped quietly. It was a cold night. Rain was expected.

Julia held her cup before her in both hands. Over the rim, she said, "Rather a momentous evening."

"I hope the whole hypnosis business didn't disturb you —"

"Oh not at all!" she said, smiling quickly. "I'm quite used to the trance state and all that. How do you think I manage my visits to the deadworld, I mean..." She saw the look on my face at the mention of that word, and she trailed off. "Well," she said, "it was quite fine. No trouble. I'm just sorry I couldn't provide better information."

I told her it was all right. Some information was better than none, at least in this context. Better to know something was going on. She said, "I could go under again, if that would help? Mr Duncombe could—"

"I suspect Gordon would be willing, if I were to ask him, but I do not think it would be wise. Next time, we might inadvertently arouse the attentions of whatever is going on in that cellar."

She nodded, looking grim. "There was no chance I was getting to sleep tonight."

I watched her. She was circling a middle finger around the gold rim of her porcelain cup; I could hear the tiniest squeak of sound, despite the wind outside battering at the rustling gum trees. She said, "I rather fear that things got stirred up anyway, Ruth, dear."

"Oh?"

"I feel things whirling around inside my head. Since waking after Mr Duncombe's procedure, I've not felt at all 'right,' if that makes sense. Like water and sand, usually calm, water at the top, sand at the bottom, but now it all feels like a busy sort of mud, if..."

I blinked, thinking about Julia's striking image. "Yes, quite. Has this sort of feeling happened to you on other occasions when you have had access to the 'other bits' of reality?"

She nodded, putting her cup down carefully on its saucer. "Indeed. It often takes me a day or two for everything to settle again."

"And this has come about entirely as a consequence of Gordon's hypnosis?"

She looked alarmed for a moment, realising. "No, dear. Not entirely. Something has not felt quite right since my arrival here. Like an off-key musical note only I could hear, ringing all through the town. I had scarcely even been aware of it, until tonight. That's when I noticed it. And, lying in bed, tossing and turning, at first I thought it was simply the unfamiliar bed, the strange sounds of the house settling, the way the very air smells different in this country, but it soon occurred to me that it wasn't any such thing. Or, that is, all those things were there, but they were not what was disturbing me. That was when I noticed—as strange as this must sound to the scientist in you—the disturbances."

"Intriguing," I murmured. "It might be worth determining if this disturbance you feel is constant throughout the area, or if it grows more or less intense in certain places. How would you feel about that?"

"If it would help sort out what's going on, I would be all for it! Do you think Mr Duncombe might be interested in coming along?" Here she smiled a little slyly, looking as if she hoped I would not notice.

I suppressed a smile. "Gordon made an impression on you, Julia?"

She looked pointedly at her cup. "I say, another cocoa would go down well!"

I set about organising it. "You do realise," I said as I warmed the milk at the range, "Gordon has very little money, and his house is nothing at all on the scale you are used to."

She looked surprised, even a little shocked. "Ruth, my dear, I am baffled by this line of conversation. How's the cocoa coming along?"

"He's also," I said, "setting about automating as much of his life as possible."

"You said he invents machines?"

"Yes. Only, he doesn't invent just one machine at a time and then move to the next one. He invents several at once, moving about his projects as inspiration strikes. Then there are his many dogs…"

"I love dogs, dear!"

"He has twelve dogs, and they have the run of his property, including the house, and the bedroom."

"The bedroom, you say?"

I said nothing and presented her fresh cocoa. "I wonder if Murray's got any decent biscuits hiding in the pantry…"

When I returned with a glass jar containing several ginger-snaps, I caught her looking, for a moment, as if trying to decide if multiple friendly dogs in the bed was something she could or could not abide. She was grateful for the biscuits, and quickly took to dunking them.

We talked about other, ordinary things for a while. Julia told further stories of remote relations and their endless intrigues. I sighed discreetly and sipped my cocoa.

Then, she said, "It must be terribly late. How will we get up for Mass tomorrow?"

I stopped, biscuit dunked and dripping on the polished karri table. A shot of cold ripped through me. I recovered swiftly, and hoped Julia had not noticed. "Mass, Julia? Oh, well..."

"We shall need toothpicks to lever our eyelids open!" she said, smiling.

"Yes," I said, feeling growing awkwardness. "Julia, did I tell you about my current novel?"

"Yes, of course you did. The poor chap trying to sort out the infinite threads of the universe, and all that. I'm sure you can work it all out."

I went to elaborate, hoping to divert her, but she went on. "So tell me, dear," she said, "what's the problem with Mass tomorrow? Hmm?"

"Problem?" I said, trying to smile behind my cup.

"You look as though you received a dead fish in the daily post. What's wrong?"

I sighed. "Ah." Might as well explain. "It's rather a long story, Julia. Very boring."

"I don't feel the slightest bit sleepy. Do you?"

I did not. Damn. "You will think this very silly, I'm sure."

"You were always devout in your observances back home. Are things not done quite the same way here? I must say, that would not at all surprise me, considering everything. I feel certain the flies alone would drive everyone to sin, if nothing else!"

"The local priest, Father William—he and I have had something of a falling out, one might say."

"Indeed?"

I took several breaths, trying to work out the best way to explain.

The nub of the matter was that I was, even before the War, very much against war. When I lost my husband to the organised, mechanised slaughter of the Great War, my opposition to war, and to the glorification of it, intensified. One might say I burned white-hot with my hatred of war, and of that particular war.

Then I moved out here to Australia. I had, as Aunt Julia said, always been a devout Christian back home in England. So once I was settled here in Pelican River, I set about finding a local church at which to attend Mass, and found one right here, run by the elderly Father William. Let me say, as simply as possible, that he and I did not see eye to eye—on anything, from the start. On our first meeting, over ten years ago, I noticed that when he laid eyes on me, and my appearance, for the first time, he visibly paled. When I asked about service times, he gave me the schedule with the greatest reluctance, as if hopeful, perhaps, that I might go elsewhere. Even with a simple question–reply situation such as this—"When are your services?", "Everything is laid out in this leaflet we've prepared."—there was tension and hostility. He peered at me as if I were a fly that had the misfortune to land in his much-too-weak cup of milky tea. He refused to make eye contact with me throughout the entire encounter. You could see his nostrils flaring; and it was impossible not to notice the rate of his respiration (astonishing bad breath, too, it must be said, which he tried to moderate with peppermint humbugs) increased sharply every time he took in my appearance. It was all he could do to get rid of me. He did ask me if my husband would be attending with me. I said no. He pointed out that I wore a wedding band. I explained that my husband was killed in the War. "I see," he said, rather than anything soothing or compassionate. "So you're in mourning, then?" he said, indicating, with the slightest gesture and tilt of his head, at my clothing. I gathered what he was trying to suggest—what he was trying to sort out in his own head—and said, "Yes, I am indeed still in mourning. But I wear what I wear because it's comfortable and I like it."

I do despise a man who refuses to make eye contact with a woman when she's speaking to him. Who refuses even to shake my hand. Who, even as we are engaged in conversation, is attempting to ease me down the aisle towards the entrance, as if I'm a foul contagion he must eradicate from the premises. Who asks me for details about my late husband's service during the War, and when I say my husband worked for the War Office, he then has the temerity—*the gall!*—to inquire how then might a man working in an office find himself killed during the War, and, I am afraid to say, I slapped the swine. "How dare you!" I said, and stalked out of the dark church and into the warmth and light before he could say a word. At that moment, vibrating with fury, I could have killed him with my bare hands. As it was, I hit him so hard he almost toppled over, but he managed to grab a pew as he spun. He came to the door, and shouted after me, forbidding me from attending his church for Mass. Forbidding me! In this day and age. As if it were the previous century. He had implied that Antony was a coward for not being a regular soldier serving in the Army. I could never forgive Father William for that. If he came to me on bended knee, weeping and full of remorse, I could never forgive such a suggestion.

But that was not why I slapped him that day. I slapped him because I, too, had wondered exactly how someone working as a civil servant in the War Office could find himself killed in the middle of the Somme. The telegram the Office sent informing me of Antony's death did not say. It said only that he had died in the course of carrying out his duty to King and Country. That he had died an honourable death. I had to write letters, many letters, to the War Office in order to find out what happened, and this was all I had managed to extract from them: that he, a civil servant, had been in the Somme that day, "on assignment", during an enemy artillery barrage. I wrote and asked if he had been delivering a written order, perhaps? They would not say. They would not answer any more of my letters. I kept sending them, and demanding to know what had happened to him, and how he had died. But my letters were met only with cold silence. On two occasions, walking through the village near the Black estate, I could have sworn I saw a man following me. On one occasion, while walking through the garden at home, I saw a nondescript brown truck, near the gates, which had been sitting there for some time. I asked Rutherford to go and ask the occupants if they needed anything. The truck left before he reached them.

*

Julia said, "So did you try to make it up with Father William?"

"I did not, no."

"Ruth!"

"I saw there was no point." Already I could feel myself getting overheated all over again. I got up from the table and found myself pacing, just as I had been pacing in my bedroom earlier. At a very basic level of my mind, I knew it was poor form to be on bad terms with the clergy. It would not do. It wasn't done. Yes, I should have made an effort to apologise to the old man, but an entire decade had now passed. When I had need of spiritual counsel or worship, I went north to a tiny church in Rockingham. Father William was hardly the first such man to take exception to me over my clothes, my manner, my line of work, my failure to marry again, my—who knows, perhaps even my hat size! I had dealt with such men many times, and I had always put aside such criticisms, overt and implied, without a worry. But when it was the church, when it was a *priest*—yes, a priest who had insulted Antony's memory, I reminded myself.

Aunt Julia gave me a hug. She was much shorter than I was, so it perhaps presented a humorous spectacle, and that helped. She was very warm, as I had always remembered. "I'm sorry, Julia, about, back home, the funeral, the—" I was close to tears.

Julia let go a moment so she could look up at me. "It's quite all right, Ruth. Think nothing of it. I should have been more sensitive. My timing was dreadful. I've regretted that day so many times, all these years. But I never stopped loving you, dear. I have always been your father's sister, and I have always looked out for you."

Twelve years before, on the day of Antony's well-attended funeral, a day in which I felt a numb, cold fury whirling through me, Julia had approached me after Antony was interred and asked me, with great tact, how I would feel if she ventured across to what she called "the deadworld" in order to find Antony's spirit, so she might ask him, personally, what had happened. In those days, with the War still raging, I was younger and much more certain of my rationalist, empiricist views than I was now, at the age of thirty-eight. When Julia proposed her idea, I was furious. I told her never to speak to me again. I would not be party to any sort of nonsense childish superstition meddling with my memories of Antony. I did want to know what had happened to him, and what he had been doing on the battlefield that day, but Julia's method was not the way to find out.

I wiped my eyes. Julia dabbed at hers. We stood there, sniffling.

Time passed. We had some more cocoa and chatted about neutral things. Julia believed I should apologise to Father William. I believed he should apologise to me. But someone would have to go first. Someone had to "be the better man", as it were, even after all this time. Someone had to take the high moral ground. I was very partial to the high moral ground: the view was marvellous. You could see for miles. Which was all very well, and very glib, but it was a distraction from the crux of the matter: that somewhere not far from here in Pelican River, a quiet little fishing town where nothing much ever happened, someone, possibly someone I knew, had a cellar under their property, and in that cellar they were trying to work some magic in order, I was starting to believe, to kill me. Gordon had referred to it as an accumulation of "foul energy". It was preposterous! This was not the Middle Ages. The world was in the grip of a scientific revolution, with an entirely new way to think about reality struggling to be born, right now, in Europe. Science and progress were advancing. We were leaving behind superstition and the old ways of doing things. And yet here we seemed to have someone resorting very much to those old ways in order to deal with me. One would think it would be much easier simply to show up at my house with a gun and shoot me. If you had a problem with me, why not do the straightforward thing? Why all the nonsense? Just come and get me! I wanted to shout. I'm right here.

I chanced to look at the east-facing window over the kitchen sink. The sky was faintly lighter; a deep greyness was stifling the weak light of distant stars. A new weather front was coming in from the sea. Such things were not altogether unusual in May; winter would properly set in only a few days hence, at the start of June. But right now, on this night, it seemed altogether troubling. I felt cold, despite sitting only a few feet from the range. Julia pulled her blue crocheted shawl tighter around her shoulders. "Is it that late?" she said, turning to see the dim light growing out there.

It was indeed late. I only hoped it was not too late.

8

I rolled a sheet of my personal letterhead stationery into the big black Imperial typewriter and tapped in today's date and the church's address on Sullivan Street. I noticed that my typing today was worse than usual; I was making foolish, elementary mistakes, which was quite unlike me. *Indeed*, I thought, as I slapped the carriage return lever a few times to bring up a good amount of white space, *it's not as if, after all this time, I still care what Father William thinks, is it?*

Dear Father William,

I wrote. The slap of keys on paper sounded louder than usual; I found myself thinking of machine-gun fire, even to the point of almost smelling the discharge smoke, the impression was so intense. I pressed on.

I am writing to you today in order to discuss my outrageous behaviour

Wait a moment. I could see the point of being conciliatory, and even humble. Humility doesn't cost anything, after all. And I had slapped the vile old trout. But did I want to be this conciliatory? I could hear my mother's voice in my head, telling me that assaulting one's local priest is not only appalling behaviour, unbecoming a lady, but also counterproductive in the long term.

Gossip will spread, and a man so central to a community is in a perfect position to spread said gossip. Therefore, Mother would counsel, grovel abjectly, or, at least, play the part of abject apology, even if you do not feel it. It is hard enough being a single woman in the world without having an entire town arrayed against you. I knew Mother was right about this. But to grovel? After all this time? I still felt the shock of that moment as if it had happened only today. I would sooner die than make a grovelling apology to that man, I thought. And yet, if that feeling in my chest was any guide, it was the required course of action. Then again, a perhaps less conscientious side of my nature argued, there had been no detectable decline in the way the people of this town saw me. They thought then, and they thought now, that I was a very odd fish indeed. Was it possible that Father William had not been spreading disgusting rumours about me? Was it possible he hadn't told anyone about it? In all this time I'd not considered that possibility—I'd not thought about it at all. I remember worrying a great deal at the time, but nothing came of it. There had been no campaign in the press against me, no-one came to my door to express their outrage, no "gentle hints" that possibly I was no longer welcome. Then an even more shocking thought arrived in my head: what if other people in this town hated him as much as I did? That gave me pause. I sat, thinking it over, staring out the window, unsure what to think. I pulled that draft out of the machine; I had always enjoyed the satisfying *riiiiiiip* sound. Still, I rolled in a fresh sheet and resumed work.

> Many years ago, you and I had a conversation at your church on Sullivan Street, I

Hmm. He already knows his address. Do I need to include that "Sullivan Street" reference? At this point it would mean starting over again. It stayed. I pressed on.

> I assaulted you without provocation or justification. It was an appalling thing to have done, a shameful breach

Not bad. Not marvellous, but it would do for the moment. Keep going. Though, I was not sure about "a shameful breach", which looked and sounded clumsy. It would be easy to fix on the next draft.

> Since that occasion I have had time to reflect on my dreadful behaviour and now I feel the need to offer you, indeed the entire community of Pelican River, my most abject apology. My actions were inexcusable. I am sorry, Father William, for my outburst. I do not expect you, even after all this time, to allow me back into your church. Certainly not. I do, however, feel it would be wrong of me to leave this matter unresolved. Naturally, I should be willing to make a formal public apology in the *Pelican River Record* if you believe that would be appropriate as well.

> Again, please accept my profound apologies.

> Thank you for your time. I remain, as ever, your humble servant,

How I hated having to say such things as that! Humble servant! Bollocks!

> R. E. Black (Mrs.)

Half an hour later, I pulled the seventh and final draft of the letter from the machine and set it on my desk next to the beetling tower of over three hundred manuscript pages that so far represented my next novel. The letter seemed, on balance, a more important document.

I quickly typed up an envelope, signed the letter with my favourite fountain pen, the Black Tethys with solid gold nib, and placed it in my Out tray. For any other correspondence, I would ask one of my staff to post it for me. This one, I would deal with myself. I knew, and my mother's voice in my head agreed, that I should have written this letter when the incident was fresh. That I had taken all this time was, I'm sure she would have thought, and told me, unforgivable. But it was done now, and better late than never. I had a strange thought: what if he'd forgotten about it? What if he felt ashamed of having said what he said to me that day? I'd never previously considered this. Perhaps that was why I hadn't seen any sign in all the years since of any kind of campaign against me and my presence here?

Leaning back, I stared out the window. From here I could look down over the town and across the estuary. The new wooden Traffic Bridge extending Estuary Road across the river was a white arc to the far left, teeming with all manner of vehicles, both motorised and horse-drawn. The estuary itself looked like hammered pewter on this overcast, bleak day; strong westerly winds stirred the chop. I saw terns hovering above the water, and knew they would be hunting fish with eyes more powerful than I could imagine. And, of course, there was always a pelican or two, somewhere to be seen, enormous white and black birds, ridiculous-looking on the ground but impossibly graceful in the air. Beyond the far side of the estuary, the broad white beaches of Hagan's Head lay, inviting even on a day like this, when I knew the fine white sand would be thick with brown seaweed, and the smell would be near-overpowering. Many times I had gone out there, rugged up against the elements on days just like this, and sat on the sand, wrapped in blankets, taking in the cold, gusting sea winds.

I never wanted to leave.

*

Later, Rutherford brought Julia home from the noon Mass.

"How was it?" I was in the lounge room again, sipping black coffee and poring over manuscript pages, armed with my vicious red pen. My protagonist was having a very bad day indeed.

Julia allowed Rutherford to take her heavy coat and made her way to the fireplace, to warm her hands. "There were only seven people there, including myself. Is that usual?"

Rutherford inquired if Miss Templesmith would care for something warming to drink. She asked for a cup of tea.

I said, "Hmm, well he does have three sessions on Sundays, as well as each night during the week, including a midnight Mass on Saturday nights. Or at least that was the way he used to do things." I spotted Sally Hall bustling through the hall armed with a load of folded linen. "Sally? Could I have a word?"

Sally deposited the enormous pile of linen on one of the armchairs, and pulled a loose stray blonde hair from her eyes. "Ma'am?"

"Father William, he's still doing all those services during the week and so forth?"

"Not as many as before, ma'am. He's cut right back lately."

"Do you know why?"

"Think he's tired, ma'am."

I nodded. "Thank you, Sally."

She bobbed, scooped up her linen and got back to work.

Father William tired? Even though I had not set foot in his church for years, I heard about him constantly, and now and then ran across him in town—not that he acknowledged my existence. He was always in the local newspaper, indefatigable, a force to be reckoned with, doing his bit—serving on committees, organising fundraising activities, making home visits for the handful of parishioners who could not get to Mass. "How did you find him?" I asked Julia.

"I rather thought he mumbled a lot, actually. Looked like he hadn't been sleeping well. There was one surprising thing, though," she said. "The service itself. It was just so, how to put this...? So shabby, if you'll excuse me saying so. Back home, and you'll remember this, nothing's changed since you left, back home churches are like palaces of God! Statues of the saints carved from the finest Italian marble, gold leaf on everything, the most beautiful tiles, vestments sewn from the finest fabrics. You know you're there to marvel at God's glory, and to feel humble in His presence. It's an awe-inspiring sort of experience."

I remembered. It had always bothered me that the Church possessed such astonishing riches, while elsewhere in the world there were people who couldn't afford to buy bread—and yet these same paupers nevertheless could sacrifice a few coins for the Church! It was something else I had often been sorely tempted to protest about during services back home, where things were indeed as Julia described. When I had read somewhere that the Church was the richest single institution in the world, I wasn't at all surprised.

"Shabby in what way?"

Julia looked as though she hardly knew where to start. "Well. For a start, there were hardly any other people there. A miserable bunch, too. Sour-faced, downcast. And then of course, the roof leaks. There are draughts because two of the stained-glass windows are broken. Cheap gold paint rather than gold leaf. The pews looked in need of a good varnishing, and the floor hadn't been swept properly. And the wine was sour. I nearly choked!"

I had not been aware things were quite so poor. I told Julia about my letter. She was pleased. "When will you post it?"

I had planned to post it tomorrow, Monday.

She said, "Why not post it today? You only have to drop it in the box."

I called Rutherford, who took Julia and me into town, pulling up out the front of the granite Postmaster General building at the corner of Estuary Road and Lewisham Street. He offered to deposit the letter in the big red postbox pillar, but I wanted to do it myself.

Outside, few people were about. My view of the estuary was obscured by sheoak and jacaranda trees lining Estuary Road. The wind was cold and fresh; I had to hold onto my hat.

Feeling surprisingly nervous, I pushed the letter into the slot, and heard it land, softly, deep down near the bottom of the pillar.

And, immediately, I found myself worrying: had I done the right thing? Had I been apologetic enough? What if it didn't work? I would need a plan. Worse, what if he simply ignored it, and didn't even open it—I could see that happening in a great many of the possible future worlds that would arise from this moment. Why should he open a letter from That Woman, especially after such an unconscionably long time? What could she possibly have to say that would be of interest to a busy man like him?

*

Later, Julia asked when we would be getting back in touch with Mr Duncombe. "Strictly professional interest, Julia, I'm sure," I said, allowing a tiny smile. We were at the Pelican River Old England Tea Rooms, where Mrs Battersby bustled about us, her only customers at the moment.

Julia flushed, and insisted that she was only thinking of my plan for us to drive her around the town and surrounding areas to see if she experienced anything "untoward" in her other bits of reality. Though thinking about it now, I was starting to wonder whether this might be too dangerous for Julia. She could have another attack of whatever had caused her recent seizure. "Are you quite sure you feel up to it?"

"Wouldn't miss it!" she said.

I looked at Rutherford, who stood quietly nearby. "I am available whenever you require my services, ma'am, of course."

He was a fine man, Rutherford. Yet, I had the oddest feeling in the back of my mind that it might be best, if we were to try out this plan, to do it alone. We could take my other car, a blue Renault Tulip, the sporty French roadster I used when I needed to take off on my own and didn't want the huge black Bentley, which required enormous effort merely to steer. The Tulip, by contrast, was quick and nimble—though rather lacking in passenger comforts.

I explained this idea. "Please feel free to take the evening off, Rutherford. I think we can manage."

"Right you are, ma'am."

Julia said, "These scones are awfully good, I must say!"

*

Gordon took a long time answering the telephone. He said, puffing for breath, "Just been out in the shed. Had a bit of a thought about the control mechanism—see, it occurred to me I needed to think about the entire vehicle moving in Einsteinian four-dimensional space-time, so I would need more than three control sticks, you see, one for the engine throttle—though I've had some thoughts about the throttle design, too, which I need to study more closely—and the others to control temporal direction and frame of whatsit!"

I listened to all this breathless outpouring with some difficulty: I could hear the many dogs, as usual, swarming and barking around him, and I could picture him being buffeted about. Some of those dogs were on the large side, too, and could easily knock a man over if he wasn't sufficiently braced. Still, he almost never yelled at them, and they all, Gordon included, seemed very happy. "Gordon, would you be available this evening for a spot of research into Julia's mysterious disturbances?" When he asked, I explained what she had told me early this morning.

"Of course, of course. Sounds like a winning plan. Shall I bring a map?"

I didn't have one. "The very thing! Would you care to join us for dinner first?"

He hesitated. "Dinner, hmm. Well…" He would be thinking about how he didn't want to impose on my hospitality two nights in a row, though he had done exactly this many times in the past. He was good about not presuming, but sometimes he could take it too far.

I insisted; he gave in. We collected him on the way home.

Julia, squeezed up next to him in the back of the Bentley, looked pleased, and asked him all about his work on the time machine. All the way home, Gordon went on about the complexities of creating a machine that could not only shift about in time, but which offered the potential to, as it were, choose realities, he said. Julia, all agog, made the error of asking, as we turned onto our street, "And what would you do with it first, Mr Duncombe, should you get it to work?"

Gordon did not yet know. He frowned. "I just thought it would be, you know, handy." He shrugged, as if "handy" said it all.

Murray performed well that night, providing us with roast goose and garden vegetables beyond superlatives. We all complimented the chef on her fine work. Murray, of course, protested that the gravy wasn't right, the meat not quite done all the way through, and many other points, none of which any of us had noticed. One hour in, Julia was still working on seconds. Gordon reported, slapping his belly, that he was "full as a goog!"

The evening meal over, Sally and Vicky cleared the dishes, and Gordon produced his map of Pelican River, and laid it out over the table. We gathered around.

"Miss Templesmith," he ventured, looking at Julia. "Are you still aware of that off-key sensation?"

"I believe I am," she said, looking back at him, round-eyed. "I feel all out of sorts, one might say."

He ignored the look on her face and glanced back at the map, where he indicated my house, up on Frenchman's Hill, overlooking the town. "Here's what I have in mind..."

9

The night rushed and swirled close around us. The Tulip's canopy kept the worst of the cold wind from infiltrating the car. In the back, Gordon and Julia talked animatedly; she was doing a good job of drawing him out, and keeping him from droning on about machinery. One thing she did ask, however, struck something of a nerve.

"Mr Duncombe," she opened.

Trying, by lamplight, to pore over the spread-out map draped over his lap without getting carsick, Gordon said, "Mmm?"

"You said last night, when you worked that protection charm for Ruth, that you had made a 'deal' with the 'Powers' which provide the, so to speak, service, in altering the universe. Is that right?"

"Of course," he said, a new tone in his voice. He sounded wary. "Why do you ask, Miss Templesmith?"

"It's just…Please, you must excuse me, I shouldn't be sticking my beak into things like this, but I just have this sense that you and I, Mr Duncombe, that we're almost kindred spirits. Do you know what I mean?"

Gordon coughed. "Oh, ah. Right. Yes. Ah. You wanted to ask something?"

I could hear her smiling. "It's just, you said that your part of the deal involved you having to give up something."

"You want to know what it was I gave up, to complete the terms of the contract?" He sounded rather businesslike, saying this.

"I hope you don't mind my curiosity. The sorts of things that I delve into in the course of my practice, sniffing around the other bits of reality and so forth, well I don't often come across people working actual magic, it's all rather...what's the word I'm looking for? Ruth, what's the word I'm looking for?"

"You're fascinated, Julia," I said, trying not to smile too much.

"Fascinated, yes! Exactly! Anyway, Mr Duncombe, I—"

"A lock of my hair, Miss Templesmith. I had to burn a lock of my hair in a very particular pure flame, while saying certain things I would rather not reveal, if that is quite all right."

Julia, surprised at his tone, said, "Oh. All right. Please, I should not have stuck the beak in. I'm a terribly nosy sort; it's always getting me in trouble. It's—"

Gordon said, gently, "It's quite all right, Miss Templesmith. I am happy to chat with you about anything you like, and I quite agree that we seem to have interests in common, but there are things about magical practice that are terribly private. It's rather a difficult business, really. As well, and here you must accept my apology, for all my hobbyist reading and study of certain volumes of lore, I'm still rather a novice, and not very good yet. I can pull apart and rebuild a motorcar engine while blindfolded, but this magic business, it's almost an art, and requires a similar level of, so to speak, subjective experience."

Julia sat and said nothing for a long moment. I sensed she had no notion of what she might say next, but that she very much would like to come up with something to keep the conversation going. She had never met a man like Gordon. And, yes, she was a renowned stickybeak. When things interested her, there was no stopping her craving for more and more knowledge. Unfortunately, the ordinary and rather quiet world in which we lived was altogether too dull and unexciting for her. She could not give a toss about politics, cricket scores, popular music—and she would rather not talk about the weather just for the sake of talking. International news of revolutions, war, horrific famine, floods or other disasters stirred her to some degree, and she made a point of donating substantial sums to charitable causes, and once a week back home volunteered with her parish church on various matters. But, the truth was, the things that truly interested her were the things other people did *not* talk about.

Gordon, perhaps sensing things were a little on the quiet and awkward side, asked Julia how she slept last night. "I trust there were no ill effects from the..."

"To be quite honest, Mr Duncombe, I hardly slept at all. Ruth and I stayed up almost all night chatting away in the kitchen. I lost count of how much cocoa we put away. I say—"

He interrupted her. "You couldn't sleep? Ruth mentioned that you were suffering strange mental disturbances, things all stirred up? Is that right?"

"Yes, I'm afraid so. It was lovely sitting up talking with Ruth, but I'm afraid it has left me feeling rather weary and strange now. That huge dinner, too...my goodness!"

I heard Gordon moving his map around; he asked Julia if she would take charge of the lamp, to make it easier for him to see the map. He said, "Right now we're on Old Hitchinbury Road, heading south-south-west. Is that right, Ruth?"

I called back, "It is, yes."

Julia said, "I'm not feeling any of that same off-key sort of sensation I told you about, Ruth."

Gordon said, "We may have gone too far in this direction."

"Head back towards town?" I asked. The road was empty. The electric headlamps on the Tulip showed that we were moving through farmland, with tall white ghost gums looming over the roads. The Tulip's tyres were handling the gravel road surface better than the heavy Bentley, too, which was pleasing. Much as I liked having Rutherford drive me about, there was still a certain enjoyment to be had out and about like this. Never mind that almost no other woman I knew, either here or back in England, could drive a car.

I stopped and turned the car, and soon we were heading back towards Pelican River. Right now we were perhaps fifteen miles outside town, and Julia was claiming no particular sense of disturbance. I knew Gordon would be marking this spot on his map with his always-reliable and badly chewed pencil stub. The problem would arise, however, that there were not many other roads leading out of town. There was this one, heading more or less south to Bunbury, and there was the Pelican River Road, which lay to the north and led through Rockingham and back up to Fremantle and Perth. There were only a few small service roads leading east from Pelican River. Gordon's map suggested there were some "unofficial trails" threading through the local farming districts. I did not relish taking the Tulip into such conditions. Would we need, at some point, simply to get out and walk all night?

In the back, Gordon and Julia were chattering away once again—or, rather, Julia was chattering about her "other bits" of reality, and Gordon was listening, making attentive noises periodically. I shook my head, hoping Gordon did not mind too much. I rather suspected he might not mind too much at all, as long as Julia kept to topics that were "safe". I had already warned her not to approach Gordon with her tales of the deadworld, offering to try to find Gordon's late wife Alice as she had offered to find Antony for me. For her such things were an adventure into realms where few others could ever go, exotic and exciting in rather the same way as climbing great mountains, perhaps. But there were profound feelings associated with this particular notion of hers that, never married, she did not seem to appreciate. Once I asked her, when this subject had come up, if she had ever gone looking for her own parents, who had died in a boating accident when she was a schoolgirl. "No, dear, of course not!" she'd said. "That would be grotesque! Good Lord!"

So Julia chattered on with her stories of ghosts, seances, ominous tea-leaf readings, abandoned houses, and the few times when local police had come for her help with the deadworld, and she had been able to contribute to the investigations. The police, though, regarded her as something a little less than freakish and a little more than disturbing, and did not call on her unless they were completely baffled, and then only with the greatest reluctance.

Soon we were in sight of the few lights of Pelican River—and almost immediately Julia stopped in mid-sentence. "Oh!" she gasped. "Oh dear..."

Gordon said, "Miss Templesmith?"

"Julia? Are you...?"

She said, "Oh, oh dear. Please—stop—the—car, would you?"

"Ruth?"

"I heard!" I hit the brakes. Fortunately we had not been travelling too quickly; the speed gauge had been steady on twenty miles per hour. We came to rest on the side of the road. Gordon was already out of his door and had darted around to help Julia out. I'd never seen him move so fast.

She leaned against Gordon and against the frame of the Tulip. The engine ticked. Heavy south-westerly winds rushed over us, stirring the lofty canopies of the white ghost gums. The sky was not completely suffocated with cloud; a few constellations were visible: the Broken Crown; the Sceptre; and part of the Begging Dog.

Julia was soon able to speak again. "I say, that rather hit like a train! My goodness me!" She was holding her head, as if afraid it might topple from her shoulders. "I do wish it would stop moving like that..."

"Miss Templesmith? Do you see something...?"

"The world, Mr Duncombe, the whole ruddy world!"

Gordon produced a small silver hipflask. "I have some twelve-year-old brandy here, if you think that—"

Before I could suggest that this might not be a good idea, Julia took it from him and took a long draught, after which she looked at first refreshed, but then much worse than before. "Oh dear..." She gave Gordon back his flask. He looked at it as if it had betrayed him. He went to have some, but then remembered his manners: "Ruth?"

I had a feeling I should keep my wits about me, and declined.

On Gordon's map, we were six miles from the town boundary. The ground all through here was quite flat; millions of years of weather had hammered this landscape into submission. There were no real mountains in the entire continent, certainly nothing that would match even the more modest alps of Europe. Here, our mountains were mere rounded humps The land fairly stank of profound age. The trees and vegetation looked so unlike anything from England or Europe. Back in England, we did not have trees whose bark was always peeling away like dead skin. We did not have bushes that thrived on almost no water at all, or which sported such riotous colours in the springtime. Plants in England were pretty and bright, but their colours blended tastefully.

Julia said, "It's not far from here."

And then she passed out.

*

Dr Lawrence Munz, who seemed as ancient and worn down as the land, was the only doctor in Pelican River, with rooms on Sullivan Street, not far from the church. The doctor lived in a small adjoining flat, with his monstrously fat Siamese cat, Willoughby. Dr Munz, I had learned, had delivered almost everyone living in the town, and many more who were no longer with us.

Gordon stayed with Julia in the Tulip while I hammered on his surgery door. The red electric light bulb next to the door cast everything in a strange, unearthly light. It was so cold I could see my breath.

I heard him muttering as he came to the door. When he pulled the door open, and saw me standing there in my driving gear, at first he looked annoyed. Then he saw Julia.

"It's my Aunt Julia," I said, feeling about twelve years old, "she's had something of a turn."

He nodded in a resigned sort of way. "Bring her in, then, we'll have a bit of a look at her. And hurry up, you're letting a cold draught in." He was clad in a tartan dressing gown and faded brown slippers.

Gordon and I brought Julia inside. She was starting to come round. The house, small but extremely tidy, smelled "good" in a way that is hard to characterise. Once through the door, I felt much better about everything. The drive back to town, racing as fast as I dared push the Tulip on the gravel, was fraught with panic. Gordon, in the back, did what he could to keep Julia warm, breathing, and upright enough so she wouldn't swallow her tongue.

We helped Julia up on the narrow, hard bed in the surgery office. She was prattling on and on in a flat, almost incoherent tone, apologising for taking up the doctor's time at this late hour, and how she wouldn't have bothered him but for the fact that she was feeling "ever so peculiar".

Dr Munz told her to open her mouth and say "Ah". He stuck a tongue depressor down her throat, which had the virtue of shutting her up for the moment. He made "hmm" noises, and put a cold thermometer under her tongue. "And keep your trap shut!" he said, perhaps unnecessarily gruff, even considering the hour.

"So what happened?" he said, looking at me from behind his desk.

I glanced at Gordon, who looked anxious. How to explain what we were doing? At last, a thought. "We were out trying to find a good spot to watch a meteor shower."

The doctor looked at Gordon, who was well-known for his odd interests. "Your doing I suppose, Mr Duncombe?"

"Ah, yes, Doctor. All my fault. Terrible night."

"I wouldn't have thought there'd be much to see tonight. The next big meteor shower isn't due for another three weeks or so, isn't it?" He gave Gordon a hard look, who brazened it out, and said nothing. Julia, still woozy, and holding her head, made faint moaning noises.

"Anyway," I said, to fill the silence, "we were out driving around the countryside, and we were coming back home, when this happened. She said she felt rather ill, and then passed out."

The doctor was inspecting Julia's eyes with a small electric light. "Has this happened before? Anything like this?"

I explained that Julia had had that incident during the flight out here, and that she had spent a few days in hospital up in Perth.

He said, looking at Julia with some interest now. "The doctors there said epilepsy, did they?"

"They were not entirely sure, but that was their opinion. The symptoms passed, however, and she's been fine since arriving here."

"Until tonight," Munz said. He retrieved his thermometer and inspected it. "Hmm..." he said, and set about taking Julia's pulse and checked her respiration. "Hmm..."

"Am I going to be all right, Doctor?"

"Is your head still giving you curry, Miss Templesmith?" He nodded at her, seeing she was still holding the back of her head.

"It's just rather on the sore side, if you know what I mean. And my eyesight, that's a bit..." She moved her head slightly from side to side. "A bit strange."

"How does this attack feel compared to the one you had on the flight?"

"Not as bad—but then, with that one, I was unconscious a lot longer. And I'd been enjoying a nip or two of cognac during the flight, because of my nerves, you understand."

"So you'd say this attack tonight feels different to the one you had on the aircraft."

"Somewhat, yes, Doctor. Is it serious?"

He looked worn out. "No, Miss Templesmith. Your temperature is up slightly, but that could be nothing, and your pulse is also slightly elevated, but that too could be due to a number of innocuous things..." He was tapping his old fountain pen against his chin, and looked very thoughtful.

"Doctor?" Julia asked, as if wondering why she hadn't been sorted out yet.

"I'd like to get another opinion, Miss Templesmith, and we might see about admitting you to the hospital up in Rockingham for a day or so, so we can run some tests."

Julia looked shocked. She glanced at me.

"Are you sure that's prudent, Doctor?" I asked.

He was already bustling us out into the waiting room so he could have some privacy while he used the telephone to arrange everything. To me, though, he said, "Just wait out here, thank you, Mrs Black. I'll be with you in a few moments."

So we sat and waited, Julia between Gordon and me. She was whispering quite loudly, "This isn't good, Ruth. I just know it. This is all happening at the wrong time, and I won't be here to look after you!"

I tried to put her mind at ease. "It's just for a day or two, Julia. It won't be too bad. We'll come up and see you, and keep you informed. It'll be fine!"

She looked at me with a disturbing fierceness. "Ruth, I felt it tonight."

"Felt what," I asked, feeling foolish as soon as the question left my mouth.

Julia went on, "Going out earlier, along that road, I felt nothing. Nothing at all. No disquieting feelings of any kind—which itself was rather strange, you must admit. Anyway, coming back, it hit me like a Number Nine bus. Do you see?"

Gordon nodded, as did I.

Julia said, "Something happened tonight. Something *arrived*."

10

By the time I dropped Gordon at his house and brought the Tulip home, it was a little after three in the morning. The night howled through the treetops; from far out to sea, I heard the crack of thunder. Leaves whirled in hectic circles around my feet as I crunched up to the front door.

Inside, Rutherford sat by a roaring fire, reading a book. He got up, "Good morning, ma'am. May I fetch you a warming drink?"

He was a wonder. "Thank you very much, Rutherford. That would be lovely."

"Right you are, ma'am," he said, heading for the kitchen. I followed him, still much too awake to consider sleep.

The milk ready, he poured, stirred and presented the finished cocoa, all with flair no-one would believe possible at this awful hour. I asked if he was having one, too, and he said he had just finished his.

I sent him to bed. I took a seat at the table, and held the hot cup in my cold hands. This time the previous night, Julia and I had sat right here and talked and talked. She seemed fine, and no doubt she had been fine, too. The thing that had now arrived was, last night, still on its shambling way. I shivered, thinking about it.

So now what? Gordon and I could go over his map with a compass and ruler, and determine the number of properties in the general vicinity of where we had stopped tonight. There shouldn't be that many. Pelican River was a small place; there could not be more than a handful of homesteads around that area. We could hardly visit each one in turn, knock on the door, and ask the occupants, "Excuse me for asking, but are you involved in demonology in any significant manner?" There were public records about property ownership and titles and such on file in the archives of the Town Hall. We could start there, perhaps. But then, what would we be looking for?

Sooner or later, I could see, we would find ourselves faced with the prospect of sneaking onto other people's land in the middle of the night and simply having a look for anything that might conceal a mysterious cellar. I did not relish this prospect. It seemed highly likely that we could wind up not only mauled by large dogs, and perhaps shot at by hostile farmers, but also arrested by the local police.

I gripped my mug, exhausted but not remotely sleepy. Also nagging in the back of my mind: now that Something had arrived, how long would it be in making its nocturnal visit to my house? I did not like thinking about this. How could one defend against such an unearthly visit? And what if the local elves really were behind it all?

One plan of action would simply be to clear out for a while. Take an extended holiday somewhere scenic, relaxing and sunny, where a harried author might finish her novel. Except, of course, an aeroplane journey to all such places would take at the very least a few weeks or longer. The prospect of sitting in cramped aeroplanes for all that time lacked a certain appeal. Somewhere in the midst of whatever would happen now, I had to finish the book.

Tomorrow morning—later this morning—I would work like a woman possessed. Visiting hours at the hospital did not begin until two in the afternoon. This would provide ample work time.

Sometime after four, I retired.

Sleep did not come until after six.

*

I woke Monday altogether too early considering the aching exhaustion I still felt, and when Rutherford inquired if I would be coming down for breakfast, and even though I could clearly smell bacon sizzling and coffee brewing, I said I might have a sandwich and coffee later. I felt like a load of wet laundry. I could not remember such weariness since my student days at Cambridge. I did ask Rutherford if there was any news, and he said there was not, or at least, not yet. I had hoped to spend today working, but getting organised for it, settling down to it, was nigh impossible. Instead, I spent much of the morning visiting Julia, and we talked about everything other than the matter at hand, the Something that had Arrived. If only I could think about anything at all other than the nagging feeling that whatever I did, whatever actions or precautions I might take, I would soon be dead. How long would the Something take, now that it was here?

*

As I settled in the dining room for breakfast on Tuesday, Vicky appeared, looking much more alive than I felt, carrying a modest bundle of post. "Gordon's been, ma'am!" She curtsied and disappeared.

Yawning, I checked through the post. A telegram from my publishers, inquiring after the progress of my novel. I put it aside. I could answer it later, when things were quieter.

Amongst the rest of the day's post was one from a reader in England, a young scientist named Hastings, studying at Cambridge, who told me I "have not the foggiest notion" about de Broglie's work on the wave-particle duality of matter and energy, and that it was "dangerous and foolhardy" of me to pretend that I did, and that I should "apologise to all readers of the world" for misleading them. Also, "why did the dog have to die?" I shook my head reading all this—it was in very small, precise handwriting. Well, I said to myself. I did read the latest scientific journals dealing with reports of early research in quantum theory, which did speculate about the possibility of wave-particle duality. Gordon had been only too keen to help me through the more difficult areas. As for apologising to readers everywhere, well, now that was amusing. I would respond to young Hastings later.

Then there was a letter addressed to Mrs R. E. Black. The postmark stamped on the envelope showed it was posted only this morning here in Pelican River. The stamp, showing a black swan, had been placed upside-down and at an odd angle. The address was typed in fading ink, which was not all that unusual, in mail coming from companies or offices of various kinds. Most ordinary people, though, did not have typewriters, which were expensive and cumbersome. And there was no return address anywhere to be found. The envelope smelled...it smelled of something slightly familiar, but I could not quite place it. Young Hastings' letter, by contrast, had been drafted on cheap, thin paper, in cheaper ink that reeked of fish. It "felt" cramped and intense, and there was a very faint air of beer about it that did not lend respect. The envelope of this last letter was inexpensive, and pale cream in colour. Opening it, I found a small sheet of octavo bank paper folded twice. Again, there was that familiar but baffling smell.

Then there was what I found typewritten on that paper:

WHY WAS YOUR FATHER KILLED?

Something very cold shot through me. I blinked a few times, and I think I laughed a little, smiling the way one does when things have taken a distinctly strange turn, but you have not yet quite realised how strange, or how disturbing. I read the note once again, and indeed several times. I inspected the back of the small piece of paper, finding nothing but the raised imprint of the typed characters.

Rutherford appeared, no doubt having heard my uncharacteristic laughter. "Ma'am?"

Not looking up from the note, I asked him for black coffee. I had a feeling I would need a lot of it before today was done.

I peered at the envelope again, and tried to identify that odd smell, without success. As Rutherford returned, bearing my coffee and two gingersnaps, I said, "But Father died of heart trouble."

"Ma'am?"

I took a sip of the coffee. It was steaming hot—just right. I showed him the note. Like me he sniffed at it, and exhibited a minute frown. "There appears to be some sort of soapy aroma, as well as something else..."

Soap! Yes, he was right. He gave back the note; I had another sniff, and this time could pick out the soap smell: it smelled like the sort of cheap soap one finds in public conveniences. But there was also that other smell, so faint...

Rutherford said, "I was under the impression that Sir Gustav suffered from a weak heart."

"That's right," I said, perhaps too hotly. "He collapsed almost exactly a year to the day after Mother passed away. And he'd not been well for months, in any case. It was the grief. He said so himself. Without Mother he wasn't half the man..." I felt myself starting to remember that whole terrible time, how I thought I would never stop crying, and how Antony had been such a tower of strength—until he, too...

I took a few moments to gather my strength again.

Rutherford waited before asking, "But why would anyone send you such a cryptic letter?"

I looked again at the envelope. At the local postmark. "All that happened back in England, more than twelve years ago..." I was speaking more to myself than anything.

"Will there be anything else, ma'am?"

I suggested a sandwich, and more coffee. Rutherford soon brought me an impressive sandwich, stuffed full of last night's leftovers, and a fresh pot.

The peculiar note occupied me throughout the morning and two cups of Murray's blistering best coffee. Once finished, I took the note, thinking I would show it to Gordon. As postman, he would have delivered it, so he might have noticed something odd about it. I had arranged to collect him before visiting Julia, and I was sure he would be at least intrigued. The arrival of this note so soon after the likely "arrival" of the "Thing" seemed ominous, though I suspected it could simply be a bizarre coincidence.

Correlation does not imply causation, I thought. And yet...

Rutherford took me out to Gordon's property. Sitting deep in the well-upholstered rear of the Bentley, I had time to brood. For one thing, I had never had cause to question my father's death. There had been a post-mortem examination of his remains, which found that he had suffered an extensive failure of his heart. His coronial arteries had been clogged to the point where such an outcome was, the coroner said, "inevitable". It had probably been something of a miracle that he had lived as long as he had, even as he pined away for Mother. So what was I now to think? My first impulse was to disregard the entire thing as a strange and tasteless prank—except that it seemed like a very specific, targeted prank. Someone wanting to play with me could choose any of a large number of things about me to mock.

But who here in this tiny seaside town at the most remote end of the civilised world knew more about my father than I did? It seemed to me that if such a note was going to arrive, surely, it would have come from home!

Rutherford spoke up. "Mr Duncombe's residence, ma'am."

11

Rutherford got us to Rockingham in short order, perhaps half an hour. I tried to discuss the disturbing note with Gordon.

I started off by asking him if, when he delivered the item in question, he had noticed anything odd about it. He said no, not at all. "Thought it was an ordinary item of post. Posted locally, of course. Nothing remarkable at all." He peered at the small sheet of thin paper from all angles, and took his time sniffing it, as I had done, noting both the soapy aroma as well as the other, more elusive scent. He read the typed question several times, a fierce frown knotting his forehead. Gordon did surprise me, though, when he produced a large magnifying glass from his too-large tweed coat's pocket and inspected both paper and question closely. He mumbled things to himself that I had learned, after all these years, not to ask him to explain. He was making notes, of a sort. Gordon was incapable of reading or studying anything without this mumbling. It had taken me some time to grow accustomed to this practice. When I was at Cambridge University, twenty years earlier, students tormented those unfortunates who made such noises as they read, regarding them as ill-bred simpletons. There was nothing simple about Gordon. He lacked impressive degrees, but I would stack up his accumulated knowledge and wisdom against that of any graduate of any university, and never mind how he went about acquiring that knowledge. At last he said, not looking up from his magnifier, "He's not a professional typist, for a start."

"The uneven pressure of the characters?"

He looked at me, and pointed at individual letters. "Women trained to use typewriters in businesses are taught at painful length to achieve an even pressure on the keys, in order to produce the best possible result. Even the harder letters, like Q, Z, and the question mark. From what I've gathered about such things, this can be tricky, to say the least. The human hand simply does not appreciate such contortions."

"So we can rule out aggrieved secretaries?"

"I think, based only on this evidence, we may have to consider a jealous rival of some sort."

"That's preposterous! I don't have jealous rivals!"

"You don't know that," he said, reasonably.

"Who on Earth would want to be *my* rival? It's nonsense! If I were writing conventional fiction, on the other hand..."

"There are other authors out there working in your field."

"And one of them not only knows something about my father's death, but is also quietly lurking about in Pelican River, plotting evil against me because of my fabulous success? I mean to say..." I stared out the window, annoyed. In a way it was disappointing *not* to have jealous rivals.

Gordon resumed his minute study of the note. "All right. What about this? Look at the 'A' in 'FATHER' and 'WAS.' What do you notice?" He handed me the glass and the note. I squinted into its depths. And noticed what he meant: the 'A' was not registering properly, and the triangular space in the top of the letter was mostly filled in—someone had been negligent in his or her typewriter maintenance. Such maintenance was filthy business and something I had almost to force myself to do.

"It sounds like something out of one of those popular tales of intrigue," Gordon said, amused despite himself, "but it's true what they say about typewriters. Find the machine that produced this note, and you'll find your mysterious correspondent. How said correspondent could possibly know about your father—and be here in Australia, and more than that, they would also have to know how to find me—well, that I don't know. It does seem rather elaborate to travel all this way just to engage you in clichéd intrigues. If they have something to tell you, why not simply tell you?"

"Ah," I said, having thought about this very question. "That's obvious. At some point there will be a promise of information in return for a sum of money."

"You think extortion's the plan?"

I nodded, feeling tired. "That's my thinking."

"And then what will you do, if you receive such a demand?"

I did not know. It had occurred to me simply to take this note to the local police, and see what they might do for me. I had little confidence in them, which seemed reasonable when it always appeared to me that they would far rather spend time fishing or crabbing on the estuary than patrolling through town. "I suppose it will depend on all sorts of things. What they claim to know, how much they want, if there are any threats. Who knows?"

Gordon said, "We can hardly put a notice in the newspaper asking all Pelican River residents who own typewriters to bring them, say, to your house so that we might inspect them…" The idea seemed to entertain him.

"The writer might be using a borrowed machine—or, indeed, a stolen machine."

"Which would at least lend itself to the idea that the writer is not a professional typist." He was making "hmm" noises again.

"What do you make of the aromas?"

"Well, there's clearly a soap of some sort. I would suggest that you're dealing with a person very conscious of cleanliness, or possibly someone like a cleaner, perhaps…" He didn't have to say it.

"Perhaps someone like a maid, who does a lot of cleaning?"

I thought about Vicky and Sally, whose lives were almost completely taken up with the many and varied cleaning duties my house required. They were quick and efficient, and they chattered away like parrots when they worked together, but I generally did not think about them much. I had always been extremely pleased with the standard of their work, particularly since neither had had any training as maids-of-all-work before coming to work in my house. I thought I paid them more than the going rate for the work they did, and I thought I treated them well, particularly considering the terrible way the servants in my family's home were treated. My mother, in particular, was inclined to regard the staff as annoying machines that were always in the way, never did a good enough job, were always after more money, and probably stole things. I was determined, when I moved here, that any servants I might employ would not be treated so poorly. So far, I thought I had done well by them. And yet Sally and Vicky would be close enough to me to issue mysterious messages. But how would they know anything about the circumstances of my father's death? And where would they have acquired something as bulky and expensive as a typewriter? Would I not know about such things, since they lived in my house?

I discussed all this with Gordon, who shared my concerns. One thing he did say, though, was helpful: "The local library, I'm pretty sure, has an old typewriter that it hires out to people, if they need to write something official, that sort of thing."

"The library?" I would have to pay a visit to my friend Jane.

Rutherford announced, speaking loudly over the noise of the wheels, "Entering Rockingham, ma'am!"

"Thank you, Rutherford," I said, now wondering if Rutherford ever felt resentful towards me. It seemed inconceivable. Rutherford, since the day I had hired him before I left England, had always demonstrated great keenness for his work, even back when I had had to train him in the buttling arts. His enthusiasm for the work always won me over, even when his technique was somewhat lacking. Then I remembered arriving home in the middle of a grim night, finding him sitting up by the fire, reading a book, awaiting my return. That did not suggest a man resentful of his employer.

Then Gordon, who had been staring out his window, said, "Then there's the other matter."

"Gordon?" I thought we had covered everything.

He held the note up. "'Why was your father killed?' You've said that your father died of natural causes. You've said that the coroner assured you of this, because the post-mortem confirmed it. The poor man simply dropped dead one day, probably from pure grief."

"That's right…" I was starting to see where he was going.

"But this correspondent of yours is telling you that your father was killed. Do you see?"

"Yes, yes, I think I do. Is it really possible, though?"

"I have heard of methods, involving exotic compounds, which, once administered, can rapidly bring about what looks most convincingly like heart failure."

"But he was just my father!" This was getting ridiculous. Who would want to kill my father?

"Your father was Minister of War, wasn't he? He was always in the papers. 'Sir Gustav Templesmith in high-level meetings with officials from France', that kind of thing, wasn't he?"

"Yes, that's right. He was Secretary of State for War, in the Cabinet — he'd served six years. Made great changes."

"Rather a sensitive position, I would say…"

"But he was my *father*!" I protested, too loudly, and with too much feeling.

Gordon looked at me. He said, quietly, "How well did you really know him?"

I went to speak, but stopped. There had always been things about my father that I had never quite understood, though one thing I had always understood only too well was that I was daughter to a man who wanted a son. Mother had had quite a deal of trouble in my birth — or, rather, our birth, I should say. I was one of a pair of identical twins. My sister, Elizabeth, had been stillborn. I thought of her often. As a writer of speculative fictions, I had often daydreamed about Elizabeth's life, unfolding in another time, hidden from this one, and I wondered what she was like. It was strange, growing up an only child, knowing there had been this other, always around, but never present, ghost. Meanwhile, in my own world, I was a daughter in a world that valued sons, and thus, at a fundamental level, a disappointment, with the thin consolation prize that perhaps my family could make a good strategic sort of marriage with another family and produce an heir, but otherwise my value was limited. Father nevertheless did his best to make a man out of me, which is probably where I acquired the peculiar notion of dressing as I did. Almost all the interesting people I met were men, and they all dressed in expensive suits. The women I had been introduced to were, on the whole, frilly, shallow, and frequently vicious young things. I learned quickly that if a man did not like you, he would be quite straightforward about it; if another woman did not like you, you would be put to a metaphorical death by gossip, and you would never see it coming. I spent altogether too much of my time at that age wondering where were all the interesting women, the ones whose transporting books I read and re-read? In the end, despairing, I learned to drink and shoot and hunt; I learned to converse and have opinions, even if those opinions, at first, were not always my own. I did my best to adapt and thrive, always despite knowing, when my father looked at his freakish offspring, that as hard as I tried to be a boy, I was, still, a silly foolish girl, and of no use to him. We did not have long talks far into the night. We were distant, and this worsened over time. He held me at arm's length, as he also did with the rest of his influential, rich, well-bred chums. I fit in and I did not. By the time Antony came along on one of Father's shooting parties, I had been thinking of packing it all in and taking off overseas, where I planned to travel for months or years at a time, and perhaps find a real identity for myself. Perhaps find someone who could see me without also seeing the grand country house and the imposing bank balance, who could see me as Ruth, and not as The Heiress.

Antony saw me, from that first moment, only as Ruth. He didn't give a toss about the way I dressed, the way I smoked cigars and drank my father's best single-malt. He saw the woman my father had always tried so hard not to see. Antony only wanted to hold me close. Though one might say it took me a long time to realise this.

"Ruth?"

Blinking, I looked up at Gordon. He was a plump, rumpled, poorly presented middle-aged man. He wore tweed that needed patching; his shirts always looked like they needed ironing. His mousy hair was never brushed, and he never polished his shoes. There was always a great deal of dog dander on his clothes, and he was just as likely to pull a dog biscuit out of his pocket as stray coins, bits of scrap paper infested with doodles, keys to things I did not know about, rubber bands, sticks, or boiled sweets. He was almost everything Antony had not been. And yet, Gordon, in many ways, was a better friend than even Antony had been. Gordon and I had been able to talk without any effort from the day I met him. His mind worked so differently from the minds of the kind of people I had known back home. It was a blessed relief.

He said, "We're here, Ruth. Are you quite all right?" I realised I had been crying a little, and dabbed at my eyes, glad I did not bother with beauty routines. "What would be the point?" Father used to say.

"I'm fine," I said, squeezing his hand. "Thank you."

Rutherford opened my door and helped me out. I looked closely at him, trying to see traces of secret resentment or hostility, but all I saw was professional respect. "Rutherford?"

"Ma'am?" He was straightening my clothing, adjusting my hat against the glare from the overcast sky.

"Vicky and Sally. Would you say they are...how to put this? Would you say they are content in their employment?"

"Ma'am?"

I tried again. "Are they happy, Rutherford? Are there any complaints about which I should be informed?"

"I believe they are fine, ma'am. Is everything quite...?"

I waved a gloved hand. "It's nothing. Just a stray thought. Nothing at all."

"Of course, ma'am."

Rutherford stayed with the car while Gordon and I went inside.

The hospital smelled like hospitals everywhere, almost frighteningly clean, and yet there was something else that wasn't quite clean, and that was a little worrying. The floors were polished—indeed, we saw a man struggling to operate a gigantic industrial floor polisher down one corridor. Nurses in white, with starched white caps on their heads, darted back and forth. There was a rattle of trolleys, and, as we entered Julia's ward, there was an elderly lady propelling a large trolley carrying a hot water urn, making cups of tea for patients and staff. In other words, everything seemed normal. I asked at the main desk if we might see Julia.

We found Julia sitting up in bed, sipping a cup of tea. She wore a thin cotton gown neither fetching nor quite large enough. Fortunately, I had brought a bag of necessaries for her. "Ruth! Mr Duncombe! Oh I say, thank goodness you've come." She beamed at us, and then turned to the lady in the adjacent bed, saying, "This is my niece and her marvellous friend Mr Duncombe, the noted inventor!" The other lady looked nonplussed and very ill. Gordon looked rather bashful. I perched on the side of the high bed and Gordon found a rickety-looking chair. Julia was nattering at me about how pleased she was to see us and what a strange night's sleep she had and how once she was asleep there were all these people wanting to know if she wanted anything to help her sleep, and would she like a cup of tea, and did she want the bed linen changed, and all the usual sorts of thing. At length, I held up my hand, said, "Good morning, Julia. It's lovely to see you looking so much better." I handed her the bag of necessaries, in which I'd concealed some biscuits and pastry treats from Murray. Julia looked very pleased. I suspected there were aspects of hospital life that she quite liked, and being spoiled like this was certainly one of them.

Julia got down to business, and told us all about what the doctors were saying, the tests she had been through, and what the people in nearby beds were all suffering from, and had we noticed that funny smell? If I had felt tired before we arrived, now I felt doubly so. Gordon maintained a polite, rather fixed, smile, and tapped one of his feet.

Julia's mysterious symptoms had subsided. She had had X-rays done of her head. Nurses had been by to take her pulse, temperature and respiration at thirty-minute intervals throughout the night and day. Doctors had frowned at her and asked her a great many questions about her apparent difficulties with visual perception, and there had been a lot of whispered conferences just far enough away from her bed that she knew they were discussing grave matters but not close enough for her to hear details. So far, she reported, the doctors were "waiting and seeing". Which meant they wanted to see if the symptoms manifested again. There was talk of the kinds of horrific drugs she had been told about up in Perth, which was a matter of great concern for her. I said, "Julia, if it comes to that, heaven forbid, we shall seek a second opinion. Worry not."

I was inclined to think, despite what doctors had told me previously, that she most likely did not have epilepsy. I was given to understand that sufferers experienced attacks both much more frequent and more severe. And besides, there was the supernatural aspect of which these doctors would be unaware, and about which I was not the person best suited to inform them. How would I even begin to broach the idea? I could only barely comprehend it myself. It ran against everything I believed, except that I had always tried to accept that there was more to what we called reality than was commonly thought. The tumult in the world of physics, happening right now, was evidence of that! I had always understood that event B was *caused* by event A. Yet the latest findings in the new quantum theory suggested, bafflingly, that event B could simply happen, on its own, with no prior cause. It was more than merely counterintuitive. There were suggestions that electrons, far from picturesque little planets orbiting the central star that was the nucleus, were blurry, chaotic things, as likely to be found *here* as *there* and *elsewhere*. That there was no longer such a thing as *certainty*. There was no telling what further strangeness might be shown to exist. Reality, in a sense, was up for grabs. Perhaps Aunt Julia's way of perceiving "other bits of reality" was not supernatural nonsense, but a unique capacity to sense something in the bowels of reality which science would one day demonstrate. There was no denying that she had a remarkable way of knowing things she could not possibly know. The whole business gave me the willies, but I was prepared to go along with it. But how to broach the entire matter to Julia's doctors here at this hospital?

Then I told Julia about the strange note I'd received, and showed it to her. She put on her reading glasses and peered at it. "What, that's it? Gustav died of heart failure, didn't he, the poor dear?" She had taken her brother's death hard. It had reduced her, as if a large piece of her physical substance had been removed. "Who would send such a thing?" she said, and asked me to hand it to her. I passed it to her. She grabbed hold of the note but immediately paused. "Oh dear," she said, "oh, that does feel most peculiar, I must say..." She flinched, as if a sudden shiver went through her, glanced at Gordon and me as the colour drained from her face. Gordon asked if she was quite all right. "Quite all right, Mr Duncombe, thank you. But this letter..." She blinked slowly and went ashen. "This is..."

She collapsed.

12

We summoned the nurse, who summoned doctors. The nurse asked us to wait in the waiting area, and drew the curtains around Julia's bed. I tried to explain, to tell them about Julia, that she wasn't just a slightly dotty lady, but the nurse, very much all business, would have none of it.

It took hours. Julia had "only" passed out, with another seizure, or something like a seizure. I sat and paced and sat in the waiting area, furious with myself. That damned note. I should have realised. What had I been thinking? What I had been thinking was that it was just a strange message typed out on a sheet of paper. It never occurred to me that it might be full of the sort of resonances and emanations that might set off Julia's condition. Gordon, the sweet man, tried his best to comfort me, to not much avail.

"What if I'd killed her?" To which he said, "But you didn't. She'll be fine. And besides," he went on, "now we know something else: the person or persons out there doing that summoning in the cellar could also be the author of that note."

"Yes, fine, good, but why?" Why all this stupid, melodramatic nonsense? Why not just come to my front door and kill me with a gun? It was a thought I'd had too many times. The whole thing offended me. It was ridiculous. Even if there were genuine demons beyond the pale of reality, and even if they could be summoned and employed to do vile things on one's behalf, it was simply too much work, too much bother, surely! It wasn't sensible. It wasn't what people did. If you wanted to murder someone and conceal your involvement, you could use poison; you could use a third party, witting or unwitting. Someone in Pelican River was prepared to go to all this absurd trouble, just for the likes of me. And what of all the people I had in my employ? They were surely in danger as well. And yet, if I were to say, "All right, that's enough, it's time to leave town, at least temporarily," there was no way to know for sure that my enemies would not simply bide their time until I returned. And if I were to leave permanently—if I were to return to England, for example, or the Continent—there was no way to guarantee they would not pursue me there and pick up where they left off. This was unacceptable. Julia, my dear Julia, positively relished the adventure of it all, the mystery. But the way things were going, it would be the most sensible thing to put her on the next flight back to England, well away from me, the strange woman with a giant target painted on her back.

More than two hours later, a middle-aged male doctor named Rainer appeared, adjusting his thick, wire-frame spectacles, to tell me, the designated next-of-kin, what was going to happen.

"You are Miss Templesmith's niece, is that right?" he asked, consulting a ragged-looking notebook, flipping pages back and forth. He had a tendency to bite his lower lip as if nervous, I noticed.

"I am, yes. Mrs Ruth Black. How is she?"

"Miss Templesmith is conscious, but in considerable pain. We've prescribed analgesia and a light sedative to help her sleep through the night."

"Of course," I said, nodding, feeling cold and numb—and responsible. "When can she come home, Doctor?"

He rubbed the back of his neck, frowning. I saw he had a nasty scar near that part of his neck. The clatter and rattle and booming rumble of noise around us in the ward was crushing me. It was hard to concentrate on what he was saying. What he seemed to be saying was that he wanted to send Julia back to Perth for more serious tests, perhaps some exploratory brain surgery. Failing that, and considering this was her third attack in only a few days, they were considering using Luminal, or phenobarbital.

I could not speak. My mouth was dry; my tongue stuck to my palate. The press of noise was unbearable. It was hard even to think. My only thought was that all this was my fault. I was not sure quite in which way, or why it was, but it felt very much like if it had not been for me, somehow, Julia would be perfectly fine, chattering away, eating other people's food, living a happy life.

Gordon took my arm. "Ruth, it's…"

I shook him off. The thought of surgeons probing about inside Julia's quivering brain made me ill. It was unbearable. It was all unbearable.

Dr Rainer offered me a chair and asked if I would like a cup of tea. I took the chair, but shook my head about the cup of tea. The doctor got down on his haunches. "I do understand how distressing this must be to you, Mrs Black."

"Is that right?" I said.

He had done this before. "These are very hard things to face."

I looked at him. He looked away.

He went on. "We do believe that Miss Templesmith's condition could be manageable, with the right course of treatment, the right conditions."

"On Luminal? With the awareness of a parsnip?"

"Ruth…" Gordon said.

"It's either that or the ketogenic diet—"

"I beg your pardon, the what?"

"It's an experimental treatment for epilepsy. We—"

"No-one, understand me, is experimenting on my aunt. Is that clear?"

"Ruth," Gordon said to me. "You're shouting."

I had not been aware of this. "Thank you, Gordon."

"Mrs Black," Rainer said, speaking in a low, measured tone, and looking as baffled as I was. "Your aunt's condition is not cut and dried. It looks somewhat like epilepsy, but not completely. There are other features. Unfortunately, there are limits to what we understand about the workings of the brain."

I looked up, wanting to scream at him (scream at myself),

but I said nothing. I wished I could tell this doctor about Julia's special talents, but I knew that was hopeless. Nothing good could come from such a revelation. I said, "Is she awake? Can I see her?"

He nodded, smiled a little, and bit his lip. "Of course. Just for a moment." Julia was lying down. She looked peaceful. The curtain was all the way around her bed; we had some privacy. The noise in here was less oppressive. "Ruthie..."

I took her hand. It was cold. I was cold. I did not know what to say.

She smiled slowly, like a ghost. "Don't be upset. I do not blame you. I came here on my own. Remember that."

Nodding, I said, "I know." She could not help what her antenna picked up out of the ether; nor could she help her need to warn her niece who might be in serious trouble. I knew that. Of course I knew that. It did not help. If I had just not shown her the note, if I had left it at home...

"You'll sort it out," she said, her eyes sleepy. "I really must get some of this for home..." She gestured at the bottle of painkilling compound. "It's better than champagne."

"Could I ask you about the note, Julia?"

She smiled again. "'Course, dear."

"Did it feel... the same? Like last night? And on the aeroplane?"

Julia looked at me as if trying to locate my face, as if trying with enormous difficulty to concentrate, to tell me this. "He's so angry, Ruth. He could kill you himself. With his bare hands..." She gestured a weak sort of throttling motion. She subsided, exhausted.

"He? Not a they?"

"There... may be others involved. It's hard to see."

"Ruth," Gordon said, poking his head awkwardly through the curtain. "That's enough. Leave her be, eh?"

I turned, meaning to snap at him. How dare he tell me when I was finished talking to my aunt when she had something to tell me! But the look on his rumpled, lined face... He looked so kind.

I said to Julia, "I'll be back tonight, if you like." Visiting hours resumed at seven o'clock.

"I'll be fine. You sort it out. See me tomorrow."

Tomorrow she might have been sent off to Perth Hospital. I nodded. It would be easy enough to find out where she was. Perth was only a four-hour journey from Pelican River.

I heard light rain rattling against the corrugated iron roof, and at the windows. Julia was already asleep.

*

Rutherford drove us home, taking the roads with great care. We made slow progress. Rain spattered against the car. Gordon and I hardly spoke.

With his bare hands. I thought I had been shocked before. I was no stranger to other people's anger towards me, but this? There were, in town, several people with grudges against me, none of which I took all that seriously. But it was one thing to have a grudge, to have had words, to have had a public argument with someone, to be full of resentment and even hatred, and quite another to be prepared to take that person's life. How many marriages were there in town that seemed only held together by the mutual hatred of the man and woman? I knew there were a few. No-one said anything much about this. Women whom one might see going about their daily business sporting a poorly concealed set of facial bruises shrugged and muttered about clumsily hitting doorknobs or falling over a child's toy and hitting a table corner. Some people, one could conclude, had extremely dangerous furniture. Some people should be persuaded, perhaps, that they needed new furniture.

I watched water run down the glass. Listened to it pounding the car's steel roof. Inside, the car was warm, smelling of expensive leather and imported wood polish.

With his bare hands.

It was a striking thing to learn. Such an intimate way to kill a person, close enough to feel their warmth, smell their heated breath, reeking of passion and fear and whatever they'd last eaten.

Chills flashed through me, thinking about it. It seemed impossible. It seemed, in fact, like the kind of thing that might occur back in England, where extraordinary, operatic passions seethed beneath the veneer of polite and mannered discourse. Where a thoughtless remark could inspire the darkest revenge. Things were not like that out here in the colonies, I had always thought. That was why I had come here, why I had endured ten months at sea.

Yet the colonies were full of people who either had come from parts of Britain or who had been born here of British parents. How could I have been so stupid and blind? I had not left behind the raging passions and lethal intrigues of British society; these had come along with me, with all of us who had journeyed out here to start new lives. We could not help but have brought it with us; it was as much a part of our way of life as the food we preferred to eat, as the heavy and cumbersome clothing we preferred to wear, the songs we sang around the piano, the prayers we mumbled in church—and even those poor benighted wretches, the elves. Not that we'd stowed them in our ships like cargo; they'd come here in our dreams and idle thoughts and memories of childhood faerie stories. We'd brought them with us the way we brought our prejudices, our hatreds and loves and fears.

"Hatreds and fears." There was a thought. Whilst it was true that several people in town held grudges against me for various largely imaginary infringements of their delicate sensibilities, one Father William Dennis certainly hated me. Indeed, he'd banished me from the premises, me and my ungodly ways.

I told Gordon the salient details. That I had gone to the church that day to inquire after service times, and for my trouble was sneered at, and the courage of my late husband impugned. He had been lost in thought, staring out the windows, perhaps watching for bands of elves by the side of the road. "I say," he said.

I said, "What about Father William?"

He scratched at his head and frowned. "I hardly think so. If he were any more devout and pious, he'd turn to marble and become one of his precious bloody statues. Besides, I mean, look at him. He's feeble. He's old. He's bitter, of course, about the

War, and being stuck in a tiny country town, but he's angry with his superiors, the bishops and archbishops, the entire ghastly superstructure of the Church itself. I'm sure his grievance with you is nothing so serious as those other matters."

"I suppose..."

"Besides, if he was your villain, how could he know anything personal about your father? He's been in town, what, how long? Longer than you, for a start."

That was an excellent point. My father's identity—that I was the daughter of Sir Gustav Templesmith—was known to many in Pelican River, as such matters inevitably are in small towns. But I always considered my personal matters just that, and the circumstances of my father's and Antony's deaths, and their lives, for that matter, were not something I had shared with any but those closest to me. "Well, who then?"

Gordon shrugged. "Anybody at all. Every man, woman and child carries the potential for the most horrific violence. You mark my words."

I had heard him say this before. Though he had been deemed unfit for military service due to back problems and flat feet, Gordon knew about the things that lay in the human heart. I did not agree with this bleak view of our fellow human beings. I believed, when one got right down to the nub of the matter, that we started out innocent and noble—and that the circumstances of our lives caused us to become what we became. We begin as blank slates. Gordon, on the other hand, pointed out cases from the newspaper and from history books which described brutal, unthinkable deeds committed by ordinary, peace-loving people, and even by children.

The huge car swerved; I was flung across at Gordon.

A terrible bumping sensation went through the front wheels, then, a moment later, the two sets of rear wheels.

"Rutherford?"

"God!" he said, working to slow the car to a stop on the side of the road.

"What...what hap...?" Gordon said, as I righted myself. I could still feel that bumping.

We stopped. "Ma'am—are you…?"

"Did we hit something?"

Rutherford looked back at us through the glass. He looked pale, quite unnerved, his dark eyes wide. He started to climb down to the road. I got out. I looked back.

We had hit something.

It lay spread out in the muddy gravel. I gasped, and crossed myself.

Several elves, perhaps nine or ten of them, stood either next to the body or by the side of the road. In the rain, their flimsy clothes, much of it stolen from local clotheslines, clung to their emaciated bodies. There was, almost literally, nothing to them.

They watched us approach, standing quite still, staring with eyes that were all white, but for the tiniest black pinprick pupils, as if even this overcast grey light was far too strong for them. Closer to, one could see suggestions of bones beneath their tissue-thin colourless flesh.

My heart sped. I felt sick. The smell was shocking.

Gordon said, "Is it dead?" He sounded close to tears.

Rutherford went up to the elves standing over the body. There were four children—I assumed they were children, as they were smaller, but I didn't know—of various ages. Rutherford said, "I am so terribly, terribly sorry. Please, is there anything I can…?"

They stared at him. I could not describe the absence of expression on their alien faces. I could just barely make out the spiral tattoos etched into the peeling skin of their faces. They stared at him, and they stared at us.

Gordon was saying, "Oh God, we hit an elf…" over and over. He looked like he would be sick.

The cold rain fell hard.

Two elves—males, I think—scooped up the body. It was hard to watch.

They took the body to the other elves, by the side of the road.

It looked like they wanted to do something, but were waiting for us to leave.

"Look," I said, "I'm…this is my fault. I shouldn't have been out in this weather. I…Is there anything I can do, anything?"

My words fell into a void. I knew they understood me. I knew they understood our feelings of horror and profound regret. I knew they could answer me had they wanted.

I could hear the car's engine tick.

They stood there, holding the body, staring at us. Staring at me. They knew that the car was mine. They knew it was my fault.

"For God's sake, speak to us!" I said. "Let us help!"

The body was *dissolving* in the rain. The rain was even dissolving the rags it had worn. Soon there would be nothing left. I could hardly believe what I was seeing. Where did the body go? What happened to it?

Why wouldn't they let us — let me — help?

"We can't just stand here in the rain all day!"

But it looked like they could.

Rutherford, weeping silently, turned to me. "What should we do?"

They stood there like trees. They did not even blink. I could not see them breathe.

"Please! Please let us help! Can we take you back to town?" I did not know how we would put them all in the Bentley, but I was willing to try.

Rutherford took a step closer, close enough to touch them. "I am sorry. I didn't mean to…It was the rain, I couldn't see…"

They glanced at him, then resumed staring at me. It seemed to me that the children showed more animation, but I could not say what it was — it could have been happiness; it could have been hatred.

This went on for some time. I don't know how long. Trying to engage them, to apologise, to try to convey our horror and sadness, but it was hopeless. They wanted to be on their way. That much we understood. I said, at last, "Let's go, Rutherford. There's nothing we can do."

"Come on, mate," Gordon said to him. Rutherford looked terrible. His hands shook.

We got back aboard the car.

I turned to look back through the rear window. They were still there, part of the fabric of the world, and yet also not part of it, marooned here in this plane of reality, far from home. If anything, I imagined they envied their lost comrade.

Rutherford put the car in gear. We drove off.

I turned again to look.

They were gone.

13

All that afternoon, every time I closed my eyes, even simply to blink, I saw the elves, saw their unearthly faces and pinprick eyes, and felt again that awful series of bumps as the enormous Bentley rode over the elf's body. I tried to keep busy. Sitting at my desk, the desk I had bought with proceeds from my first novel, *Eliza Paine*, I stared at the worn keys of the typewriter for a long time. At some point I rolled in some paper. After reading back over the previous three or four pages of *Too Many Worlds*, I started work. I'd missed too many days with all the panic and intrigue. So I started typing.

I lasted half an hour before giving up for the day. I had no concentration. There was no way to focus on my stricken protagonist and his make-believe troubles when my mind was full of the sight of dead elves dissolving in the rain. I cannot even recall now what happened in those pages.

Pulling out the completed pages without releasing the platen made a loud zipping noise; it startled me to hear it. By the time I quit for the day, I had done eight pages, double-spaced. But it was, as I say, all typing. There was no writing there.

Downstairs, restless, still with no appetite for dinner, I tried to read last week's issue of the *Pelican River Record*. It was only a handful of pages, written, printed and distributed by Bill Cox. His mates called him "Blue" because of his receding red hair and freckled skin. The local news was, as ever, quiet. The Pelican River Association of War Veterans was holding public meetings over whether to join the national Returned Sailors' and Soldiers' Imperial League of Australia; opinion seemed divided. Certain kinds of fish were running off certain parts of the local coast. There was a reminder from the local police that it was indeed an offence for stray cattle to roam through the town, and a further offence for said cattle to eat the posted signs pointing this out. That one made me smile. I had only seen roaming cattle on a few occasions. They made quite a mess that had to be cleaned up, but otherwise seemed harmless. A Mr Ronny Fitch fell from the estuary footbridge while on his way back to the Foreshore from the Commercial Hotel, out on the Point. This was the third time this month. There was a supplementary note suggesting it was high time the local Council decided "once and for all" just who was responsible for maintaining that footbridge. The police had caught some crab poachers. Mrs Violet Eglee, eighty-six, reported "funny noises" and "goings on" in her front yard last Monday night. Ted "Nobby" Mack was selling his booming fish-canning and export business, due to ill health. In the War he'd been exposed to mustard gas. His lungs had never been right since. It was understood a group of wealthy Perth investors was interested in taking over the business. The Lavelle family's pet dog, a beagle named Max, had now been missing for four days. A reward of two pounds was offered. An article largely dictated by Pelican River Mayor Fred "Dipper" Trevaney, known throughout town to be "a top bloke," reported, as always, that the town was "thriving," and that in the last quarter four new families had moved here (names included) and five new businesses (same), and he urged the townsfolk to give the new arrivals a big Pelican River welcome. I recalled no such urgings when I moved here, nor any mentions in the local paper. On the other hand, the town's richest farmer, Jack "Nugget" White, who had the biggest sheep station in the entire region, had placed an advertisement in the "Help Wanted" column for a "butler/

driver. Decent wages. Two days off per week. Duties to include helping Mrs with grocery shopping and general errands."

It occurred to me that Rutherford might be tempted by the job offer. I decided to have a quiet word with him, take a sounding. On the back page, where Bill Cox ran colourful coverage of local, national and overseas sport, I learned that the local football team, the Pelican River Pelicans, was poised to "cripple and maim" rival team, the Rockingham Warriors, this Saturday, which would take the Pelicans to a six-game winning streak. The rest of the local competition were said to be feeling "nervous". And, the weekly chook raffle at the Commercial Hotel had been won by Mayor Dipper Trevaney again, for the eighteenth time this year. Trevaney was quoted as saying, "Crikey, what a turn-up for the books this is! You beauty!" He was then said to have shouted the bar, to general acclaim.

It all read like reports from a far-off land. There was nothing about the haughty rich Englishwoman whose enormously expensive car had run over a poor helpless elf. Not that I expected there to be anything. Most people had never seen an elf, let alone a whole group, and certainly almost no-one would have had any sort of encounter with them, as we had now. They avoided us; we avoided them. There were sometimes signs that you might be in an area occupied by a band of elves: dead or dying trees, failing crops, an absence of wildlife. Sometimes it was simply an overwhelming sense of dread. British anthropologists had, from time to time, attempted to study them, or even approach them, without success. I suspected scientists from outside the historical sphere of influence of the British Empire might do better. The elves were manifestations of everything we British had done wrong, of how we had violated the very Earth itself with our existence. I wondered if other historical empires had had similar shadows following them around the globe in their conquests? Had there been elves of some sort trailing after the Romans? After Alexander the Great? Or was this a manifestation of purely British shame? One could only imagine what the planet must have "felt" about the atrocity of world war raging across its face.

*

Sitting there on the sofa, not seeing anything, feeling numb, I realised I could hear voices in the kitchen. Rutherford was unburdening himself to Murray and Sally. They were listening, telling him, "It was just an accident. You couldn't help it. It's just like when you run over an animal. You didn't mean to. It's all right, John, it's all right. Stiff upper lip, love. You'll be right." I could not quite make out what Rutherford was saying; his voice was muffled; he sounded profoundly distressed. What should I do? Was it proper to provide a shoulder to cry on for a man in one's employ? I could not imagine anyone in my family showing such compassion for an upset servant in similar circumstances—and that was the perspective I needed. I got up and went to the kitchen. Rutherford and I talked for half an hour. He looked like he appreciated it.

Why was I not crying, as he was? In a way, I felt far too upset for mere crying. The wet gloom of the day had infested my bones.

I wondered how Gordon was managing. If I knew Gordon, he was working extremely hard on his time machine, or on something, at least. That was how he managed. When we had spoken, briefly and just once, about his wife's death, he told me that in the month following her loss, he designed and built nine new devices, including a scale model of a new sort of locomotive engine, powered by electricity transmitted through the air. I therefore expected, when I next saw Gordon, that his time machine, a bare framework and collections of odd components when last I visited, would be just about ready for a test jaunt.

I telephoned Gordon. The evening switchboard lady, June, hearing my voice, asked, "Mr Duncombe, ma'am?"

"Please, if you would."

It took a very long time for Gordon to answer. When, at length, he did, he sounded as if he had just woken up. "Mmm...? Ruth? Is that you?" Even though June would have just told him that I was calling. This wasn't like Gordon.

"Gordon, I was just...are you quite all right?"

There was a long pause. I could hear his slow, heavy breathing.

"Mmm. I'm...I'm fine. Just fine. And you, my dear?"

My dear? Gordon didn't speak like that to me. Concerned, I said, "I thought you might need some company..."

"No, no, that's fine, no. I'm fine."

"Perhaps I'll just pop over, say hello. I could bring some sort of afternoon tea?"

"If you like, dear. That's fine."

*

Driving out of town to Gordon's house in the Tulip, I went very slowly in the bleak, overcast light, over the sodden roads, and gripped the steering lever with both gloved hands as though my life depended on it. I peered through the rain, alert for the slightest problem or obstacle. I could not remember ever feeling more alert, or more nervous, while driving. In my mind, that horrible sensation of the Bentley's wheels bumping over the elf's body kept playing out. I felt certain I would run across another one. Every turn of the narrow road concealed imminent tragedy. Making these turns, and finding nothing but the odd fallen branch, was disturbing. I kept "seeing" wandering elves. The car's brakes were suffering with my constant application; the journey was a stop-start misery. When I finally arrived at Gordon's, it was late afternoon, the feeble sun low in the west behind thick cloud, and his small house looked as gloomy and tense as I felt. I brought the Tulip up to the front of the house.

Where were all the dogs? The place seemed deathly quiet. By now I should have been drowning in dogs.

At the door, bearing a basket of hastily constructed afternoon-tea treats, I did hear dogs barking, far in the background. Gordon opened up and let me in.

The stink of alcohol was all over him.

"Ruth!" he said, smiling, and closing the door. "What brings you here?"

The dogs sounded like they were going mad, locked out the back.

"I thought you might like some company."

He unveiled an enormous smile, completely lacking his usual

reserve. "What's in the basket?" He lifted the lid. His eyebrows lifted. "Oooooh," he said. "Please come in!" He led me through to his lounge room. I found two empty wine bottles on the floor next to his favourite chair, and another just opened on the table in front of the chair. He was using a jam jar for a glass. "Fancy a drink?"

"Why don't I put some coffee on? I could use a strong one, and I think you could, too." I squeezed past him into the kitchen, such as it was. One wall was dominated by towering stacks of old newspapers and scientific journals, bundled up with twine. The smell of cheap paper dominated the room. The din from the dogs was extraordinary, but I did not want to talk about it. I pretended everything was normal.

Moving a stack of dirty dishes from the sink, I filled the battered kettle and put it on the range. I did not feel up to attempting to operate the automatic coffee machine. The range was still going, which was a relief. Gordon stood in the doorway. He said, making a big show of it, "How do you like the name, 'The Navigator'? It's got a certain something about it, I think."

"Gordon?" I said, glancing up at him as I searched for clean cups. If ever a house needed a woman's touch, this was it. However, the woman whose touch was needed here was not myself, I was certain of that.

"I'm calling it 'The Navigator'!" He said the name over and over, enjoying the sound of it in a way that was so unlike him I could hardly believe it. I kept busy, getting the percolator going. The smell of coffee was sharp and comforting in the musty room.

Then I realised what he was saying. "Oh, you mean the time machine!"

"Of course the time machine, you silly woman! What else? It's only my life's ambition to visit Ancient Greece, Ruth!"

Keeping my back to him as I busied about, I said, "'The Navigator' sounds reasonable. I thought you liked 'Time Hopper'? What changed your mind?"

He didn't answer, but I heard a strange flat sound coming from him. Turning, I said, "Gordon?"

He was asleep, standing up, leaning against the doorjamb.

*

I took Gordon back to my house. He managed to walk most of the way to the car on his own two feet. He slept most of the way. When he struggled to the surface of wakefulness, he jumped, startled, and swore. Then he saw me driving. "Ruth!" He sounded a little more sober.

"You need a decent meal, Gordon." The late afternoon sun, to the extent that it could be seen for all the cloud, was muted. "I hope you don't mind."

He blinked several times, and saw that we were nearly at my house. He said, "The dogs!"

"I left them some food and a bucket of water." A lot of food, and a lot of water.

Gordon discreetly burped into his hand. "I do beg your pardon, Ruth. Oh dear."

"Something the matter?" I was keeping my eyes on the wet road, and driving much more slowly than ordinarily I would, even on gravel. I think I was making about ten miles per hour, and even that felt reckless.

He fidgeted and tried to straighten up his clothing. "I'm...sorry you had to see me. Like this. I'm not..."

"We are all having a bad time with it. Rutherford, too. It's understandable." Which was easy to say, but I was still completely surprised at Gordon's response. I did not think he drank at all, much less that he could put away two bottles of red in an afternoon.

At home, I sat Gordon in the drawing room. Rutherford, doing his best to look his usual self, asked if there was anything he could do. I told him he could take the evening off. Later, at seven o'clock, I would be calling Rockingham Hospital to inquire after Julia. If we were going to visit, I would drive. This was partly because I felt vile at the thought of Rutherford's guilt when what happened had been my fault. I did not like that he should feel so wretched on my account, even if that meant that I did my own driving for a while. Rutherford, however, looked shocked. "I will not hear of it, ma'am. If you require my services later to visit Miss Templesmith, do not hesitate to call on me." He looked resolute, but I could also see the shock and sadness in his eyes.

"I take it you are insisting, Rutherford?"

"I am, ma'am."

I looked at Gordon, then back at Rutherford. "It would appear I do not have a choice."

"Quite so, ma'am."

After a light dinner, and a considerable quantity of coffee, Gordon was looking better, though very rumpled indeed. I could see he also looked increasingly embarrassed, and it was difficult trying to tell him it was all right. He did not mention the incident with the elf; neither did I. We did not need to mention it. The whole terrible thing seemed almost to squeeze us out of the room, it was so big and so awful. We told ourselves that elves did not belong in this world. Over time the sheer grinding forces of entropy, the slow unwinding of the universe itself, were erasing them from the world. But not quite yet. I did not understand them, but I would not deliberately hurt them out of sheer ignorance. Accidentally killing one seemed to me a grievous sin. Their implacable response; the way they had stared; the complete lack of anything comprehensible in their faces; was difficult to bear — and impossible to forget. How did they feel about what had happened? Did they feel anything? It seemed to me they must have emotions of their own, but that their feelings must be of such an alien character that they and we would never reach any sort of understanding. They did resent us, I knew that, we who fit in to this world so well, while they did not. We knew that much, but that was all.

And, deep in the dark well of my brooding, I remembered my worry that elves might have plans to kill people in this town. The incident today had not helped. If they needed a reason to come after me, or more reason than perhaps they had had already, this would be it — if, that is, they believed in revenge.

*

Shortly after seven o'clock, I telephoned the hospital, to ask after Julia.

It took some time to find someone who could talk to me, but at last a Doctor Samuels came on the line. "I'm terribly sorry to report this, Mrs Black. I am afraid your aunt has slipped into a coma."

"I beg your pardon?"

Dr Samuels repeated himself, and apologised for the bad news. "We have her on a round-the-clock watch. So far she's stable, and breathing on her own."

She was breathing on her own. In a coma.

"I...God...!" I felt weak; dizzy.

"Mrs Black, are you quite...?"

"I'm..." My legs gave out. I fell. I hit my head on the edge of the sideboard. The telephone's earpiece dangled on its cord. I heard the doctor asking, in a tiny, crackling voice, if I was all right.

14

Gordon and Rutherford struggled to help me up, each trying to be more helpful than the other—it was almost comical. If only my head had not hurt quite so fiercely; if only this had not been such a profoundly bad day. Rutherford brought me a stiff drink. Gordon fussed.

With the help of June at the exchange, I was soon back in contact with Dr Samuels, and apologised. I still felt out of sorts. But that was the least of my troubles. I told him I would be there as soon as possible. He said, "There really is very little you can do, Mrs Black. She's receiving the best care. Tomorrow, if there's no improvement, we'll be sending her up to Perth."

"Yes, of course. A doctor there said that they... that you... right. But are you sure? It would be no trouble to come up..."

Dr Samuels was firm and quiet. I think he knew more about how I felt than I did. He recommended that I should perhaps get some rest. I tried again, feeling like I ought to be there. The doctor insisted.

This went on for some minutes. Then Rutherford took the phone from me, thanked the doctor, and said, "Mrs Black will be in touch in the morning." Turning to me he told me that he was sending me to bed, and that he would send Vicky or Ryan up with a hot toddy shortly. He also told me that he would run Mr Duncombe home to his cooped-up dogs. Gordon looked rather at a loose end, hearing all this. "I know when I'm beaten, Mr Rutherford."

Once installed in the bedroom, I sat up in bed. The sheets were cold. The room, too, was chilly. I remembered the old house back home, which boasted a grand fireplace in each of the bedrooms. Those were the days. Sitting in front of the roaring fire with Antony, sipping mulled wine, talking long into the night. The way his eyes caught the firelight...

Someone was knocking on my door. "Just me, ma'am, Vicky, you know?"

I had hired Vicky only seven months ago, when Sally reported that she needed help in her duties. I suspected what Sally had really wanted was just some company, to help pass the time. It seemed a reasonable request. Vicky still needed some polishing. I let her in; she handed me the hot toddy; I thanked her. "Rarely have I needed something like this quite so much," I said, smiling at her.

She hesitated, looking uncomfortable—which was normal—and tense—which was not. "Ma'am? Is it all right if I say something to you?" She rushed the words out, as if they were much too hot for her mouth.

"What's on your mind, Vicky?" I was far too tired, and too worried, for a new crisis, but I couldn't bring myself to be rude to her. I urged her to sit on the end of the bed.

Sitting uncomfortably as though her working-class bottom would somehow cheapen the antique bed, she looked at her fidgeting hands. "It's just...I'm really sorry, ma'am, about what's happened? About the elf and that?"

"Vicky..." I had not been expecting a vote of sympathy. I smiled. "Thank you for saying so. It's been a bad day in every respect."

She nodded, "And I'm sorry, you know, about your auntie."

I agreed. "She really needs our prayers now, Vicky."

"Good night, then, ma'am. Sleep well."

I watched her disappear behind the bedroom door as she eased it shut. How, I wondered, had I managed to hire such a sweet girl? After the endlessly miserable day I had been through, this brief moment of warmth was enough almost to push away the gloom and the anxiety. The hot toddy finished, I lay down, shuffling my cold legs to generate some friction heat from the sheets.

Things were not all bad.

No, that would be later.

*

Morning came all too soon. Rutherford appeared with a scalding hot cup of coffee. He opened the curtains, revealing the promise of a clear sunny day. He said that the time was twenty-five minutes to nine o'clock, and that Murray's breakfast would be served promptly at nine o'clock, and that he had already begun running me a bath. A fresh suit of clothes had been pressed and laid out, awaiting my approval.

"Thank you, Rutherford. And how are *you* this...disturbingly sunny...morning?"

"I am in good health, ma'am. Thank you for asking." This was what he always said. I had a feeling that he would say this even if he lost a leg.

Breakfast in the expansive and cold dining room had always been a solitary business. Rutherford took the food from Murray and laid it out on gleaming silver trays on the sideboard. Next to the food he left the latest newspapers, each freshly ironed and still warm and fragrant. There was the *Daily News*, from Perth, always two days late thanks to the trouble of getting it down here; and once a week there was the esteemed broadsheet, *The Times of London*. This latter was flown out from England and thus was always at least two months out of date, but that did not matter. What mattered was the remarkable sensation of being in some sort of contact with a piece of the mother country. One could smell it in the ink, which smelled different from the ink used in local newspapers. There was much that I had been very glad to leave behind in England, but there were also things I missed, and proper newspapers were one such.

I sat down and worked through my porridge, my ham and eggs, and a generous pot of black coffee, and, between bites, peeled back the tabloid-sized pages of the *Daily News*, reading about events in Perth and across the country. The large pages crackled and rattled as I turned them. The noise boomed in this too-large room. The tink of steel knife against ceramic plate sounded like it might crack the windows or disturb the chandelier.

Not far away, I heard a chorus of muffled laughter from the kitchen.

I looked around. This dining room was intended for feasts, for grand events with a dozen guests, perhaps more. The tabletop was built from local karri wood, brought to a remarkable lustre by Sally and Vicky's relentless polishing. Eleven other chairs stood empty.

All this had never bothered me before.

I missed Julia. She filled rooms all by herself, in a way that I never would. I would always be the quiet, watchful one who sat back, who didn't want to dance, who observed from the corner, and who told herself she did not envy all those vivacious people.

I rang the bell for Rutherford to come and clear away breakfast. I was done.

*

After breakfast, I asked Rutherford to prepare the Bentley for the journey up to Rockingham Hospital. Whilst I waited, I finished dressing, pulling on a warming coat over my black suit. From outside, I heard the rumble as the car's great motor came to life; I imagined the thick clouds of steam its exhaust would produce in the brisk morning air, the sound of those big wheels crunching over gravel as he brought the car to the main door—

And I realised, feeling suddenly more uneasy than before, that I was no longer hearing the engine, nor the crunch of gravel.

At the window, I looked down.

My breath caught.

Six elves stood in the driveway, blocking the way out.

Rutherford lay before them. He was spread across the gravel. I saw no blood. He did not move.

They all looked up at me.

"Rutherford!" Calling the staff out to assist, I raced downstairs and out the main doors.

By the time I reached Rutherford's body, the elves had gone.

It was disturbing, the way even their absence felt like a great presence.

I knelt next to Rutherford, checking him over. He felt clammy, and I could feel a pulse at his throat. "Vicky—call Dr Munz!" She ran back into the house.

Sally squatted next to me, examining Rutherford with me; Sally had previously worked as a nurse in Perth. She said, "Get him rolled over, so the silly bugger doesn't swallow his bloody tongue."

We took care of this. "Ryan?"

"Yes, ma'am?" He shuffled his feet about, unable to stand still in a crisis.

"Put the kettle on. We may need boiling water."

Murray, arriving late, took Ryan under her wing. "Failing that, a cuppa'd be very welcome, eh? Come on."

"Right you are, ma'am!" They scooted inside. Ryan had the purposeful stride of a scared young man given something to do to ease his nerves. Murray followed behind at her own pace. She said, "Give us a shout if you need anything else!"

Sally and I were examining as much of Rutherford as we could without disturbing his immaculate clothing. We could find no marks, scrapes, cuts or bruises. There was no indication that the elves had hit him.

"That doesn't mean they didn't do nothing, though, ma'am," Sally said, glancing at me significantly.

By the time Dr Munz arrived in his rickety car, Rutherford had regained something resembling consciousness. He was sitting up, with his back leaning against the side of the Bentley. The doctor nodded good morning and said, not pleased to be here, "Ah, Mrs Black. Your girl says your *butler*—" He made a point of emphasising the word, to let me know he didn't approve of such genteel affectations as having one's own butler. Kneeling down on knees that made audible clicking and popping noises, he winced and gasped and said, "Mr Rutherford, good morning. I hear you've had a bit of a run-in with our fey friends."

Rutherford looked embarrassed and held his head as if willing either it or the world to stop spinning, which was something to see. Rutherford never looked embarrassed or disturbed by anything.

Gritting his teeth against his knee pain, Dr Munz checked him over. Rutherford provided an account of what had happened. He said everything had been perfectly normal. He'd come out to the garage to get the car started. With the motor running, he noted that it sounded like it would need a tune in the next two or three weeks. He then went to reverse the car from the garage. He eased her back, executed a three-point turn and eased the vehicle up to the house's main door.

Which was when he saw a group of six scruffy elves standing in front of the car.

He had not seen them arrive, had not seen them walk up the driveway from the gate, had not seen them in the course of manoeuvring the car around to the main door. They had simply appeared before him, looking as if they had been there all along.

"I didn't know what to think, but I knew what they were here for. They'd come for me, like I thought they would, I bloody *knew* they'd come for me! I know about elves, they're like that, they believe in eye for an eye, and they were going to have me because of yesterday…" I was not sure if this was true, that they believed in eye-for-an-eye-style retribution; this allegation was part of the dense soup of confusing folklore regarding the elves.

I explained to Dr Munz about yesterday's incident. He said, "Bloody hell… That's a bit unlucky. The car all right?"

Rutherford, in great distress, tried to tell us what had happened this morning. He'd climbed down from the car, and he tried again to apologise to the elves for what had happened yesterday, to little avail. "I was just trying to tell them, I was *sorry*, that's all I could think of to say, that I was sorry, I didn't mean to hurt their mate, it was an accident and, and…" It looked like he was going to pass out again. I was glad he was still sitting.

Dr Munz prescribed a few days' strict bed rest. He had nothing that would cure a case of profound guilt. Sally, Vicky and Ryan took charge of Rutherford and led him back into the house and upstairs to his quarters, reassuring him all the way. As he was going, Rutherford looked mortified, to have come undone like this, again, in front of his employer and everyone else.

After a moment, Dr Munz and I stood alone next to the car. I said to him, "What do you think I should do if they return?"

"I could recommend a shotgun," he said, and he was only half-joking. "Failing that, of course, you could ring the coppers and get them off their fat backsides. You can't live your life in fear, Mrs Black, you know that."

I nodded. He was right about not living in fear, of course. After that an awkward silence hung between us in the cold air. Crows nearby cawed in a way that sounded mocking. "Could I offer you a cup of tea, perhaps?"

"Thank you, but I must be going. Let me just scribble out my bill." He produced a notepad and pen and started writing out the details of his consultation, such as they were. I had my purse with me; we were able to settle up quickly. I think he preferred it that way, particularly when he had to deal with me. As he counted out the money I gave him, he asked, "And how's your Auntie Julia doing?"

"Actually, I was just on my way up to Rockingham to see her. She's had another nasty turn, I'm afraid."

He raised his wispy white eyebrows. His blueish eyes looked watery and bloodshot. "She's not having much of a holiday, eh?"

"No, I'm afraid not," I said, not wanting to go into details. Munz's yellowing false teeth were rattling around in his mouth, and, up close, he smelled like sour antiseptic.

"You might consider sending her back home," he said as he was getting back into his car.

"I hardly think that's warranted," I said, starting to feel that a tide was beginning to turn against me.

Munz tipped his head to the side, conceding the point. "You know best, Mrs Black, I'm sure."

"Thank you and good day." I watched his car drive off, boiling inside, breathing hard.

15

Before setting out for the hospital, I needed coffee. I sat in the kitchen alone, attempting to collect my thoughts.

Out in the drawing room, the telephone rang. Vicky answered, saying simply, "Hello?" I sighed and made a loud coughing noise. She quickly said, "Oh! Sorry! Black residence. Good morning!"

I took my coffee into the drawing room, in time for Vicky to look at me, her eyes wide and worried. "It's the hospital, ma'am..." She held out the telephone for me.

"This is Ruth Black," I said, once I put my coffee down.

"Mrs Black? This is Doctor Rainer. We spoke yesterday."

"What's happened?" I shooed Vicky out of the room.

There was a hesitation at the far end of the crackling line. "Er, well, this is rather hard to explain..."

"What's happened, Doctor? Tell me." I was aware of gripping the telephone's earpiece so hard it might have broken under the pressure. I could smell the warm bakelite.

"Well, your aunt is awake and she's asking for you."

I frowned, staring at the telephone. "I beg your pardon? Last night I was—"

"Mrs Black, we're as puzzled as you are. All I know is that she's awake and lucid, but rather anxious. She wants to speak with you as soon as possible."

Confused, I said, "Last night I was told she had fallen into a coma."

"People do recover from comas. Meanwhile, we're running tests and keeping her under observation."

"Is she in any pain?"

"She says she's not. She's been awake for only twenty minutes."

"I'll be right there."

*

I found Aunt Julia sitting up in bed in a small intensive care ward, enjoying a cup of tea. She also looked like she was bursting to talk to me. On seeing me she beamed, "Ruth! Ruth, I'm so pleased to see you, I've got ever such a lot to tell you!"

Still trying to overcome my great shock, I kissed her hello and dragged up a chair. "The doctor just called," I said. "I came as soon as I could." It was a clear, sunny day, the roads were not too bad. I made good time in the Tulip, but kept careful watch for wandering bands of elves. It was hard driving past the spot where yesterday we had killed that elf; I felt myself go cold and was still sick at heart. I thought again about Dr Munz' advice to use a shotgun to deter future visits.

Julia said, "You didn't bring Mr Duncombe?" She peered around, in case he had hung back to buy a bag of jubes or something. I said Gordon was recovering from a hard day.

At length I adjusted to the sight of my aunt sitting up and looking reasonably lively, despite not having bathed and so forth. It was hard to believe, looking at her, that only hours earlier she had been comatose, gravely ill, and faced with the prospect of brain surgery and worse. Instead, they were giving her tea. She looked like a nice cream biscuit would be welcome. Between this and the business earlier with Rutherford, I hardly knew which way was up.

"I've got so much I need to tell you, Ruth!"

Blinking at her, I said, "Oh?"

She looked mock-cross at me. "Ruthie, dear! I'm *fine*! Everything's all right!"

I stared, and felt myself suddenly on the point of tears, of all things. I swallowed that back and tried to breathe my way back to self-control. "I just can't believe…" I said, working hard to control my voice, "…you're just *sitting there*, after…what happened." I used a handkerchief to dab at my eyes and nose.

"Oh that! Nothing at all to worry about. I tried to tell you while I was away, you know, but I couldn't get through to you, you were so fast asleep."

"Pardon?"

"During the night. I came to visit you during the night, to tell you I was all right."

"Julia, you were—"

"My dear Ruth, I was *travelling* all night!" She said this quietly, but with a certain familiar glee.

Travelling. Ah, I thought. "All right, then. Where did you go?"

"Well, since I had the opportunity, I thought I'd have a wander around town, to see if I might see who's had the very poor taste to have it in for you. You know, just snooping here and there."

I pinched my nose. "Right. Um. Listen, do you remember the note I showed you yesterday?"

"Oh yes, frightful business, absolutely frightful."

"The attack you had after touching the note…"

"Yes, dear?"

"Was that anything to do with why you fell into that coma?"

"Oh, I expect so, yes. I was quietly sort of sniffing around the edges of the feelings I remembered from touching the note, you see, and I seem to have got rather more of a sniff than I planned, as it were…" She looked amused, as if it were a fine old jape on a rainy Sunday afternoon.

"So you inflicted the coma on yourself? Is that what you're saying?"

"Please, dear," she said, frowning, and glancing about. "Keep that booming voice of yours down!" Fortunately she was the only occupant in the ward, but nurses and cleaners and other miscellaneous staff kept bustling about, stripping and making beds, cleaning everything in sight, and there was a sharp odour of carbolic acid.

I lowered my voice. "Well? Is that what you're saying? That your coma was in some way self-inflicted?"

"In a manner of speaking, dear. "

"We were worried out of our minds last night!"

"Thank you, dear. But that's why I was trying to contact you! I knew you'd be worried."

"*Worried*...?"

Julia rang her nurse-call bell. Presently a young nurse appeared, and Julia asked if the nurse would be kind enough to fetch her another cup of tea. The nurse sighed and said yes, ma'am, of course. Won't be a moment. After the nurse disappeared to bother the tea lady, Julia turned back to me. "The tea here's very more-ish, isn't it?"

I paused a moment to concentrate. "You said you had a lot to tell me, Julia. About your travels."

"Yes, yes, of course I do. I found out the name of your demon, for one thing."

A cold flash went through my belly. "Oh?"

"I sort of met him."

Smiling the too-bright smile of a woman unable quite to believe what she was hearing, I asked, "And how do you go about 'sort of' meeting a demon?"

"Oh, well. In that state, things are less complex. You could say I followed my nose, as it were."

"Your nose, Julia?" I said.

"Demons carry something of an odour about them, one might say."

"Ah."

Julia's calm, jolly acceptance of such things was disturbing. I said, "So, you met the demon that's been summoned to come and get me... What's his name?"

"His name's Ukresh Nor."

"Sounds very exotic."

"I tried to find out who was controlling him in our world, but he wouldn't say."

"Even though you knew his name? I thought once you knew something's name, you—"

"Ah, well, dear. The name he gave me is, if you will, it's what's known as his 'work name'. Something of a code-name, one might say. So it's not much use. Only his summoner knows his true name."

"So that's not very much use at all then, is it?"

"I did find out from Mr Nor, though, that he has nothing personal against you at all. He has no interest in the goings-on in our world."

"Hmm. So this demon's allowing himself to be ordered about so he can earn some extra pin money? Is that it?" I could not believe I was even having such a conversation. I did not know whether to be horrified or bitterly amused.

"No, silly. He's allowing himself to be ordered about because the summoner knows his true name. He has no choice. He's got as much choice as a hammer has when you want to bang in a nail."

"I imagine Mr Nor is none too sanguine about this."

"He said he'd be very interested in learning his summoner's true name. But he doesn't even know the man's, er, regular name, as it were."

"How about a physical description? Does he know the address where we might find that cellar?"

The tea lady rolled her rattling trolley into the ward. She was a thin but happy sort of lady, middle-aged, a volunteer, the sort of woman one can always rely on to muck in with everyone to get the job done. "A little bird tells me you'd like another cuppa, love?"

Julia switched from telling me about her supernatural travels to chatting with the tea lady with an enviable smoothness. "Yes, dear, that'd be lovely. One sugar, that's right."

"You can certainly put 'em away, eh?" the tea lady said, grinning as she prepared the fragrant tea. She looked at me. "Anything you'd like, ma'am?"

"Nothing for me, thank you. I'm fine."

Julia flashed me a Look. I suspect she thought I was being unnecessarily curt. Soon she was set up with her tea once more and the tea lady was propelling her trolley elsewhere.

"You were saying, dear?" She smiled at me, looking every inch my eccentric Aunt Julia, despite her recent travails.

"Right. Yes. I was asking if Mr Nor the demon could give you a physical description of his summoner, or perhaps an address for the mysterious cellar." It was difficult to keep a sarcastic edge out of my voice.

"Well," she opened, looking away for a moment and thinking hard, "I could go back and see if I can find him again. It would be easy enough to ask, I suppose."

"Why doesn't he just kill you for bothering him?"

"Because it's not done, dear. It's not done. Besides, he hasn't been told to harm me, so he and I can chat away." She smiled again in that way which meant I should have realised this for myself. The other world was as much bound by elaborate codes of manners and customs as my world, it seemed. All the same, it was still hard to consider that my delightfully strange Aunt Julia was having mystical chats with otherworldly entities. But then, Aunt Julia could talk with anybody, it was a knack she had. Why should demons be immune?

Which gave me a thought. "How would it be if I were to meet this demon fellow? In the other world, that is, so he couldn't just attack me. Would that work?"

Julia smiled at me again, this time looking as if I had just asked a very perceptive question at long last. "Of course, dear. It would require quite a lot of intensive preparation on your part, but a meeting could certainly be arranged, and you could certainly ask Ukresh Nor if he would kindly mind not coming to your house and killing you." Now she was looking at me with the sort of ironic edge I might employ.

"But?" I asked, sensing a problem.

"But, Ruthie, whilst Mr Nor would be only too pleased to chat with you, he would also tell you that he has no choice about coming to kill you. As I say, it's nothing at all personal with him, and in fact he would rather not be bothered with the whole thing. He finds it very disturbing and painful."

"Poor lamb!" I said, annoyed. "All right, then. What's the delay? Why hasn't he come already? That would be nice to know. I could make sure I'm suitably attired and bathed. I could have the house straightened up. I could perhaps get my book finished!"

"Do try to keep your voice down, Ruthie. You're in a hospital, for heaven's sake!"

I tried to control my breathing; my heart raced. "This is just a *very* bizarre conversation to be having."

"That is understandable, dear. It really is."

"I deal with rational concepts. Logic and scientific method. Quantifiable results and inferences."

"Of course you do," she said, and managed not to sound patronising.

"Then there's this prospect of my brutal murder coming up at some indefinite point in the future! How do I deal with that? How can I stop it happening, for instance? I take it I can't simply wait for the chap to show up and then just shoot him with a gun?"

"I would say not. However..."

"Julia?"

"However," she said, thinking things over, "the obvious way to stop him coming would be by finding the summoner and stopping *him*. Or, perhaps, getting the summoner to unmake the spell. That would set Mr Nor free, you see."

"So he can get back to pruning his roses, say..."

"Better he prunes his roses than you, I would say, dear."

I felt as though I carried a terrible weight. And besides all this supernatural nonsense, there was the business of that letter I received the day before, with its ominous question about my father's death. I had not forgotten about that, nor had I forgotten that the problems with Julia's health seemed linked to the letter's author. The logical conclusion towards which I felt myself drawn was that the author of the card would send further such notes, intending that I would get increasingly agitated, perhaps, and then, when things were at a suitable pitch of anxiety, he would send this Ukresh Nor around to visit me one night.

I remembered what Julia had said yesterday, that whoever it was hated me so much he could kill me with his bare hands, given half a chance. Such hatred, as I understood it, could take on a life of its own, and could be relished like a fine brandy. The man behind all this would want to savour the experience, draw it out, taste every subtle hint and nuance, before bringing the matter to a satisfactory close.

The thought that somewhere out there, perhaps someone in this town, felt so strongly against me was hard to accept, as hard as all of Julia's peculiar insights combined. Hate I could comprehend; magic and the supernatural remained sealed books to me.

Besides which, I thought, what possible revelations could there be about my poor old father's death? All right, so my father might have been killed in some mysterious bit of business. Men were murdered every day. Father, as a Cabinet Minister, no doubt had his enemies. I may well have even met his killer at the old family home, if it came to that. It was a chilling thought, but I grasped enough of the subtleties of high-level government intrigues to realise that sometimes such men had certain things done. One such thing had perhaps come home to roost, and Father got in its way.

*

I left Julia at lunchtime, and drove home, my head awhirl with disturbing thoughts.

When I arrived, Vicky told me Gordon had been by with the day's post.

Another note from my secret correspondent had arrived. It said:

WHO IS REALLY BURIED IN YOUR HUSBAND'S GRAVE?

16

My husband Antony was killed in the War, in the Battle of the Somme. He was a civil servant attached to the British government's War Office. He travelled extensively, usually throughout the various nations of Europe. He was often away for a month or six weeks at a time. When he returned, we would celebrate. We had marvellous celebrations. One day he told me he would have to go to France "on business", which was the way he always spoke about his service. I knew never to ask any questions. I read all the latest reports of the fighting in France in the newspapers, and, during his absence, pored every day over the long, long lists of the killed and missing in action. The only thing that made life tolerable during his absences was the daily arrival of letters from him, usually telling me about places he'd seen, people he'd met or seen—and nothing at all about his official business, or even anything from which his official business might be inferred.

But one day, four weeks into his latest trip, there was no letter. There had been letters, as usual, on each of the previous days. Sometimes only a postcard dashed off in haste, but there was always something, to let me know I was in his thoughts, and that he wished he was here with me. That first day with no post from Antony was very strange. A step had been missed. There was a gap in the normal rhythm of life. But, I thought, it was wartime, and Antony was somewhere in Europe, stuck on a train perhaps, or otherwise unable to get to a postbox. No doubt the next day, or certainly in the next two days, there would be a long letter explaining the whole thing, with copious apologies for worrying me.

Next day there was still no letter, nor even a postcard, and the situation two days later was no better. After three days with no word from Antony, I felt a heavy cold stone deep inside me. I had words with the postmaster. I hardly ate. I took long agitated walks around the estate. Sleep became a stranger. Indeed, I hated going to bed (too many reminders of Antony), and if I slept at all I slept on sofas in the drawing room, in front of the fire.

Each morning the local postman would come to our door with the day's post at around ten o'clock. My entire day revolved around the postman's arrival. When, sometimes, he was as little as ten minutes late, I would be found waiting, heart racing, smoking thin cigars too quickly, nervous as a foolish schoolgirl despite my great pains to look calm and detached, next to the post slot in the house's main door, prepared to intercept the day's post as quickly as possible. The house staff, including Weatherton, the aged butler, tolerated this as they tolerated my other peculiar ways. The younger maids sometimes confided that they wished they had a gentleman who would write as faithfully and frequently as "Sir". These were strange encounters for me: I could never recall a time when anything about my life had been the envy of anyone. Antony's letters were always necessarily vague about what he was doing each day, but always vivid and specific enough when it came to what he was thinking about, and longing for.

But when that day came with no letter from Antony, and when the silence continued, first for days, and then weeks, with no word, no message—and when spending hours and hours, and days and days, going over the endless published lists of men killed or missing in action yielded no trace of him—

My life no longer made sense. When six weeks had passed, with no word of any sort, and I entered the time when ordinarily Antony would be home from his trip, my life broke open. I went over all his previous letters, searching for traces and clues, hidden signals and signs that something "funny" was going on, something he'd tried to tell me. I imagined terrible, mad things,

things I dared not mention to anyone. The house staff were very kind, but did not know what to do with me. I did not know what to do with me, either. How could my husband simply disappear? I knew—everyone knew—that from time to time people did sometimes, for no apparent reason, simply vanish. Their families and friends would be left with nothing but a frustrated, endless ache inside them. Some of these later turned up dead, often murdered. But there were some who never reappeared. I was familiar from popular accounts and newspaper reports that such things happened. But they did not happen to me. They did not happen to people like Antony. He was assured. He knew the Continent of old. He spoke several languages fluently. He had money. He was not the sort of person simply to go missing like this. Therefore, I believed, or at least mostly believed, he must be dead. But if he had died, why had there been no word from the War Office?

The telegram from the War Office arrived the next afternoon. Antony had been missing—which was to say I had received no word from him—for almost two months. In those two months I had gone from a young woman simply missing her husband to a woman losing her mind. I had been sleeping too little, eating hardly at all, and I was wasting away. Almost two months. The time had dragged, yet it had also flown. It was confounding. The world was confounding.

I buried Antony in the Black family estate's modest graveyard, amongst his ancestors. The weather was good; it did not rain.

*

I felt like a frame of film stuck in a projector's gate, burning, charring and bubbling away to nothing. Time stopped. People whirred and hummed around me, doing things, arranging things, providing things. I observed it all, but saw nothing.

I slept too much. Sometimes I slept for three or four days. Sometimes I did not bathe for more than a week. For some reason the house staff allowed all this. I ate little.

It never occurred to me to lose myself in drink; I don't know why.

One day, during a rare bath, it occurred to me to lie back and inhale the water. It could not hurt more than I already hurt, though what I felt was as close to a vacuum of feeling as I could imagine. It was a fire that burned cold. So I lay back in the water, and felt it rise up over the hollow planes of my face, over my lips, down my ears, up my nose. My hair drifted around my face like seaweed. Distantly, I heard traces of sound from the rest of the house: parts of voices; the flat crack of a dropped dinner plate; a private moment of laughter. My heart boomed like artillery. Soon I would need air. Through my hair, I could see the wavering image of the ceiling moulding and the antique light fittings. The ceramic of the tub pressed against my arms, my back, my legs. All I would need to do, if I were to do it, would be to inhale. Simply breathe it in, as if it were that first fragrant waft of morning coffee.

My heart boomed faster. Tension gathered in my belly.

Opening my mouth, water flooded in. I took my fatal breath. Never afraid in life to do something wholeheartedly, I took a *deep* breath.

The coughing! The panic! Suddenly I was sitting up, water streaming from my skin, and I was coughing up water, coughing to the point of vomiting. Weatherton appeared. I heard him calling out orders to the staff. He helped me out of the bath, even as I bent double, barely able to stand for the coughing. The taste of bathwater and bile shook me like nothing else had for a long time.

Later, I sat in the kitchen, shivering in a dressing-gown and slippers, wrapped in a thick woollen blanket, clutching in shaking hands the hottest cup of disgustingly sweet tea in all Christendom, while the local doctor, one Barbara Witcham, went over me from top to bottom. Weatherton supervised the rest of the household staff out in the hallway. Dr Witcham looked at me with sensible grey eyes. "You do know how lucky you were today, don't you?"

I sipped my tea. My throat hurt.

"When was the last time you weighed yourself, Mrs Black?"

I never weighed myself. There was never any need.

Dr Witcham produced a hand mirror. She held it up so I could see my face.

Who was this person who looked like a starving Dickensian waif?

She arranged for me to stay at a certain health spa on the south coast for three months. The weather was mild; the view of the sea crashing against the rocky cliffs was unmatched; the sight of sea birds hovering in the cool updraughts was marvellous. They let me eat whatever I wanted — as long as I ate something, and as long as I kept it down. Others stayed there, too. Some told me about their "cases"; others did not, and spoke only about the weather. I read silly popular novels. I worked on crossword puzzles. I stared out the windows for hours and hours at a time, watching the sea.

The three months was not nearly enough time, but it was enough to get going. I bathed regularly, and slowly gained weight and shape.

I did not want to go home to the family estate. In my mind the entire property loomed like a vast mausoleum, with a howling Antony-shaped vacuum deep in its black heart.

But back I went. Every day I visited a "friend" of Dr Witcham's, a Dr Faulkner. We talked. I told him how it felt being back in the house, about the lethal lack of my husband. He told me the feeling would eventually pass, so slowly that I would hardly feel the change. I would never get over it, he said, but I would one day find that it was bearable. The house would feel something like comfortable. Dr Faulkner and I talked a great deal, and not only about Antony. I told him about my surprise on learning that Antony had left me an extraordinary sum of money in his will, and that his life insurance policy was also worth a substantial sum. I had never been poor, but now I was a woman of independent means.

Dr Faulkner asked me one day, as we sat in his cluttered office that smelled a little like a greengrocer's shop because some of his patients paid in sacks of vegetables or fruit, why I never cried. Caught by surprise, I said, "I just don't."

"No, seriously, Mrs Black. I'd like to know." He leaned forward in his overstuffed and rather disreputable-looking old chair.

I was holding a cup of coffee. Holding it very tightly. "Why do you want to know that?"

"It's just, it's a natural part of grieving."

"I know. I...just...don't." I shrugged and affected a cheeky smile.

"Sometimes," he said, after a long silence, in which he sank back into the comfortable recesses of his huge chair, "sometimes we can be so terrified of the consequences of losing control of our feelings, mmm? That...we keep them under such tight control that we wind up magnifying them. To the point that when they do break out — and they always do — they're every bit as terrifying as we originally imagined, and even perhaps worse, mmm? Do you see?"

From outside I heard church bells, distant motor traffic. "I've been toying, recently, with the notion of becoming a sort of writer," I said at last, to break the tension.

Dr Faulkner said he thought that sounded like a marvellous idea.

"I'm also thinking, and this is just at the level of being an idea, it's nothing concrete, with specific plans and so forth, but I've also been thinking about leaving Britain."

"Leaving?" he said, not looking too surprised. "Where would you go? Somewhere in Europe? Perhaps France? Strong literary traditions there."

I nodded, and said, "Actually, I was thinking about the colonies, possibly Australia."

He could not have looked more surprised. I smiled.

*

Again, I looked at the note.

WHO IS REALLY BURIED IN YOUR HUSBAND'S GRAVE?

I needed to sit. The rest of the day's post could wait. Sally appeared. "Would you like some coffee, ma'am? You look like you could use it, if you'll pardon my saying so."

My thoughts were a blur.

Inside, my guts tangled in cold knots.

Sally reappeared, bearing coffee. She set it down on a minute lace doily and went away. I remember the piercing aroma of the coffee.

I kept seeing, in my mind, his burned remains in that temporary casket. The figure had been curled around on itself. The hands and feet were not there. The head was little more than a lump—with the suggestion of teeth.

I remembered saying, *"That could be anybody..."*

The words rang in my head like a cracked bell.

Who was this person, this *bastard*, sending me these notes?

How could he possibly know that I had always, since that day, secretly wondered if that had really been Antony in that casket?

I started to think that the reason I had never cried for Antony was that, in the most secret, most suspicious corners of my heart, I had never believed in his death.

How could this person know that about me, when I had hardly been aware of it myself, until this moment?

How could this person know that and be here in Pelican River?

I checked the envelope. It was the same as the envelope from yesterday. The only difference: today the black swan stamp was the right way up. There was still no return address.

Up and pacing, clutching the note, I was alive with thought. Central in that tangle was this: *If those had not been Antony's remains in that casket, where was he?*

17

Wait. Take a deep breath.

I looked at the note again. It was just a question typed out on a small sheet of paper. Despite its eerie specificity, it could all simply be a hoax, or a prank. Most people who knew me well would also know what I knew about Antony's death, which, it must be said, wasn't a lot. Thinking about it, it occurred to me that the list of people who could possibly know these things was quite extensive. Newspaper writers of a certain sort would probably have no difficulty extracting this sort of information from my former staff for a modest fee. And it would be exactly the sort of worry that would weigh on anyone's mind. I had been shown a set of remains so damaged that even dental records were no help. One only knew they were one's husband's remains because one had been told so by the War Office. Why, I wondered, would they lie to a grieving widow?

All the same, why now? Antony died twelve years ago. Surely the time for such melodramatic intrigues was back when it was all still fresh, and when I had been in such a very fragile, suggestible state.

Then I thought about the previous note, and its effects on Julia. Somehow all this was tied up with some disturbing supernatural business. It made little sense.

And yet, there was that pool of icy doubt I felt about Antony's death deep down inside. If only, and I hated to admit this even to myself, because it meant that one day I might be with him again...

I was shivering; I felt sticky. "*Sally*...?"

She found me leaning against the karri table, head low, legs trembling. I forget what she said, but she soon organised me into bed. "I'll call Dr Munz," she said. Vicky, next to her and looking upset despite her best efforts to maintain professional poise, said, "God, what a day!"

Ignoring Vicky's outburst, I told Sally not to call the doctor, but I did ask if she would arrange to pick up Gordon from his house.

Sally glanced at Vicky, then said to me, "Pardon me for pointing this out, ma'am, but none of us can drive a motorcar."

I said, "Oh," and was about to resign myself to my clammy fate when there was a quiet knock on my bedroom door.

Rutherford, back in his uniform suit, wearing his driving gloves and carrying his goggles, leaned around the door.

Before he could say what I knew he would say, I said, "No, Rutherford. You need your rest. The doctor was very firm."

"Ma'am," he said, coming into the room and looking like a reasonable, though pale, facsimile of his former self, "I insist. If I can be of service to you in your hour of need, please allow me to do so."

It had only been about four hours or so since I had seen him unconscious in the driveway, surrounded by elves. I hesitated. Sally and Vicky said nothing, but looked between Rutherford and me. He added, "Mr Duncombe's property is not far, and the roads should be quiet at this time of day. If I may be so bold."

I felt dreadful. Perhaps a visit from Dr Munz would be a better idea, but I wanted to speak with Gordon. Of course, I could have simply telephoned him, but with the telephone one had always to worry about people listening in. With a bit of luck he would have recovered from yesterday's excesses.

"Very well," I said, shaking my head. "But you may not hurry, rush or in any way go briskly. There's no prize for reaching Mr Duncombe's house in record time. If you need to stop and sit for a while, please take the opportunity to do so. We'll be fine back here."

"We will, ma'am," Sally said with a conviction that did not bear questioning.

In time, Rutherford ducked out of the room. Soon I heard the Bentley rumble to life and the crunch of the tyres on the gravel as he left. I realised I was listening for unexpected interruptions; I was listening for elves. So far, so good.

Sally fetched me a cup of sweet tea. "No coffee?" I said, looking at her.

"This is better for you, ma'am."

I nodded and behaved like a good patient for her, but in my mind I was thinking that the only thing that would make me feel better right now was the truth about Antony, one way or the other.

If Antony was alive out there somewhere, I would find him.

And I would kill the bastard.

*

Gordon, when he arrived an hour later, looked better—or at least, less catastrophic. He made all the right noises, inquiring after my condition. I was sitting wrapped in a Hepburn tartan-patterned woollen blanket in the drawing room, enjoying the fire roaring in the fireplace. Neither Gordon nor I spoke of his condition yesterday; indeed, he seemed to be making an effort to seem jaunty, and the effect was rather like a man on stage, playing the part of himself. Gordon asked after Julia's health, too, and I was pleased to report that she was much improved, thank you for asking, making a pest of herself on the ward, and probably drinking far too much tea.

At length, the staff disappeared and set about their tasks for the afternoon. In their absence, Gordon fell quiet, and peered into his own cup of tea.

"I've been talking to Julia, actually," I said.

"Oh yes? "

"Yes. It transpires she's on good terms with a certain demon."

Gordon blinked and looked at me. "I beg your pardon? "

I explained the conversation I had with Julia about Ukresh Nor.

"I see," he said, looking thoughtful, staring off to one side. "That's very interesting." He pulled out a scrap of notepaper and a pencil stub and made a note of the name, perhaps planning to "look up" Mr Nor in one of his dusty volumes of arcane lore. "Very interesting," he repeated, speaking to himself, frowning now. "Did Miss Templesmith say anything else about him?"

"Only that they had had a lovely chat whilst she was comatose." I could scarcely believe what I was saying. It was preposterous!

"My word," he said, now looking at the floor, deep in thought.

I changed the subject. "I also received another of those notes today. Didn't you notice when you were sorting the post?"

"Another?" He looked up, at once curious and apprehensive. "No, I was busy today. Young Debbie Hewitt sorted today's post."

I showed him, and he took both note and envelope for close examination. "He got the stamp right," I said. Gordon smiled vaguely, nodding, still looking like his mind was elsewhere.

Gordon produced the magnifying glass from his coat pocket, and peered at the items. "It rather looks like the same typewriter at work. But did you notice this—he's cleaned the strikers somewhat." He showed me what he meant. "The previous note had 'A's where the triangular gap in the 'A' was full of muck—today it's clearer."

"He's aware of the identifiability of typewriter print? Trying to cover his tracks?"

"Either that or he's just fastidious," Gordon said, looking at me with a small smile. "I mean to say, there's that aroma of some sort of soap again…" He held the note beneath his nostrils for a long moment, concentrating intently. "I wish I knew what that other smell is, though. Have you had any thoughts?"

"To tell the truth, Gordon, I've been much more preoccupied with the question itself."

He looked surprised, as if the question itself was a clue he had not yet noticed. Reading it, his face fell. "Oh, Ruth…Ruth, you can't allow yourself to believe this! He's…it's obvious he's just trying to upset you. It's so obvious!"

I explained something about my lingering anxieties about

Antony's fate, and how this note had touched a very specific nerve indeed.

"Well, it's just as you say, it's someone who has knowledge —rather detailed knowledge, I grant you—of the circumstances surrounding…"

"I keep thinking, what if it's true?"

Gordon forced a laugh, which emerged sounding more like a bad cough. "No! No, don't be silly. He's toying with you. He might know this very particular thing about the funeral and so on, but it's just a lucky punt, he doesn't know anything, really." The look on my face must have alarmed Gordon more than I expected. He came closer, leaning forward. "Ruth—this is the pathway to madness. You know it is. First there was the insinuation about your poor father. Today this nonsense about Antony. This, this, tormentor of yours, he's not interested in your money. He wants to make you unpick all the threads of your life! He wants to unravel you! And remember what Miss Templesmith said, that this is someone who hates you so much he could strangle you with bare hands…" He made a throttling sort of gesture that, on him, looked strange, jarring.

For the merest fraction of a moment, less than a second, the dark and suspicious part of my mind thought, *What if it's Gordon? He's so close to you. He knows so much about you. He probably owns a typewriter*…I felt so shocked by this stray thought that my breath caught, and I sat, on the point of coughing, feeling a blush steal up my neck and over my face. I looked at him, only a few feet away. He had some money, but not much. He supported himself by working part-time in the post office, as well as doing repair work on farm machines, fishing-boat motors, and on the handful of motorcars in the area. Could he secretly be filled with envy at my comparative success and comfort? This did indeed seem like the pathway to madness. Gordon cared more for his beloved dogs and the memory of his lost Alice and his odd contraptions than anything else.

And yet…

"Ruth?"

He looked concerned. I smiled, made myself laugh lightly,

and apologised. "Away with the faeries. Sorry. All this business, it's getting to me, I think."

Gordon nodded, smiling like a good, true friend doing his best to be helpful.

I leaned back into the recesses of the sofa and pulled the blanket more tightly around me. Outside, off in the distance, I heard a kookaburra cackling. Gordon looked up and out the nearby porthole window. "I've never gotten used to the noises these birds make, you know. I've been here all these years, and sometimes it seems as if every single wild bird is out there screaming and squawking. They always seem like they're making fun of us, and telling us we'll never survive here. We're too soft, too bookish, too, I don't know, civilised, perhaps. To make it here, you have to be like them, loud and rude and a bit on the mad side, have you noticed that?"

I said I had noticed that, but that I rather liked it, most of the time. "It's not like back home. None of the birds there has anything you'd mistake for a sense of humour, do they?"

"I used to think geese were nature's humourists..."

We talked about birds for some time. It was marvellous simply to have an ordinary conversation about ordinary things with someone who understood.

And as we talked, I looked at Gordon, as he went on about rare owls and red kites and bearded tits. I had not realised before that Gordon had been quite such a birdwatcher in his former life. He said he loved British birds for their soft, muted colours and their pretty, tuneful calls. So unlike the raucous and vibrant birds here.

After a long while, and some reviving hot beverages, we returned to the matter at hand. Gordon once more had his magnifying glass out and he was poring over the envelopes of both notes. "I would not have thought there were any shops in town where you could buy such stationery, would you?"

"I had the same thought."

He nodded. "Nevertheless, it wouldn't hurt to rule out a local supplier."

"In the interim, what am I to do with the notion that my husband deceived me?"

"You don't know that for certain. Until such time as you see him in front of you, you can't know that for certain. I mean to say, it is entirely possible that you did bury the poor blighter, and that he did indeed come to a bloody awful end on that battlefield, along with so many others."

Gordon added, "Let's leave aside the question of who might be sending these damned notes, and look at what he's saying to you. He's talking about your late father and your late husband. You've told me they were friends, that you met Antony at one of your father's shooting parties."

"That's right. I had been attending only sporadically at that point, and I cannot say anyone particularly missed my presence when I didn't attend. I was the peculiar, grumpy, sarcastic girl who never wore proper attire and who did not know her place."

"Or, who knew exactly how to get a lot of attention?" Gordon smiled.

"It was attention I did not care for!"

"All the same, but it certainly got you noticed, including, as you've said, by one Antony Black."

"I did once wonder if he would have noticed me at all if I were a proper young heiress and dressed in pretty frocks and wore my hair just so and all the rest."

"I doubt he would have given you a moment's thought. He probably saw hundreds of girls exactly like that everywhere he went."

"That's what he actually said, the one time I asked him." I smiled at the memory, and at the memory of what he did after telling me that.

"So, who was he? How did he know your father?"

This was old news. "I'm sure I've told you before. Father was Secretary of State for War, and Antony was a civil servant in the War Office. He and Father would often moan about all the boring parties and receptions that correct form and official business dictated they needed to attend. It was the height of tedium meeting all these old generals, and listening, again, to their old war stories. As well, of course, Father just had a sort of knack for finding rising young men whose careers he could sponsor and encourage. That sort of thing."

"And you've said that Antony spent a great deal of time overseas, particularly in Europe, on official business."

"There was never a great deal that I wanted to know. It sounded deadly. Antony told many amusing stories, though, about the various people he had to deal with. He was a great mimic, and he could 'do' all these other people, with their voices, the things they said. It was sometimes like watching a play with a cast of thousands, all played by him."

"That's very interesting," Gordon said, and I did not, then, know why he said it quite like that.

I went on at some length, describing some of Antony's better performances, but it was frustrating, because though I could see it and hear it all in my mind, I could not reproduce Antony's talent for voices and so forth. Gordon, in any case, looked rather distracted, and I worried, stupidly, because my confidence had been disturbed, that I was boring him. Which was a first for me. I had never in all the time I had known Gordon been bothered for a moment by the notion that I was in some way boring him. He had always behaved towards me like a perfect gentleman, and like a man who cannot quite believe that someone as strange as I am had come along and fallen into his life. I suspect he worried at times that *he* was boring *me*.

"Did they spend much time together, your father and Antony, when you weren't around?"

"Oh heavens yes! They were always out riding, or huddled around the fire in the drawing room playing chess, or...Why are you looking at me like that?"

He looked surprised, and blinked the expression away. "Oh, pardon. Sorry. I'm just trying to get clear in my head the sort of relationship these two men had. If you know what I mean."

Puzzled, a little worried, I said, "Actually, no, I do not know what you mean. Explain."

"All right. When you learned of Antony's death, you had a pretty grim time of things for a while. Ultimately, you wound up being sent off to that spa or solarium or whatever it was for a few months."

"That's right. I don't follow."

"When you eventually returned home, had anything strange happened? In your absence."

I did not remember this period too well, and told him. "My life was still rather a difficult blur, I'm afraid…"

"All right. Was anything missing?"

"What do you mean, missing? Are you suggesting one of the staff—?"

"No, no, not that. I mean," and here he looked concerned, trying to find delicate ways to phrase things. "Were any of Antony's personal effects missing?"

Seeing his point, I smiled and laughed a moment. "Oh! Oh, I see! Ah. I see. Right. Actually, when I returned home, I did notice that many of Antony's personal things were gone. I asked Weatherton about it, and he said that the staff had taken the opportunity, in my absence, to collect up some of these things and put them up in the attic, in storage. They thought too many reminders of Antony would be distressing for me. I was furious. They had no right."

"And when you went up to the attic to see everything?"

"There were several steamer trunks, full of Antony's things. The smell, when I opened them, Gordon…"

Gordon would not be deterred. "Does this sort of thing happen often?"

"How do you mean?"

"I mean—how do I put this?—when people in the aristocracy pass away, is it usual to put their things away into storage like that, for the sake of the remaining family, and so forth? Do you see what I mean?"

"Erm," I opened, thinking about it, trying to remember. "I suppose. Some families do, and some don't. Some families I knew had quite the opposite idea, and turned whole wings of their houses into rather chilly shrines to the departed, with everything arranged just so, as if he'd only just stepped out for a moment, but would be back any moment. That sort of thing. It's rather disturbing, seeing things like that happen."

"What about your father, Sir Gustav? What happened to his things?"

"What about his things?"

"Did his personal effects, you know, his books and papers, his toiletry items, his clothes, all that kind of thing—what happened to all that? Did the family store it all, or what?"

I thought back, still puzzled and rather disturbed by Gordon's dogged interest in these things. "As it happened, I believe there were specific terms in his Will governing what should happen to his papers and books. It had to do with the Office, I think. Anything he'd brought home to work on, and there were always alarming great stacks of signal boxes, as I recall, full of briefing papers and reports and files about this and that—all of those things had to go back to the Office, of course."

"So they just took all these official documents and boxes and whatnot?"

"Gordon, what on Earth are you driving at? I'm having a rather dismal day, I'm tired, and I'm dreading there's going to be another one of these damned notes tomorrow, and here you are burrowing about in ancient history!"

He looked horrified that he'd upset me and set about apologising profusely, telling me he never meant to upset me, that he was only thinking about possible reasons for what was going on. We went back and forth, with him apologising and me telling him it was all right, of course, and then I would apologise, and then he'd apologise back, and so it went. Ultimately, we called a truce and I sent Sally to fetch us fresh cups of tea. While we sat, blowing on the surface of the scalding tea, Gordon spoke, very quietly, and at first I was not sure I had even heard him properly.

He said, "It's just...it's just, I'm wondering if your father and husband might have been involved in the espionage business."

18

I laughed so hard I had to put my tea down on the table. "That's preposterous!"

"Oh dear. Er...I'm terribly sorry, terribly..."

"I've never heard such an absurd..." I couldn't finish the thought. It took some time before either of us settled back down to anything resembling coherent conversation again, by which point Gordon looked more embarrassed than I had ever seen him, and my initial disbelief and shock had subsided into some sort of amusement. Sally appeared, not saying anything, but looking like she was just checking to see if everything was all right. I smiled at her. Gordon looked like he wanted to conceal himself under his chair.

We said nothing much for quite some time. I believe there were comments about the weather, which was starting once again to look bleak; another storm front was on its way. The clock on the mantelpiece over the fireplace ticked through the awkward silence. The fire popped and hissed. My tea cooled. Gordon excused himself to visit the privy out the back of the house. As he left, treading lightly, as if to draw as little attention to himself as possible, I watched him, thinking, *You poor man*. It wasn't a kind thought. I was annoyed now, perhaps more than annoyed. I would never have expected Gordon, of all people, to say such a thing. And yet, I knew, he was only trying to help. He was trying to see patterns in the evidence. Patterns that I had never seen, it was true, and, looking back over my history with Antony, and his relationship with Father, it still did not seem likely. Father would never have sold secrets to a foreign power. He was a fine man, for all his faults. As for Antony, what could I say? He was Antony. I was fortunate that my husband and my father had established such a rapport. Earlier in my life, during my time at Cambridge, I had gone through a period of seeing starving artists and intense young writers, all of them quite penniless but almost equally dashing in a slightly seedy sort of way. They were all scruffy, like lost dogs, but they saw things in the world that I never saw, and I remember longing to see through their languid eyes, just for an hour, to see my too-familiar world as it looked to them, to see the familiar transformed and exposed. My parents, when I brought this one or that one home for the summer, reeled in a kind of horror that manifested itself as extreme politeness. Mother spent a lot of time in bed. Father, terrified that I would allow myself to be attached permanently to one of these lost causes, and yet also terrified that he might lose me if he acted too harshly, did his manful best to get to know them. The boys, for their part, many of whom came from the same sort of family background as I did, and who stood no chance of inheriting short of a calamity involving the death of almost everyone else in the world, found my parents *amusing*. And I found I did not like that. Whilst I did not often see eye-to-eye with my family, it was another matter for others to regard them in this way. It was true that these boyfriends of mine did have a certain way with borrowing small amounts of cash that I never saw again. I seemed always to be the one coughing up change for train fares and cheap wine and morsels of food—even rent on a few "I promise this'll never happen again, it's just that..." occasions.

I heard the phrase "it's just that" more often than I cared to admit.

Allowing, for the sake of argument, that Gordon was correct to some extent in his allegation, exactly when would Antony even have had *time* for this alleged espionage work?

I sat there, wrapped in my blanket, and wrapped equally in

my foolishness, thinking things like, *Surely Antony was far too busy on official business to be a spy...*

I liked to think I had more than my share of intelligence, and understanding of the wider world, but there were times, and this was one of them, when I could be thicker than the oldest trees in the world.

*

Gordon returned, still doing his best to look as small as humanly possible.

He went once more to apologise, to tell me he was foolish to have even mentioned it, that he was just a silly old duffer, and so on. I said, "It's all right, Gordon."

He looked so upset. I got up and poured him a single-malt; he looked like he could use it. Handing it to him, I allowed him a small smile, and I sat back on my sofa, wrapped in my blankets. I said to him, after a long moment, "Imagine if one day, in confusing circumstances, I suggested to you that your beloved Alice was really a murderer, or an anarchist bomber, or something like that—"

"I say, Ruth, that's—" He went to stand, face flushed, and then he stopped, glancing first at me and then back into his drink. He sat back in his chair, landing like a sack of potatoes. "Oh, dear..."

I knew mentioning Alice like this was playing with fire, but I wanted him to see how I felt.

He saw. We sat quietly again.

"What am I going to do about these notes, Gordon?"

"You could talk to the police."

"For all the good that would do," I muttered, watching the fire, chewing over and discarding poor ideas, such as trying to watch the postbox out front of the post office building all day. "There's still the idea of checking public land records, to see which properties could be near that spot where Julia had her turn the other night."

"I could do that tomorrow, if you like. It would be easy enough, and I've got some errands to run in town anyway."

Tomorrow would be Thursday. If the note-sender was

keeping to his apparent pattern, there would be another note. God only knew what the next one might contain. I was starting to feel anxious about even the most innocuous elements of my past, wondering if I would soon find out that not only were my father and husband not what they seemed, but that absolutely everything I could remember was false. It was enough to make one want to hold onto the floor, in case it should shift suddenly. It had already occurred to me, in the wake of today's note, that I could contact my lawyers in England and ask them to arrange to have Antony's grave exhumed — but to what end? He had been unidentifiable then; he would be even less so now. What about Father's grave? Was there something about his death that the doctors and coroner missed?

I held my head. I felt a headache looming, the sort that confines one to bed, longing for sleep, and hoping for relief by morning.

Gordon started; his eyes snapped open. "Oh! I say!"

Alarmed, I said, "Gordon?"

"Fingerprints, Ruth!"

"Pardon?"

"Fingerprints. The police, they could examine the notes and the envelopes for fingerprints. We could give them our own fingerprints, so they could eliminate us, but whatever prints remained would be those of our man!"

"Could we do that?"

He looked dubious. "I'm not sure, to be quite honest. We are talking about our local constabulary. On the other hand..."

"And how would we go about identifying my correspondent from his fingerprints? We would need, presumably, to take samples from everyone in town!" Which, I knew only too well, meant more than one thousand men, women and children. Although I was almost completely certain we could eliminate the children immediately.

"It would certainly take time, making sure we collected every set. It's easy enough getting fingerprints from cups, plates, glasses, anything like that. We could set up a collection of files, matching names and print samples." I could see his mind working on the details.

"I could invite people for dinner, perhaps," I said. "Though that would mean, at twelve guests per dinner, divided into over a thousand residents..."

"Yes, perhaps a hundred dinner parties. I think perhaps that may not be the most efficacious approach. To say nothing of causing a great deal of suspicion in the townsfolk. 'Why's that Mrs Black having all these dinner parties, then? For years she's done bugger-all for us, and now she's our best friend!' That kind of thing."

He had a point. I lived in this town, but I was not quite *of* the town. I was not exactly a part of its fabric. This I was inclined to put down to the nature of my work, which required me to spend long hours alone. When I needed contact with people, I knew where to go. The Ladies' Lounge of the Commercial Hotel was a haven on Friday afternoons, particularly in the warmer months. But it wasn't as if I saw all the locals every day; my staff, on the other hand, were often in town, shopping for groceries or paying bills or running other errands for me.

I wondered if I was perhaps too solitary. Which was a peculiar thing to wonder, I thought. It was like wondering if I was too right-handed, or if my hair was too brown.

*

Shortly after dinner I telephoned the hospital to ask after Julia's condition. They told me she was still doing well, and had been moved back into a general ward for further observation. They expected to keep her in for "a few more days, just to make sure".

Rutherford drove us up to Rockingham, though I noticed he seemed more cautious, and took the roads with greater care than hitherto. I could not blame him; the weather was starting to hit; a light rain was spitting down. The vehicle's headlamps lit the road ahead almost like day, and made the looming ghost gums shine with unearthly light.

Gordon said little, but he looked more relaxed than he had earlier. I was busy with my own troubling thoughts. Chief amongst these was this: there seemed to be only one way to learn the truth about the deaths of my father and husband, and Julia would probably clap her hands in glee when I approached her about it. It seemed to me that I would need to investigate Julia's "deadworld" just as she had offered me all those years ago, when I had been so affronted that it had damaged our relationship for years afterward. She said everyone who had ever died, and for that matter every animal, too, passed through that strange realm. There were records, of a sort, she had implied, but had never explained, because I had never wanted to know anything about such nonsense. Now, needing to know the truth for my own peace of mind, so that I might begin striking back against the note-sender, I would have to face this other truth, if truth it was. It is said that the truth will set you free. I was more concerned that this truth would destroy my life.

19

"Whatever's the matter, dear?" Julia asked, once we got through all the chaos of greetings and the handing over of boiled sweets and flowers. "You don't look at all like yourself!" She was sitting up in bed, one of the Perth newspapers spread out across her lap. I noticed she had somehow acquired a fresh bag of grapes. It was easy to imagine Julia befriending other patients' families during earlier visiting times. I would never impose on someone else's private time with their family like that, and wondered how she managed it.

At length, I told Julia about the new note. "But I didn't bring it along this time. The last thing we need is for you to have another turn," I said, trying for a light sort of tone.

Julia smiled, saying, "Ah, but I might have been able to learn a bit more! One never knows!"

While she explained what she meant to a baffled Gordon, I tried once again to deal with the veritable glee Julia exhibited at the prospect of going forth in the "astral plane" to learn more about demons and other monsters. The glee was understandable: all her life her entire family had discouraged, sometimes with considerable force, these "flights of fancy" of hers, insisting that she live only in the same world which confined the rest of us. To her it was like being told she could not see particular friends because they lowered the tone.

And I had not yet proposed to her that, once she was discharged from hospital, we might set about letting me explore this deadworld of hers.

I realised Julia and Gordon were deep in hushed conversation.

"I seem to recall reading," Gordon was saying, as he peered vaguely at the ceiling with its slowly rotating fan blades, "something about a particular ritual in which you could physically prise a true name from someone or something, rather as if you had a sort of supernatural crowbar...I'm sure I read about this somewhere, not that long ago, too..."

And Julia was saying, "Wouldn't you need to locate the original summoning and—?"

"Hmm, yes, probably you would, hmm. I think so. I'll have to have a bit of a read. Hmm..." He looked concerned, and said to me, "I might need to have a look in a particular library up in Perth, actually, Ruth..."

I gathered, suddenly, that he was subtly asking if I could provide him with transport should this prove necessary. I said, "Just say the word, Gordon," smiling a little uncomfortably, caught as I was between the racing river of their conversation and the need, at the moment, to show Gordon I was not still cross with him.

After a long moment, I had a useful thought about Julia: "Erm, is it at all possible, Julia, that because you've done all this 'travelling' in the other realm, and spoken to these various entities, that someone from there might follow your trail back here? Is that possible?"

Gordon scratched at his chin, thinking about this; to my surprise, Julia said, "Why ever would they do that, dear?"

"Is it possible? Could something reach down here and hurt you?"

"You're not worried about Mr Nor, are you? Because, I mean to say, I've already explained that he's quite safe in the—"

"Actually, no," I broke in, "I feel quite reassured that Mr Nor is the nicest demon he could possibly be when he's just chatting with you over cucumber sandwiches—"

"Oh, Ruth!"

"I'm not finished. I'm talking about other things. Things not perhaps quite so particular about the rules of interdimensional etiquette, things that might use you as a convenient conduit into this world. Could it happen?"

She saw my point, and looked disappointed. "Well, if you put it like that. Of course, there's..."

"Gordon," I said. "The protection charm you worked for me?"

"You want one for Miss Templesmith?"

"Could you?"

Julia looked between us. "Oh dear..."

Gordon fidgeted with some of his hair. "Well, of course I could. It would be no trouble. Of course. If you think it might help."

"I should have thought of it earlier," I said, irritated with myself for being so self-absorbed, thinking little of the price others in my life might have to pay. Already Julia had suffered in the course of all this. I should have acted sooner to protect her.

Gordon said, "When should I...?" He was looking around the busy hospital ward. All around, clusters of family sat and stood around other beds, talking softly. Sometimes there was a brief cough of not-quite-relaxed laughter. Nurses patrolled about, seeing to various needs, taking observation readings, carrying away bedpans, finding jars for flowers.

"I hardly think this is necessary, Ruth. I mean to say, I've been visiting the other world all my life, I've—"

"I'm afraid I must insist. And besides," I said, feeling a twinge of cold nerves as I worked my way up to my other point of business.

Julia noticed the odd look I must have worn, and she said, "Oh yes?"

"I think I may need to call on your expertise regarding the deadworld..." I felt myself blushing as I said it.

"Pardon?" Julia stared. "Did you just...?"

Gordon also stared. "I say, Ruth. Are you sure?"

"No," I said, not looking at either of them. "I am not sure. I'm starting to feel unsure about a great many things, and it seemed to me...it just seemed that I might..."

"Oh, I say..." Julia said.

Gordon said, "How can I help?"

"Can you do it?" Now I looked at Julia, though it was hard.

She was about to say something, and it looked like it was coming from a long way down in her mind. Something she'd wanted to say to me for the longest time. However, at that precise moment, the tea lady wheeled her rattling, clattering old trolley up to Julia's bed. "Fancy another tea, love?"

*

Gordon worked his protection charm before we left. I chose not to ask him what he would have to sacrifice in order to complete the "deal". The charm he provided Julia was different in character from the one he gave me, I saw. He explained, after doing it, that Julia's needed to be stronger; I did not argue with him, and neither did Julia. She watched him going through the strange motions, steps and mutterings of the charm with ill-disguised happiness; she was placing her faith entirely in Gordon's abilities. When he was done, at last, I heard her sigh dreamily. "Thank you *so much*, Mr Duncombe," she said, her voice slightly thick with feeling, "I feel ever so much safer already." For his part, Gordon looked surprised and distracted at her gratitude. I suspected he was already wondering what he would have to give up when he returned home tonight, and, from the look of him, it would need to be something more substantial than a lock of his hair.

We rumbled home through the lamplit raining darkness. Gordon told me he would be going into town tomorrow to see about land and property records.

We dropped Gordon at his property. As Rutherford pulled the car back onto the road, I heard the din of his dogs yapping and barking. I did envy Gordon that he had such a warm welcome when he returned home. My staff were always polite and pleasant, sometimes quite demonstrably so—but it was also part of their job to welcome their employer and inquire after her health and so forth. I had not dwelt on this feeling in a long time. Indeed, for a very long time now, since coming out here on that hellish ten-month sea journey, I had been safely cut off from the emotions I had felt in the wake of Father's and Antony's deaths. These ominous notes were affecting me more than I had realised. Coming home tonight, I felt myself wish, if only for a moment, that someone like Antony were there awaiting my return, keen to hear about my troubles and adventures. But who could ever replace him? Even if Gordon's hypothesis proved true (which still seemed preposterous, I kept telling myself), and Antony was little more than a spy, and even a traitor, he was still the man who had loved me. It was hard to imagine another man accepting the strange catastrophe that was me so easily.

I went up to bed. Sally or Vicky had left me a hot toddy on my bedside table — it was still steaming.

Despite the toddy's effects, I lay awake a long time. Finally, I gave in, got up, wrapped myself in a thick woollen dressing gown, and went to my study, floorboards creaking at each step. *Might as well work on the book.*

*

Thursday broke bleak and cold. Rutherford woke me later than usual, aware no doubt that Ma'am had been working most of the night. I think it had been about half past three when I dragged myself back to the cold bed, and another hour beyond that before sleep came for me. It took that long for my whirring mind to settle for the night, as often happened when the words came easily.

By the time I came downstairs for a late brunch, the day's post had already arrived. Vicky had left it stacked tidily on the sideboard.

Abruptly, my appetite for Murray's superb eggs, ham and toast was gone. Rutherford said something I did not hear. With cold hands I picked up and sorted through the morning's post.

That's odd, I thought, examining return addresses.

I sorted it again, and then again. And again. I was aware of breathing very hard, and muttering something. "*Where is it? Where is it?*"

There were three letters from readers. Two postcards from

relatives, off somewhere exotic on holidays. Another enterprising young author with intense, blocky penmanship had sent me his latest short story, no doubt wanting my guidance on how to get it published. That one I took out and dropped in the bin.

"Ma'am?" It was Rutherford, next to me. He sounded concerned.

I sorted through more envelopes, certain that I had missed it somehow.

Then I found one I had not previously noticed. It wasn't from the note-sender, as far as I could tell. In fact it was, if anything, even more surprising: a personal letter from Father William. "What on Earth is this?" I said, ripping the end off the envelope.

Inside, two small sheets of blue-tinted notepaper lay folded.

Rutherford said, "Is there anything I could...?"

I was busy pulling out the note, unfolding, reading his shaky but precise copperplate handwriting.

It was a reply to my apology note. I'd forgotten that I had sent, let alone written, an apology, though it was only two or three days previously. Rutherford disappeared somewhere. I stood next to the sideboard and read what the bastard had to say.

20

My Dear Mrs Black,

Thank you ever so much indeed for your recent and highly surprising letter.

I say surprising because I had not thought you were the sort of woman who would try to make amends for such an outrageous breach of decorum, as you did on the occasion of our last, and first, meeting, but I am grateful, and even humbled, to learn that you are not quite the ill-mannered woman I thought you must be.

Having said that, I must tell you that whilst I do appreciate your apology, I am not quite ready to forgive you. Forgiveness is no trifling thing. It must be earned. I will have you know that the neuralgia I developed in the aftermath of your attack, and which had been quiet for many years, has in recent times flared up once again. My aged flesh never did quite recover. The pain, I can assure you, is debilitating, but I must, of course, soldier on, as I have always soldiered on, lo these many, many years. It is not as if I can ask you to come in and take my place whilst I recover.

If you should feel the urge to come back to the church, perhaps to apologise in person, I would be very pleased indeed to meet with you. Perhaps we could have afternoon tea, and you could tell me how you have been praying for forgiveness, and that you are contemplating a modest contribution to our efforts to raise funds for necessary structural repairs to the church and grounds. I think that might help a great deal.

Thank you, again, Mrs Black, for making a tired old man smile.

Yours in Christ,

W. F. Dennis (Fr.)

I needed to sit. I read through Father William's letter again in a state of mounting dread. Rutherford provided me with a fresh cup of black coffee—so strong, in fact, that the aroma punched through my fresh horror, and I glanced at the coffee, and then up at him. He looked concerned. "Ma'am?"

"Rutherford? I, erm..." I waved the letter. "Some disturbing post today."

"Of course, ma'am." He left the dining room.

"Rutherford?"

He turned at the kitchen doorway. "Ma'am?"

"How are you feeling today? Did you sleep well?"

It was his turn to look surprised. "Thank you for asking, ma'am. I am quite restored." He worked to suppress a pleased smile from the professional face.

That swine! Attend in person, equipped with a generous donation for his roof repairs? To *beg* for forgiveness, with a *bribe*? I did not think so. His bloody roof could rot.

*

Breakfast finished, newspapers read, dishes cleared away, I sat thinking about recent matters over a fresh cup of coffee. What was going on? Mysterious notes on Tuesday and Wednesday, but not today? Perhaps, I thought for a moment, there would be no further notes. That made even less sense. Where was the hook, the climax? It was hard to believe that someone in this town was going to a great deal of trouble over me, because they hated me so much—but now they were finished? Such things did not work this way. I suspected that the note-sender was not finished at all; he was preparing the next phase of his operation, whatever that might entail. Which led me to wonder about the long-term efficacy of Gordon's protection charm. And about one Mr Ukresh Nor, with whom Julia got on so strangely well, to the point that they could chat about me and his summoner's plans—at least to some extent. That all felt extremely wrong to me. I could not believe that a notional "good" person, under any circumstances, could be in contact with a notional "evil" person (such as I presumed Mr Nor to be) without suffering some sort of erosion of her...her very self, her, in this case, "Julia-ness". Evil contaminated all it touched, even if the touch was only at the level of minds conversing. Evil tempted. It persuaded. As often as it presented itself through anger and hatred, it also presented itself as a form of love. Evil could show itself as the very last person of whom one would expect evil.

Gordon, if he were here, would criticise me, as he had done in the past, about my use of such naïve terms as "good" and "evil". He did not believe in either, he said, and that belief was a fundamental part of his studies in magic. All there was, he said, was what people did, and what people felt. It was why he believed that "innocent" children were capable of murder, why he believed that everyone was capable of the most grievous acts, under the right conditions. It was why, when he first told me about his protection charm, he had said that it would protect me from "malicious" entities, rather than "evil" ones. I wondered if this distinction offered more or less comfort. Then again, if it saved my life...

*

I decided to spend the afternoon working on the novel and made reasonable progress. The calendar over my desk showed that today, Thursday, was the thirty-first of May. I still had two and a half months in which to complete Eastlake's adventures. In ordinary circumstances—that is, without ominous questions from beyond the grave and the awareness of a genteel demon biding his time in a separate dimension before coming to kill me—I might have managed the task with time to spare, but now I was no longer so sure.

Gordon telephoned shortly before dinner. We chatted for a few moments about nothing much before he said, "I think I may have found the property."

"You found the cellar?"

"There are only two farms in the area, where Miss Templesmith had—"

"Are they occupied?"

"One is, it's, ah…" I heard him rustling through pages of notes. "Wait a moment…" There was more rustling. "Right. Yes. Here it is. The occupied one… do you know the Dawkinses?"

"I think I've seen Frank Dawkins at the Commercial Hotel on the occasional Friday. Big chap. Very large beer belly. Squinty eyes that don't miss anything. Looks like he could sling a bull over his shoulder without disturbing his beer. Looks after his chums. I think he has a wife and a horde of unruly children—I've never seen Mrs Dawkins."

"She's a bit of a funny old stick, the Mrs of the piece. I see her sometimes when I'm doing the post. Always invites me in for a cuppa, talks my head off."

"What about the other property, the abandoned one?" It seemed at least reasonably obvious to me that our man would make use of an abandoned property, where he would not need to worry about encountering curious homesteaders.

"It used to be a sheep station run by…" He checked through his notes. "The Cahill family. They went back to Europe, and put their lawyers in charge of selling off the property for them. This was, ah, six years ago. I have no idea why they all left , nor why their lawyers haven't been able to sell the place since."

"Wool market collapse?" I wondered out loud, but privately I wondered about the pernicious influence of local elves, perhaps poisoning Cahill's land.

"It'd be easy enough to find out. Current wool prices are listed in the newspaper each week. Perhaps a search through the archives might be worthwhile..."

I thought about this. It sounded promising, though what I wanted most of all at this point was simply to get out to these properties to look around. Searching the Dawkins property, however, would be tricky. Tonight I had promised to visit Julia again, too, which meant the earliest opportunity to look around would be either tomorrow, Friday night, or, possibly, much later this evening, after the hospital visit. Even as I formed the thought, I realised that it sounded like the thought of a desperate woman, someone who had taken leave of her senses. I suspect I was still keyed up after the outrageous letter from Father William. As for the prospect of sneaking around these two properties, after midnight, in this weather, with little notion of what I was trying to find, other than "a cellar"—it all seemed a little foolish.

Then again, the little voice argued, what if doing so led you to information that could save your life?

Oh yes, and what if, in the course of finding this information, I was apprehended? It was easy to imagine Julia loving the idea of sneaking about in the dark, searching for hidden clues; I was not so sanguine. I had a reputation, of sorts, to protect. The locals accepted me, more or less, even if they did think I was, one told me, "an odd sort of bird". I did not want to be known instead for mysteriously lurking about on farms in the wee hours of the night with no good explanation for what I might be doing there. *"Oh sorry, officer. I was just in the neighbourhood and had a feeling I might be able to locate a demon on this property. Yes, that's right, a demon. By the name of Ukresh Nor, said to be a shy, retiring type, and also said to be planning to kill me in my bed any day now."*

I told Gordon about these concerns. He said, without pausing, "Don't worry about it. You'll be fine!"

Indicating I was unclear on what Gordon meant by this, he clarified: "No-one will know we're there, I guarantee it. A wee little shadow glamour, combined with the protection charm you're already wearing, and you could practically walk around naked in full daylight, and just about no-one would see you. They might have a feeling something funny's going on, and it's true that certain animals won't like it, but you'll be fine."

"Walk around naked, Gordon?"

"Figure of speech, sort of thing. You know."

"So, this magic of yours is really that good, is it?" It seemed unlikely.

"Hasn't let me down yet," he said, and I could hear him smiling.

"What if we run into the demon-chap? What then? Could he see us?"

"Ah. That is a different kettle of fish, that is. I would say, hmm, yes, absolutely. I mean, this little glamour thing, it's just meant to keep regular people from seeing anything odd going on. And people are terribly unobservant to start with, you see, you're only enhancing what they already have, or don't have, so to speak ... Most people wouldn't notice if their trousers had fallen down, they're so vague."

"I'm sure I'd notice," I said.

*

Later, up at Rockingham Hospital, Julia had some good news. "They're letting me come home tomorrow!"

I had not even sat down yet. "Tomorrow? That soon?"

"Oh yes. The medicos have been giving me quite the going-over, and they can't find anything wrong with me, or at least nothing that losing a few pounds wouldn't fix, that is!" She beamed. I was surprised anyone would see Julia as "plump". "They say they can't find any trace of the peculiar brain-activity I was apparently showing before, and they feel I'm rather taking up a bed that could better be used for someone who's actually sick. How about that, then!"

"Are you sure they aren't more concerned about their tea budget blowing out?"

She smiled again. "Oh, Ruth!" Though, it must be reported, she was midway through a cup as she said all this to me. "And how has your day been, dear?"

I told her about the letter from Father William.

Julia was displeased. "He said that?"

"He did. The price of my forgiveness would be a nice cheque, and suitable grovelling, no doubt at his very feet."

"I can't believe a man of God would say such a thing to you!"

"At this point, I would not be at all surprised to learn that our Mr Nor had been summoned by Father William, or someone in his employ." I'd been thinking about this during the drive up to Rockingham today.

"Do you really think so?" Julia said. "I can't really see a harmless old man being your villain, dear." After a moment's contemplation she added, "And what's new on the intrigue front?"

"A harmless old man?" I said, remembering the look on his face that day as he sneered at me, and threw mud on my husband's memory. "I hardly think so. I think he could be just bitter and miserable enough to be the culprit."

"Well, quite," Julia said. To smooth things over, I explained that Gordon had identified two possible locations for the cellar. Julia, hearing of Gordon's discoveries, beamed. "He's so terribly clever!"

"He certainly has his moments, I must admit," I said, thinking about yesterday, and Gordon's stunning suggestion that Antony and my father had been somehow involved in espionage. I was still trying to work my mind around that one. Of course, though, here I was talking to the lady who would be able to put all such ideas to bed for good.

As though reading my mind, Julia's next question was, "So how do you feel about dipping your toes into the deadworld?"

"How do you think?" I said, and I must have looked rather amusing as I shuddered, because Julia laughed.

"Ruth, you silly thing! It's not like that at all! Not at all! You'll be surprised at just how much it looks like this world, in fact. You'll be wondering why you ever made such a silly fuss about it, I guarantee it."

"I do find that hard to believe, Julia, it's just..."

"How would you feel about a small wager on the matter?"

"Pardon?"

"Just to make it interesting—and to show you I'm serious about this. I'm willing to bet one pound that you'll be shocked at how ordinary it all seems, and embarrassed at all the fuss you put up over the years. How do you like that?" She stuck her pale hand out; it did not shake.

"Julia..." I did not know what to think. I certainly had not expected this development. And, I felt a sizeable part of my mind protesting, and fighting the idea that there could be anything "normal" or "ordinary" about what still seemed irredeemably ghoulish and macabre. There might be useful answers to some particular questions, but I also did not want actually to see members of my family, people whom I had long ago consigned to the deepest parts of memory. I had no desire to dredge all that up. It felt, in a word, like we were going to set out, all jaunty and merry, to exhume various deceased members of my family. The idea was revolting. I did not understand why Julia treated the entire thing like a trip to the zoo.

She took away her hand, disappointed. "You'll see. You mark my words, you'll see."

This was part of what scared me about the entire thing. I did not *want* to see. I did not want to see that the realm of death was not so different from the realm of life. How could I explain to her that I was used to thinking of my family and lost friends as *gone*? To say nothing of all those soldiers, and, more recently, all those poor wretches who had died of influenza. Julia was talking about a whole teeming *world* of death. I could hardly stand the thought.

Then there was a very specific fear: that we would go there, consult whatever records Julia said they kept, and we would find out that Antony was, indeed, *not* there. That he had never been there. Twelve long years I had spent believing in his death, and mourning for him. I still missed his body and his heat in bed. I still had some of his clothes; sometimes I wore his shirts to bed, and my own warmth would bring out his personal scent. For a dreamy while, on the edge of sleep, I could almost imagine he was still with me. Realising, of course, that he was not, and had not been for a long time, was a hard thing, and it was why I did not often do this. Could I really face that disappointment all over again?

I worried, too, that we would find Father, and that he would know things that would be terrible for me to learn. I did not know if I could stand to find out that my father had been a traitor. What possible reasons could justify treachery? It was beyond rational thought, at least to my outraged mind at that point. This was my *father*, not a normal, vulnerable, flawed man. A man who perhaps did have his reasons, though they might not have been good ones, for doing what he did. I was not ready to have my memory of him destroyed like this.

Julia was looking at me. She leaned forward and hugged me. She was warm, and she smelled comforting, almost the way my mother used to smell. Julia rubbed my back and told me it would be all right. She told me I did not have to go with her, if it bothered me that much. She could go by herself, or perhaps with Mr Duncombe, and they could report back with their findings. It would be fine, she said. I did not have to worry so. She would never make me do anything that I really did not wish to do.

*

I did not sleep well that night. On the other hand, though I lay awake a long time listening to wind and rain in the trees, to the faint sounds of the old house settling into its foundations, I did not meet Mr Ukresh Nor. He, or whoever controlled him, was biding his time.

21

Rutherford woke me late Friday morning. I did not know how, but somehow he knew that I had neither slept well, nor for very long. The coffee that morning was extravagantly strong, and seemed to hit my brain like a mailed fist. As I dressed behind a screen, Rutherford said, "I must inform you, ma'am, that Mr Duncombe has delivered the day's post—"

I bolted downstairs, still buttoning my shirt, still struggling with the waistcoat, feet still bare. The polished wooden steps were cold; their edges sharp. Rutherford came along behind, trying to get my attention. "Ma'am?"

Vicky had left today's bundle of post on the sideboard. Breakfast had not yet been served.

Sorting through the modest bundle, I soon found it.

The note-sender had returned.

I slit the envelope with my thumbnail and retrieved the folded octavo note.

There was that aroma again. Soap and…what was that smell?

Opening the note, I saw there was more than the traditional stark question:

WHY DID YOUR HUSBAND KILL YOUR FATHER?

YOUR FATHER SIGNED A CONFESSION.

IT IS VERY DETAILED, INDEED.

WOULD YOU LIKE TO READ IT?

WOULD YOU LIKE TO KNOW WHAT IT SAYS?

COULD YOU BEAR NOT KNOWING?

PLACE THIS LETTER IN YOUR LETTERBOX BY MIDNIGHT TONIGHT.

INCLUDE ONE THOUSAND POUNDS IN CASH.

WE WILL BE IN TOUCH SOON.

I tried to telephone Gordon. The morning-shift operator, Val, told me, "No can do, love, sorry. Looks like some trees fell over last night, over Sloat Road way? 'S buggered up the whole works, I reckon."

"Can't you do anything?"

"Not much. Some blokes from up in the city are on their way to have a bit of a look at it."

It was easy to imagine the rest. "And they'll take at least until tomorrow just having a look at the problem..."

"Sorry, love. Is it urgent?"

I hung up. Rutherford said, "I shall ready the car, ma'am."

*

Gordon was in his workshop, in his oft-patched and filthy overalls, surrounded by a dizzying array of bits and pieces, all of them, he would have me believe, destined to one day form part of his elusive time machine. The whole place reeked of oil and electricity, a worrying mixture. Gordon looked as if he had been there all night. His face was a smear of dark smudges. And, as ever, too many dogs leaped and barked around me. Something looked not quite right about them, though, that was hard to spot. And in my haste to get here I'd forgotten to bring them any treats.

He said, seeing the look on my face, "I'll just get cleaned up. Be right with you."

This took a further twenty minutes, but when he emerged from the laundry room he was clean and fresh-faced, now reeking of the better odour of degreasing oil, wiping his large, pale hands on an old rag.

As we waited for his old kettle to boil, I showed Gordon the latest note, and its envelope. He held each by corners and edges, and peered closely at every surface. "Smells the same," he said. "What are you going to do about that?"

"What do you mean?"

"He's wanting money."

The kettle boiled. Gordon set about making tea.

"Do you believe it, this business about Antony killing your father?"

I shook my head. "I don't know. I don't want to believe it, obviously. It's just—"

"You need to know the truth."

"Julia's coming home from hospital this afternoon."

He brightened, "That's marvellous! What a relief that must be!"

"Yes, and she's planning to take me, and of course you're invited, too, on a little jaunt to..." I couldn't finish the thought. It was still too much to face.

"The deadworld?"

"Yes," I said. "The very idea curdles my blood."

Gordon was more philosophical. "From Miss Templesmith's descriptions, it doesn't sound too horrifying."

"Perhaps that's exactly the problem."

"I expect it's practically overrun with lost soldiers," Gordon said, staring into his tea.

"Yes."

"Still, I'm sure you'd rather, as it were, die than visit..."

"Quite. In any case, Julia says it's the only way to find the truth about everything."

Gordon paused a long moment, and blinked. He sipped his tea with great care. "The deadworld, eh?"

"She says we just have to find the records on Father and Antony—"

"If he's there."

"Precisely," I said, perhaps more bitterly than I'd intended.

Gordon put his chipped teacup down and took up the note again. "Or, of course, you could just pay this bugger the money."

He was right. It had occurred to me that potentially I could avoid a jaunt in the deadworld by simply paying my correspondent his thousand pounds—except, where was I to lay my hands on one thousand pounds, in cash, at short notice? I had the money, but withdrawing it would most likely mean going up to my bank in the city and arranging an appointment with my bank manager, who would then have to arrange for that amount of cash to be available, and that could take some time.

"The problem there, though," Gordon went on, speaking softly, even as his dogs snuffled and squabbled under the table, "is that the money might just be for 'opening the account', so to speak. He says he's got a very detailed confession—though who knows *how* he's got it?—what's to say he doesn't give it to you in pieces, and each piece costs you more money?"

This had crossed my mind, too. Equally, I was baffled by the implication that I was so wealthy that I had great piles of cash sitting around, perhaps in jam tins, in my house! It was ludicrous. Whomever my extortionist might be, he clearly had no idea about such things. On the other hand, I would be prepared to part with a considerable sum of money if it meant I would not have to visit the deadworld. This was a shameful thought on my part, one that I did not share with Gordon. I wanted the truth very badly. The question was, how badly?

However, the *other* question was: what did Mr Nor have to do with it all?

"Interesting that he's asking you to pop the money in your own letterbox," Gordon said, thinking out loud. "Surely he must realise we could simply sit by the letterbox all day and all night, waiting for someone to come by and collect it."

I was thinking about Gordon's sideline business. "He's got a demon at his beck and call. He could send that along at any time and take the money and probably we'd never see it. Or at least I wouldn't…"

"I have heard of wizards using demons as various kinds of thugs, enforcers, and errand-boys. You owe the wizard a bit of money for doing something for you on the shady side of the law. If he sends some bag-man type fellow around, you might or might not feel like paying up, depending. But if he sends Mr Nor, you might feel much more inclined to cooperate."

"Wizards and demons are involved in organised crime?" This was new to me. It was strange enough thinking about such things in these Modern times at all.

"Oh yes, very much so. Wizards, I mean, they're just men, for the most part. Some women. But they're human. They have the same urges and desires and dreams and schemes as anyone else. It's just they also have…other things."

I thought about this. "How would we go about finding another wizard living in this town?"

"You're still keen to investigate those properties?"

"Of course!" I said, too brightly.

Gordon smiled, amused at my fib. He returned to the table with a fresh cup of tea. He also had a small plate of Empire Cream biscuits. "Forgotten about these—silly me!"

I remembered that I had come out here to Gordon's without stopping first to have breakfast. Two of the biscuits helped a great deal.

Gordon sat, dunking a biscuit in his tea, thinking things over. "So Miss Templesmith is returning from the hospital today?"

"Yes, and will probably require mechanical restraints to keep her from jumping straight into you-know-where as soon as she gets to the house."

Gordon concealed a smirk as he chewed. "And we have these properties to prowl about, getting up to no good at all…"

"I'm sure Julia would be keen to join us on that as well. I swear, she never got over being eleven years old."

"And now there's this new note." He was looking at it again. "What do you think might happen if you don't pay the thousand pounds?"

"I would expect him—or, rather, them—to keep at me until I do pay."

"Risky sort of gambit, for them, at least. They don't want to give away all their secrets, but if you steadfastly refuse to pay, they need to find ways to encourage you to play along. And yes, that 'we' business there at the end. I thought we were just up against one lunatic!"

"I thought so, too, Gordon," I said. "But what if the extortionist simply wants to create the illusion that there's more going on than one person with an extraordinary grudge? Is he trying to intimidate me?" Gordon looked thoughtful again, and picked up a third Empire Cream. This one he split into its two halves and absent-mindedly licked the cream. He seemed quite to have forgotten that I was there. Biscuit eaten, he rummaged about in a drawer until he found his magnifying glass, and set about examining the type on the letter. "Looks like the same machine again. But he's—they—are still trying to get the strikers clean, see? Here, and...here?" He pointed with his little finger, showing me where the note-sender had been busy removing dirt from the spaces inside the letter-forms.

One of Gordon's dogs latched onto my right leg and began working with great keenness. I muttered something in disgust and prised the animal off me. Gordon shouted and chased it out of the kitchen. I think it was a dachshund. Gordon apologised.

I was thinking again about Gordon's suggestion that Father and Antony were somehow involved in espionage, the mere suggestion of which had upset me — and still upset me — so much. I still believed that Father died of heart failure, compounded by profound grief following the loss, the year before, of his wife, my mother. The note-sender's question—WHY DID YOUR HUSBAND KILL YOUR FATHER?—like his other questions, assumed certain things while asking about others. He assumed that there were things between Father and Antony, and that there were intrigues concerning their deaths. It was difficult to resist these assumptions when they were so plainly posed. I felt as if I were living in a world of refusal, insisting again and again that my, admittedly simple, view of their relationship was true. All else were lies aimed more at disturbing me than at exposing suppressed truths. But the more I refused to accept these assumptions, the more they occupied me. I had no objective, straightforward means of refuting the claims, which did not help. The only two ways I now had open to me by which I might learn the truth were both things I could not bring myself to follow. Either enter the world of the dead—I had noticed that Aunt Julia had never spoken of the Christian "Heaven"—and consult shades who might prefer not to see the living, or accede to the note-sender's demand. What I wanted was a way to learn the truth without having recourse to either of these choices. I wondered out loud when Gordon's time machine might be ready. He shook his head. "Oh, Ruth," he said. "No time soon."

I said suddenly, "At the hospital yesterday, you said you thought there might be some wizardly means of extracting the true name of the demon's summoner..."

"That's right," he said. He was doodling with a chewed pencil in the margins of a sheet of newspaper, drawing some kind of elaborate device whose purpose I could not guess.

"But with the summoner's true name, we could get him to tell us things?"

"Correct. It's just that..." He was concentrating on his drawing.

"Just that what?"

"We still need to locate his circle of power." He did not look up.

"All right. How does tonight strike you?"

"Tonight?" He looked at me now. "Are you sure?"

"I refuse to pay the money, and I wish very much to avoid the deadworld. So, yes, tonight."

*

That afternoon, Rutherford took me up to the hospital, where Julia signed her discharge papers. Her doctors had advised her to return at the first sign of renewed trouble, and she assured them that she would. "I wouldn't *miss* it!" she said, finishing a last cup of tea.

On the way home, Julia was keen to discuss our venture into the deadworld. I cut her off. "Julia, before we go that route, there are fresh developments, and a new plan of attack." I informed her of the new note and its demand for money. She looked at once shocked and also a little excited, and she listened, saucer-eyed, as I explained what we would be doing this evening. "You are most welcome to join us, though I really think, considering this ghastly weather, you would be far better waiting at the house, with the fire going and my staff taking care of your every whim."

She surprised me. "You may well be right about that. I am feeling a little weary, I must say."

I paused, surprised. "Pardon, Julia? Are you not feeling...?"

Julia yawned. "Up all night travelling, I'm afraid. Snooping about, trying to find your summoner."

"No luck?"

"Not as such. Whoever it is, he's got some excellent protection charms of his own, I can tell you that. The entire town seems completely dead, and yet at the same time it fairly tingles with some sort of activity that I can't isolate and follow. Most perplexing!"

I thought about this. "Are you sure the source of whatever it is is actually *in* Pelican River? It's not someone or something elsewhere?"

"Oh, quite," she said, nodding, and looking very convinced indeed. "That would be relatively easy to trace. But that's enough about me and my nonsense, dear. How are you holding up? You're looking not quite your best—though it's a little hard to tell, sometimes, what with the way you dress and your lack of, well, *polish*."

I glanced out the large window to my left. Scrubby bushland studded with skinny, diseased-looking trees rushed by. To the right, dunes strewn with struggling coastal vegetation blocked my view of the sea and the western horizon. Brooding cloud smeared out the afternoon sun. I felt cold, looking at it all. To Julia, I said, "Things are piling up, somewhat."

"I'm sure they are, dear," she said, patting my knee.

"I mean to say," I went on, "I still do not know just why this note-sender bastard, and these alleged chums he may or may not have, is even doing this! Clearly he wants money, as clichéd as that seems, but why does he want it? And why do all this to me? Why can't he simply take out a modest bank loan to cover his shortfall? Is he picking on me because I stick out, so to speak, around here, because in some fashion I do not quite fit in? And where on Earth did he get all this alleged information? He says he has a detailed confession written by my own father, who never, to the best of my knowledge, set foot in this country. How does one acquire such information?"

Julia looked at me, and she looked sad. "My dear Ruth," she opened, speaking more softly than I had, "he's some sort of magician. He can visit the rest of reality. He may well have found your late father and obtained his confession that way. It's entirely possible, though very much in the way of things that are simply not done."

I could hardly speak. My heart raced. My insides felt like knots of steel, and I thought I might be getting carsick. I wound down the window for some fresh air. It did not help. There was, I realised, one thing worse than having to visit the land of the dead in order to ask Father about things he had done and which he must have thought were done and finished, and that was learning that someone else had already been there and visited him, and probably coerced the information from his wretched spirit. All for the sake of extracting money from me, and hurting me? If I found out who was behind all this, I could not imagine letting them live. I far preferred the thought of such a swine trapped in the deadworld, where the other shades could punish them for violating the sacrosanct barrier between the world of the living, and the world of the dead.

22

Rutherford volunteered for letterbox-watching duty that night. Sally and Murray provided him with hot soup and coffee. The weather prospect looked bleak so he wrapped himself in a sou'-wester and took a black umbrella. I told him, "You can't do this on your own, Rutherford. You'll catch your death!"

He insisted. I argued. He continued to insist. He had that determined look which said he would man the letterbox even if it did, indeed, lead to his death. I had only mentioned the situation to him, that I was the victim of an extortion attempt, and so forth, and he had done the rest. There had been no need to concern him with all the supernatural aspects of the situation. He did ask, "And what sort of character am I looking for, ma'am?" I told him I did not know. I explained that I was not going to play along, and that whomever the extortionist sent by would be disappointed. As to who it might be, I said it could be anyone, or it could be no-one. I also said to take note of strange occurrences, anything peculiar or unsettling that might give a moment's pause or concern.

"Strange occurrences, ma'am?"

"It's rather hard to explain, I'm afraid, Rutherford." I felt glum, and wished I could reveal the whole matter.

He said, "If you are being extorted, ma'am, the police should be notified. This is very serious business."

I agreed. "All right. I'll talk to them in the morning."

"Very good, ma'am," he said, then looked at the rest of the gathered staff. He had the air of an explorer setting out for the remotest parts of the world. He flashed a jaunty salute and headed out the door.

I wondered if he would be all right out there alone. Suppose the note-sender did send his tame demon along. How would Mr Nor react on learning that I wasn't playing along? How much latitude did he have for bringing mayhem to my staff? I did know, however, that Rutherford also had his Webley Mk VI .455-calibre service revolver on his person, and professed great confidence in its "man-stopping power". That was some help, I supposed, but I knew that I would be worrying about him all night long.

*

Julia did indeed take to her bed. She announced that she would attempt a catnap or two, and, failing that, would catch up on her correspondence, of which she had a great deal, more even than I had. She also tried to get me to let her read my unfinished *Too Many Worlds* manuscript, but I drew the line at that. It was bad enough that I was starting to have doubts about the thing without having Aunt Julia offering me critiques over breakfast.

*

After dinner had been cleared away for the night, I wrapped myself in my warmest, darkest clothing and stepped out of the house. The Tulip roadster was a vivid royal blue with white stencilled markings; it hardly looked like the sort of vehicle one would choose for a night of illicit adventures in the bush, but I did not want the cumbersome Bentley. The Tulip, small and light, not too noisy, would have to do.

*

Gordon was ready when I arrived. His dogs went through their usual deafening and enthusiastic routine, even as he herded them into a back room while we talked about our plans for the evening. There was, I thought, still something wrong about them, but in all the bustle and noise I could not place it. Over coffee hot enough to scald my palate, we studied the maps Gordon had managed to procure from the offices of the Shire of Pelican River. He pointed with his little finger. "The two properties are here, and here."

"Right," I agreed, noting that the abandoned Cahill property was located about one and one-quarter miles from the spot where Julia had had her disastrous turn the other night, along Country Road Three, a one-lane gravel strip in dire need of repair. The Hawkins property was two miles outside town, on Hawkins Road, another narrow strip, named after the family whose property brought about the need for the road. The Hawkins property was draped over the side of a broad, low hill and surrounding flat pasture land. The Cahill property, on the other hand, occupied a modest allotment of perhaps one hundred and twenty acres of what once would have been ideal grazing land. Now it was probably a hundred and twenty acres of waist-high weeds. The buildings were clustered together near the centre, at the end of a driveway perhaps one hundred and fifty yards long. Gordon and I had agreed that any cellars would be under the kitchens of the main homesteads. Unfortunately, he had not been able to obtain copies of either house's plans. Gordon shrugged and muttered something about imperfect intelligence, and also said, chewing on a nail, "We should be prepared for the possibility that this cellar is somewhere else on the property, too."

"I was already thinking along those lines," I said. "Which do you want to look at first?" I knew which I wanted to look at first, particularly if it involved sneaking around kitchens. That rather raised some delicate problems. I could not see how we could enter the Hawkins kitchen without giving the game away and winding up arrested. Even though Gordon insisted that his shadow glamour would work wonders, the entire prospect daunted me. He had said, for instance, that certain animals could see through it. I'd asked him if that included guard dogs, and he'd allowed, rubbing his chin, that guard dogs might be a problem.

Gordon said, leaning down over the maps, and pointing, "I say we try the Hawkinses first."

"I disagree!"

He said, looking up at me, "Look, it's late. They're farmers. They'll have already turned in for the night. And besides, this is the one you really don't want to visit, the one you're most nervous about, so I say we get it over with quickly and move on to the other one."

He had a point, but I didn't like it. "And if they catch us?"

"They won't catch us, Ruth." He seemed eerily calm and confident about this.

"I expect their dogs will go spare!"

"I know about dogs. We'll be fine."

"What if their dogs smell your dogs on your clothes?"

"They'll be distracted."

"You're very sure of that?"

"I'm sure."

I did not like it one bit. All I could think of was my future career in prison for breaking and entering. The chance that we might, in fact, locate the summoner's circle of power, and gain an advantage over him was there in my mind, but it was not uppermost, where perhaps it should have been. I had always, at least in my youth, been the kind of girl who liked to take risks, particularly if it alarmed or even offended the stuffy establishment types whom my parents were always trying to get me to impress, and whom I could not have found more loathsome. I still shudder at the memory of the time, not long after I had graduated from Cambridge, when Father took me aside one afternoon and explained how he had found me "a suitable young man". The suitable young man in question was the vicar Charles Fawley, all of forty-four years old at that point, who emitted noxious odours, and who "would be an excellent steadying influence" on me. I had no doubt at least some of my "difficulties" with organised religion, and men like Father William here in Pelican River, stemmed from the explosion of horror I experienced on that day, and which only grew stronger and more intense the longer Vicar Fawley stayed in my orbit.

"Ruth?" Gordon was looking at me, worried.

I apologised. "Lot on my mind. Beg your pardon."

At length, Gordon persuaded me that sneaking onto the Hawkins property first would be the wisest course. I could certainly see the merit in getting the worst part over quickly. I had always found it wise, when volunteers are called for in any situation, to be the first to leap forward. Volunteers are never called for when something enjoyable is in prospect, and the only thing worse than going through the dire experience itself is the worry about how bad it will be, which only worsens for those whose turn comes later.

"What are we going to do for light?" I asked.

"I have taken the liberty of purchasing a pair of lamps, which should do nicely."

"What? No magical mystical light on a stick?" I smiled at him.

"Sadly, no. I'll need my strength in the event we find the circle."

This cleaned the smile right off my face. "Why would that be?"

"If we need to destroy the circle, it can take a certain amount of effort to overwhelm the power of the summoner. The universe has adapted itself to the circle's presence and what it's doing. That creates a good deal of resistance or inertia, you see…"

"The universe? The whole universe?"

"Oh yes," he said, without elaborating further.

*

It was just after midnight when we set out. Our breath steamed around our faces. So far the expected rain had not arrived; the sky was a misery of low-hanging cloud, obscuring stars and moon. Around us, as I drove us out of town, along Old Hitchinbury Road, heading south, the bush felt more still than usual. I kept thinking of Rutherford, loyally sitting there in his heavy-weather gear, sipping soup, awaiting the arrival of anything out of the ordinary. I considered giving Rutherford an increase in his salary.

Gordon spotted the Hawkins Road turnoff and pointed.

Tension was knotting me up inside. I made the turn.

Two miles to go.

"It'll be all right, Ruth."

"I shall be very cross if you're wrong, Gordon Duncombe."

"Me, too," he said.

We soon found the Hawkins property. Their letterbox was constructed out of second-hand bricks and lengths of wood that might have been left over from a destroyed house, perhaps by fire. It was customary out in the countryside, I knew, for people to build their own letterboxes out of whatever items came to hand.

From the main gate, shaded by tall gum trees, we could see the sprawl of the homestead, its outhouse, and an impressive corrugated iron water-tank perched on the flank of the hill. Nearby stood a barn, a large shearing shed, a rickety garage sort of arrangement that looked temporary at best, and some other more modest structures. Two motorcars, both past their prime, and one in pieces, stood near the garage. Not far away was a heap of old machinery, and another great heap, bristling with the twisted and burned roots of torn-up old trees; the Hawkins clan had been clearing some new land, by the looks. We also saw sheep clustered here and there across several paddocks.

"Leave the Tulip up here?" I asked Gordon, not meaning to whisper.

"Might be an idea," he said, also whispering. "If only the thing wasn't so recognisable…"

It was the only French roadster in town; one of only a few in all Australia, I thought. Up until now, that had always been a good thing. Now it was like an electric sign advertising my presence to all passersby. "Is there anything you can do, Gordon?"

He looked at me, "It's a bit big, Ruth. I'd have to sacrifice something pretty significant to complete the deal." He looked very reluctant. We settled for pushing the car off the road more and into a thick stand of trees and bushes, and set about trying to conceal it. No matter what we did, it looked like a car, and it looked like something rather more exotic than the plain and box-like motorcars seen elsewhere in town. Even standing some distance away, I could still see the brasswork around the headlamps gleaming. I muttered unladylike things and decided simply to press on with our mission.

Gordon, meanwhile, had unchained the freshly painted main

gate and was waving at me to go through. Once properly on Hawkins land, my nerves intensified. I expected at any moment to hear large dogs barking in protest and hurtling at me, all white teeth and rippling sinews. Gordon said, "Here, time to add a little glamour." I wish I could describe what he did next, but it was over before I could even see him clearly. All at once, I felt warmer, and there was a little more light, as if the moon were visible. It was a confounding sensation, right on the edge of perception; faint, but so constant that one could not ignore it. It was a little like a mild toothache, without the pain, but with the urge to keep poking one's tongue at it, so to speak. As I tried to adjust myself to this new, mystical state of being, Gordon quickly went through the motions for himself, and then murmured, "The deal is done." He shook his head, looking distressed for a long moment. I suspected he was thinking about what he would have to sacrifice to the universe, and that it was something costly to lose. I hated to think what that might be, and didn't ask, as I should have done.

We ventured down the driveway, keeping to the grass next to the gravel.

23

Nothing disturbed us; and we appeared to disturb nothing in return. I trod as softly as I could, thinking about the almost-weightless steps of a kitten, as if that might help. Gordon, however, simply strolled along towards the house as if he were ambling by the side of the road on a perfect autumn day. For his part, he looked at me as if amused at my great efforts at stealth.

In the too-quiet stillness, I saw, nearby, an owl dive for the grass, and then flap effortlessly away towards the trees, something small and helpless struggling in its lethal claws. If I had not been looking that way, I realised, I would never have seen it. It reminded me that, despite appearances, the world was neither asleep, nor friendly.

The Hawkins house was a large, flat homestead, with broad verandahs all the way around. A few chairs and tables stood here and there in places where one might catch what was left of the afternoon sea breeze. The yard was well maintained: as well as an extensive vegetable garden they had a modest garden of flowers featuring some well-pruned roses, all of them asleep for the night.

Two impressive German shepherds slept on a patched old chaise longue on one verandah. Around their necks were substantial leather collars connected to long, heavy chains fixed to a bracket on the wall nearby. One of the dogs was dreaming, feet and tail twitching; the other dog lay on her back, forelegs stuck straight up in the air.

"Now what?" I whispered to Gordon.

"How do you mean?" he said, in a much louder stage whisper that I thought would alert both dogs at once.

"Well, look! What about these dogs?"

"Beautiful animals, I must say. Excellent condition."

"When will they realise we're here?"

"Depends."

"Depends on what exactly?"

"How much noise we make!"

He took some delicate steps forward. Nothing happened. The dog with her feet up rolled on to her flank, legs still stuck out. Gordon lifted his right foot, preparing to try the first of the wooden steps. I stood with my hands over my face; I could hardly watch, and I did not want any accidental sounds I might make in my anxiety to give us away. My knees felt weak. Gordon tried the step. It held his foot's weight. He nodded to himself. He leaned in, and still the step remained silent. He shifted himself up and soon stood on the lowest step. "Come on," he said.

I approached. I could hear the dreaming dog snoring. It was surprisingly loud.

Behind me, I was aware of a light wind soughing through the treetops.

Gordon was up on the verandah.

I shivered. I made my way up the steps. I could feel the wood flex a little, but it did not creak. Soon I was up on the verandah with Gordon. The sleeping dogs were perhaps four feet to my right. They had rather more than four feet of chain—that I could see—and probably more.

Gordon pointed at a door to his left. "Kitchen door," he said.

So far we had had no need of our lanterns. The silvery glimmer of the shadow glamour provided just enough illumination.

Gordon strolled over to the kitchen door. Unable to believe his casual air, I stepped as if my life depended on it.

A board under my right boot emitted a mild squeak.

I stopped, heart hammering in my throat. I watched the dogs. The dreaming dog opened his eyes a little and glanced about, ears twitching, but he soon subsided, making loud snuffling and grumbling noises.

Gordon looked at me and smiled.

I could hardly move.

Gordon took my gloved hand and drew me to the door. There was a flywire panel in the upper half of the outer, light wooden door. Gordon pulled this aside; it made a small squeaking sound that disturbed neither dog. Behind the flyscreen door, the heavy main door stood locked against us. Gordon produced a set of iron lockpicks, and soon we heard a *clunk!* and he turned the brass knob of the door, which opened without a sound. He put away his tools; I heard them *clink* in his pocket.

"Have you done this sort of thing before, Gordon?"

"I am a man of many talents," he said, without further clarification.

From the kitchen I smelled recent cooking: fried meat, boiled potatoes, peas and beans, something that was probably pumpkin.

It was a large kitchen, with workbenches all around, and cabinets above and below. The black iron range quietly roared and hissed in its alcove. Glass jars held banksia heads. Everything was clean and tidy.

Gordon glanced about the room, edging around the great, scarred wooden chopping block that dominated the centre of the kitchen. He was looking at doors, trying to figure out which one led down to the cellar. I could hear two adults snoring not far away. Less clear, but somehow more piercing and immediate, was the sound of a small child crying softly, probably in its sleep. As Gordon tried the three other doors, all I could hear was this crying. At the moment it was not loud, not hacking sobs and wailing, but it was loud enough.

"Here," Gordon said, pointing at an opened door with black nothingness beyond.

The child's crying gave way to calling its mother. *"Muuuu-uuuuum…? Muuuu-uuuuum…?"*

I went to the cellar door as quickly as I dared.

Gordon showed me a rickety-looking flight of narrow steps leading down.

The Hawkins mother called out, "Hang on, love, hang on..."

Gordon went first and I needed no encouragement to follow quickly; I eased the cellar door shut behind me. The mother did not pass through the kitchen, but I heard her padding along a hallway, saying something, and I heard her child say something in halting tones. I was thinking, *We should not be doing this!* At any moment we would be discovered, I was sure of it.

Gordon lit his shuttered lamp. This took longer than I would have liked. I heard someone, probably the mother, come into the kitchen. It sounded like she was filling the iron kettle with water and I heard it go *clank* on the range. Gordon's lamp lit; he closed the open shutter. I was sure the mother, even half-asleep, would notice a strange glow from under the cellar door. She was moving around, and I heard her open the icebox, rummaging for something.

Gordon started down the steps.

The second step emitted a loud squeak.

From the kitchen, I heard no change in the mother's activity. I assumed she was making her child something to eat.

Gordon had stopped cold on the steps, looking back at the door. Ahead of him, the dim glow from around the lamp's shutters revealed a stone wall. It was impossible to see what lay below.

"Do you feel that?" he whispered, this time with no trace of his previous confidence.

"Pardon?"

"It feels colder than it should."

"We're underground."

When we could no longer hear noise from the kitchen, Gordon risked the next step. It groaned faintly. I wondered if I could somehow avoid the loud step. As Gordon ventured further down the steps, I followed, trying to keep to the edge nearest the wall, where they squeaked least.

Gordon reached the floor. "Flagstones," he said. As he held the lamp out, one shutter slightly open, and looked around, we saw that the cellar was full of big wooden tea chests, each one smelling of its original contents. Now they seemed full of odd bits and pieces. Gordon looked distracted as he examined a few to see what interesting items the Hawkinses might be storing. I was pleased, as I reached the floor, to have avoided spiderwebs so far. Gordon aimed the light at the gritty floor; two large cockroaches scuttled out of the faint glow.

I managed to suppress the disgusted squeal that I felt, and resolved to crush any such creatures I found. I have never been able quite to believe the cockroaches in this country. The first time I saw one after arriving here, I had been so horrified that I had very nearly turned around and sought the first boat home. Such creatures were unnatural, I was sure. Now I had to suppress my revulsion as I thought I felt them crawling over my boots. When I got home, I would need a long, very hot bath.

Gordon was peering around in the small cellar, studying the floor, sometimes touching it with the palm of his hand. He was deep in frowning thought.

When I could break my mind away from its fevered imaginings, I asked him, "Any luck?"

"Not so far, I must say," he said, sounding not as annoyed as I thought he would be. "There's nothing down here..."

"Are you sure? Is it possible the summoner could conceal it from you?"

"Not a circle of power. It would fairly hum with its energy, particularly if it was employed in manifesting an entity like...well..."

"So it's not as if he's just shifted a tea chest over it."

"The tea chest would have extensive charring all over it, and might even have caught fire."

He was examining the stone walls, as best he could with the tea chests stacked around here and there. I saw him rapping on the exposed stonework with his knuckles, and he was listening, perhaps for a hollow sound. At length he shook his head and looked disappointed. "Just a cellar," he said.

"In that case, we can...?"

"We can go, yes."

I did not need telling twice. We worked our way up the steps, keeping to the edges of the ones that creaked. At the top, standing at the kitchen door, we listened. I could no longer hear the child crying. The mother seemed to have gone back to bed.

Gordon doused the lamp; it reeked of oil and a little smoke.

He eased open the door, peered about, and stepped up into the kitchen. "Come on," he said.

I joined him. The silvery light was a welcome change after the cold blackness of the cellar. We edged towards the door by which we entered. Close by the sink, I heard one of the snores abruptly stop, followed by a vague muttering, and then footsteps. The other snoring, which I assumed was the mother, stopped then, too, and she murmured something. He murmured something back. Heavy footsteps pounded down the hall, heading for the kitchen.

We were about five feet from the verandah door. Gordon was still moving. I stood rooted to the spot, staring at the door.

Frank Hawkins, his beergut preceding him, lumbered into the kitchen, crossed the room, did not stop at the icebox, and kept going, heading for the door that would lead outside, to the outhouse. In the strange light, it was difficult to tell, but it looked as if he was almost asleep, even as he plodded about the house. Certainly he spotted neither of us. As he pushed open the back door, which led out onto the verandah on that side of the house, Gordon dragged me out onto the verandah on this side.

The two dogs were awake and barking, pleased to see their master, even if he was only on his way to the privy.

"Run for it?" I asked Gordon.

"As soon as he shuts the privy door...Right. Now!"

We ran. The plan was to cover as much ground as we could, and with a bit of luck get beyond the reach of the dogs' generous chains. My lungs burned; I was not used to this kind of exertion. Gordon, though he was always tinkering and fiddling with machines, was equally unused to such efforts. By the time we reached the property's main gate, we were both wheezing and coughing, slumped against the fence, perspiring freely. And, as we pushed the Tulip down the road away from the Hawkins property, it was all we could do to keep from giggling like naughty schoolchildren.

*

We found the circle in the cellar of the abandoned Cahill house.

It took us a long time simply getting to the cellar on that property. Our efforts were not helped by the house's dilapidation. Where the Hawkins house had been clean and tidy, and where the cellar featured nothing worse than cockroaches scuttling across the floor and over my feet, the Cahill house was a flimsy death-trap wreathed in the webs of very large spiders and full of rotted floorboards. Even wading through the long grass up to the house was fraught with peril; with every step I worried I would disturb a sleeping snake. Gordon, by contrast, pushed through the weeds without any apparent caution.

It was only when we stepped inside the ruined house that our problems began.

"The summoner must know a safe route through this place," Gordon said as he looked around. We stood in the central hallway of the house, off which doors to all the rooms could be seen, at least in our faint glimmering light. It helped us see where the floorboards had either rotted away or been taken away by people looking for free lumber, and we could see where walls were crumbling and would not support us if we leaned on them. Worse, the entire house felt alive with what I suspected were very active insects, spiders and presumably nervous rodents. With each hesitant step, I heard things scuttling and scrambling out of our way—and what I was sure were other things coming to fend us off. Gordon, however, was unconcerned. When I asked him, he said, "I wouldn't worry too much, Ruth. Most of it's illusory, courtesy of our friend the summoner."

"It might be illusory, but I can feel these illusions in my hair and down my neck!"

Gordon ignored me. He was studying the floor with great care, and placing his feet in particular places, even where it looked very much like there were no floorboards. He advised me in a tone I had never heard from him before, "Only step where I step. I can see the summoner's path and you can't, all right?" And saying this, he took two small, precise steps across empty space. Under what was left of the floor, I knew, was only about two or three feet of relatively empty space and then the ground. It was not a great fatal fall that I feared; it was slipping or crashing through in such a way as to break my legs. I kept my eyes on Gordon's feet, and did my level best to match his steps, even though my legs and back were cramping up with the strain of it. In this manner we worked our agonising way towards the kitchen, which was located in the centre of the house.

There was no floor in what had been the kitchen.

Gordon had explained that the shadow glamour enhanced what feeble light was already available, which was why it worked outside and in the kitchen of the Hawkins house, but not in the cellar, where there was none. By that logic, we should have been able to see down into the pit before us, even if faintly. But we could not. The pit was as dark as the Hawkins cellar had been, and somehow seemed darker. I had been shivering, but now I was almost convulsing I was so cold. "H-how do we g-get down there?"

Gordon was trying to warm his hands in his armpits. "I don't recommend jumping, I can tell you that right away. I have no way to determine the pit's depth."

I found a loose, rusty nail and tossed it in.

The nail never struck bottom, as far as I could tell.

"This has to be the place," I said, wishing very much I had stayed at home.

"Oh, it's the place all right."

"What do we do next? We didn't bring any rope or ..."

Gordon lit his lamp. Once it was going, he crouched on our tiny patch of safe ground and waved it out over the gaping square hole. The lamp's light was swallowed whole. He swore.

With the lamp's shutters wide open, he reached out over the edge of the pit, and waved his hand around below floor-level, looking for something. "Ah," he said.

"Ah?"

"A step."

"A step?"

He stood up, holding the lamp in his left, gloved hand. "I think I've found a way down."

"But we can't see the steps."

"Where's your sense of adventure?"

"Sitting up in bed at home, reading a good book!" It occurred to me that Julia was probably doing just this. Now *she* would have enjoyed all this tension and anxiety. I only wanted it to be over.

Gordon smiled at me. "You'll be fine!"

This was not reassuring. All the same, and feeling as though I might fall to my death at any moment, I followed Gordon's advice. Down on the safe bit of floor, on hands and knees, I started climbing down the invisible steps and into the frigid, lightless depths.

24

With extreme care, we crab-walked our way down these phantom steps. Gordon went ahead, the handle of the lantern gripped in his teeth. It threw out a yellow light that did not so much fail to illuminate as that the illumination was stolen by the surrounding darkness. Gordon also kept muttering at me, with considerable difficulty, to please stop kicking him in the back of his head.

Minutes later, we had still not reached the floor. Instead, we had found first one corner landing leading to another flight of steps, and then still others. I managed to keep a rough count: we had descended more than fifty steps and four landings. Peering up revealed only the faintest suggestion of a smudged silvery illumination, concentrated in a small square, perhaps the size of a stamp. My hands, wrapped in thick leather gloves, ached with the cold. I fancied that the invisible steps were constructed from ice. My shoulders, knees, upper arms and legs all ached with unfamiliar exertion. From time to time I needed to stop and rest, but the steps felt so insubstantial that it was too easy to imagine them melting away or simply collapsing if one stayed too long in one spot. And, in the air itself, rasping in and out of my lungs, something smelled awful in a way I could not quite place. There was another faint aroma, too, which was familiar: it was the mysterious "other" smell from the notes, the scent we had tried to identify but could not. It was here, whatever it was. I asked if Gordon had noticed it.

He said, "It's like a sort of mildew sort of…rather a sweet odour…" I could hear him struggling for breath, too. And this was the easy part, going down these endless steps. Climbing back up, I knew, would be far harder.

"It's not any sort of rotting meat stench, or anything like that," I said.

"No," he managed to say, with a firm casualness that surprised me.

We kept going. With ten landings passed, and with no hint of light from above, I started wondering if we had stumbled into a trap. Perhaps I should have wondered this earlier, but I had not. I had been too busy counting steps and landings and gritting my teeth against the muscle pains. When I asked Gordon if we might be caught in such a trap, he said, "Poshibly. Hld n a mmnt."

He took the lantern's handle out of his mouth. "I say, that's much better," he said. "As for the possibility that we're caught in a trap—I fear you may be right. If so there's only one thing to do."

"I know just what you're about to say, Gordon," I said, and felt the icy dread rising through me. The only thing worse than inching our way down these lightless steps this way would be jumping out into the void, hoping for the best.

"The best way to beat a fear, Ruth…"

I had stopped my descent and now sat, awkwardly, with my legs dangling into the pit. The prospect of leaping into that pit, having faith in…what, exactly? The perversity of evildoers? It seemed to me the obvious thing to do would be to make the pit just as bottomless as the steps. "Perhaps we could climb down a little further," I ventured, keeping the shivers out of my voice. My teeth desperately wanted to rattle together in my mouth.

Gordon waved the lantern over the pit. Nothing had improved there, either. The darkness stole the light. He said, "Well, if we're going to do this…"

"You're not going to leave me stuck here, Gordon Duncombe!"

I could feel wafts of cold air rising from the pit. My lungs burned with the cold.

"One of us needs to test the theory, though, and I'm the logical candidate," he said, not sounding too worried.

"Is there nothing magical you could do that might help us?"

I could barely see, in the eerie ghost of light left in the immediate area around the lamp, the outline of part of Gordon's face. He looked reluctant. "I've got quite a debt going already, Ruth."

"Even so, Gordon. I mean, if we're stuck in a magic trap, surely we should use—"

"Ruth, you don't understand. It *costs* me, to do things. That protection charm only cost me a lock of my hair. That's not much of a change to the fabric of the universe. To fix this problem, on the other hand, I'd need to break what's probably a very powerful enchantment. It's a different order of cost. The sacrifice rises to the point of severity. As it is, I've already had to..." He broke off, unable to speak further. When he resumed, he spoke with great, slow, caution, a word at a time: "I can't lose more, Ruth. I can't. It would be either one of them, or...pieces of me. I can't do it, I just can't." I heard him discreetly wipe his nose.

We sat in silence. I did not ask him what he meant by "one of them". I knew how he loved his dogs.

Later, sounding perhaps too confident, even a little rash, he said, "Well, here goes nothing!"

"*Gordon?*" The darkness choked my scream.

He jumped.

"Gordon?" I had not heard him hit anything. He had not called out as he fell.

He had left me alone. Terror took hold. I found myself pressed against the wall, as far as possible from the abyss. Clinging to the frost-slick surface.

"Gordon!"

There was nothing else for it. I could keep climbing down these infinite steps, or I could follow Gordon. The thought of staying put, terrified out of my wits, was not acceptable. I took a deep, cold breath—and jumped into black nothingness.

*

Gordon's voice came as if in a dream. "Here, let me help you up."

It was another trap. I refused. I was on some kind of ground;

a solid floor lay beneath me. I did not recall how I got here. My eyes were squeezed shut. It felt like a long time since I had heard from my heart.

"Come on, Ruth. It's all right. Really. It's just me."

My teeth were rattling to the point of shattering. Hard coughing had set in. I was curled so tight I could not imagine standing upright again.

"Just open your eyes. It's all right. Look, it's all right. It's the floor. We're on the floor. Look! There were only the two flights of steps, and we were going around and around..." Then he said, in a quite different tone, "Come *on*, Ruth!"

He'd never raised his voice like that, and that surprise made me open my eyes, just to see what was happening.

Gordon hunched before me, one gloved hand on my shoulder. I saw that I was pressed tight into a dark corner of a small, square room. There was light down here, but not any kind of light I understood or recognised. There was a quality to it, as if we were deep underwater.

The centre of the room contained a glowing circle, perhaps two yards across. I could smell it. It had that strange smell from the notes. To one side, I saw there was a small wooden table, painted a colour that might have been blue, the paint peeling with age, on the surface of which sat an old typewriter; on a shelf beneath lay a packet of octavo bank typing paper, and some typewriter maintenance tools I recognised only too well.

As I was about to point out the typewriter to Gordon, I saw him peering at the walls all around the room. Made of stone blocks, the walls were painted and etched with small, intense writing. Gordon said it was an occult script, one he did not recognise, but which was likely the spell used to create the circle; that the entire room was a magical construct, in effect. "I shouldn't look at it too closely, or for too long, Ruth."

He helped me stand. The pain was remarkable. Something in my head boomed and boomed.

The ceiling pressed down on us like a winter sky threatening storms; there were perhaps only a few inches of clearance. It did not feel like standing in a room so much as being trapped in a box. Then I looked up again at this ceiling. I saw that perfectly ordinary stone steps led down here from upstairs. Gordon said that, in some ways, being on the other end of an enchantment was like looking through the wrong end of a telescope.

It was still extremely cold. Even in this peculiar light, I could see my breath, but it seemed to plume differently. It was unsettling to see.

"So," I said at long last, "here's the circle Julia saw."

Gordon had not ventured near it. "Can you feel it?"

I could feel something terrible going on just behind my conscious awareness, a sensation that what I perceived with my ordinary senses was only the merest hint of what there really was here. I had never quite understood what Julia meant by her "other bits" of reality—until now. I had a profound sense that my ordinary faculties were, in some ways, blinding me to some greater, bleaker truth.

My head hurt so much I was almost in tears. I imagined I was not made to comprehend experiences such as these.

Gordon appeared seasick: pale and clammy and very cautious in his movements.

"Gordon? Are you...?"

He swallowed and tried to breathe through his mouth. "It's just a little difficult, being close to a point of contact between the...the brain isn't sure if it's here or there..."

"We should go then."

"No," he said. "No."

"Gordon, you look terrible!"

He fished from an inside pocket a small paper envelope. His hands shook.

"What's...?"

"Take this. You don't need to know what it is. It's better if you don't. Here, take it."

I would far rather have taken hold of an electric eel, but I took the envelope. It felt light, as if it were filled with the finest dust. I could not reliably describe the smell; it changed by the moment, erasing the previous impression with each new one.

"You need to pour this into the circle."

My head howled. "Into the circle?"

"We need to see Ukresh Nor, don't we?"

We did, if we were to extract his true name, and with that to extract the name of his summoner, my tormentor — or tormentors. Yet at the moment this did not seem such an important goal. All I wanted was to take one of my antique trap-shooting guns and blow my head off. My insides were in turmoil. And at any moment, I would need to be quite unladylike in front of Gordon. It says something about how little had really changed in the deepest parts of my mind that I felt waves of incipient embarrassment at this mortifying prospect.

"This," Gordon said, picking slowly through his words, and nodding towards the small envelope, "will get his attention."

"We really are going to do this, then."

"Yes," he said. "And the sooner the better, if you take my meaning, Ruth."

I looked at the circle; it was emanating an unsettling black light. "Wish me luck."

"You don't need luck. You need strength."

I took two steps towards the circle, and felt something like an underwater current push back at me. The current worsened the pain in my head, and deepened the turmoil in my belly. I managed to swallow back the first few attacks of vomiting. The bitter taste of bile helped clarify my thinking.

Gordon was calling after me, urging me on, standing well back, his hands on his knees, and he was breathing very hard.

Telling myself I was doing this for my own ultimate benefit, I pressed on. The currents pushed at me again, and tried to spin me around, tried to confound me. Focusing on the evil light rising from the circle, and that intense stink, which now made me think of flowers, but not any blossoms of this world, I kept on, taking tiny but firm steps. The circle loomed ahead. Reaching out, I saw that I was close enough. Two more small steps. More buffeting, more confusion. Nausea like an ocean storm through my body and mind. Keeping one hand clamped over my mouth to catch the surging bile, I leaned into the circle. The circle, I saw, was a drain, swirling with something alive, a throat; I heard it gurgling in the back of my mind.

I upended the paper envelope.

Some kind of *water*—gallons of it—poured out, and kept pouring as I stood there. Stunned, feeling on the verge of collapsing, I watched a river of water crash out of the envelope and fall down into the living drain between worlds.

The black light flashed into nothingness, knocking me backwards, dazed and stunned. The circle became an ordinary circle painted in something that might have been blood on worn flagstones. Faint light shone down into an ordinary cellar—and I saw the writing on the walls unwriting itself, as though dozens of busy unseen hands were working at it, in every part of the room.

Gordon gasped, suddenly, and pointed at the far corner.

An elf stood there, but not one we had seen before. This one was different. He had the same peeling, translucent skin, covered in tiny spiral tattoos, and that same deathly look about him as if it was all he could do just to stand up, to keep his huge head from lolling to one side. But where the other ones we had seen had horrible white eyes with pinprick irises, this one had no eyes at all, as if they had been scooped out of his sockets. He wore, incongruously, a black felt bowler hat, not quite the right size, no doubt stolen, but was otherwise naked, and piteous with it, no more than skin and only too visible bone through that wrinkled tissue of flesh.

The eyeless elf pointed something at Gordon. In the weak light, it looked like a triangular device made of sticks and black feathers.

"Good Christ—" Gordon said, his voice faint and tight, as he dropped to his knees, clutching his belly.

When I looked back at the elf, he was gone.

But Mr Ukresh Nor had arrived.

25

The demon stood in the circle. He wore dark trousers held up by braces and a cheap-looking brown shirt. His shoes were brown, and looked worn, as if he'd walked a thousand miles in them. He looked like a middle-aged man back from the War, where he'd seen too many terrible things. And his hands—I had never seen such enormous hands. The sight of them, having heard about them from Julia, was shocking. How could a demon look so much like a man, yet have such hands? He pointed his eyes at me but did not look at me.

His mouth was stitched closed.

My knees gave way.

The demon caught me and helped me to the floor without hurting myself.

His giant's hands were rough, and cool.

He had that smell about him, like a cologne.

I looked at Gordon. Gordon was curled up, on the floor, clutching his belly, not speaking, in profound pain.

Now what? I said to myself, trying not to panic. A lady must maintain her poise no matter the provocation, after all. Where that had come from, I did not know. It sounded like my mother.

I sat and tried to think. My own belly was protesting. I felt ready to be horribly ill at any moment. I held my head. Mr Nor did not seem threatening, so far. It looked as though I could spare a moment to collect myself.

What about Gordon, though? He looked in a very bad way, like he'd been gut-shot. I should be getting him to some sort of doctor, I could see that, but to what kind of doctor, and what could I say? He was not bleeding. And something that looked very much like it might have been an elven shaman had pointed some sort of magical device at him.

Which left me with Mr Nor.

"Are you…are you Ukresh Nor, the demon?" I said, working to keep bile—and terror—out of my voice. It is not every day one encounters one's intended assassin, prior to the deed's performance. It seemed reasonable, in an insane sort of way, to see what information I might extract from him.

He nodded. He nodded slowly, as though it was a great effort and he would rather not.

"Do you recognise me?"

He looked down at me. After a moment, he produced a small notepad and a stub of pencil from a pocket, and, slowly, his great hands seeming to swallow the pencil and notebook, wrote something. He showed it to me: "YOU ARE MRS BLACK."

"That's right," I said, swallowing more bile, trying to breathe. "I am."

He looked at Gordon, but not with any visible concern. Gordon continued to make awful noises. In my mind I was willing him to do some sort of deal with the universe. Anything.

To the demon, I said, "Someone summoned and bound you, is that right, Mr Nor?"

He nodded and looked desolate, which surprised me.

"I understand that this person summoned you to kill me. Is that right?"

The demon looked concerned for a moment. He scratched out his last message and wrote a new message. "NOT PRECISELY. I RUN ERRANDS FOR HIM."

"Errands?"

Nod.

"And these errands could include killing me?"

Nod. He wrote: "IF YOU DO NOT COOPERATE."

It occurred to me I had refused to pay the initial, absurd sum of one thousand pounds. That Rutherford was patiently and loyally sitting near my letterbox tonight, waiting for whatever might happen.

Oh...

"I have already refused to cooperate, though, Mr Nor..." I said, my hard-won sense of almost-normalcy dropping away into chilly chaos.

He wrote: "I HAVE ALREADY ACTED."

"Y-you've already...?" I was backing away from the circle.

Mr Nor wrote, "YOU DID NOT COOPERATE. YOU NEEDED A LESSON."

"Rutherford...Oh, God..."

I wanted to leave. Turning, though, I almost tripped over Gordon. Through his own agony, he held a scrap of crumpled paper in his right hand. He was trying to get me to take it. "Please, Ruth..."

Opening it, a torn-off bit of butcher's paper, I saw that Gordon had written three nonsense words, and the demon's name, in shaky printed writing.

Gordon looked up at me. He was dying. It was plain to see. His eyes were losing their focus. He screwed up his remaining strength and said, "Say the words...to him. Now, Ruth..."

Looking again at the words, and back at the demon, and thinking about Rutherford, I was not sure what to do. "Gordon...you're ... *Do something! Help yourself!*" I had not meant to shout at him like that. He struggled to focus on me. "It's cold, Ruth. So cold." I could see his breath, feeble though it was.

"Save yourself! Good God, Gordon, save yourself!"

"Ruth...I have always..." He was making an extreme effort now to look at me, in a way he had never looked at me before. There was a fleeting candour in his expression that was new.

"Please, Gordon!"

"I'll be right. I'll be fine. You...you sort out Mr... Nor..."

"Promise me! Promise me you'll save yourself!"

"The cost...I can't..." He looked so helpless, holding onto a thread of life, and, in his extremity, he was still not prepared to sacrifice his dogs to save himself.

"Then take something of mine, for God's sake! Take my good right arm! Take it! It's yours!"

His failing eyes almost burst out of his head at this suggestion. "Ruth?"

"Take the damned thing! I would rather have you back than keep this arm. All right? Is that enough for you?"

He saw now that I meant it. He was speechless, and looked ashamed. I saw tears forming in his eyes. "Let me...get started. You..." he gestured to the demon. I looked again at the paper, now a tiny, hard ball in my fist. Gordon's eyes were closed now. He was mumbling something under his breath.

Now it was my turn. I went back to the demon. "Mr Ukresh Nor?"

Again, with the deepest reluctance, he looked down at me. His eyes were somewhere beyond sadness.

"I need to know your true name."

He pulled out his notebook, flicked to a fresh page, and he wrote, with great care, "I CANNOT REVEAL MY TRUE NAME TO YOU."

"I understand," I said, though it must be admitted that my understanding of exactly why this was the case was thin to the point of vanishing. "My friend has given me some words to say to you. Is that all right?"

Suddenly the demon looked very interested. I saw him trying to see what was written on Gordon's bit of paper. I was, oddly, reminded of a dog who knows there's something tasty in one's hand, and is trying to sniff it out.

The demon scrawled, "I WILL HEAR YOUR WORDS, MRS BLACK." He wrote this more quickly than I'd seen him do anything else. For the briefest moment, I thought I saw him bounce on the balls of his feet.

This monstrosity hurt Rutherford earlier tonight. Remember that. He'll hurt other people close to you if you don't stop him. He is a monster. He will kill you, if given the instruction.

I needed the reminder. The demon had those enormous, square hands. It was too easy to imagine him throttling me as I lay in my bed. I would never stand a chance.

"Kashlat vio Nytholor, Ukresh Nor," I said, trying to pronounce the words clearly, and worrying that if I pronounced them incorrectly, they would not work.

The demon staggered, as if something had hit him hard in the chest—like a train, perhaps. He emitted a terrible grumbling noise that started out so low it worsened my feeling of nausea. Soon it rose through audible registers. I wondered if he was dying.

I chanced a glance at Gordon. He lay still, with his eyes closed. "Gordon!" I shouted, and moved to run to him—until I saw the faint movement of his chest. He was alive, in some way. It would do.

Ukresh Nor had slumped to the floor. Kneeling, he looked at me, eye to eye. Taking up his notebook and pencil again, and with his great hands shaking, he glared with concentration as he wrote, "VARIEL".

I was short of breath from sheer astonishment. It had worked. Gordon had done it. I now had the demon's true name. My knees turned to water once again, and I sat down quickly. I tried to re-gather my wits. But not for long. I still had things to do.

What has he done to Rutherford? I wondered, looking at him. Would he tell me, now I could control him? I did not see why he would not tell me.

I took a deep breath and cleared my throat. My voice wavering, I said, "Variel—"

The demon stood quickly and with admirable rigidity. I was reminded of a soldier coming to attention. It was difficult to comprehend having any sort of power over a creature from another world. It was easy to understand why humans had dabbled in demonology. People were weak; demons, at least ones like this, were strong. Having such a thing at one's beck and call would be irresistible, even intoxicating. One could have enemies killed or maimed and no policeman in the world would be able to trace the crime back to the source.

"Variel," I opened, "tell me what you did to my servant Rutherford earlier this evening."

He nodded and began writing. At length, he showed me his

answer, squeezed into a blank corner of the page: "I HAVE DONE NOTHING TO MISTER RUTHERFORD. I BELIEVE HE IS WELL."

The shock hit me hard. I wanted to tell him he had to be mistaken.

But I had only assumed he must have attacked Rutherford. The demon would have gone to my letterbox and found it empty of the money. He would have found Rutherford sitting there guarding it, and no doubt very handy with his revolver.

A fresh fear began to stir. Rutherford was capable of defending himself. There were others at my house, however...

"Variel, you said you had already acted, to teach me a lesson."

He nodded, and looked so sad.

"So you hurt someone in my house?"

Another nod.

I asked him if he had hurt any of my staff, and named each one. Variel shook his head. He wrote, "I HAVE NO BUSINESS WITH YOUR STAFF, MRS BLACK."

By this point I was baffled. The only person left in my house was Aunt Julia, and she was safe from harm because of Gordon's protection charm. So who was left? I had no pets.

I asked him whom he hurt in order to teach me a lesson.

Variel looked more desolate than ever. He wrote, slowly, on a fresh page, "MISS JULIA TEMPLESMITH."

*

I should have seen it, the huge gaping risk. The demon had shown it to me himself throughout my entire encounter with him tonight.

I was now sitting once more, leaning against the wall near Gordon's unconscious body. I was exhausted. There was a hot blue fire screaming in my head and guts. The fire burned away the nausea, the confusion, and most certainly any remaining "thrill" I might have felt on gaining control of Variel. Now there was only the simplicity and clarity of anger—almost all of it directed against myself.

Gordon's protection charm offered protection from "malicious" entities.

Julia, when she told me about her encounters with the demon in the other world, had told me, in so many words, that there was nothing personal in the demon's plans against me. It was, indeed, all business. There was no malice. Indeed, tonight all I had seen, though I had failed to take note of it, was that the demon was a melancholy figure trapped into doing someone's dirty work, work the demon probably would not have done, had he any sort of choice. The very nature of the demon meant he could not refuse the orders of his summoner and master. I could see that now. So he had done something to Julia, and, because of Gordon's specifically worded protection charm, she had been defenceless.

I tried to concentrate. I needed to focus. The anger gave me clarity, but not the sort of clarity that allowed for thinking through plans of action.

So I did not ask just exactly what had the demon done to Julia. Whatever it was he had done, I was in no position to do anything about it. With a little luck, Rutherford and the rest of the staff would have taken the necessary action. In so far as the situation could be said to be "in hand", it was, at least for now.

Instead, I asked my tame demon, "Tell me the name of your former master. The man who brought you into this world, and who got you running all those errands."

Variel nodded, and he began writing. It did not take him long. When he was finished, he showed me the page.

It was a name I knew. It was someone I knew. Someone I knew only too well.

It was hard to breathe. My heart galloped. I wanted to ask him if this name was correct—but how could he lie to me? He could no more lie to me than he could defy the specific orders of his former master, even as complying with those orders sickened him with his own notion of regret.

I did what seemed at the time to be the only just thing. I put aside my impulse to send Variel to wreak havoc on my tormentor as he had hurt me. I could not bring myself to use Variel as he had been used by my enemy. That would have only compounded the sin. Variel needed one thing and only one thing.

"Variel," I said, standing up. "I am not sure how to go about this, but I hope it does the job for you. Erm..."

The great demon stood there, crisp and smart, alert to my every whim. It was a terrible thing to see. I said to him, "I release you, Variel. I no longer want or need your services. You're a free...ah, you are a free demon."

He looked shocked, full of disbelief. He wrote, "ARE YOU QUITE SURE? IS THERE NOTHING ELSE YOU WOULD HAVE ME DO?"

"No," I said, "nothing else. You're free. Go home. Go."

Still, he stared at me. I had a feeling no-one had done this to him before. He had presumably been handed from one master to another for who knows how long, and now he was mine.

He wrote again, "THANK YOU. I AM SORRY FOR WHAT I HAVE DONE."

With that, he vanished.

The air swirled around, cold and reeking of that stink.

I thought my troubles would now be over. As I went to Gordon and tried to pick him up, I was thinking how I would deal with my problem. Was it possible I could somehow get Variel's former controller to confess to what he had done to Julia? Could I involve the police in some way? At that moment, it did not seem likely.

Gordon was tremendously heavy; unconscious and cold, he was a dead weight. I had to haul him up the two flights of steps into the ruined Cahill house. I am not sure, now, how I got him outside, though I do recall the great difficulty of driving the Tulip through the towering weeds, wet with pre-dawn dew, heaving Gordon into the back of the car, and very carefully easing the Tulip back up towards the road. We were nearly bogged several times. Only judicious use of the throttle lever and brakes saved the day. By the time dawn washed the eastern sky that certain shade of cold metal blue, and the local crows were awake and cawing in apparent protest at the sight of the new day, we were back on the gravel road, and motoring back to town.

Julia...

I had been concentrating on the physical difficulties of manoeuvring Gordon out of that pit, concentrating with what probably looked like a frightening intensity.

At that point I could not falter. I could not give way to my fears for Julia. A natural pessimist, I assumed the worst had occurred, that Variel had done his work thoroughly, if not with any great delicacy. Driving home along quiet roads hardly occupied, the sounds of the Tulip's motor and solid rubber tyres on gravel in my ears, I did my best to ignore the booming of my heart, and the cold dread pooling in my belly. This night had been exhausting. There had been too many shocks, too much strain, too much terror. And, of course, I was not yet done.

Should I take Gordon back to his house? Perhaps taking him back to my house was the better course, because my staff could take care of him—

There was a stirring in the back seat. "Mmrgh..."

"Gordon?" I stopped the Tulip by the side of the road. It was so quiet. "Are you all right, Gordon?"

He was rubbing at his stubbled face, and looked like death, pale and grey. "Ruth, where are we?"

"We're heading back into town."

"The demon?" He was starting to sit up, his eyes squeezed shut against the morning sun. One hand clutched at his stomach. "What hit me? Good God."

"We freed him, Gordon. He's free. We—"

Gordon nodded. "Fine. Good. Could you take me back to my place, please? The dogs..." As soon as he said it, he remembered last night. I'd seen film of icebergs calving from the side of glaciers. Gordon's face, ordinarily a sagging, rumpled mess, now seemed to collapse, darkening. His breathing changed. He stared out the window, seeing nothing that was actually there.

"Gordon, I'm..." Not turning to look at me, he lifted a hand, as if to dismiss my concern, and perhaps to dismiss me, as well. I hurt all through, seeing that look on his face, and seeing that hand.

I was glad we were no longer on the road. The dogs. Those poor, beautiful, lively dogs. "There must be something else—"

"Please, Ruth. Take me home. It's all right. It's fine." His voice was gentle.

"Julia's dead." It was true that I did not know this for sure. It was possible the demon had only hurt her somehow—a whole world of horrifying thoughts flickered past at that—but I doubted it.

Gordon looked at me. "I beg your pardon?"

"Julia. She...Mr Nor, he—"

We sat in our own solitudes, lost.

I found myself thinking about the elven shaman who'd attacked Gordon. What in the world was an elven shaman doing down in that cellar? I wondered if my enemy, the extortionist, had resorted to elven magic, somehow, in order to construct the gateway between our world and the world of Variel? I thought about the unexplained abandonment of the Cahill property six years earlier, the failed crops. It made a certain insane sense. Nothing one could explain to anyone else, of course, but in the context of everything else happening around me lately, it seemed quite reasonable. I sensed that my future self would be resorting to a very stiff gin and tonic, and don't worry too much about the tonic. Variel's eyes, those achingly sad eyes. The way he'd caught me when I fell. His apology. Demons, I was told, were fallen angels. It was something Gordon reminded me about earlier. Yes, I could see it now. I felt sorry for the poor blighter.

*

Later, I took Gordon home, his noisy, raucous home. I offered to come in with him, since I could see he was still in considerable pain, and walked stooped over, clutching his belly. He could barely walk on his own. "I am quite all right, thank you," he told me when I tried to help. I wanted him to scream at me. I wanted him to blame me. God, I wanted him to look at me. We reached his door. The noise of the dogs was unbearable. They were so full of boisterous life. Growing up, back in England, I had known many occasions when it had come time for beloved pets, a favourite riding horse, even, oddly, a chicken, had come to a point when they had to be put down due to ill health. I had always been the sort of child who took it hard. It never seemed fair, even if it was the kindest thing to do.

I had expected, in a way, that when we got here the dogs would already have gone, as if the forces of cosmic balance would somehow have leaned down into this plane of reality and simply erased them, as they were troubling figures on a balance sheet. But the fact that they were all still vibrantly here, and that Gordon—my God, the poor man—would have to carry out that balancing task himself.

I headed home, hardly able to see where I was going.

"Oh, Julia..." I whispered, fighting fresh, cold, tears.

26

Rutherford was running down the driveway. *"It's Miss Templesmith!"* I had not heard him actually scream before, but he was doing it as he hurled himself towards the Tulip as I drove up. It was unnerving, seeing him so distressed. Last night, before we set out, Rutherford had looked the very image of a resolute man on a just mission. Now he looked like a scared boy.

He ran alongside as I brought the Tulip up to the door.

A police vehicle, a black boxy sedan with POLICE stencilled on the doors, and the Shire of Rockingham coroner's wagon, were already there.

Rutherford said, without my having to ask, "They've been here approximately—" he glanced at his pocketwatch, "—forty minutes, ma'am. This time…"

This time?

I could see he wanted to ask me where I had been, but knew this was not the time to ask.

I said, "And you've directed the staff to see to the gentlemen's needs in my absence?"

"Of course, ma'am. They have asked us some questions, I should point out."

"Which you all answered to the best of your ability?"

"Yes, ma'am, as far as we were able."

I felt very strange, playing this part. It felt that way to me, like a performance of calm composure and control in a crisis.

In truth I felt the way Rutherford looked—which was like death itself.

Inside, standing by the grandfather clock, listening to its unhurried clacks, I noticed the time. It was twenty minutes before six o'clock. I realised, as I heard heavy footsteps along the upstairs hallway heading towards the stairs, that Gordon and I had been out last night for over seven hours.

No wonder I felt exhausted.

And seeing two of the local policemen carrying what must have been Julia's draped body on a stretcher down the stairs, negotiating the landings with no skill at all, did not help. I could not look away from the stretcher. The Julia-shaped figure under the sheet was still. One could not have mistaken it for sleep, even the deepest, darkest sleep one could experience, simply lying there, barely breathing, not even dreaming. Death was something else again, a profound lack of everything that had ever made Julia the person she had been. I watched, nevertheless, for the merest hint of breathing. There had been too many stories in the popular press of dead people who had returned to some sort of life, because they had merely been comatose. I knew there once were places where bodies were stored and watched for a considerable time, to make sure they were dead, and where they were assaulted with sticks and whips and flails, in a desperate attempt to bring about some sort of vital response. It was the most ghoulish business imaginable. So I watched her, as the young uniformed policemen brought her to me and asked me quietly if I would "do the honours, ma'am", which meant, could I just make sure it was who they had been told it was. Horrified in a way that must seem surprising, considering how I had spent my evening, I consented and, when one of the officers pulled the sheet away from Julia's face…

"It's her," I said, hand over my mouth. Tonight I had conversed with a demon from a realm I could not directly perceive and in which I had never particularly believed. For the first—but not the last—time in my life I had worked magic. But I had never been more heart-in-my-throat terrified than that moment, when I had glanced at what was left of Julia.

I forget what happened after that point.

The next thing I knew, I was sitting on a sofa by the fire, with a blanket over my lap, and I was holding onto a cup of steaming, very sweet tea, as if my life depended on it. Shivering, I looked around. On an adjacent couch two plain-clothes detectives sat. The older one asked if I was all right, and when I said I was not quite sure, the older one decided to get on with it. He made the introductions. He was Detective Inspector Carmody, a mild-looking man who seemed unhappy at having been called all the way down here to Pelican River. Carmody was tall, with the build of a former football player gone somewhat to fat. He spent a great deal of effort stroking his gingery moustache into correct shape. Carmody was assisted by Senior Sergeant Sills, who hung back and concentrated intently on his notepad, flicking pages back and forth, always checking things, as if every secret of the universe lay in those pages, and it was all his to know. Once he saw that I was capable of being interviewed, a look of determination stirred into his bland face; he led the initial interview.

"We've just got a few questions, ma'am. We're hoping you can help us with our inquiries."

"Will this take long?"

Sills said, "Oh no, I shouldn't think so, ma'am."

Inspector Carmody sat back and watched me.

Sills asked, "Now let's just check some facts here, all right? You are Ruth Elizabeth Black? Is that right?"

I stared at him, wishing the whole miserable business were over. "I am, yes."

"And you are a widow?"

"Yes, that's right."

"A War widow?"

"Yes."

All this, I thought with a bitter amusement, was somehow to do with Antony, and his "alleged" lies to me. And now it had claimed the life of my harmless, talkative aunt. I had been furious with Antony—at least in so far as one could be furious with someone who *might* be alive—but if it should turn out that a consequence of his intrigues meant not only the death of my father but also of my aunt, then he had better watch himself. When I found him…

"Mrs Black? Are you all right?" Sills waved a hand up and down in the path of my vision. I had been staring at the fire, quite unaware.

I composed myself. I wished the shivering would cease. "Sorry."

A flash of memory shot through my mind: the image of the elven shaman, tattooed with spirals, wearing that bowler hat, ancient as the earth itself, its eyeless sockets swollen black with *malice*, pointing that device at Gordon.

Pointing it at Gordon because it could not see me, because I was protected by Gordon's protection charm.

"Er, Mrs Black? I'm sorry, you must be tired…"

Blinking, I looked up. "I am terribly sorry. It's just…" I let my voice trail away.

"Of course."

Inspector Carmody, doing his best to look avuncular and mild, smiled gently at me. "Mrs Black, you've been nursing that cuppa for nearly half an hour. Would you care for a top-up?"

Indeed, my tea had gone cool. Nodding vaguely, I saw the inspector turn to Sills, telling him, "Get the lady a fresh cuppa, would you? There's a good lad." Sills took my half-finished cup and clomped out to the kitchen. I knew Murray and Ryan were up, preparing the day's meals, working out what to purchase from the markets, clinging to routine. Vicky and Sally would be about somewhere, too, in case they were needed, and probably in shock just as I was, hoping they could be helpful. As for Rutherford: I had not seen him since he went out to put away the Tulip.

Carmody smiled. He said, "It is a beautiful house you have here, Mrs Black. Would I be mistaken in believing this must be the most expensive home in this whole town?"

I shrugged. "I do not keep track of such matters."

"Your staff tells us that you are something of an author. Is that right?"

I looked at him, annoyed and tired.

He went on, "Oh don't mind me. I'm just chatting whilst we wait for the sergeant."

Sighing, I went to say, "Yes, I write popular novels—"

But he interrupted me. "Ah, Sergeant Sills to the rescue!"

Sills had returned, large shoes clicking on the polished floorboards. He bore a steaming cup of tea, with an Empire Cream biscuit perched on the saucer, and handed it to me. "There you go, ma'am," he said, showing a polite smile. "Get that into you."

Carmody was saying, "Sergeant, I was just asking Mrs Black about the value of this house."

Sills was already deep into his notebook. He said, "Built twenty years ago, Federation style, formerly owned by the Westland family, who were graziers, though not for long. They returned to England, er, twelve years ago, unable, apparently, to accept the local insect life, most particularly the bull ants, I believe."

I sipped my steaming and very sweet tea. It helped.

Then Sills said: "Mrs Black—where were you this evening?"

Ah, it was time for this question. I looked up at Inspector Carmody. "I was out."

"Just...*out*?" Carmody glanced at Sills, who made a visible point of spelling, under his breath, as he wrote, "O...u...t. Out."

Carmody said, "And was anyone with you last night, who could verify your being 'out'?"

I said Mr Gordon Duncombe was with me. Sills nodded. "Of course, of course," he said, scribbling. Watching him scribble, I could not help but be reminded of Variel scratching in his own notebook.

"So," Carmody said after a pause, "Mr Duncombe could conceivably corroborate your story that this evening you and he were both 'out'."

"He could."

As I sipped the tea, I felt some of my faculties restoring themselves. I realised what was going on, at last. "You believe that *I* was involved in Julia's...?"

Carmody gave Sills a serious look this time. He said, "Not at all, not at all. I'm terribly sorry if we conveyed that impression. Your staff has been very loyal in your defence, and they have told us at considerable length that you and your Auntie Julia were quite devoted."

I felt a fleeting moment of great pride in my staff.

Then Sills said, "We're only trying to eliminate you from our list of suspects."

Then, before I could protest, Carmody said, "And, of course, there is the other matter."

He noticed my shocked pause. He looked as though he could smell my fresh dread. "Oh?"

"The other murder," Sills said, businesslike, flicking pages.

"It's been rather a busy night, Mrs Black," Carmody said. "Busy, busy, busy." He stroked his moustache.

"Someone else has...?"

"An acquaintance of yours," Sills said.

"Judging by your correspondence," Carmody added.

I was confused. "I don't..."

"Mrs Black..." Carmody said, staring at me like an entomologist at an insect.

"Inspector?"

"Where *were* you last night?"

Sills said, "We are prepared to obtain a court order permitting us to take a specimen of your fingerprints, unless you voluntarily provide us with same."

I opened and closed my mouth. I set the teacup down on the saucer. It landed badly on the edge of the uneaten Empire Cream. It spilled. The sound of porcelain scraping porcelain seemed far too loud. I frantically fiddled with the cup, and tried to clean up the mess. I knew I was muttering things. I knew Sills would be jotting it all down in his quick and spidery shorthand. All shorthand looked spidery, I knew that. Panic built. I struggled to fight back hot tears. Where had they come from? Nothing made sense. Outside I knew the sun was rising. I could hear a flat chorus of crows. They did this every morning, but today it felt worse. It felt like they were laughing at me, telling me I was done for. I held my face; my hands were cold.

"Mrs Black," Sills said, softer this time. "We need you to account for your movements of last night."

"Just to rule you out, of course," Carmody said. "It's only a formality."

"Purely routine," Sills said.

"We're not accusing you of anything, are we, Sergeant?"

He sputtered a weak laugh. "Of course not."

"But we would like you to tell us what you were doing last night."

Then Carmody asked, very softly, "Tell us about the extortion letters."

"God..." I said.

"Mrs Black?"

"Your butler, Mr Rutherford, he told us you have received a series of notes. He said that the most recent one included a demand for money in exchange for some sort of information?"

"Oh...God." Of course Rutherford would have told them about the notes. He would see no reason why the police ought not to know.

"May we see these notes, Mrs Black?"

"It's just...they're..."

I almost said: *potentially extremely dangerous to the psychically inclined*, but I stopped myself.

Carmody, nonetheless, saw that I had held something back.

He said, "We really do not consider you as a suspect in what happened to your aunt, Mrs Black. I can give you my word as an officer of the law. Fair dinkum. It's just that your staff mentioned them, and it seemed strange that all these things should happen in the same short period of time."

"Of...of course," I said, at last, looking at the inspector, and starting to believe that he might in fact be as decent as he was pretending to be. "They're upstairs. They're in my study, in the top drawer of the desk. Shall I...?"

Carmody nodded to Sills, who left to go upstairs.

"Why would *anyone* try to extort money from you, Mrs Black?" The irony in his tone suggested that, in his view, people would be foolish *not* to try to get money out of the eccentric rich author woman who wore men's clothes.

I shook my head. Where was his nice-copper routine now? "I do not know. I wish I did."

"And what *were* you and Mr Duncombe doing last night?"

"We were just out! We were out driving around. We were talking. We talk. Is that all right with you? That two people should just drive around talking?" I needed to take a breath after that.

"Bit of a chilly night for driving, wasn't it? I heard it was going to get down around thirty-five degrees or so. Good night for staying tucked up in bed, I'd have said. Actually, I was tucked up in bed when the call came…" He made it sound like he was wryly amused.

"I like cold nights. Reminds me of home."

"I see," he said, "of course. It would, too. Yes, I can see that."

I said nothing, and sat feeling foolish for my outburst. I sipped tea.

"Not me, though. No, not me. Born here. Local lad."

I wished the whole miserable experience would cease.

Sills clumped down the stairs. He had the notes. They seemed to cause him no discomfort, as the first one at least had caused Julia.

Julia… My breath caught; fresh shivers washed over me.

He handed them over. Carmody said, looking at them, "This is it?"

"That's all so far."

"You're expecting more?"

"Yes…" Oh yes. My correspondent would not be pleased with my activities last night. Taking away his demon—he would not like that. He would need to strike back. That was something to consider. Presumably his anger towards me, which now would be doubled, would drive him to strike at me—but Gordon's charm should see to that. So what else could he target? Gordon? The house?

God, my house…

Carmody said, "What's all this—sorry, I don't mean to be tedious about this, it's just my job, you understand—what's all this about your father and your husband? Eh? What's that about?"

I groaned. I tried to explain something about Antony and Father, but I was so tired.

"And this character, he was going to tell you something in exchange for money? Is that the deal?"

"I just want to go to bed, Inspector. I'm quite exhausted."

Carmody handed the notes over to Sills, who studied them closely, even to the point of sniffing them, and looking puzzled. The inspector said, "And you don't know who sent these notes to you?"

"No, Inspector. *I don't know.*"

Sills said, "Your Mr Rutherford said you had resolved not to cooperate with the extortionist. He said that he spent the evening sitting by your letterbox, waiting for a courier in the extortionist's employ. Seems a bit strange. Why not use some remote dead drop? If he just fronted up to your letterbox, surely you'd get a good look at him, maybe even catch him, and the game's up. So why would he do that?

"I do not know," I said. "Perhaps he's simple."

"It's still rather odd," Sills said, consulting his notes, looking like this one element would keep him awake for days as he worried over it.

"And why might that be, Sergeant?" I asked, wishing only these men would go away and leave me be.

"Nothing, really, ma'am. It's just that your Mr Rutherford told us he did not recall seeing anything of a suspicious nature during the entire time he sat out there in the cold for you. Not a sausage."

"Funny, that," Carmody said, nodding a little, looking at me.

No-one had come by to check the letterbox? That was not right. Variel had told me he had been here and seen that there was no money. He was incapable of lying.

But then, I thought, he would only respond to the questions asked of him. He would not volunteer information.

Something was terribly wrong, more wrong than I had thought.

"Mr Rutherford also said that your Aunt Julia had come out from England in something of a hurry, that she had something important to tell you. What was that?"

At this rate, Rutherford would put me in prison. Still, I could not fault him for doing his job. I said, "She had a premonition."

"I beg your pardon, ma'am?" This from Sills, who looked up, amused, from his note-taking.

"She had a premonition, in which I was in some sort of danger."

"Was she right?" He smirked some more.

"No! She's inclined to the dramatic, she…" I held my hands over my face.

"But as soon as she arrived, these notes started arriving?"

"That's right, but—"

"And this last note contains an implied threat, doesn't it?" Carmody was peering at me now.

I did not know what to say. I was tired, confused, sick at heart.

At last, I managed to pull myself together enough to say, "If you're not charging me with anything, gentlemen, I would appreciate it very much if you would leave me be. I should be only too pleased to discuss things with you once I have had some sleep."

"Yes," Carmody said, nodding and stroking his moustache. "Driving around all night long must be very tiring. Yes, I can see that."

"It's only natural," Sills agreed.

Checking with each other, they prepared to leave.

As they reached the door, however, Carmody turned back to face me, and he said, "Can you think of any reason why someone might murder Father William Dennis?"

27

Carmody turned back to face me. I struggled up; my legs did not want to support my weight; then I managed, leaning against the back of the sofa.

Carmody and Sills watched me as I tried to right myself. Sills seemed to have his thin face tilted over to one side slightly. The inspector said, quietly, "It's like I said, ma'am. Father William Dennis—he's dead, too."

"That's...that can't be right," I said.

"Why would you say that, ma'am?" Carmody looked very awake, very perceptive—quite the opposite of how I felt.

"I don't know, entirely. It simply seems wrong. It makes no sense."

Carmody said, "I quite agree. From what we've gathered so far from his housekeeper..."

"Mrs Rioli," Sergeant Sills supplied.

"Thank you, Sills. Yes, Mrs Rioli. She found the body. She says he was a quiet, humble sort of fellow. Devout, of course. Pious as the day is long."

"Pillar of the community," Sills added. "No enemies, nothing like that."

I stared at them. I remembered my recent business with him. His "suggestion" that I make a generous donation towards the church repair fund by way of atoning for hitting the swine all those years ago. Yes, I remembered only too well.

I felt dizzy.

"Where *were* you and Mr Duncombe last night, Mrs Black?" Carmody was studying me.

"Why don't you tell us what's really going on here?" This from Sills, who looked impatient.

Carmody added, "The sooner you tell us, the sooner we can all get some sleep."

"You're looking a bit ordinary there, Mrs Black," Sills said. "Why, if you'll pardon my asking, have you got...is that *spiderweb* on your clothes, and dust?"

Carmody smiled. "Driving around inside haunted houses?"

"It's all through your hair, too, look," Sills said, pointing.

I reached up and felt my hair, and he was right. The Cahill house had left its mark on me.

"What the hell were you two *doing* all night, ma'am?"

"*Nothing*!" I said, and knew as soon as I said it that it was both the wrong thing to say and the wrong way to say it. The way I looked—all in black, thick gloves, boots, and of course covered in spiderwebs, dust, and God only knew what else I'd picked up in the course of my adventures—wasn't helping my case.

Carmody and Sills exchanged looks. They were not quite sure what I had done, but they were sure I had been up to no good.

Then Carmody said, "You wrote to Father William..."

Sills said, "On the twenty-seventh of this month. Last Sunday."

"He's very good, isn't he?" Carmody said to me, smiling. "Never forgets a thing. Not a thing."

I said, "Yes. Yes, I wrote to him last Sunday. I wanted to apologise to him."

"Mrs Rioli says you and the Father have been at odds over the years."

I stared at Carmody, feeling sicker by the moment. "You think I...?"

Carmody laughed. "Oh no, oh no, Mrs Black. I'm sorry. Did we give you that impression? I'm so sorry. No. As I said about this bizarre business involving your aunt, we're only trying to sort through what's been quite the unusual evening in this very small town. You do understand. We're only trying to find the truth. That's all. We're not the enemy." He did his best to appear unthreatening, and essayed a bit of a laugh. Sergeant Sills tried to do the same; on him it looked like he had a dirty secret that he found amusing.

"In that case, gentlemen, as entertaining, and even disturbing, as this has been..."

"Father William wrote back to you, didn't he? Just this week?"

Sills said, "We found a carbon copy of a letter he wrote to you on Monday."

"Good," I said, feeling growing anger. "That's marvellous." Then, after a moment, frowning, I said, "Wait a moment." Monday did not sound right. Wasn't it just the other morning that I...? I was too tired to think straight. Could it have been Monday? Now I wasn't sure. Whereas I was certain that the police were trying to catch me in a lie or inconsistency—there was Sills with his notebook, jotting everything down. That boy was so observant he should take up a side-career as a novelist. Deciding to change tack, I said, "All right. You've seen my correspondence with him, and his with me. You'll know that he and I, we have a history going back some years. I even hit him—"

"You hit a priest, Mrs Black?" Carmody said, pretending to be surprised, and sharing a glance with Sills, who was still jotting. "Surely that's some sort of bad luck, wouldn't you say?"

I pressed on. "Yes, he impugned my late husband's honour. So yes, more than ten years ago, I did in fact hit him. But I did not kill him last night."

"Yes, of course, Mrs Black. Quite, yes," Carmody said, walking around me as he talked.

"He solicited a bribe from me."

"Is that right, Mrs Black?"

Sills said, "That's a very serious charge, ma'am."

"I still have his letter. You're welcome to see it."

The two policemen, however, looked confused. Sergeant Sills was checking through his notebook, and showing entries to Inspector Carmody, who raised his eyebrows and stroked his moustache. "Is that right, ma'am?" he said, still looking at the notebook.

I was losing my patience again. "Gentlemen, please. Can't this wait until after I've had a little sleep? I would be only too happy to entertain any number of alarming questions and improbable hypotheses you might assemble, perhaps this afternoon. Right now, however, I..."

They were still staring at me.

"Sergeant?"

Sills consulted his notes. "We found a carbon of Father William's reply, ma'am. He most emphatically refused to accept your apology. He denounced you, and threatened to have you excommunicated from the Church, and said you were a moral threat to the good men and women of this town. More or less. He went on a fair bit."

I stared, and then, feeling giddy now, I laughed a little. "Now that's just silly. Look. I have Father William's letter here. Or, at least, it would be upstairs in my study, where you found those notes. Please, feel free to go and have a look, or, if you like, I'll go. I shan't be a moment."

"Sergeant? Your stair-climbing legs feel up to another challenge?"

"Raring to go, sir."

Carmody smiled, and Sills set off up the stairs with a speed and vigour that was to be envied, particularly at this hour.

"Do you mind if I sit down again, Inspector? I feel quite..."

He looked embarrassed, momentarily, "Oh, I'm sorry. Yes, of course. Please. I understand completely. I'm feeling a little that way myself." We sat. He said, to fill the silence, "It's been a hell of a night, ma'am, if you'll pardon my French..."

By now I was holding my head up. "Oh?"

"Oh yes. Very odd. Strange. You see, what appears to have happened here is this: your Aunt Julia fell asleep last night and left her room light on. She'd been up late, reading, but she'd nodded off. Happens to me often enough," he said, smiling, doing his trick again, trying to make me like him, or at least find him unthreatening.

"One of your servants, I believe it was Miss Tool, I'm pretty sure, anyway, Sergeant Sills'll know, nothing escapes that boy, mark my words. Anyway, she was up late, and noticed the light under Miss Templesmith's room door. She went to see if Miss Templesmith was all right. This must have been about half past twelve or so. Pretty late. So Miss Tool knocks on the door, gets no response, and she eases the door open, just to make sure your aunt's all right. But…"

"You need not dwell on the details, Inspector."

"Ah, but listen. I'm trying to tell you why we're not trying to fit you up for your aunt's murder, Mrs Black. See, Miss Tool opened the door, peeked in, and she saw that, well…The deed had been done. The victim had been strangled as she slept. She would have had no opportunity to…"

"Inspector, please…"

"What I'm getting around to telling you, Mrs Black, is that the marks left on the victim's neck—the killer's hands, the killer's hands were *immense*! Much bigger than yours—bigger than *mine*!"

I thought of Variel, labouring to use his tiny pencil on the pages of his notebook. His giant hands seemed to swallow the pencil stub.

I wondered what was keeping Sergeant Sills. The inspector went on. "So Miss Tool alerts the rest of your staff. Your butler, Mr Rutherford, calls the local boys. They come out and have a gander, and they reckon it's a job for the d's, up in Perth, and they get on the horn. By the time I hear about it, it's after one in the morning. It takes us until after four o'clock just to get here, going flat-out, mind you. And then we get here, and the local boys show us the body, and we see the marks on Miss Templesmith's throat. It's these gigantic hands, as I said. We asked your servants: 'Could someone break in to this house and come upstairs and do this without being heard or spotted?' and they all said they didn't see how that could happen. Someone like that would have made a lot of noise. So we were puzzled. How did this bastard get in without disturbing everyone? Bit of a mystery. But then the local boys get the call about Father William. His housekeeper found him at five. He likes to get up early and go for a long walk by the water, she says, get some thinking done, plan his sermons, things like that. So she goes to wake him up, and he's not in bed. He's in his office, and he's been knifed, with a letter-opener. Big mess everywhere, place really torn up. We look around, take notes, and we call the forensics boys up in the city to get down here. Quiet little fishing town suddenly turns interesting. Still, at least what happened to the poor bloody priest looks like a straightforward murder. Back here is where things are a bit on the funny side, so we come back. The Rockingham coroner's boys have turned up, and they need us to tell them they can take the body off..."

Rutherford appeared, a most welcome sight. He looked like he knew I needed rescuing. He also looked better than he had earlier. "Inspector? Could I interest you in a fresh cup of tea or coffee?"

He looked surprised. I was thinking that a good hostess maintains her poise no matter what. No matter what. Very English thinking. Carmody asked for coffee, no sugar, black—just as I have it. I asked for a cup, too. Rutherford swept out to the kitchen.

What could I say at this point? He did not think I had killed Julia, but he suspected I knew something about it. He suspected these notes from my secret correspondent—the enemy whose name Variel gave me—had something to do with it, and I knew now why he thought so. I also knew who the large-handed brute was, of course, but how to explain how I knew it?

Then there was this bizarre business with Father William. The inspector knew I was involved in that, too—and this peculiar letter business only implicated me further. That Father William should have a copy of a different letter to the one that I had received seemed odd. That the "new" letter was a profoundly angry and serious rebuff of my apology seemed doubly odd. Why was there this other letter? I was not too worried. I knew his reply letter, the one I had received, was upstairs in my desk drawer, where I had left it.

Inspector Carmody called up to Sills, "Any luck, Sergeant?"

"Not yet, sir. There's a lot of correspondence to sort through."

We were still awaiting Rutherford with our coffee. I offered to show the inspector up to my office, so that I could find the letter. Carmody agreed. Feeling a peculiar sense of second wind which no doubt had to do with a sensation that things could not get much worse, I led the inspector upstairs. In my study I found the sergeant sorting through my filing cabinet, and going through piles of papers, bound manuscripts, official documents pertaining to the house, my insurance policies, bank records, car registration forms, and so forth. I said, "Did you look in the drawer?"

Sills muttered, "Couldn't find anything in the drawer."

I opened the drawer in question. The letter was right there, tucked in its envelope.

"I believe this is the letter, gentlemen," I said, offering it to the inspector, who took it. Sergeant Sills, surprised, said, "I looked there, I'm sure I bloody well looked there!"

Carmody read, nodding. "This is it, ma'am," he said, and showed it to me.

I snatched it from his hands, and read.

This wasn't right.

This wasn't right at all.

No!

"There's some mistake," I said, looking at the letter and then at the policemen. "It's..."

They had been right. This was not the letter I had received. In this version, Father William was *vehement* in his outrage, scornful of my apologetic words, furious at me in general. And he did threaten to have me excommunicated.

"This isn't right," I said, shaken afresh. "This isn't the letter I received."

"You recognised the envelope," Carmody said, pointing.

"Well, yes, I did, yes...It's just..." My hands shook.

"Mrs Black," Carmody said, "I think it would be best if you popped around to the station later, and gave us a bit of a statement about your movements last night, and about your business with Father William Dennis. At that time we will also be asking for your fingerprints. The forensics people are going over the house as we speak, as I said. Do you have any questions?"

Questions? I had questions!

After experiencing what had felt like every other known emotion during the course of this endless night, all I had left was numbness. The damning letter, the letter that supposedly inspired me to murder a man, dropped from my fingers.

"I'd like to contact my lawyers," I said, hardly making a sound. It was only too easy to see how it would play out. Everyone knew about my very public feud with Father William. Now I was on record seeking to bury the hatchet. And Father William now was on record, telling me to burn in Hell! How dare he refuse my apology? The bastard! I would show him! I, the strange, eccentric rich woman with her strange ideas.

Carmody said, "That's your right, of course, Mrs Black."

They took both the copy of my initial apology letter, as well as Father William's letter, with them when they left, sealed in large yellow envelopes.

I slid to the floor of my study. I was surrounded by piles and piles of paper.

Blocks of brass-coloured dawn light shone on my walls.

Even in this state I could see what must have happened. When Variel came to kill Julia, he had also swapped the letter I had actually received with this new letter. He would have had a shadow glamour much like the one Gordon and I had used.

Father William's new letter was different, though, in more ways than one, I had noticed. It had a certain faint aroma about it; no doubt it had rubbed off from the demon, the source of that odour. And Father William Dennis, who I had learned last night was the one who had sent me those notes, would carry that odour around with him because of his time spent communing with his tame demon. Father William, a bitter old man, passed over for promotion, stuck out here in the boondocks of Pelican River, seeing his congregation decline over time, unable to raise sufficient funds to repair his run-down church. How had it gone with him, I wondered, thinking in the dreamy, cold fog of fatigue. How had such a devout, such a pious, old man reached a point of such desperation that he turned to those books forbidden by his church for answers? What had it cost him?

I did not know. But I did know the forensics people would be finding my fingerprints all over his house, and all over the murder weapon. Father William Dennis hated me so much that he would use black arts and a tame demon to frame me for his "murder". But why now, after all these years?

And how could he do it? I could not imagine a situation in which it would be better to have myself killed in such a way as to implicate some bitter enemy than to kill that enemy myself. But who knows how different people make their decisions? I was a writer of novels. My bailiwick was character motivation. It was my task to unravel the tangle of motivations that lead a person to do extraordinary things, to make the contrived and manipulated seem plausible, natural — even inevitable.

I did not know, at that moment, at that bitter hour, sitting, feeling defeated, in the shambles of my office, how on Earth I could fight the priest's scheme.

28

I woke later on, not noticeably refreshed. Washed, dressed, coffee consumed, I came downstairs. The police and their forensic people were gone. The Yellow Room, Julia's room, was sealed off. I remembered the sight of Julia this morning, her remains, on that stretcher. I could hardly breathe.

Sitting in the drawing room, I asked Rutherford to contact Gordon for me, but he came back shortly and said he was unable to get through. The poor man. He must be still fast asleep. I thought of his beautiful dogs, and what Gordon did — and would have to do — for me the previous night.

"His dogs..."

He had made his choice, I told myself, and he had chosen not to take my offered arm.

I heard Murray quietly telling Ryan off about dropping some expensive plates. I could also hear Sally or Vicky out the back, beating rugs into submission. The repetitive whacking was starting to sound like the headache forming in my head.

I tried the telephone myself. June interrupted me, "Sorry, Mrs Black, but Gordon's asked me not to put through any calls from you. I'm really sorry."

"But that's — All right. All right. I am sorry to bother you, June. Good afternoon."

I hung up the telephone.

Rutherford appeared, bearing a fresh coffee. I took it from him and downed a great gulp of it at once.

"Ma'am?"

For long minutes I stood there, gasping, eyes wide, feeling the scald boiling the delicate tissues of my mouth and throat. Rutherford quickly returned with a jug of cold water and a glass. I took the jug from him and guzzled, in a very undignified fashion, as much of the water as I could manage. At length the initial pain died away, but my palate and tongue still felt sore and delicate. "That will serve me right for acting without thinking, won't it, Rutherford?"

"It did seem ill-advised, ma'am," he said quietly.

Looking at him, I said, "Prepare the car."

"Right you are, ma'am."

*

The main gate at Gordon's property was locked—for the first time I could remember.

I instructed Rutherford to wait with the car, while I climbed out and down, and walked over to the gate. It was not a high gate—only perhaps waist-height—and it would be easy enough to climb over it, but instead I stood there, hesitating.

For the first time in a very long while, I heard no dogs barking. No dogs swarmed up to the gate to jump and yap at me. All I could hear was the car's engine ticking, some nearby magpies carolling, and a few insects chittering.

"Damn it!" I muttered, and vaulted the gate.

Walking down the gravel driveway, past the heaps of rusting metal parts, it occurred to me that Gordon, if he really was this angry with me, might have gone to the trouble of installing elaborate machines to prevent me reaching his house. Fortunately, this seemed not to have been the case, and I reached the porch in one piece.

As my boots clumped on the bare grey boards, I heard two dogs barking. They sounded like small dogs, and they sounded frightened. Shivering from head to toe now, and feeling terrible dread worse than I had felt even last night, I pulled the brass lever next to the door, to activate the bell mechanism.

Soon, over the yapping of the dogs, I heard heavy footsteps.

"I've got nothing to say to you, Ruth," Gordon called from behind the solid door. "Get off with you!" This latter he did not say angrily; he said it with firmness, but with a certain heavy sadness, too, that was worse to hear.

I stared at the door, then turned to look back up the driveway to the gate, and the waiting Bentley.

Gordon opened the door a crack. "Go on, get off my property." His face was worse than angry; it was cold and blank.

"What have you done, Gordon? What did you do to—?"

"It's none of your concern. Now kindly leave my property."

His two dogs howled and yelped behind him somewhere. I assumed he'd trapped them in a room.

"Gordon—you could have taken my arm! I offered it in good faith!"

He paused a moment, and allowed himself to meet my eyes. He looked sad, and shook his head. "Just go. Please." His voice was small and weak. He pushed the door closed.

I wanted to talk to him. His footsteps retreated. The two dogs howled.

*

Back at home, feeling my whole world coming apart, I decided it was time to contact my lawyers up in Perth. It was a quarter to four o'clock in the afternoon. Rutherford was working on the cars in the garage; Murray and Ryan were in town shopping; Vicky and Sally were doing the week's laundry. The house felt too big, cold and empty. There was a cold draught through the drawing room.

I tried the telephone, but kept dropping the earpiece. When June asked me what number I wanted, I stood there, unable to think of anything to say, and felt like I would burst into tears at any moment. I hung up. I would need to apologise to June.

At length I returned to the telephone, feeling a little restored. I apologised to June, who said, "No worries, love. What can I do you for?"

She put me through to the law firm of Pembroke and Associates. And, of course, there was no-one there. Of course. Fortunately, I had my solicitor's private telephone number, so I asked June to try that—and there was no answer, until a little girl answered. She told me I had reached the residence of the Campbell family, and recited the telephone number in a very polite quavery voice. I asked if I might speak to her father. She said, "May I ask who's calling, please?" and I told her I was a client of her father's, Mrs Black. There was a heavy clunk, and distantly I heard, "Daaaaaad!" Then Campbell came to phone, and I briefly explained my business, and apologised for telephoning him at home on the weekend.

He said, "I'm tied up somewhat at the moment, but I will ring you tomorrow morning, and we can talk things over then. Would that be all right, Mrs Black?"

"That would be splendid," I said, playing it much cooler than I felt.

*

After dinner that night I took to bed earlier than usual. My head throbbed with dull aching pain and I could feel it threatening to spread down my shoulders and down my back. Sally prepared me an analgesic draught of salts and urged me to call her at any time during the night if I should have need of anything. Before she left me she said, by the door, "Ma'am, I just wanted you to know, if you'll pardon me saying so, that is, that we're all really sorry about Miss Templesmith? If we'd had any idea, any notion... If we'd just known... He just got in and out so silent..." She tried to hold back tears.

"There was nothing at all any of you could have done, Sally. Not a damned thing. Please try not to worry."

"It's just..." She looked desperate and frustrated.

"Good night, Sally. Thank you."

She left, and I heard her take a great sniff as she padded down the hall outside.

The salts carried me off to sleep faster than I would have thought possible, considering how I felt after this awful day.

Sleep was very welcome indeed.

So it was most surprising when I woke up, with the sensation that it was only moments later, and that I had not been asleep at all, to find Rutherford wrapping a thick woollen blanket around me—and that I was sitting at my desk, in my study. I stared. "What...?"

He said, "I heard you writing, ma'am, and thought you might need—"

I glanced up at him. "You heard me *writing*?"

He indicated the big Imperial typewriter.

A sheet of paper had been rolled in; it was not quite straight. There was no backing sheet.

Someone had indeed been writing.

RUTH RUTH RUTH RUT6H RUTH

It went on like this, my name over and over, line after line. The typing was not elegant. Overstrikes and mistakes abounded. It did not look like something I had typed; the text was uneven—some letters were dark and heavy, while others hardly registered. It looked like something a child might do whilst playing with a typewriter. But there was more.

HELLO HELLO HELLO HELLO HELLO !!

Again, line after line of this, badly typed. Then:

ITS ME ITS ME ITSME

JULIA JULIS JULIA JULIA

HELLO HELLO HELLO HELLO??

HEAR ME HEAR ME HEAR ME!!

"Good God..." I said, hardly breathing. "What on Earth is this?"

IVE FOUND HIM IVE F0UND HIM

THE PRIEST THE PREIST THE PRIEST THE PRIEST!!

HELLO HELLO HELLO HELLO!

LISTEN LISTEN LISTEN LISTEN!

IVE FOUND THE SWINE THE SWINE THE SWINE
THE SWINE

IVE GOT HIM FOR YOU!

WE CAN TALKK
TALLKKKTTTALLAALLLLKKKKXXXB

RUUUUTRRRUUUUUTTHHRRRRRRUUUUU
UUUUTTTTTTTTTTTHHHHHHHHHHH
HHHHHHH!!!!!!

29

I stared at the page. When I pulled it free from the typewriter, the paper did not exhibit the curvature it would have had it been sitting in the machine for a prolonged period; it looked very much as if someone (me?) had just typed it. I sniffed the page. It had occurred to me that, despite what the policemen had told me, my phantom note-sender might still be at large. There was no unearthly waft about it. It looked and smelled exactly like something I had just typed—though I had no recollection of having sat there and produced it.

I looked up at Rutherford, who stood next to me, doing his best to maintain composure. "You said you heard me writing?"

"Yes, ma'am. It rather sounded like you were having a bad time of it."

"In what way?"

"Hitting the keys very hard, ma'am. Not like your usual manner—if you'll pardon the observation."

"What on Earth is the time, anyway?"

"Five minutes after three o'clock in the morning, ma'am."

My head still throbbed with pain. Holding my head with one hand, and the mysterious note with the other, I asked Rutherford, "Didn't you think it was rather odd that someone should be in here using my typewriter at this peculiar hour—particularly in light of what happened last night?"

"You have been known to work through the night. It would not have been unusual, particularly given your looming deadline."

I stared at the message.

JULIA JULIS JULIA JULIA

Rutherford was correct regarding my occasional fits of late-night writing. It had been known to happen, particularly on hot summer nights, when the temperatures and humidity were unbearable. It was better, on such nights, to get up and do some work than lie in the soggy bed, tossing and turning.

This was not one of those nights. This was the beginning of winter: cold, wind lashing the ghost gums and jacarandas and the sheoaks, with the threat of rain to come perhaps tomorrow—later today. This was the weather for staying tucked in bed reading good books, or catching up on one's correspondence.

I had seen some odd things lately. Julia herself had told me of many such odd things, things which, to her, were part of her ordinary experience of life, as uncontroversial as bumblebees and bluebirds.

Her body was still with the coroner's office. I had not yet even begun to think about funeral arrangements, nor had I contacted the family back in England to arrange the shipment of her body.

Her body...

I was not ready to start thinking of her up to no good in some other realm of existence when I was still in shock from learning of her murder in this one.

And yet, if there were truth in this, if it really had somehow been Julia operating my hands at the typewriter tonight, she would not understand how I felt. To her it would simply be another day. To her, she would have gone on another jaunt to some other country, just as she had come out here, in her desperate bid to warn me about my impending demise—when it had been her own demise in my house that she had seen in her visions.

My mind was not constructed in such a way as to calmly accept such things. I could not accept that Julia was, on one hand, lying cold under a sheet in the Rockingham mortuary, and, on the other hand, rather enjoying herself in the deadworld. And, more than simply enjoying the sights, actually working on my case for me, tracking down the late Father William! He, a devout believer in Christian teaching, would have expected—exactly what kind of afterlife? Surely not free access to the Heaven in which he had believed for most of his life. Given his recent, filthy dabbling in demonology—and only God knew what else—it seemed reasonable that he expected to spend his eternity in Hell. He might even have thought that a fair enough result, all things considered. So what would he make of the deadworld? Julia had told me that it was the one true afterlife, the final destination for everyone, regardless of Earthbound faith. Whereas Julia would take to her new surroundings with verve, I could imagine Father William, braced for an eternity of suffering, being extremely confused indeed.

It defied sense.

And yet here was what purported to be the truth. I could not believe any of my staff would have gone to such elaborate lengths to fool me—even to the extent of carrying me into my study. After the business of the night before last, it was tempting to think that somehow another enemy was using shadow glamours to get up to tasteless mischief in my house.

But that seemed even more insane than the idea that Julia had used me like a puppet. She had told me of the phenomenon of "automatic writing", just as she had told me about mysterious somnambular movements of which the person concerned could not recall anything afterwards.

"Will you be requiring anything further tonight, ma'am?"

I had forgotten that Rutherford was still standing there. Looking up at him, I saw him doing his best to stifle yawns. "Oh, I say…" I said. "Yes. No. That is all. Go back to bed. I'll be fine, thank you."

He nodded, essayed a modest but surprisingly crisp bow, and left.

I was left alone in the night with what amounted to a telegram from the land of the dead.

Believing it was what it claimed to be was the simplest—and

yet also the most insane — course. Even allowing for Julia's bizarre beliefs, it was hard to accept. And yet, she was the person who had told me how, while in her coma, she had travelled about, a disembodied spirit, trying to find out the truth about the demon's summoner.

"Julia? Is this really you?"

I wanted to believe it was true. To believe it would be to cancel out my grief, at least to some extent. I would have lost her, but only to another place, rather than an absolute loss from the entirety of existence. It would almost be bearable, to think she was still somehow herself — somewhere.

It also raised the old bugaboos, though: if this was evidence that Julia still lived, in the land of the dead, and that she had also encountered the shade of Father William, then that would imply that if she looked hard enough she might also find other long lost people.

She might find Father.

She might find Antony.

She might find that Antony was *not* there, and never had been.

*

I was still sitting there, wrapped in the blanket, staring at this note, as dawn arrived, bringing the morning chorus of crows with it. A lot had passed through my thumping head in those few hours. Sometimes I wanted to believe it was all true, and at other times I refused to believe it, that it made no empirical sense. Where, for example, *was* this deadworld? It was the same sorts of things I had always wanted to know about Heaven, and in which I had never quite believed. It seemed too improbable, and disappointingly vague. No clergyman I had ever met could tell me anything about the details of Heaven, or, if they were well read, they might refer me to Dante and his meticulously detailed vision of the afterlife. But what did it really look like? Was there a sense of time? Did everyone really sport haloes and angel wings and just float about?

So where was the deadworld? From another perspective, I believed in the exciting though confounding reality of the quantum world over which physicists everywhere seemed at war. Quantum mechanics suggested that, when a thing could take a number of different paths to a destination, it actually took all possible paths. I had drawn on a lot of this still largely unproven research for some of my own novels. It was exciting and strange and defied expectation. It went with the recent findings regarding Special and General Relativity, which told us that space and time were two aspects of the same thing, space-time, and that this combined space-time was "curved" in ways that were hard to grasp, due to the effects of mass, conveying the sense of gravity. Yet, even without experimental findings to support all this exotic theory, I was prepared to accept it and make use of it. I was prepared to accept it because it was the word of Science, and I had the kind of faith in Science that Father William once had in God, and in which Julia had in her "other bits" of reality. One day in the future, I expect, there will be scientific verification of the truth of quantum reality, as bizarre as that prospect now seems to me. Julia, by contrast, already knew the truth of her faith. She had pointed out to me, years ago, that the truths of science change all the time. Whole bodies of thought come and go over time as new findings emerge, and scientists quarrel with each other over whether the old is still true or whether the new findings are merely aberrations. Scientific truths only gain wide acceptance when the old scientists die off; Julia's truths, she said, "are simply *there*, dear!"

Julia had always carried that air of the know-it-all, the smug attitude that she knew what was really going on in the world, and that it wasn't what the newspapers reported each day. Now, vindicated, she would be insufferable. Thinking this, and missing Julia to the point of physical pain, I smiled. Good for you, Julia.

She said, in her note,

IVE FOUND HIM IVE F0UND HIM

THE PRIEST THE PREIST THE PRIEST THE PRIEST!!

HELLO HELLO HELLO HELLO!

LISTEN LISTEN LISTEN LISTEN!

IVE FOUND THE SWINE THE SWINE THE SWINE
THE SWINE

IVE GOT HIM FOR YOU!

All right, I thought, let's take this at face value. She and Father William are in the deadworld together. She can get him to talk about what he did to me—and why. That was all well and good, I thought, even if Julia somehow managed to extract a signed confession from him—

I stopped at that point, cold and shivery again.

The thought of signed confessions from people in the deadworld made me think of Father William's last little note to me, the one in which he said he had a confession from my father about his activities prior to his own untimely but not completely surprising death.

Leaving aside the horrible nature of what Father William had done to my father, the question arose: how did he do it? If he only died the night before last—how had he made contact with Father? One could not quite see my Father, consumed with earthly guilt as he roamed the mysterious landscapes of the deadworld, turning to a "visiting" priest from somewhere on the other side of his world—or would he? Was he so encumbered with guilt and sorrow that he would confide in someone like Father William?

My best guess was that he had not known. I suspected he was experimenting with some means of making contact with the deadworld, and he had chanced to come across the guilty shade of my father, and recognised him. Even so, Father William would not necessarily realise that Sir Gustav Templesmith was the father of Mrs Ruth Black, widow of that known coward and duty-shirker, Antony Black. From the priest's point of view, my father would be a guilt-ridden old man who might have betrayed his country. I could imagine him talking and talking, for hours. All the things he'd done wrong in his life.

So how did he do it?

How could I ask Julia to make some inquiries for me?

I needed to find out how the priest had made contact. I could not simply wait for Julia to send me notes like this.

Then, quite apart from all this, there was the hard question: How on Earth could I get the police and the courts to believe all this?

Obviously, I could not. The testimony of what would amount to a ghost would hardly be admissible.

I needed Gordon's expertise. Somehow I needed to find a way to show that the fingerprints the police forensics men had found were not mine. My alibi for that night was already useless—"It couldn't have been me, guv, on account of how me and me mate Gordon were sneaking around enchanted ruins and working magic, and that..." Yes, I could see how that would sound. And now Gordon was no longer speaking to me. I had no notion of what he might say if questioned by the police about his movements that night. Would he tell the police exactly what we had done, or would he not? And if he told them everything about that night, did that mean they would soon find out about our raid on the Hawkins property?

My head boomed with pain. It would not stop. Tired all over again, I went downstairs to see if I could find where Sally kept those salts.

Murray sat at a counter in the kitchen reading the newspaper, and if I had not been in so much pain, and my world so much in turmoil, I might have paused a moment to think that it was very odd indeed for a newspaper that was lucky to come out once or twice a week to have a fresh edition out on a Sunday morning, something it had never previously done. But I felt like a walking corpse, wracked with pain, so I did not stop to consider all this. Outside, I could hear Young Ryan chopping wood for the range. The sound, the rhythmic chopping, added to my headache. Murray looked shocked to see me up at this early hour, and guiltily pushed the newspaper away and stood. "'Morning, ma'am!" she said.

I stared at her. "Good God, woman, do I terrify you that much?"

"Oh, no, ma'am!" she said.

Perhaps she was worried I might come at her with a letter-opener.

Then I saw what she was reading: a special issue of the *Pelican River Record*.

"Oh..." I said. "Would you mind passing that over? Murray?"

She looked like I might eat her if she didn't, and shoved the paper down the counter.

The Record was a newspaper in which someone catching a fat mulloway would get a banner headline. Today it had a better headline:

LOCAL PRIEST BRUTALLY SLAIN!

HOMICIDE POLICE QUESTION FOREIGN AUTHOR

30

Later that morning I sat alone at the dining table, my breakfast ignored and going cold. Even my coffee stood untouched. I kept seeing that damning headline before my eyes. "FOREIGN AUTHOR". I had never in my life felt so unwelcome, so much an intruder in this land. The cold, wretched feeling in my gut was starting to make me feel ill, to say nothing of my pounding headache. If it kept up like this for much longer, I would need to retire to bed in hopes of sleeping it off. Murray had given me the salts bottle, but in the same way she had given me the newspaper — as if her life depended on it. No amount of persuasion had helped. She had said, "Father William was a wonderful man! He was such a help when my Ern was killed in the War. Sorry, ma'am. It's just...He was such a fine man!" At that point she had dissolved into tears and fled out the back door.

Mr Campbell telephoned on the dot of nine o'clock. The clock on the mantel was still chiming. The telephone's jarring ring made me jump.

"Mr Campbell," I said, when the operator put his call through to me. "I'm very pleased to hear from you."

"Good morning. I am sorry I could not attend to your business sooner than this."

I explained the circumstances to him, and the police's interest.

"But they have yet to formally charge you, is that correct?"

"I should have given them a statement yesterday, but I..."

"Wait for me. I'll pop down around one-ish, we'll discuss what you'll say, and then we'll both go and have a quiet word with the constabulary. How does that sound?"

He made it sound like a bit of a spiffing wheeze, actually. Like a trifle. Like we'd go and have a chat with the coppers and then head off for celebratory cocktails at the Commercial Hotel. I explained that they probably had forensic evidence placing me at the scene.

"Well, we'll get that tossed out, for openers. Not to worry, Mrs Black, I deal with this kind of thing all the time."

*

Mr Geoffrey Campbell rolled into Pelican River and pulled up at my home at twenty-five minutes past one that afternoon. Never had a day taken so long in passing. Between speaking to him that morning and his ultimate arrival, it had been only about four hours. It had felt like four months. The headache, the awful sick feeling, the icy tension, had not helped matters. Now that he was here, looking dapper and confident in a charcoal-grey three-piece pinstripe suit with fob-chain and expensive shoes and greying hair swept back from his keen face with fragrant oil, I should have felt profound relief. He could not, after all, have looked more the part of the leading man come to save the day. To me, however, his arrival meant only that the time when I would have to front up to the police to make my statement was too close for comfort. I could not sit still. I had consumed nearly the whole bottle of salts, with little result. Sally, when she saw how much I had taken, told me I would probably be ill this evening. I didn't care. I had tried four different — identical — outfits before settling on one. It had been the ties that flummoxed me. Everything about how I dress is the same, but I do try to vary the tie. Today, however, the choice of tie was paralysing. Rutherford ultimately came to the rescue, recommending my old school tie from Newnham College. It looked dignified and conservative, and went well with my college brooch, worn on my coat lapel. Then I had trouble tying the damned thing, and Rutherford had been forced to take over the operation for me, even as I fidgeted and bounced on my toes and muttered to myself about the weather.

Anything to keep myself from seeing that headline again in my mind. "FOREIGN AUTHOR..." *Foreign*? I had been here twelve years, I said to myself. No, I was not yet a naturalised *citizen* of Australia. I maintained my British citizenship because it was useful; it opened doors, particularly in Europe, when I travelled there on research trips. I had had no idea, after all this time living here, that there was such apparent resentment, which is how it felt. The article described me as wealthy, reclusive, eccentric, opinionated, peculiar and, worst, "superior".

I had said to Rutherford, "Do I appear to believe I am somehow 'superior' to ordinary people, Rutherford?"

"Not at all, ma'am," he said, with a straight face, as he adjusted my tie.

I told him he would have to polish up his lying skills.

"Right you are, ma'am."

*

Mr Campbell and I spoke in the drawing room. Rutherford served afternoon tea. Mr Campbell enjoyed Murray's scones to the point of asking for the recipe. I told him he would sooner acquire God's personal telephone number than get Murray to give out one of her recipes. I found myself laughing a lot, but in a way that in no way conveyed any sense of genuine mirth or happiness. It was nervous, brittle laughter. Mr Campbell, I suspected, was only too used to this sort of thing. Actually, as I sat there, sipping sweet tea and pulling scones to bits, I found myself wishing for one of the cigars that I used to smoke, before giving them up years before. A good smoke would settle me, I kept thinking.

Mr Campbell eased me through the situation. I told him about the notes, and their ominous questions regarding my husband and father's relationship, and told him of the faint and mysterious odour. I wondered if I should tell him the whole story, or just those parts of it the criminal justice system of this country would understand. At first I hesitated, and kept to the "facts". It was easy to imagine that he had heard worse stories than mine. Then I went into the business with first my letter of apology, then what I called the "bribe letter", and finally the bizarre surprise of finding the letters switched. He kept saying, "My *word*..." As we went along, I began to suspect that, privately at least, Mr Campbell was somehow amused by all this. This did not help me to feel that I could entirely rely on the fellow.

Soon we had the facts laid out — minus the occult business.

Mr Campbell ran through it all quickly, to make sure his notes were correct, and to make sure he comprehended the matter fully. As he went, a minute frown deepened. By the time he was done, he said to me, "Now, Mrs Black, you can tell me the rest."

"The rest, Mr Campbell?" I said, doing my best to look calm and detached.

He allowed himself a wry toothless smile. He said, "I have no interest in whether or not you actually killed this poor man. Indeed, I do not wish to know. It's beside the point. But it is obvious to me that there is more to this story that so far you have omitted. What were you and Mr Duncombe doing that night, by yourselves, while Father William was getting himself killed?"

I hesitated. Mr Campbell looked to be in his late thirties, perhaps, prematurely grey, and he had once been athletic in some way. Perhaps he had been a quality batsman for his university cricket team. He had the gaze for it, I thought, to see how a rapidly moving ball was spinning, so that he might effectively defend his wicket. He did not look, in fact, like a man who would brook nonsense, nor did he look like he would suffer fools gladly. So I started in once again, treading carefully around the more supernatural elements of the matter.

"Ah," he said, nodding and making further notes, and drawing meaningful arrows between circled elements of his existing notes. "I rather thought as much," he said, when I was done.

This time I simply stared. "You thought as much, Mr Campbell?"

He helped himself to another scone, applying a dab of fresh whipped cream and some strawberry jam. "Oh yes," he said, pausing whilst he chewed. He smacked his lips. "My word!

These scones are quite deadly!"

I drew him back to the matter.

He said, "I read an interesting monograph some time back, which drew a connection between, on the one hand, great scientific revolutions and advances, and, on the other, increased interest and activity in matters of the occult. The more things seem to go in one direction, there appears to be an opposite and more or less equal thrust, if you will, in the other direction. Intriguing theory, I've often thought."

We talked about all this for a while longer, which mostly consisted of Mr Campbell telling me about his background reading in "this and that, you know", and chums he had known at university who had regularly dabbled that way. But then, somewhere around half past two in the afternoon, Mr Campbell, scones demolished, turned to me and wanted me to tell him all about that long night.

So I told him. Starting with the ominous telegram from Julia, and all her misfortunes, through the business with the notes, the search for the cellar, our raid on the two properties — Mr Campbell shook his finger, "naughty naughty", as I covered that part of it — and everything that had occurred deep in the ruins of the Cahill property, the business with Gordon and the elven shaman — "indeed? My word!" he said — and my encounter with Mr Ukresh Nor, also known as Variel. And then, once we returned to the house, learning that Julia had been strangled, and that Father William had been stabbed.

"This is more like it," he said, reading back through his pages of notes, nodding to himself, satisfied that now the picture made more sense. He drew more urgent arrows between circled and underlined phrases, and conveyed an air of someone planning an elaborate painting.

"I say," he said at last, "it's got rather a bit of everything, hasn't it?" He smiled, apparently trying to set me at ease, but instead making me feel worse.

I explained my theory about Father William wanting to hurt me so badly that he would resort to an elaborate plot like this, rather than, for example, simply killing me outright.

"The police won't like this at all," he said, reading through his notes again.

"What should I tell them?"

"For one thing, only answer the questions they ask, Mrs Black. And wait for me to provide permission before answering anything. They will absolutely hate being spoonfed information like that, but it's what you must do. Then there is the matter of the forensic evidence. You surmise that Father William will have arranged through his unorthodox methods to have planted your fingerprints in suggestive places at the scene of the crime—correct?"

"I would bet my life on it, all things considered."

"Well," he said, shifting in his chair, making himself more comfortable, "I shouldn't worry too much about that."

"I shouldn't?"

"I know people, Mrs Black."

Frowning, I looked at him, wondering what on Earth to make of that. "Do tell, Mr Campbell."

"Suffice to say, try not to worry overly much about the fingerprints. One way or another, I should be able to get all of that thrown out."

"Pardon me for putting this quite so bluntly, sir, but I'm afraid I do not share your confidence in this matter."

"I am sure you do not. That is entirely all right. From my initial sniffing about prior to popping down here this afternoon, I think I can safely report to you that there is a bit more to this case than some funny fingerprints and a very cross old clergyman."

"Would you care to unburden yourself of this information, at least for the sake of easing my own nervous agitation?"

He smiled. "We shall see what moves the other side plays first."

"*Moves*, Mr Campbell?" I had not meant to raise my voice. He flinched.

"Please excuse me," I said, getting up and pacing in front of the fireplace. "I am not having an easy time of it."

"That's quite all right. I do understand."

"It's just that, as things stand right now, I could find it rather difficult to remain in this town. The local newspaper this morning..." I could not finish. I covered my face and tried to hold back my tears.

He remained seated. "It will be all right. I promise."

I wanted to laugh, but it came out as a terrible coughing fit.

Once I regained my composure, he said, "We have arcane tricks of our own, we lawyers."

*

Later that afternoon saw Mr Campbell and me sitting in the cramped interview room at the local police station. The stink — of stale tobacco and nervous sweat — was appalling. Behind us, up near the low ceiling, a small rectangular window let in a bit of the gloomy afternoon light. A naked insect-spotted electric light bulb hung from the ceiling, emitting a useless glow of its own. We had been waiting here more than fifteen minutes when Inspector Carmody lumbered in, with Sergeant Sills trailing behind. Neither looked like they had slept much. Carmody, seeing Mr Campbell, muttered something under his breath that seemed to amuse Campbell. I gathered that the two had some sort of history. Carmody, sitting, said to me, "You've done well, then, haven't you?"

Before I could respond, a third man slipped into the room. He was old, perhaps in his seventies, and dressed at least as well as Campbell; he walked without visible difficulty, and stood straight. He eased into a folding metal chair in the back of the room, behind the policemen, crossed his legs, and adjusted the cuffs of his expensive trousers. He produced a gold cigarette case, from which he took a long, black cigarette. Sergeant Sills lit it for him. Soon the room was full of an exotic stench I did not like. It smelled like something from the far east of Europe. The newcomer held his cigarette in the Continental manner, between thumb and middle finger, pointing up when at rest, to minimise waste.

I leaned across to Mr Campbell, who had also noted the arrival of the third man. "Who's that?"

"An interested third party, from what I've heard," was all Campbell would tell me.

Carmody, sitting at the table, glared at me and opened a cardboard file containing a sheaf of typed documents and large black and white photographs taken in harsh light—which showed an old man's twisted body, dressed in pyjamas, drenched in what looked like black blood, sprawled face-down across a cluttered desk. It did not look like Father William. There was none of his sanctimony, or his barely concealed bitterness.

Campbell said, "My client is here to make her statement, Inspector."

"And you're here to make sure she doesn't actually tell us anything—right, mate?"

Campbell said nothing, but looked confident.

The old man in the back of the room watched the end of his cigarette burn.

31

Sergeant Sills produced a court order, signed by a magistrate in Perth, bearing the Governor's seal, permitting the policemen to take specimens of my fingerprints. Mr Campbell had no objections, but he did insist on giving the document a close reading before allowing the sergeant to produce the fingerprinting equipment. The procedure was filthy but quick; I shall remember the ink's oily reek for the rest of my life, the pain of humiliation. When Sills was finished with my fingers, he did not offer the use of a bathroom where I might wash myself. Mr Campbell reminded him of his obligations. Sills escorted me out of the room, down a short passageway, from which I could hear a group of local policemen sitting around talking about a planned fishing trip later that evening. The bathroom was tiny and dirty and smelled of mould, mildew, and something else on which I did not dwell too long. Sills dragged me out before I was finished and deposited me back in the interview room. He said nothing throughout the entire encounter, and succeeded in making me feel like a criminal.

The interview resumed.

"So, Mrs Black," the inspector opened, once he'd made himself as comfortable as he could on the nasty folding chairs, "why don't you tell me about your relationship with Father William?"

I sighed, and said, "We had no relationship!" Campbell shot

me a look indicating I should await permission before speaking. He made me feel like a child, but I supposed his caution served a useful purpose.

Carmody and Sills were exchanging glances. Sills showed Carmody typed documents from the folder; he had quite a bundle of them, as well as another folder containing what looked—and smelled—like burnt paper. I guessed that these were witness statements, and so forth. The inspector looked at Campbell. "Mind if I ask her another?"

"Let's hear it first."

"Mrs Black—do you know one Mrs Eileen Rioli?"

Campbell nodded slightly. I said, "I do, of course. She's Father William's housekeeper. Everybody knows her."

Carmody was reading through Mrs Rioli's statement. "She tells us that the late Father William often spoke of you."

Campbell said, "He was the town priest. He would have spoken of just about everyone—"

The inspector revealed his teeth. "I'm prepared to concede that point, Mr Campbell. Fair cop. However..."

Campbell asked, "My client does not have all day. She has other commitments."

The policemen once again exchanged looks. Carmody said, "Mrs Rioli tells us that Father William had, shall we say, strong views about you, Mrs Black. Were you aware of these views?"

Campbell gave me permission. I said, "He and I did not get on well, no."

"Mrs Rioli quotes Father William in her statement. She says that he said—"

"A learned policeman such as you would surely be aware of the rules governing hearsay testimony...?"

Carmody shot my lawyer a glance that would have cut bricks. He went on. "Let's just say, the deceased spoke of you often, and never kindly. He believed you were an 'abomination'—"

"That's lovely," I commented.

"—and indeed a 'disgrace to your father's good name, and a disgrace to English womanhood!'"

I did not know quite what to say to this; I could not entirely suppress an embarrassed laugh. I knew the old bugger didn't like me, but I did not know his feelings ran this deep. Though perhaps, I thought, I should have, based on everything I'd learned so far.

"You find these proceedings amusing, Mrs Black?"

"Not at all, I'm sorry. I just... Oh dear. That poor man."

"Pity from the lofty Mrs Black, Sergeant," Carmody said. "Do make a note of that."

Sills nodded and scribbled in his notebook.

So it went.

Later, Carmody was hammering at me: "You did hate Father William, did you not, Mrs Black?"

"No, Inspector. I did not. I am, however, learning to hate you."

"You hated this helpless old man, pillar of the community, a man who was poor by choice, who led a good and kind life —"

Campbell made a point of yawning. "Do get to the point, Inspector."

"He was helpless and he was old — and he was a living example of everything about the traditional Establishment that you have always rejected — isn't that right?"

Stunned, I hesitated a moment.

"Isn't it, Mrs Black? Isn't that why you left England in the first place? Isn't that why you live the way you do, flouting every convention, every standard, every *shred* of decency —"

I was on my feet before Campbell could stop me. "*I did not kill that sad old man!*"

And as soon as I said it, I knew I'd blundered. Campbell sighed. Carmody grinned up at me.

"Sergeant...?"

"Already recording the statement, sir."

I sat, feeling at once furious and worried.

"Turning back to the testimony of Mrs Rioli for a moment," Carmody said quietly, looking as if he felt good about how things were going, "she remembers that that Father William was so upset by your physical assault on his person that, later that night, she had to call in Doctor Munz. He was that upset. We spoke to Dr Munz yesterday, too, since you were not forthcoming. He had to check back through his records, but he was able to verify that he had indeed seen the deceased that night, and said that the patient exhibited..." He rummaged for another handful of paper. "Here we are. The patient exhibited signs of 'extreme panic and anxiety'. Were you aware of this, Mrs Black?"

"I was not... That all happened years ago," I said, voice small.

"Did you get that, Sergeant? She says she was not aware that she had almost killed the poor old bugger."

Campbell interrupted. "Inspector, I do not believe that you can draw that conclusion."

Sergeant Sills looked across at him. "Don't get your silk knickers in a knot, mate. I'm not writing that."

"Moving right along, Mrs Black," Carmody said. "Mrs Rioli, who sat up with Father William all that night, she said that at one point Father William said he held deep fears for his life."

"Pardon my French, Inspector, but bollocks!" I said, perhaps incautiously.

"Sergeant?"

"Bollocks, sir. Yes, sir." He made a little show of spelling out the word in his very careful handwriting.

Campbell murmured, "Is there a reason for me to be here today, or not, Mrs Black?"

"I beg your pardon," I murmured back.

Carmody went on. He revealed that Father William, fearing for his life, confided to his housekeeper that night that he was worried that I, a mere novelist, would "do something" by way of "sorting him out", in retaliation for my being banned from his church. It seemed Father William could not conceive of anyone taking such a banning in their stride. To him it was only one step below excommunication. It was about as grave a development as one could face. Banning was serious business. No truly pious person could take such a catastrophic shame and go on about the business of her life. The fact that I did, more or less, continue to go about my life, and for many years, not greatly troubled by the whole matter, only proved to Father William what he had said of me all along.

"'In his mind,' Mrs Rioli continues, 'it was only a matter of time before she'—that would be you, Mrs Black—'struck back at him. And he swore he would be ready, even if it killed him!'" Carmody put the papers down and looked at me. He said, "You do seem to have quite an effect on people, Mrs Black."

"All my previous comments about hearsay evidence," Campbell said, again, "continue to apply."

Carmody smiled at him, saying, "Hearsay evidence, Mr Campbell? I think not. Sergeant?" He glanced at Sills, who reached for the folder of burned pages, and passed it to Carmody, who opened it with the glee of a hungry man sitting down to a huge Christmas dinner. "Well, look what we have here, well well well... Just look at this!"

"Anything you'd care to share with the rest of the class, Inspector?" Campbell said, eyebrow arched at Carmody's nonsense.

Meanwhile, it was hard to see, from where I sat, what the inspector found so exciting. As far as I could tell, that folder appeared to contain perhaps two dozen sheets of paper, all of them burned to some degree, and some of them almost completely. The smell was extraordinary. The pages I could see appeared to contain very bad single-spaced typing, from one edge of the paper to the other. Carmody sat there very carefully leafing through the pages, still very pleased with himself, and from time to time pointing out what must have been "good bits" to Sills, who smirked at me.

"Very stimulating, yes, sir," Sills said, allowing himself the smallest of smiles.

Carmody went on. "What we have here, Mrs Black, is something of a miracle. In fact I think it's fair to say that God was smiling down on us that night."

"Inspector? In your own time."

Carmody confected an apologetic manner. "Oh, I am sorry. Yes, do make a note of my unprofessional manner, Sills. Now. What we have here is fragments from something we believe was called 'The Book of William'."

"Indeed?" Campbell said. "And you are planning to give me a chance to examine this document exactly when?"

"In due course, mate. In due bloody course. Now. It turns out

Father William had something in common with you, Mrs Black. He fancied himself an author!"

This did indeed surprise me. I turned to Campbell, who nodded. I said, "May I inquire as to what he wrote?"

"Ah. Well. That's a little bit hard to sort out, exactly. What we have here is all Mrs Rioli was able to retrieve from Father William's incinerator on the night he died. We believe there once was a great deal more. Mrs Rioli tells us that the deceased was—" He turned to a document in the file with all the transcripts. "'He was always at it, for hours and hours, tapping away like a bloody maniac.' Sound familiar, Mrs Black?" He leered.

It did, I had to admit, sound only too familiar. But that meant that Father William had another typewriter besides the one he kept in his demon-trapping cellar. I looked at Campbell, who was making notes. I said to Carmody, "Yes, but what was he actually writing?"

"We think it was a sort of memoir. Perhaps even a confession. I think you'll find that that document tells you everything you need to know about Father William and his state of mind. I'm sure even a reasonably competent Crown Prosecutor could make something of all this lot."

"There's only one small problem," I said, trying to brazen it out. "I did not actually hate him enough to want to kill him. His banning did not bother me overmuch. I went up to Rockingham to attend Mass on those occasions when I felt the need. It..." I felt Campbell staring at me.

"Mrs Black?" he said, quietly.

I had been doing it again, I knew. "Bad habit," I said.

We continued. My backside ached; my shoulders burned with pain.

Campbell said, "Why, Inspector, if Father William felt so terrified of my client, did he then set about trying to inflict emotional torment upon her, and then even to extort money from her? Why would a terrified man do that?"

Carmody leaned back. He said, not concerned in the least, "He wanted her to suffer as he was suffering. He was fighting back. It's all there in the diary. It's all there."

"Very well," Campbell said, nodding, "Pass it over. Let's have a look." Carmody handed him the folder. As Campbell started leafing through the burnt pages with the greatest of care, I became aware of a familiar odour. The smell of Variel. Campbell looked up from his reading. He said, "But the extortion notes—"

Carmody reached across for the document. Campbell handed it back, and the inspector flicked to a certain page. "There you go, sunshine. Cop that!" He pointed at a lengthy passage, thick with overstrikes and corrections. Campbell squinted and read. After a moment, a little more pale than before, he looked at me. "I see," he said, talking to Carmody but looking at me. He showed me the passage. It was all there. It made little sense, and was, from what I could tell, the ravings of a mind long past the last lights of sanity and out in the darkness of pure madness, but there was, nonetheless, a certain unhinged coherence to it. The salient point was that he described his extortion plan, and agonised about the notes and what to say in them. He talked about consulting Variel for suggestions.

He tried to show Carmody, but Carmody swept it aside. "It shows enough, Campbell. It shows enough. It shows his state of mind. It shows he was mad with fury. It shows that your client was the cause of his madness. Your client and her deviant practices offended—"

I wanted to hit him. Campbell somehow sensed this and leaned across the desk. "There is no suggestion, Carmody, none whatsoever, that my client is anything but a decent, God-fearing War widow."

Carmody smiled, very pleased with himself. "Perhaps we should take a short break to allow the suspect and her brief to regain their composure, Sergeant?"

"Sounds good to me, sir. I'd love a cuppa."

We took a short break. Campbell and I spent that break arguing, trying very hard not to shout, with each other. Campbell's patience with me was wearing thin. He cautioned me again to not speak until he told me to. "Why am I even here?" he said. I told him I could defend myself against outrageous bullying swine like Carmody, and had been doing so all my life. We both talked about the surprise revelation of Father William's "Book".

"How done for are we?" I asked.

"All depends on what the magistrate thinks about it."

"Talking with a demon? Asking for style advice?"

"Detailed, coherent planning. I would say, Mrs Black, that it could go either way."

"Why would he keep such a thing, though?" I said. "Why implicate himself?"

Campbell said, "I didn't get long to look through it. I think he might have been sick."

"Good God! What a bloody mess."

*

The interrogation continued in due course. The issue of my father's death years earlier, and Father William's surprisingly complete knowledge about my intimate family history, featured prominently. "How could the deceased possibly know all this?" Campbell asked. "Does it say anything about that in his book there? Does it say the 'demon' told him, perchance?"

"As it happens, Campbell, no. It doesn't talk about that. Clearly, he had a confederate either back in England or in France. This confederate could easily have located bits of information and sent it across by telegram, or even by post. Be dead easy."

Campbell raised his eyebrows at this scenario. He said, "So Father William used the business with the notes and the extortion bid to strike back at my client, of whom he was terrified?"

"That's the way we see it. And the evidence is right there, in his own words. Then again," Carmody went on, "even if the magistrate throws out the the deceased's own testimony, we've still got your client's fingerprints all over the scene of the crime, showing she was definitely there, had her hand on the murder weapon, and clearly killed that dear old man in cold blood."

"Until such time as the print evidence arrives, Inspector..."

"We've got her dead to rights, mate. Say what you like. Theorise what you like. The fact is, she went to the priest's cottage that night and she killed him."

"Why?" I said, furious again, but trying to keep from raising my voice. "Why would I? What could I possibly gain from killing this helpless old man?"

"Put an end to the notes and the extortion, for one thing. Strike back at him for banning you. Those sound good to me. Murder's been done for less than that, mark my words."

"But I didn't *care* about the banning! And why would I wait all this time?"

Campbell said, "I believe, Inspector, that you obtained testimony from Mrs Black's staff on the night in question."

Carmody shifted in his seat and looked at Campbell. "And?"

"Surely, Mrs Black's own staff would remember how she felt about the banning. Would they not?"

The inspector glared at Campbell. "They said, to the best of their recollection, considering it was some time back, she was upset and agitated afterwards. They said she stopped working on her precious bloody books, and slept poorly."

"They did?" Campbell said, sounding doubtful. "Which ones?"

"Sergeant?"

Sills pulled out another notebook from a coat pocket and started flicking through pages. "We asked each of them if they remembered anything about this from that time. Had there been any changes in Mrs Black's behaviour? That kind of thing. Mr Rutherford said that Mrs Black was moody, slept poorly, ate poorly, and so forth. Miss Tool said, 'Mrs Black's like that all the time.' Miss Hall said, 'She works herself too bloody hard, that's for sure, doesn't look after herself properly, and doesn't eat a proper diet and I'm always at her to make sure she gets her proper sleep, and she won't listen to reason...' It goes on like that at some length, I'm afraid."

"You omitted to report on my cook and her assistant, Sergeant."

"Er, what they said agrees with what the others said. I can read it back...?"

Carmody frowned. "Thank you, Sergeant. I think we can skip that for the time being."

The interview went on. It made me think of trench warfare.

There was my side and their side, and a deadly no-man's-land stretched between us. Carmody fired his withering, repetitive questions at me; I shot back terse refusals; Campbell only sometimes interrupted to "prevent you hanging yourself!" We were making no progress. The truth was not unfolding. The truth, of course, from my perspective, could not unfold in this environment. Carmody knew there was something fishy about my relationship with the priest, and my movements that night, but he could not quite make his case fit together. He was getting even more agitated than I was, which surprised me. If the fingerprint evidence, once it arrived, was as solid as he seemed to believe, it would almost certainly convict me, regardless of all the extraneous business. Yet he did not look like a man who would soon win. I wondered, idly, during a moment when he and Campbell were shouting at each other, did Carmody really want to know all the occult business, as well? Just how seriously did he take the business in Father William's diary about the demon and all of that? It would not be admissible, but it would make everything make a certain bizarre sense. Or almost so: there was still the question of why Father William changed the game that night. He had started out planning to milk money out of me by feeding me intimate details about my husband and father. But then he had chosen to have Variel kill him, hoping to implicate me. What changed his mind that night? Was it that he must have realised, after sending the note demanding the sum of one thousand pounds, that I had no chance of putting my hands on such a sum in the time allowed, but by then it was too late? Any why did he try to burn his precious book? To conceal his motives?

Carmody, meanwhile, who really did look like a furious man stuck in a small box made of his preconceptions and biases, plainly wanted to see me convicted. I had the impression his motivation was not to serve justice, but to remove me from his tidy and ordered and conservative world. I was an aberration, and he had an opportunity to remove me from society. He and Father William, I saw, had very similar views when it came to people like me.

We went on, getting more and more bogged down in the same questions, the same answers. It was taking on a feeling of unreality. Time seemed to stop, and hang in the air like the bitter black smoke from the old man's cigarettes.

Sills took pages and pages of shorthand notes.

The old man in the back listened but said nothing; his unreadable expression did not alter.

Slowly, around six o'clock, we came around—again, for the nth time—to discussing the night Father William and Julia were killed. This time, however, Inspector Carmody wanted to probe into exactly what Gordon and I had been doing that evening. Clearly he liked the prospect of fitting up Gordon as an accessory.

I had tremendous pain across my back, up my neck, spreading into my head. This chair would be the death of me. When Carmody asked, again, what Gordon and I had been doing that night, I said, also for the nth time, "We were out driving around, taking my car for a spin."

Carmody turned to a sheaf of typed pages in the back of the file. He said, "We have spoken to Mr Duncombe about that night..."

It was suddenly hard to breathe. "Is that right," I managed to say.

"What did Mr Duncombe have to say, Inspector?" Campbell asked, quite unruffled.

Carmody glanced across at Sills, who shrugged and twiddled his pencil. Carmody said, "He said you were out for an evening drive, and that you talked about books and his plans for his 'time machine.'" Carmody could not have injected more ironic venom into the phrase.

Campbell said, "Is that all Mr Duncombe had to say?"

"It is," Carmody said. "He was...very insistent."

"Wouldn't say boo to a grasshopper," Sills added.

I could not keep the feeling of extreme relief I felt at this from showing itself. Mr Campbell shot me a look, urging me to keep such displays to myself. Even so, I had been worried about what Gordon might say if he was questioned; the way things were between us, I had even worried that he might tell all, revealing our involvement in all kinds of pursuits.

Campbell drew my attention for a moment. He pointed. The old man in the corner passed a small note to Carmody, who read it with a brief, angry look, and passed it to Sills, who made a cryptic notation before pocketing it.

Campbell said, "Is there any chance you good chaps might reveal the content of your little note there?"

"Oh you'd love that, wouldn't you, Campbell!"

"If it's germane to the matters at hand..."

Carmody just looked at him, his face like tired rock. Sills discreetly shook his head, and did not look up. The old man lit another cigarette from the burned down end of the previous one, which he crushed against the floor with his shoe. The atmosphere worsened.

There was a knock on the door. Sills got up to answer it. A young man in plain clothes handed Sills a folder, and glanced at me for a moment before flicking his gaze away. It had been enough to surmise that this new folder was probably the fingerprint comparison report.

Sills handed Carmody the folder. He read the half-page typed summary and glanced at the collection of enlarged photographs showing prints found at the scene of the crime, and the prints from my fingers, taken earlier. The forensics chap had circled several areas on the photographs and on enlargements of the actual prints taken from me earlier.

Carmody allowed himself a humourless smirk and showed the report to Sills, who made notes. Mr Campbell requested a chance to examine the findings.

He explained things to me without patronising me too much.

"They like to have eleven or twelve points of identity," he said. "Here they've managed to find, at best, eight, here with this thumbprint taken from the letter-opener, see?" I looked at the photograph, and saw where a blood-smeared hand had gripped the engraved steel handle of the opener.

"They've got me," I said. Even I could see it.

And before Campbell could stop me, I said again, *"But I didn't do it! I didn't kill him!"*

Carmody grinned. He looked wickedly satisfied. "Ah, Mrs Black, but you did."

32

"Mrs Black," Campbell said to me during a brief break, even as I felt the icy draught from the vast hammer plunging down to smash me apart. "Remember what I told you. We can get evidence like this disallowed. It will be all right. You just need to hold yourself together now. Believe me."

I could think of nothing more to say. I'd protested my innocence, and it had not been enough.

And yet, something else was going on here, other than the main show. It was all about the old man in the corner, sitting there quietly, killing his disgusting cigarettes under his shoe. I wondered if Carmody's earlier agitation and his excitement now had anything to do with this man. He did not look like a policeman of any sort. There was something "other" about him that I could not place, and rather felt that I would regret finding out. Still, he took no part in the proceedings. He had offered no further notes.

Once back in the stifling box, I sat next to Campbell, and did my best to shut up. It was not something which came naturally to me. I believed I was finished. Campbell, if he managed to change the way it would surely play out at all, would most likely only succeed in reducing my sentence. I thought, a sarcastic voice in my head, about prison novelists. All that time to do nothing but sit and write.

Carmody said, at one point, sitting back in his chair, his arms folded across his chest, "You know we've got enough. You might as well confess, love."

Campbell felt me bristle. He said, "It would not be the first time one of your perfectly airtight cases fell completely apart in court, though, Inspector, now would it?"

Sills looked unhappy about that barb, but Carmody kept on smiling. "It's all over, mate. You know it. I know it." He turned his gaze on me, and smiled. "Even you know it, Your Highness. It's all over. You're done, and done properly. This isn't bloody England, where nobs like you can go about living as you like because you're all born to rule and the rest of it. This is here, this is Australia, a whole country full of convicts and the grubby spawn of convicts. We take this sort of thing rather seriously, *m'lady*. Here, we don't let the upper classes get away with rank arrogance and foul deeds like yours. We put people like you away for a bloody long time. A long time. And when you go and murder a man of the cloth, a helpless old man, in cold blood, like what you done—well, we take a very special interest, don't we, Sergeant? Isn't that right?"

Sills did look smug, in a subdued sort of way.

The old man considered his black cigarette, and took a long, long pull on it. The black smoke jetting from his big nostrils looked like poison.

"At this point, Mrs Black," Campbell was saying to me, "what you need is a rock-solid alibi, to prove you could not have been at the scene that night. So far we only have your story that you and Mr Duncombe were out all that night driving about the countryside. The fact that Mr Duncombe tells the same story does not help you much—you both had long enough to agree on your story. What you need are witnesses or documents which demonstrate you were nowhere near Father William's cottage..."

I looked at him, trying to convey things to him without speaking. Campbell knew where I was that night. I had told him. He knew, as I knew, that the only possible witnesses were, on one hand, a demon, and, on the other hand, what might have been an elven shaman. Even if we could find this latter individual, it did not seem likely that he would provide helpful testimony. Thanks to Gordon's protection charm, there was a high likelihood that the elf had not even seen me. And it was hard to believe a court of law would accept testimony either from a demon, no matter how "tame", or *about* a demon, particularly considering the demon's own role in what had happened to "poor" Father William. As tempting as it was to think that a magistrate would laugh the demon evidence out of court, I knew it was foolish to count on such things. A good Crown Prosecutor, it seemed to me, could possibly find a way to make the evidence in Father William's book work.

All of which left me trapped like an insect in a killing bottle.

I knew how the legal system operated. I could be charged with either Manslaughter, Murder, or, worse yet, Wilful Murder. Then, once I was formally charged, the police would transport me up to Perth, where I would appear before a magistrate at the Supreme Court, and plead "Not Guilty". There was little to no prospect of bail; they would remand me to sit in prison until the trial started. It could take a long time.

So, this time tomorrow, I could be in prison.

I was still no closer to learning the truth about my father and Antony.

Julia had said in her note from the deadworld that she had somehow found the shade of Father William. And he had all the answers I needed — and no reason on Earth to tell me.

My staff would lose their jobs, and their home.

I could not imagine seeing Gordon again, or that he would forgive me. I truly had been willing, that night, to sacrifice my right arm. Had I not made that clear enough to him? There had been no need to sacrifice his dogs. No need at all. I would have managed. I meant what I had said. I could type with one hand. How could he not have understood that? Was it pride? Idiot male pride, not wanting the help of a woman? But how could his pride have been stronger than his devotion to his beloved dogs?

Mr Campbell offered me a silk handkerchief. Not looking up, I thanked him.

Inspector Carmody smiled, seeing me brought so low, and soon lower still. He said, "Well, since you don't seem to have anything much to say, m'lady, we might just move to the exciting part, and work out the formal charges. How does that sound?" He rubbed his hands with vicious glee. Sergeant Sills looked as though he did not share his superior's taste for humiliating women.

Mr Campbell, still not looking troubled, said, "This won't pass muster, Carmody. No magistrate is going to accept the fingerprints."

"Nothing wrong with them that I can see. What about you, Sergeant? Looks pretty straightforward, eh?"

Sills made a show of looking at the prints. "Looks tickety-boo to me."

"Yes," Campbell said, his tone making clear what he thought of Sills' analytical skills, "you would think so."

Sills bristled. Carmody looked at me. "We just have to get the paperwork typed up. Shouldn't be more than a few minutes. Feel free to wait here." They left. I could hear Carmody chuckling as they went up the hallway.

The air was unbreathable. I felt as if I were choking.

The old man sat forward in his chair, legs apart, holding his cigarette, burning end tilted up. He continued to look thoughtful, even a little amused. It was hard to tell. I wanted to know what on Earth he was doing there, but no-one was talking to me.

I asked Campbell, "What makes you think you can get the fingerprints excluded?"

"Well," Campbell said, "seventy-five per cent."

"The police don't seem too worried."

"The police," he said, smiling thinly, "don't know who my fingerprint expert is."

"You have a fingerprint expert." It seemed like something he would have.

"She's particularly good at spotting shonky prints like these."

"They're more than shonky," I said, trying to keep my voice down, and trying not to cough.

"Precisely. That's the sort of thing she does."

"She knows about...?"

"Her bread and butter, Mrs Black."

"The inspector won't be pleased."

"The inspector should be accustomed to this sort of thing. I've rubbed his nose in it often enough."

"I see," I said. "What about what happened to Aunt Julia?"

"Separate business. The inspector is still snuffling about, I expect."

"So it'll go unsolved, and Aunt Julia will get no justice, you mean."

"It's an imperfect world, I'm afraid." He looked not much bothered by this. Julia's brutal, terrifying death meant little to him. He was terribly sorry about it, but it was not his problem. After all, he understood, from my story, that it had been likely committed by an entity from another realm of existence. "Bit hard to serve an arrest warrant where no Earthly jurisdiction applies," he had said.

Which left me to deal with it.

I knew that Father William had given Variel the instructions that led him to kill Julia.

I knew where Father William could be found.

Carmody's heavy footsteps came charging down the hallway outside. He was a big man; it was easy to imagine him, decades earlier, many stones lighter, intimidating smaller players on the football oval. And now he was back, bearing fateful papers. Sills brought up the rear, looking considerably less excited, and glancing worriedly at the old man. It occurred to me that Sills did not know who this was, either.

Carmody did not sit. He slapped the sheets down before me, and, pointing with his stubby finger at the typed text as he spoke, informed me that under the laws of Western Australia, I was being charged with Wilful Murder in the matter of one Father William Arthur Dennis. As he read it all out to me, Mr Campbell held my hand, and told me that it was all nonsense, and that I had nothing to worry about.

I did not believe him.

I believed I was finished.

*

Carmody finished explaining everything, and showed me where I needed to sign and initial the papers in recognition of the fact that the arresting officer had indeed told me of the formal charge against me, and that I understood everything. He showed me where I needed to put today's date, as well. It was all very proper. The papers, with layers of carbon paper between each sheet, smelled very official. The inspector's fountain pen moved well across these papers. My hand shook, however, and I left unsightly blobs of purple ink everywhere. Carmody muttered about the mess I was making.

Then, at last, it was done.

"Please stand, Mrs Ruth Elizabeth Black," Carmody said to me.

I tried to stand, but my legs were weak. Campbell helped me up.

"A car is being brought around as we speak. Once it is ready, Sergeant Sills and I shall take you into our custody, place your hands and feet in irons, and we shall transport you to Perth, where you shall be housed temporarily in the Roe Street police lock-up, prior to your appointment tomorrow with the magistrate for the preliminary hearing. Is this clear, Mrs Black?"

Sergeant Sills produced a set of iron manacles and chains.

I stared at them. A stray part of my mind, still aware and thinking, wondered where Carmody had been hiding those. Another angry part of me wanted to scream that I was damned well innocent! Instead, all I could coax out of my dry mouth was a feeble noise. I had kept the kite of my unorthodox life aloft for a long time, colourful and beautiful, a rare and exotic thing, but now its wreckage lay at my feet, everything ruined.

33

"Inspector; Sergeant? That will do, I think."

My eyes had been fixed on the black iron manacles. All I could hear was the heavy chinking sound they made in Sills' hands.

Carmody swore. "You bloody bastard."

"I've made up my mind," the new voice said.

Carmody swore quietly and said, "You said you bastards needed more time!"

"I said, Inspector, that I have decided."

"*I knew it! I bloody knew it.*"

"Surrender the prisoner to my custody, as per the Act."

Confused, I looked around. Carmody was shouting now, at someone. Campbell indicated the old man in the corner. He was standing now, very still, holding his current cigarette upright in his left hand, down at his side.

"You can't do this to me. Not now!"

The old man said, quietly, "Do not test me, Inspector."

"You said you hadn't decided—"

"I needed time."

"But we've got her—don't you bloody see? She's done!" Carmody was shouting again, waving the forensics report at the old man. "Dead to bloody *rights*!"

Sills looked as confused as I felt. He was looking around, perhaps for somewhere in which to disappear. Carmody was swearing and punching the stone wall.

"Mrs Black," the old man said. "My apologies." His voice was quiet and hoarse; he spoke with some sort of European accent that I could not place.

"What's...?" I looked at Campbell.

Campbell sighed. "This is what I alluded to previously. There are other interested parties."

Carmody was saying, *"Dead to bloody rights!"* over and over, and flicking through the arrest documents. His knuckles were bleeding.

The old man turned, looking slightly pained, and said, softly, to Carmody. "Wait outside. Both of you."

"So help me I'll bloody kill you, mate, *you mark my words, mate. You watch out, I'll bloody kill you!"* Carmody said, but he went. As the door closed on him and Sills, the inspector shouted, *"I'm not finished with you, m'lady! You mark my bloody words! I'm not finished with you by a long chalk!"*

Campbell said, "My *word...*"

The old man said, "Please, sit, sit." He gestured with his free hand, and sat himself in Carmody's chair. He closed both case folders and, carefully, set them to one side.

"You took long enough to show your colours, sir," Campbell said to him.

More confused than ever, I stared at Campbell, and then at the old man. He looked as though he would like to dismiss Mr Campbell as well as the policemen.

Minutes earlier, facing the prospect of iron manacles and immediate imprisonment, my future had acquired a certain bleak simplicity. I could not then see how things could play out differently from how the inspector described. I was going to prison, and that would be that. The terrifying threat to the Establishment would be taken away forever. The world would once more be safe for ordinary people. And even if, by some miracle, I had been acquitted of the charge, my future in Pelican River did not look favourable. In the minds of many townsfolk, I would always be held responsible for Father William's death. No amount of proof would suffice. People, I knew, were like this.

They could hold onto their prejudices as if they were lost at sea, clinging to life-preservers.

Now things looked very different.

"Mrs Black..." the old man said.

"I do not believe I have had the pleasure, sir," I said, relying on my poise to get me through whatever was happening.

"You do not need to know my name," he said slowly, "but if it would help, please call me Mr Brown."

"Mr Brown," I said, "charmed, I'm sure."

"I regret...that you had to endure all of that," he said, not looking at me. He continued to stare at his cigarette, and at the case folders. He looked deep in thought, squinting through smoke.

"May I, sir?" Campbell said.

Mr Brown waved him off with the merest shake of his head.

"What...?" I looked at both of them. Mr Campbell seemed to have lost much of his confidence.

Mr Brown turned back, and almost faced me; his cigarette still seemed more interesting.

I said, "I demand to know what on Earth is going on. Am I arrested, or am I not?"

He said, nodding, "Oh, yes. You are indeed arrested. You have been charged with Wilful Murder. It is quite official." He looked tired, having said all that.

"Then...Why am I still—?"

"Mrs Black," he interrupted, and now he looked me in the eye. His eyes were not good to see. They were cold, like the space between the stars. He said, "I am here to provide you with a choice, of sorts."

Campbell shifted in his seat, uneasy. I wondered how much I really wanted to know about this choice, but I said nothing. It seemed wise to wait, even though Mr Brown was not someone to be rushed.

He said, "I am assuming that you do not relish the prospect of imprisonment."

"You assume correctly."

He nodded slowly. "I can make certain that you do go to

prison, and that you stay there for the term of your natural life. Do you understand me? I can make certain that this nonsense fingerprint evidence is accepted. I have an authority, of a sort."

"Go on." I was hardly breathing anymore, and it was not because of the smoke.

"I have read two of your novels, in translation, I should mention, prior to going on. Or, more precisely, I had them read to me, aloud."

He could not have surprised me more by hitting me in the head with a brick. I stared.

"Yes. I quite enjoyed *The Star Twins*. *Eliza Paine*, on the other hand, I thought was..." He looked bothered for a moment. "Weak." He made a dismissive movement with his cigarette hand, and leaned back to suck on the thing again.

I did not know what to say to this, but experience has shown that the best thing to say on receiving bad reviews is to say, "Thank you, sir."

"You seem quite entranced by the possibilities of the new physics."

"I would say intrigued, certainly..." I wished someone would explain what was happening.

He stared at me, looking like an artist who thinks there is something wrong with his painting but cannot spot the flaw. I knew the feeling. "I wonder if you are who we need, though..."

We? "I wish I could tell you."

"You have blundered into a larger game," he rasped. "High stakes."

Campbell took a deep breath.

Brown went on. "I, and the people I represent, know that you did not kill the priest."

"Oh..." I said, impressing even myself with my sharp dialogue in a pinch.

"The priest, however... The priest was involved with some people, and in some things in which he should not have been involved."

"The demonology?"

270

"Amongst other things, yes. My people were watching him."

"How did he know things about my father and my husband? Was it through the deadworld?"

"This is what attracted our interest. He found your father there. He was looking for something else at the time. He recognised your father, and he saw—it was hard not to notice—that your father carried a terrible burden of guilt."

I made a helpless sound. Then, thinking about what Mr Brown was saying, I asked, "You're speaking about my father in the—"

"Past tense. Yes. My apologies. My sincerest apologies, and condolences. Father William eliminated your father's spirit—"

"Pardon?"

Mr Brown nodded and leaned towards me. "Father William used your father's soul to consecrate his cellar."

Blinking in shock, I tried to stand. "I beg your—"

Brown said, "I have no reason to lie."

"He killed my father...*again*?"

"Your father was filled with a foul corruption of the spirit. It was eating at him, like cancer. Taking his soul was almost a kindness, and the balance of probability suggests that the priest presented it as exactly that. 'Here, Sir Gustav, allow me to absolve your sins...'"

"Good God." I could hardly speak. Mr Campbell provided his handkerchief again. The phrase, "foul corruption" resonated through my mind. I remembered Gordon telling me that the cellar was filling with a "foul energy".

"Mrs Black, there are laws against the living tampering with the spirits of the dead like this," he went on in the silence of my shock.

"My *father*...?"

"This priest, he was a problem. We watched him for many years. He developed a network of associates over time, people who assisted him with his occult studies."

"Years? He was...for *years*?"

"Once it became clear to him that his life was not moving in the right direction. Whereas, he knew, your life was going rather well. You dressed as you liked, you earned considerable money writing your shameful books, you espoused alarmingly liberal views, you did not behave like a proper lady of means."

I did not know what to say to this.

"In his eyes, you were unworthy. You were not a good Christian. You were neither humble nor pious. You were not a good example to others."

There were some things I could say about this, but they were not polite. I sat and kept my mouth shut. Rarely, however, had it been so hard to do so.

Mr Brown went on. "Do not take offence, Mrs Black. I only report the priest's feelings. You were not the only one about whom he felt this way; you were merely close at hand. You lived under his nose. You had everything handed to you, whereas he was losing everything. His outrage was profound."

"My Aunt Julia said the note-sender — Father William — hated me so much he could strangle me with his bare hands," I said, once I finished wiping my face. I felt cold all over.

Mr Brown nodded. "It did not help that you attacked him physically, humiliated him in his own church."

I was beginning to see how it must have been with him. "He killed my father? When...?"

He did not answer me. He said, "Compose yourself, Mrs Black. There is something which we need you to consider."

I nodded, wiping my nose. "And if I do not cooperate, I go to prison?"

"You have a satisfactory grasp of the situation, I see. Good." He sat back and lit another of his disgusting cigarettes.

"My God, must you smoke those ghastly things?" I could contain my feelings no longer.

He surprised me by not getting angry. He said, "It rather seems I must."

Mr Campbell said, "It's getting late, sir. Could we...?"

Brown nodded. "Of course. I am keeping you from your dinner. My apologies. I did not expect Carmody's questioning to take so long."

I was tired, and in a great deal of pain, and not all of it from the chair. I could see how this was going to play out. I simply could not believe that it was happening to me. "You have something nasty you want me to do for you. Why don't you just tell me what it is?"

He managed a smile. His teeth were orange from smoking. He said, his breath vile, "Mrs Black, we want you to die."

34

I nearly choked from laughing. Mr Campbell pounded my back, as if that might help. It was hard, suddenly, to breathe—and I wanted to breathe. I wanted to keep breathing. It took a long time to recover from the laughing-choking fit, but when I was all right again, Mr Brown still sat there, still exhaling his bitter black smoke into the cramped room. He looked unmoved. At length I straightened up. Then I remembered what he had said to me, and I felt another fit of hacking laughter trying to kick me. This time I managed to control it.

Mr Brown said, "When you are ready, you will be transported back to the city and placed in the police lock-up—"

I was staring. "But I haven't decided yet!"

"It is a regrettable fact of life, Mrs Black, that we rarely have sufficient time to decide things—"

"I am not going to prison! I refuse!" In hindsight, this strikes me as amusing, but it is what I said.

Mr Brown sucked on his cigarette with glacial patience. He looked at the burning tip as if it might contain ancient wisdom in which he was only slightly interested. When he resumed, it was as if I had not made any foolish outbursts. Somehow this was worse than being rebuked. He said, "During your stay in the lock-up, you will experience a sense of profound shame. Though the policemen on duty will have taken your tie, your shoelaces, the braces holding up your trousers and anything else with which they deem you might try to hurt yourself, you will still have sheets on your bunk."

I wanted to protest, but I was too horrified to speak.

Mr Campbell said, "It will be all right, Mrs Black. It will."

How does he know that? I wondered.

Mr Brown continued. "In the morning, quite early, a routine check on your cell will show that you have hanged yourself with your sheet, from the bars of your high window. It will be a clumsy job, and in fact more of a prolonged strangulation. But you will be dead."

It was hard to breathe again.

"When your body is removed from the lock-up, it will be taken elsewhere, by people of mine. They will monitor your condition."

At last I found my voice. "I will *not* commit suicide. Not for you, not for anyone!" My voice was hoarse.

He sucked the last of his cigarette and lit a fresh one from the smouldering end. He took his time. I felt like I might be sick at any moment. He said, at last, "You will not commit suicide, Mrs Black. One of my people will see to the arrangements. There will be an injection of a certain drug. She will arrange the knot in the sheet. She will supervise your transport away from the lock-up, and she will propagate the news of your death to appropriate newspapers."

"At this point, Mr Brown," I managed to say, "I would rather take my chances with the legal system." Mr Campbell, after all, had insisted he could get the fingerprint evidence dismissed. I still did not have a satisfactory alibi for the night in question, but I could see a faint gleam of hope there.

"Allow me to complete my offer, Mrs Black. There is not a great deal more."

I looked at Mr Campbell. He nodded encouragingly and moved to hold my hand, presumably for my moral support. I did not let him. Somehow he knew what was happening here, and he had not warned me about it.

Mr Brown continued. "My people will not take you to the

city mortuary but to a certain warehouse in the city. There you will be cared for by the best medical practitioners in the country, particularly once you return to life."

"I don't stay dead?"

"You will be merely visiting the deadworld."

"Visiting? But...I...?"

"You will be in the state for no more than one day."

I was confused. I was far more than confused.

"A day is the best we can achieve. After that..." He did not finish. He didn't need to finish that thought.

"I need time to think. Good God..."

Mr Brown consulted his pocketwatch. It looked different. He touched things on the inside of the lid; when he closed it, he ran his narrow, orange-stained fingers around the edge, and it sealed itself, leaving no discernible crack or seam. I stared as he slipped it back into its pocket.

I was feeling very much the way I felt that night in the cellar, when Gordon told me we were at a point where different worlds made contact. *How many worlds were there?* I wondered—and only later did I realise the unintended irony of the thought, about my current work in progress.

Before he could speak again, I voiced the one concern that was dominating all others. "You said you would be telling the newspapers about my death."

"This is for the benefit of certain individuals and organisations who monitor these things, Mrs Black. It is important that they believe certain things."

"But you also said I will be coming back to life..."

"If all goes to plan, we shall issue a correction. You would not be the first person whose obituary appeared prematurely."

I thought about this. Certain individuals and organisations?

I remembered what Gordon had said that night, his wild speculation that Father and Antony might have been involved in espionage. This present business certainly had that sort of a ring about it—in a way.

"And your people can guarantee that I will completely recover from being dead?"

"If all goes to plan, then yes."

"You have done things like this before? Smuggling people into the deadworld to do jobs for you?"

"It is what we do, Mrs Black."

"In that case..." I frowned, trying to think it all through. "Why pick me? I'm merely a strange female author who offends people."

"You have a unique connection with Father William."

"And you're trying to catch him."

"He has hidden himself away."

"But you think I can find him where all your chaps have failed?"

"It is hard to overstate how much he hates you. In fact, all you have to do, once you encounter him, is simply get him to talk. That's it. Talk to him. It's all we ask."

"I need to ask him some questions of my own ..."

"If all goes to plan, you will have that opportunity."

If all goes to plan...I knew about plans. I knew that battle plans did not survive first contact with the enemy. I looked at my lawyer. "What should I do?"

Mr Campbell looked thoughtful. He said to Mr Brown: "What happens to the charges against my client in the event she succeeds and is revivified?"

"All charges will be dropped, of course, we will make sure of it. Your client may resume her life here."

If, that is, the locals will have me back, I thought. How long could I stand being called "Murderer" behind my back—or perhaps even right to my face?

Then I thought about those days I spent sitting out on the beach, watching the wind-tossed waves, the circling pelicans far above, the surfing dolphins, the huddled seagulls all facing into the breeze. I thought about the times I spent sitting by the estuary, upwind from the fish canneries, watching terns diving for fish, and pelicans joining the crowds of seagulls beggimg picnic food from me. The whole area had a feeling of peace and tranquillity about it that was hard to convey without looking and sounding foolish. It was something that, as soon as I arrived here for the first time, just to look at property, I had felt in my bones.

Immediately I felt relaxed in a way that I had never felt back home, or even up in Perth. There was simply something about being by the sea, taking the air, which was good for me. And at this moment it seemed like it had been a long while since I had taken the time to really enjoy these things.

If I did manage to get out of this predicament—I laughed inside at the very thought; I knew I wasn't getting out of this one—I would make more time to enjoy things.

But then I thought: what if, in the deadworld, I learned things about the past that I could not simply shrug off? Father William had made contact with the spirit of my father, and my father had told him terrible things. One had to presume that those terrible things concerned the truth about my husband's real life, the one in which I did not appear. I did not know if I could bear to learn such things. My love for Antony—love that I continued to feel, even now, after all this time—had always been a consuming passion. After his loss, I had not considered the notion of remarrying, and knew I never would. There would be no more men like him, as long as I lived. Had he, though, been playing the part of my husband in an elaborate theatrical production, in which I was a dupe? Everything I had learned in the past week appeared to say exactly this. It was a difficult thing to face, let alone to accept. If I did accept it, what did that make me? How much of a fool could I have been? I have always wanted, even as a child, to be taken seriously. Partly this was exacerbated by the mere fact of my gender: women were not often regarded as serious-minded people. Only men were considered capable of rational thought and decisions. I had had to resort to elaborate means and threaten legal action simply in order to establish a bank account.

I would not take it well, therefore, if I learned I had indeed been a fool all this time.

Mr Brown sat waiting for me. I would far rather face the modern horror of dentistry, with all its probes and picks and its hand-cranked mechanical drills than go to the deadworld. Even the prospect of meeting Julia again did not improve matters. However, I compared this to a lifetime spent in prison, breaking rocks or whatever women had to do for hard labour in these enlightened times. Earlier I had glibly imagined myself a prison novelist, with all that lovely free time in which to write turgid novels of incarceration and intolerance. What if prison, in fact, offered no chance to write? What if it meant my career, such as it was, would be finished? Could I tolerate that? Worse, could I tolerate never knowing the truth about my husband and my father?

I said to Mr Brown: "I'll do it."

35

Death came wrapped in sleep and dreams.

The holding cell at the police lock-up was a dark, cramped concrete box that stank of urine and fear, its walls liberally marked and scrawled with names, drawings, prayers and arcane messages I could not decipher. I sat on the bunk, sickened and mortified, as a woman in heavy eye-glasses with only one arm, and dressed as a police officer, gave me the injection. "This won't hurt a bit," she said, lying through her teeth. The solution burned up my arm, and the fire spread through my body, and up into my head, where I felt it alive and bubbling behind my eyes. "Lie down," she told me. "It hits pretty fast."

I could hear hacking sobs from other nearby cells, and at least one male voice howling out the filthiest language I had ever heard.

How could my life have come to this? I wondered, but not for long.

As sleep pulled at me, I thought of sick dogs being put down just like this.

And, thinking that, I thought of Gordon, and what he had been forced to do because he helped me that night. The thought was unbearable.

Good God...*I'm so sorry, Gordon.*

I watched the woman in glasses do a surprisingly efficient job of knotting the sheet with her left hand and the below-the-elbow stump of the other. It was hard not to stare. Standing on the end of the bunk, she managed to tie a loop around the bars up on the window. It was not an elegant way to kill oneself, I reflected, now almost beyond caring.

Even as I felt my flesh burn, I could see my breath turning to fog.

My heart slowed, and slowed even more, and as it did, I grew colder, and began to shiver.

The woman in glasses took my wrist in her cold hand and checked my pulse and respiration; she had a nurse's brass fob-watch. She smelled of cheap soap. Threads of blonde hair, escaped from under her black and white police cap, fell around her face.

"Am I really going to die?" I was finding it hard to see.

"Do you remember your briefing?"

"Hmm...?"

The burning sensation was fading.

"Do you remember your briefing?"

"Oh..." I could no longer see her. Dreams came and took me away. Part-memory and part-fabrication, I saw things I understood and things that were odd, in the way of ordinary dreams. It is difficult now to remember the things I saw. I do recall a feeling of peace. It was the most pleasant sensation I had experienced in a long time.

Then Julia was sitting next to me. We were on a tram, and the tram was trundling and rattling through the streets of a city that looked something like many cities I knew—but when I thought I recognised a landmark, a corner, a public fountain, a tree-lined park, there were other things I did not recognise at all; it was confusing. Julia said, "So you got here in one piece, then? Jube, dear?" She held out a cellophane bag containing colourful fruit jubes. She had been through half the bag already.

"Thank you very much," I said, relying on good manners to get me through this odd dream. The jube was red and crusted with sugar. It smelled of raspberries in a way that was almost overwhelming. The taste was exquisite. I sat there, surrounded by people I did not know, bunched together on the old wooden benches of the tram, while a raspberry explosion occurred within my mouth. It seemed to make everything else go pale by comparison.

Julia reached up and pulled the cord, and a bell rang. "This is our stop. Come along, dear."

I got up and threaded my way between the other people. I heard an old man say, speaking to no-one, "What the hell is this? Where's Mary? She was right here a moment ago. Have you seen her?" He was looking up at me, and I happened to catch his eye. He was dressed in loose cotton pyjamas. "Have you seen my Mary?"

The tram squeaked to a stop. Julia helped me climb down to the street. A few other passengers got off with us, and, like me, they stood there, next to the idle tram, simply staring at the surrounding scene.

On one hand, it was bright and sunny, like a spring afternoon, but the quality of the light was odd, neither the harsh yellow flatness of Australian light, nor the softer European light I knew from home. This was something else, and disconcerting.

On the other hand, the sky was a spray of stars against the infinite depth of space. I did not recognise any constellations. The stars were the wrong colours.

I could smell motorcar exhaust and horse manure and human perspiration.

The tram rattled and jingled off up the middle of the street. Other traffic, including motorcars, horses and buggies, people on bicycles, and pedestrians looking very busy, dodged around the big red trams.

Julia watched the flow of traffic and led me to the footpath. We were an island of calm as a river of other people flowed by in both directions, everyone talking at once. Julia looked around, a seasoned observer, and pointed at things. "That's the Urquhart Building. It used to be one of the tallest buildings here, until the last few years. This is Greathelm Street, I should point out, one of the main shopping districts. If you go down this hill to the corner, you'll be on Cogsworth Street, which leads to the High

Street to the *ewst* and up to Government House to the *wast*. Over there, next to Sweetling's Book Emporium, there's Purvis's, the department store."

It was a pounding rain of new information. It was confusing and frightening. I had never imagined an afterlife like this.

"I say, dear, feeling hungry?" Julia smiled at me.

"I'm asleep. I remember."

"Follow me, dear."

She took me back across the busy street and led me into Purvis's department store. It was thick with busy people, many carrying bulging paper bags which bore the stylised *P* I recognised from outside. Many of these people also had children following them around; the children looked confused and upset, even as they ate ice-cream cones and sugared doughnuts that smelled delicious. The noise in here was extraordinary. People raising their voices to be heard over other people doing the same thing—combined with occasional public announcements from overhead speakers, alerting shoppers to special sales and discount offers. The press of busy, grumpy people was hard to bear. "Where are we...?"

Julia pulled me towards an ornate wooden staircase leading up and down. We headed down. I kept holding the varnished banister as we descended two whole levels, each as frantic and noisy as the last, until we reached the basement. There was a cafeteria down here. The noise was bad, but different; the change was a blessing. Around me were scores of small tables, most occupied by family groups that didn't look quite right. There was an intense rattling of steel cutlery on china plates that jarred in my ears.

Still bewildered by the stunning press of hundreds and hundreds of busy people, I followed Julia, clutching her hand the way I imagined I must have done as a small child when my governess took me for walks on the common or by lake, when she told me stories about faeries and elves and brave but doomed knights. The memory of those walks bloomed and filled my mind for a long moment; I tripped over someone's foot and fell to the polished wooden floor. My knees and left elbow hit hard and I wound up sitting on my backside, embarrassed. People nearby stared at me and made arch remarks to those with them about "idiot new chums". Suddenly I felt upset and thought I might cry, just to make this intense experience — so like something bad from childhood — complete. The entire journey so far did indeed remind me of my first visits to London, when I was only perhaps six or seven years old. I remembered my father, leaning forward in the carriage, smelling of fragrant pipe smoke, with me on his lap, pointing at things through the windows. It seemed cities were made of vast ferocious-looking buildings, smelly horses, crowds of unhappy people, and soot and smoke and noise. It was fascinating but also frightening — just like this new place.

We were seated at a table by ourselves, up against a wall. Julia was sipping a cup of fragrant tea. She had provided me with a plate of ham and cheese sandwiches on fresh white bread, and a glass of cold water. The bread smelled warm. She said, "I would have given you milk, but it's been known to react poorly in the stomachs of the newly arrived. Hope you don't mind." She smiled warmly, and set about her own sandwich, which looked like something involving chicken and mustard, and smelled *wonderful*.

As I ate my sandwich, which was very good — and I was surprised that food here should be so good — I felt my mind beginning to wrap itself around these new surroundings. Things seemed at once only too familiar, but also subtly wrong. This conflict of impressions was disturbing, but I was starting to *see*. Julia said, at one point, "You see what you're accustomed to, Ruth. Not everyone sees the same thing. This city is so crowded, however, because so many people these days live in big cities. They're comfortable in this sort of world. Do you see, dear?"

I chewed this over and took a sip of water. The water tasted off somehow, and I put the glass back on the table. "How...*real* is all this?"

"Oh, quite real, I assure you. I say, are you staying here or are you heading out into the countryside once you've become acclimatised? I should have asked you before, but...well, you know what it's like when you first arrive, don't you? Some poor folk just about keel over a second time, just from shock! 'I say,' they say, all confused and indignant, 'where're all the angels, and where's God and whatnot?' It's something of a trial explaining to some people that it's not so much an afterlife, but *another* life. Do you see?" She went on for some time about some of these people she'd encountered, writhing on the ground, suffering "afterlife shock", as she called it.

Something was wrong about all this, though. There was something I needed to be doing, and it wasn't stuffing my face like this and trying not to inhale the rich perfumes of the ladies lunching around us.

I finished my sandwich and dabbed my lips with the paper napkin provided. Julia was still talking, regaling me with hard-to-follow accounts of her first visits here, and the trouble she had coming to grips with it all, and the famous people she'd come across, not all of whom handled the transition with the sort of poise and aplomb for which they were famous in life. The more she went on, talking about her encounters with actors, politicians, artists, "altogether too many soldiers", even horse-race jockeys and famous opera divas, the less I listened. My attention was drawn to what I assumed was a clock on the opposite wall. This clock sported the traditional circular dial, but only one hand, and—I squinted—*fourteen* numbers. The time at this moment was something after one o'clock, presumably in the afternoon.

How long had I been here now? I thought back as far as I could, and determined that perhaps twenty minutes had already passed—and all I had done was eat a sandwich and feel confused and embarrassed.

"I've got to find Father William," I said, interrupting Aunt Julia's deadworld memoirs.

She blinked and peered across at me. "Is that right?"

I got up. "You might say I'm on a tourist visa. I'm here to find that swine and then I'm heading back, erm, home, so to speak."

Julia looked disappointed. "You say you're looking for this Father William? I was talking with him just recently. I sent you that message, did you get it?"

"Yes I did. What happened? Do you know where he's gone?"

She looked surprised at my keen interest. "He saw through my cunning ruse and fled, dear. I am sorry. It's just I'd rather hoped you would get back in touch with me."

"A bit of a problem there, Julia. I had no way of reaching you. The telephone has its limitations, somewhat."

"What about that nice Mr Duncombe? Wouldn't he lend his services?"

"That nice Mr Duncombe, I'm very sorry to say, is not currently speaking to me—and I do not mean because I'm dead. We had something of a falling out." It was still bothering me.

Julia was shocked. "What on Earth happened? You two were such chums!"

"I honestly don't have time to explain."

"Don't be silly, Ruth. Of course you have time."

"Pardon me for saying so, Julia, but I really do not have time. I've already used up about twenty minutes!"

"How long do you have?"

"They told me one day is the best they can manage."

"That's not too good."

"No, that's right. So I need to get moving."

"Did they say one day there or one day here, dear?"

I stared again. "Pardon?"

"Time, dear. It's not the same here as it is back there. Bit of a funny story ..."

"What's the difference?" I managed to interrupt before she launched back into anecdotes.

"Hard to say," she said, sounding a little miffed that I had not wanted to hear the story. "It just works differently here. There's no direct correspondence, as one might expect, and it seems to vary rather a lot. Makes it all very hard to keep appointments and so forth."

"Well, how much of a difference might be involved?"

"An hour back home could last half an hour here, or possibly as much as a year or so."

I blinked. "A year?"

"Yes. Do try to keep up. It all depends on a variety of factors.

A very clever and rather fetching scientist chap named Garson Somebody once tried to explain it to me over cocktails, and I must confess I rather felt the eyes glazing over after only a few minutes of it."

I was staring at her now. "A *year*?"

"Or more, dear. It's all quite up in the air. Who knows?"

"Good God..." I needed to hold my head.

"Ruth?"

"Headache forming. Nothing unusual. Though I must say I had rather hoped headaches would be a thing of the mortal flesh."

We got up and left the cafeteria and wound up outside Purvis's on the footpath under the wide marquee. Standing there in the midst of the churning pedestrian traffic, my head felt very sore indeed. I wondered if the shops here carried Compton's Aches and Pain Relieving Salts. Julia popped another fruit jube in her mouth and chewed thoughtfully for a few moments. "So we need to find that Father William again," she said, studying people going by as if one might be Father William in a bad wig.

"Well, I do, at any rate."

"What happens if you don't find him before your time expires, dear?"

I had not considered this. Of course, I had had no notion of what to expect here in the deadworld, and no sense of what might be involved in locating someone who did not want to be found. I suppose, in my imagination, the deadworld was some sort of twee storybook sort of land in which everyone was ever so happy, don't you know, and villains would be relatively easy to flush out of their strongholds. I had not been ready for all this. But what would happen if I failed? The most obvious answer also seemed the most likely: why would Mr Brown's people even bother reviving me? If I failed, I might as well stay dead.

"Where," I said to Julia, "was the last place you saw Father William?"

"He was a guest at my home for afternoon tea, of course."

"You have a home here?"

"I do live here now, Ruth," she said, smiling indulgently.

"And you wanted to meet him, even though his note hurt you

that time? You weren't worried about what he might...?"

"Ruth, dear. I am not without resources of my own here."

"All right. Is it far?"

"Just outside the city. Let me hail us a cab."

And so we went to Aunt Julia's house in the deadworld.

36

Julia lived in one of a row of picturesque two-storey white stone terrace houses on the outskirts of this immense city. The street was broad and lined with great old fig trees with spreading canopies that met overhead. The eerie sourceless sunlight dappled through the dense leaf cover; an old man with a slight limp could be seen sweeping the wide footpath on the far side of the street. A young woman walking an odd-looking white dog was further up the street. Opposite Julia's house a cricket pitch was spread out, green and well manicured. A few strapping young men in creams practised their bowling and batting in the nets. It was like a scene lifted whole from the golden summers I spent at Cambridge. Julia saw me marvelling. "You could do worse than live here, Ruth."

Julia paid the driver; we climbed out; the cab clopped off.

"Well, here we are, Number Five Stonecastle Boulevard. What do you think?"

She had planter boxes by the door and in the windows; they were all blooming with colours more vibrant than any I had seen back home. Indeed, I did not recognise these flowers at all. They looked even stranger than the plants of Australia, whose strangeness was legendary amongst British botanists. As Julia opened the door, I said to her, "How do you manage to have such a house?"

"I am not entirely certain, dear. It simply worked out that way. Come on in! You must be exhausted."

Julia's house was very much like the homes back in England: dark and crammed with heavy, heirloom furniture, and with expensive carpets over the floorboards. It did not smell musty, but there was a familiar sense of age and time-worn traditions that seemed etched into everything. It was difficult simply threading my way between overstuffed armchairs and side-tables and bureaux and cabinets and bookcases, which were also crammed with leather-bound volumes, locked behind ornate glass doors. There was a persistent aroma of expensive furniture polish and elbow grease. "You have staff, Julia?"

"Actually, no. It's just me and Merlin, wherever he might be. He's always lurking somewhere."

"Merlin?"

"My cat. A very fat, spoiled white cat."

"There are pet shops here?"

"None that I have seen. Merlin was simply here, along with the house. I can't quite explain it all."

I thought about the time. It had taken about an hour in the cab to get here, so that gave me perhaps twenty-three hours—unless the problem with time Julia had mentioned to me was indeed in effect, and I could have...days or months or more, or perhaps much less. That was a difficult thing to think about. It rather reminded me of those faery stories I read, where hapless humans got trapped in the world of faery, and time moved very differently indeed for them. For that matter, it also reminded me of the time-dilation effect predicted by relativity. Travel fast enough, close to the speed of light itself, and while one might age at the usual rate, people back home would zoom through time. Was something like that occurring here, I wondered? Or was it faeries? I suspected, on balance, that it was something stranger still.

*

I sat Julia down by the fireplace. It was time to talk about Father William. Somehow she had acquired a cup of tea, which she sipped as we spoke.

She said, "He was in very poor shape when I met him, Ruth."

"He was an old man…"

"No. He was…he was not himself. Something was taking over his…It was quite distressing to see, I must confess. I had a difficult time simply looking at him." Her hands shook a little as she remembered the occasion.

"How did you get him to come here in the first place?"

"We arrived at about the same time. He was on the tram with me."

I remembered the tram. "Everyone arrives on the tram?"

"Most of the time, yes. There are special cases, unique circumstances."

"And you spoke to him, or he spoke to you, or…?" There was so much to learn; it got in the way of finding things out quickly. Would I know, would I be able to feel it, somehow, if Brown's people decided to leave me here? It gave me a queasy feeling to go with the headache. As gorgeous as this part of the deadworld looked, it struck me as perhaps too gorgeous, too tempting. I did not want to stay here. "All right. You're both on the tram, along with lots of other people. What then?"

"I knew his identity immediately. I remembered that note you showed me. There was that same feeling burning off him, like a dreadful illumination—"

"And naturally you felt inclined to have afternoon tea with him?"

"I wanted to know about him. The demon he sent that night. I knew it was his creature, dear. I knew it in my marrow. It stank of this man, if you'll pardon me saying so. His creature killed me the way you might screw up a page of bad writing and toss it in the bin. I presented that much of a challenge to the poor thing. I was lying there, his hands crushing my throat, and I was unable to breathe or even scream. He had too much power for such a simple job. It was like using a mallet to kill a fly, if you will, dear. There was a terrible sense of desolation about him, too, which surprised me. Even though he was killing me, I did not feel much real fear. I knew the deadworld was nothing to worry about, after all, so I found myself feeling for the creature sent to hurt me—well, clearly he was the killer I saw in my prophetic dreams. If you had been at home that night, Ruth, I am sure it would have been you who died—"

"Julia, I am so sorry, I—"

"Shhh. It is quite all right. I do not blame you. I am, however, struck by a certain bitter irony, that I should have gone to all this trouble to warn you, only to fall victim myself. But it's quite all right."

"How can you be so, so...*at ease* about having been murdered by a demon, for God's sake?"

She finished the last of her tea and set the cup down on its fine porcelain saucer. Looking at me, she said, "I was not afraid. Surprised, of course. Disappointed I would not be able to say goodbye before I left that world, and sorry that I would not soon see Mr Duncombe again—I'm so sorry you two have had your falling out. That's terrible. If you get back there, you must promise me you will make every effort to repair the breach. Is that clear, Ruth? Do you promise?"

I did not see how I might set about repairing the friendship, but I promised her that I would try, for what it was worth. Gordon and I had been friends for a long time, after all. He understood and accepted me, because he was a kindred spirit, and another runaway from the constrictions of the old country.

I brought the conversation around to Father William again. "You say you wanted to get to know him better, to see just what he had against me, that kind of thing?"

"More or less. I intended to give him a piece of my mind, I must say. Giving you all that trouble and going to such unwholesome lengths to cause you pain. That is not right. It is absolutely unacceptable, particularly coming from a man of the cloth!" Julia was much more exercised about this than I would have suspected. She went on: "I remembered him from the Mass I went along to that Sunday, so I made my way to where he was sitting, near the front of the tram. He was looking miserable and lost. I told him I knew him from his service and so forth, and pretended I was a simple new chum glad to have found a familiar face in the crowd, as it were."

"You say he seemed miserable? I would have thought he'd have been jumping for joy, having dropped me into such trouble with the constabulary."

"He was devastated, Ruth. Riddled with the most terrible guilt. And here—"

"*Guilt*? He was full of guilt?" I could not believe my ears.

"Indeed. And here such things come out. They manifest themselves and start to take over one's body. That's why, by the time I brought him out here, he was already well on the way through the manifestation process. It was guilt, and it was making a monster of him, the poor beggar."

This silenced me. I sat and thought for a moment. Mr Brown, when he told me about what Father William had been up to, that he had taken my father's soul as well as his confession, he had said that my father at that point had been consumed with guilt, which was eating at him like cancer. I had not realised that he meant this literally, that such profound feelings could manifest like this. It was difficult to accept. "Was he...was he in pain, with all the...?"

Julia nodded. Somehow she had acquired another cup of tea. "He was. He said it was killing him, though he was of course already dead."

"So you and he talked?" I tried to imagine the two of them sitting here, sipping tea, all very civilised. It made me think again about Julia's inner strength, that there must be more to her than her bubbly, chatty appearance suggested. It embarrassed me to realise I had not noticed this before.

"We did. I did not tell him that I was your aunt, dear. He had no notion of our connection."

"And what did he tell you?"

"He was, first of all, a terribly confused old man. This is not the afterlife he was expecting. He fully expected to be cast down to a literal Hell, and he had been bracing himself for all that it offered. On finding himself here, so much like home but also not at all like home...Let me just say that he was terribly pleased to have found a friendly face." She smiled thinly and sipped tea, pleased with her scheming.

"So did you ask him what he had done that had given him all this terrible guilt?"

"He could not easily speak of it. He tried. I think he wanted to tell someone. But in the end, he could not bring himself to speak of it. He said he had done monstrous things, engaged in the most terrible practices, broken his vows to such an extent, that to speak of the things he had done...Well, I think you can see what he was like. I have rarely seen such shame in a man."

I was not prepared for this. Since learning the name of my enemy, I had imagined him a gloating, malign, larger-than-life sort of figure, much in the way, during the War, it had been common to depict the Germans as diabolical monsters, every one of them, down to the smallest child. They were the very Enemy of the World, an insult to all that was decent and right and just and good. They were Villains in the most melodramatic, even cartoon-like sense. I had refused to accept this propaganda. I could not see how an entire population could be like this, and it was a view that made me few friends. But here I found myself realising that I had imagined "my enemy" in the same simplistic manner, as a mad genius bent on my destruction, so much consumed with that tremendous anger of his that he had no sense of remorse or concern that he had gone too far. That it might be otherwise had simply never occurred to me. Which led me to this point, learning, reluctantly, that my enemy was a small man concerned that he had gone too far. Indeed, who knew he had done the greatest wrongs, and was already confined to a monstrous Hell of his own making.

"So you planned," I said to Aunt Julia, "that if I could contact you while you had him here, that he might confess everything?"

"I do not think you could characterise this with so precise a term as a 'plan', dear. I thought I might possibly persuade him to explain why he had done everything..."

"But somehow, he realised what you were up to, and left."

"That's correct, dear." She looked miffed.

"Do you think he realised who you were?"

"I'm very doubtful. He was not thinking clearly, I'm afraid."

"Did you see which way he—"

Something was happening around us. Things were shifting in the air.

"I say…" Julia said, looking around, setting down her tea.

Figures of men were unfolding out of thin air.

Men with guns. I got to my feet. "Julia—come on. We have to go." I tried to grab her arm, but she would not budge from her seat. She was glancing about at what was happening. "What's…?"

The figures resolved themselves. There were five of them. They looked like commandos of the occult. Their black uniforms bore faintly legible mystic symbols. None of them had eyes; their sockets were empty. Two were focused on Julia, and had her covered from different angles. The other three were looking around, and spread through the room, and into the rest of the house. "Where is she?" one, I guessed the leader, asked.

I was standing right there, heart in my throat, and I almost spoke up and said, "I'm right here, idiot," but I kept my tongue. I soon realised they truly couldn't see me. The searchers returned. "Nothing," one said, and they all turned back to Julia. "Where is she?"

Julia, no fool, said, with perfect, well-bred poise, "Where is who, dear?"

"We're looking for a Mrs Ruth Black. Newly arrived. She was last seen with you, Miss Templesmith."

"And may I ask your names, and see some identification, perhaps?"

One of the men said, "She's plainly not here."

Another said, "She can't have gone far. Spread out."

Then Julia got to her feet. "I really must insist on seeing some identification. I will not have armed thugs bursting uninvited into my home."

I was all set to cheer, when the leader of the team shot her. Just like that. He raised his gun and fired two shots, which both hit her in the chest. The sound was shocking. The thick, hot smell of gunsmoke in the air. Julia sank to the floor, and glanced my way. Wide-eyed, wanting to scream, I saw her mouth the words, "Run, dear!" Even as she said it, she was starting to dissolve into pale mist.

I ran. As I opened the door, the men turned their guns and came after me. One yelled out, "Suppression field!"

"Re-tune to level four," the leader said, as they came swarming after me.

Outside, vaulting over the gate, I hit the pavement and ran, hurtling down the tree-lined street, trying to remember to breathe, my heart exploding—and having no idea where to go. Here I was in an unfamiliar city, where it was perfectly possible to die all over again. What would happen then, I wondered, as I ran, leaping through hedges, vaulting fences, racing across beautifully kept lawns, aware, fleetingly, of the smells of roses, and the sight of confused children. I ran for all I was worth, and was sorry that in this new existence I seemed no more fit than I had been in my former life, which was to say, not very. I was starting to flag. I ran into the flow of traffic, dodging in amongst and around motorcars and horses, trying not to slip on stinking smears of horse-dung, then pelting down another street towards the entrance to a huge and very beautiful park, where I hoped I might hide. Behind me, not far, I could hear running footsteps. Once or twice I heard warning shots fired overhead, as chilling and heart-stopping a sound as you're ever likely to hear in any life, but I kept running, sure they would shoot me as I ran, shoot me in the back, just to stop me—but they never did. Pain stinging me under my ribs on the right side, I lurched through the park, scanning everywhere, trying not to trip over nannies with babies in strollers, people enjoying afternoon tea on benches—but there was nowhere a woman dressed like me, and as tall as I was, might conceal herself. Worse, I was hearing sirens from all around. Black-clad police and more of these commando figures were massing at the other park entrances, and starting to close in. "Mrs Black," someone called through a megaphone, "it's hopeless. We are tracking your movements. Give yourself up peacefully. We don't want to hurt you." I was hiding amongst some hedges near a statue of a dead general, my breathing ragged, my heart thumping in my throat, that pain in my side nigh on unbearable, perspiration soaking my hair and running down my face and neck. My choices appeared stark: give myself up, or get myself killed. I had not asked Mr Brown, or that nurse in the lock-up, what might happen to me if I were to die again while here. Was there a further level of afterlife beyond even this one, or was this it? Was there nothing beyond this bonus life but the friction of entropy stripping my soul of its energy and meaning? One thing I was sure of: if I died here, if I died again, I couldn't see any way of coming back to my own world.

And that decided me. I got up, raised my hands, and moved out into the open, swearing and weeping.

37

I woke later, unaware that I had been asleep, to find myself, cold and trying not to shiver, in a small, white-tiled room, aware of an antiseptic smell, and strapped to a hospital stretcher, wearing only a flimsy cotton gown. I could not move, save to wriggle my fingers and toes. I didn't even know if I was still in the deadworld, or if I were back in my world. This room, from what I could see as I lay strapped to the stretcher, was lined with racks of stainless steel instruments, trolleys containing diabolical-looking white and chrome machinery, and wall charts illustrating things to do with the brain and nervous system, only the nervous system depicted looked far more complex and strange than anything I was familiar with. The tight restraints bit at my flesh, constricting circulation; I could not even move my head. An ageing nurse appeared; she looked very tired, as nurses usually looked, and took my pulse, respiration and blood pressure; staring at a dial that I could not see, she squeezed the black rubber bulb; the cuff on my arm grew very tight. I could feel my racing pulse under the cuff.

The nurse released the valve on the squeeze-bulb; the cuff loosened; she watched the mercury fall on the dial. Once she was done, she packed up the machine, smiled at me in a perfunctory manner. "There you go," she said. "I'll just get Doctor." She went to leave.

"Wait!" I managed to say, though my whole mouth felt not quite right.

The nurse stopped at the door. I could hardly see her. "Yes, Mrs Black?"

What to say, what to say?

"What am I doing here?"

"Doctor will be along shortly," she said, and I heard the door swing shut.

*

Some time later, I heard the door open. I assumed it was "Doctor".

"What is the meaning of this, Doctor?" I said in the imperious tone I normally reserved for upbraiding the likes of Ryan for some foolish mistake.

"'Meaning', Mrs Black?" It was an old, wet voice, the sound of a man dying of emphysema, or, I remembered, the men who'd been exposed to poison gas during the War, whose lungs were never the same afterwards. And there was a smell now, a disgusting, biological stink.

"Who the hell are you?" I said, only too aware, as I struggled to free myself, there was nothing I could do.

"Who am I? Well, who *am* I? That's a good question. I'm surprised you don't recognise me, madam."

"I demand to know what exactly is going on here. As a citizen of Great Britain, I have certain inalienable rights!"

"Ah, but you are dead now—yes, properly dead, not just here on holiday anymore. Your time long ago expired. You're here with the rest of us, a citizen of Thanatos at last, so it behooves you to make the best of it."

Thanatos? I thought. Freud's death impulse? The land of the dead? Well, that was lovely. I think I preferred the term "deadworld". But, of more concern: "My time's up? I had...I had—"

"It took too long to revive you," the wet, stinking voice said, and dissolved into a horrible coughing spasm. "Excuse me. Yes, the police, when they arrested you in the park, took their assignment a trifle too seriously. Terribly sorry for the inconvenience. You'll get used to it. We all get used to it. It's not so bad, living here, if you could call it living, of course."

So I was dead now, with no way back, was I? There was no way to tell if this were true or not. The pain in my joints, the pain in my head, the way the leather straps bit into my wrists and ankles certainly felt real, or at least convincing. "I'm sorry, but I don't believe we've been properly introduced," I said, straining after that performance of poise, but I could hear in my voice that it was more strain and less poise. My unseen (though not unsmelled) interlocutor coughed again. "Oh, I see. Yes, quite. How rude of us." Still coughing, he shuffled around into my field of view. The smell, up close, made me sick. Though he no longer looked in any way as he had in life, though he looked as if his entire body had become cancerous, and as if the cancer was as much without as within, I recognised the bearing of the man. I remembered that posture only too well. "You're looking well," I said.

He shrugged, and coughed again, his mangled hand over his wet mouth. "It's been too long," he said.

"I hear you met up with my father."

He nodded, and sagged visibly. "A poor lost soul. Thanatos is not kind to a man carrying that sort of guilt, Mrs Black. Not kind at all."

"So I gather. Nice of you to offer him absolution for his sins."

"You heard about that."

"I met Variel. Lovely chap."

Nodding again. "He was once a very good man, Variel."

"A lot of that going around."

"Your father was the most tormented soul I have ever encountered. It was a mercy, healing him. He went to a better place."

"You consecrated your demon-trap with my father's soul."

"I put it to good use."

"You're a poor excuse for a blackmailer, you know that, don't you?"

"And you a poor excuse for a woman, it must be said."

"Did you really hate me that much?"

He pulled up a chair behind my head somewhere, and I heard something wet and heavy shifting about as he sat. The smell was bad, and it was made worse, knowing from whom it emanated. It was hard to believe such a man could fall so far.

He said, as if aware of my thoughts, "I have made peace with my God. Have you? Oh yes, of course. You have no God, do you?"

"I want no part of a God that would have you."

"Always so self-righteous. Sometimes I think you must be angry at the entire world, Mrs Black."

"Not the entire world."

"Perhaps not."

"I cannot believe that you really thought that extortion nonsense would work."

"I was a desperate man."

"Desperate enough to...*eliminate* my father?" I shuddered, thinking about how it must have been. The confession, the penance, the blessing. "Go with God, my son," he might have said, just before ripping Father's essence from him.

"He was already dead. I eased his torment. He was grateful."

Grateful? I lay there and bit back the things I was going to say about these comments of his. "So you're saying," I said after a while, "your God will let you embark on a career in demonology and blackest magic, and even order the death of innocents, and, as long as you make all the right noises by way of confession and so forth, you can return to a state of grace? Is that right?"

"It's more complex than that."

"I'm sure it is."

"Your father had a lot to say."

"You took advantage of him."

"He needed to talk."

I thought about my father, who had always been a well-meaning old chap, fairly capable, an asset to the government, if not to his family. I'm sure his fellow Cabinet Ministers saw more of him than we did at home. During those days, he always looked like a kettle about to boil.

"Well," I said at last, "you seemed awfully keen to tell me the awful truth about my father and husband. Why not unburden yourself at last, now that you have me at such disadvantage?"

He hesitated. When he spoke, he sounded sad. "It is not an

easy thing, having neither power nor hope, is it?"

He had a point but I did not wish him to see that. "All right. Don't tell me. Fine."

"Oh, but I want to tell you. I want to tell you all about it."

"What—that my father was a traitor and my husband a spy? I know that already." Which was not strictly true, but I was growing impatient.

It seemed to have the desired effect. "You know that your father was selling secrets to the Germans?"

I had not known it in quite so many words. Again, I worked to stay calm. "It seemed likely," I said, thinking now about that late-night conversation with Gordon, in which he had first floated the preposterous notion that Father and Antony might have been involved in espionage. At the time it had seemed like such an extraordinary, fanciful notion. I had even been offended, if I recalled correctly.

Struggling to sleep these past several nights, I had spent a considerable time thinking about this, and how it must have been between Antony and my father. At some point, Antony must have made contact with Father, to let him know that he, Antony, knew about Father's little secret, but he was not there to arrest Father. I didn't know this for certain, but I knew it was common practice, to send disinformation back to the enemy. So it seemed plausible, at least, to think that Antony might have offered Father a chance to redeem himself this way. Father would have had much the same choice I had had: do as we ask, or face punishment for High Treason—which was execution by hanging. Father agreed to consider the extremely risky prospect of trying to fool his German masters. And then, one day, as Antony was working on Father, he came across me, and, possibly, saw what must have seemed like a golden opportunity. Get involved with the daughter in order to remain close to the target of the operation.

But then…Something happened. Father died. Near the anniversary of Mother's death. Naturally, it had looked like all-too-understandable grief taking him. It had been his heart. I remembered that night, as Antony drove us to the hospital, hurtling along those narrow country roads, driving like a man possessed. He certainly looked at all times like a man desperately concerned about my father.

But then he would, wouldn't he? That would be all part of the operation.

I remembered Father William's note:

WHY DID YOUR HUSBAND KILL YOUR FATHER?

I could not say, and was not sure that I wanted to know. The question still disturbed me. The coroner said, at the time, that Father's heart had failed him, and there were no suspicious circumstances. Father was getting on in years; he did not eat well; he was overweight; he liked his cigars and his wine rather too much. It all made a certain kind of sense. But, of course, it *would* make sense like that, wouldn't it, if someone wanted to kill him and make it look like natural causes? Why would Antony kill Father, the proverbial goose that laid the golden eggs? The two of them had always seemed like such great chums. Had that been a performance for my benefit? Had Antony's behaviour with me been as much a performance?

"It does rather eat at one's sense of reality, does it not, Mrs Black?"

"Reality, these days, seems up for grabs," I said.

"Who can you trust? Your husband? Your father? It's all lies."

I ignored this. "You changed your mind."

"I beg your pardon?"

"You changed your mind. You had the notes coming each day. But with the third note you asked for far too much money. Naturally I wasn't about to give you money, and when your pet demon came by to see if I was playing along, you gave him instructions to hurt someone close to me."

"I did need the money. The church is terribly run-down."

"Yes, I'm sure. But not only did you have Variel kill my helpless Aunt Julia—"

He interrupted, snorting, "—Your Aunt Julia was in no way helpless, let me assure you."

"—But you *then* had this bright idea to set up a bizarre scenario in which you would have me framed for your murder!"

"Ah yes, of course." He sounded pleased. His smell was worsening. I did not want to see how he must look now to be making a stink like that.

"Why the change of plan? Why not keep at me, picking off my staff, everyone else in my life, until I paid up?"

"Mrs Black," he said after a long pause. "I have been a sick man for many years. Very, very sick. Dr Munz had kept me alive for years, and sent me to all the best specialists, up in Perth and elsewhere. Then, more recently, they told me there was nothing more they could do. I had one month, perhaps two, if I were lucky. If I were 'blessed'. It was hopeless. Inoperable. I was riddled with it, they said. They showed me their X-rays, and even I could see it. Even I could see how God had *betrayed* me, when I needed His strength most. My whole life was collapsing around me. *My whole life!* The church was crumbling. People were no longer coming to Mass. 'Oh no, that terrible War has shown us that God is irrelevant, He doesn't matter, blah blah blah.' And there I was, imprisoned in that pathetic little town, with these indifferent parishioners, no money, precious little hope, no matter how much or how often I prayed, kneeling there on the cold stone floor, begging for strength and guidance, *begging like a pauper!* I wrote and wrote to the Archbishop, telling him about my many *excellent* ideas for making the Church mean something again, to bring the people back...But no. The Old Boys Network wanted to keep me down, stuck in Pelican River, going nowhere. I wrote so many letters, so many fawning, begging letters..."

He went on and on, angrier by the moment. It was just as I had been told. I did not dare point out that perhaps word of his occult adventures had leaked out, and that perhaps the Archbishop and the rest of the Church hierarchy were trying to keep him in Pelican River as a punishment—and perhaps as a means of quarantine. Because, and I knew this only too well, the Church would never actually sack anyone. Problematic people simply were moved out of harm's way, so the Church could keep an eye on them. Telling him this would not have helped, though I was sorely tempted.

So there he was. Banished to Pelican River, starved of

parishioners, frustrated beyond reason. And no sooner had he received his original diagnosis than I had come along, offending his every sensibility, and he mine, and I slapped him, hard enough almost to make him topple over, humiliating him in public. He sat and stewed away for years, thinking about me up on Frenchman's Hill in my castle. How it ate at him! Then, recently, the hammer had come down on him, told he had only weeks or so to live, so he must have thought, What have I to lose now? A holy man so full of furious rage that he had decided, after that day, to plot against me. Then, one day while visiting the deadworld, he stumbled across the wandering guilt-ridden spirit of my poor father.

He went on, sounding a little more reasonable, now that he'd had a moment to gather himself. "I have long been interested in the unorthodox side of things. I was recruited to the Order during my third year at the Seminary."

"The Order?"

"The Order of Pentacles, Mrs Black."

I remembered Mr Brown telling me about Father William's connections with other organisations and so forth.

My God, what have I stumbled into here?

"So you had me framed for your 'murder'…"

"*I was out of time!*"

"You were out of your feeble mind!"

"*Framing you was the better idea!* In any case, I was dying, moment by precious moment…"

"Julia said you were a poor wretch of a thing when she saw you. All confused, sitting on the tram, looking out at the city around you, wondering what on Earth had happened. You weren't supposed to come *here*, were you? You knew about this place, but you still believed in the charcoal of your heart that when it was your turn, you would go to that other place, right? This must surely just be limbo, a way-station. Maybe there were further tests for you, things to prove? How confusing for you! It was all a terrible mistake. But there was no mistake, was there? You daily spat on your precious Bible, and you came here to torment the tormented, but you nevertheless *believed* in the

Biblical afterlife, didn't you? Godless heathens might wind up here, dazed and confused, but you, you were different. You were a man of God. And yet, here you are, just like the rest of us."

All I heard for a while was his wet, sticky breathing. He'd lost his own poise. "It *was* a mistake! God betrayed me again!" He suffered another, withering, coughing fit.

"It must have been lovely, then, finding a friendly face on that tram."

"Your Aunt Julia was a fine lady. In other circumstances..."

I snorted. "My Aunt Julia pitied you."

"She was a good listener."

We said nothing for a long time. I heard him swallowing such tears as he was capable of expressing. I swallowed my own. He said, "She's gone to a better place. A better place than... than this."

"Damn you!" I managed, my voice hoarse, after a while. "Damn you and your lies."

"Lies, Mrs Black? Fair enough. I have told many lies. But I can tell you one thing that's absolutely true."

I said nothing.

He went on. "Your father."

"What now?"

"It wasn't your father's espionage for the Germans that he confessed to me. He dealt with that on his first day here, a decade or more ago. No. He had a greater, more serious burden weighing on him, Mrs Black."

"There's more? Even now, you continue to torment me?" I kept thinking of Mr Brown's instruction to keep the bastard talking. Talking was the last thing I wanted to do.

"Your father. Yes. He told me to tell you he was sorry."

I was confused. "I beg your pardon? What?"

"He was sorry, Mrs Black. The awful burden he carried with him, even after he had been absolved of his crimes, was you. He deeply regretted that he had not been a better father to you."

I could not speak. Tears welled in my eyes. My heart pounded.

The wreck of Father William went on. "He told me he had always wanted a son, but instead had a daughter, a beautiful, intelligent young woman, and he had no notion of what to do with you. It kept him awake at night. He prayed for guidance. He didn't understand. Before I took his soul, he had one final request. He wanted me to tell you that he loved you. I promised I would, if I had a chance."

I was crying, but I managed to say, "Thank you."

*

The doctor, a woman, arrived later. Father William had not left; he sat on an empty bunk nearby, spent, hardly able to breathe, wheezing moistly. I was alive with thought, and there was so much to take in, and to try to understand. Quite apart from what he'd told me about my father—could I believe him? Couldn't he have simply been telling me what I most wanted to hear about my father? It was impossible to know one way or another. It was maddening. I wanted to believe him. I wanted that perhaps more than anything. I certainly wanted that more than I wanted to know everything else he'd told me. My father a traitor and spy. Antony the spy sent to recruit him. It made me sick to think about it, even now.

Then there was this other business. This "Order of Pentacles", with their supernatural shock-troops; they were the other side, no doubt playing for control of all of reality. I burned inside, thinking about it. I seethed, like molten glass. This sad old remnant of a man was not the only one who knew about towering, all-consuming hatred.

I remembered my instructions. Had I drawn him out enough? Had I done enough to make sure Father William went down for the rest of whatever sort of life he had coming? For a moment I considered whether I should moderate my hatred, because after all he had told me my father loved me—the more I thought about it, the more it seemed like lies, and the worst of lies, for pretending at such intimacy. I could have killed him.

The doctor came in with a young, pretty nurse. Both looked worn out, as though they had been on duty for three days straight. Which made me wonder: just where were we? There were no windows in here that I could see from where I was parked. The air, reeking of antiseptic and of course Father William's suppurations, was vile. No fresh air had been through here in a long time.

The nurse moved Father William to a corner of the room. "Come along then, Father. I'm just popping you over here for a bit. Is that all right?" He said nothing in return, but I heard sticky, wet movements and I caught a fresh waft of his smell. The doctor looked competent, about middle-aged, and wore a crisp white coat with stethoscope but no name-tag. I caught her glancing at Father William, and I suspected she would have preferred to carry out this procedure without his supervision. She smiled at me. It was that cool, polite smile doctors employ to "set the patient at ease".

"How are we today, Mrs Black?" she said, snapping on rubber gloves.

"If you're going to kill me, make it fast."

The doctor smiled again; this time she looked genuinely amused. "I say, we're not going to kill you." Smiling, there was something about the doctor that looked odd. I stared at her as she busied herself with some sort of machinery behind me. I heard her giving the nurse complicated instructions, and getting impatient when the girl didn't do things quickly enough. "No, Sister—like *this!*" She leaned across me, and adjusted something on a machine.

I said, "Would you at least do me the favour of telling me what's going to happen?"

"Of course, of course," the doctor said, without coming back into sight. "We just need to decant your immortal soul. Shouldn't take more than a moment."

38

I laughed. I must have misheard her. It wouldn't have surprised me. My mind was still spinning with everything Father William had told me. It was not every day that a woman learns that she has been a pawn in matters of international, and even supernatural, espionage, for example. Nor was it every day that she learns that her husband only used her to get to her father. Presumably, too, my father knew about this, and never once told me about it, as one might expect, and which further undermined Father William's parting gift to me. So I was having a big day, one might say.

And yet, I was fairly sure that the doctor had just said that she proposed to take my immortal soul from me. It raised the question: what would become of me, once I had been relieved of this numinous burden? Would I be up and about in a few days, and taking gentle walks around the grounds of the hospital, perhaps, eating bland jellies and putting up a brave face when my relatives dropped by to provide a bit of moral support?

So, even as I heard an electric humming sound, growing in power, and as I watched the nurse, from the corner of my left eye, smearing some kind of eucalpytus-smelling gelid substance to the contacts of a thing that looked wickedly like it might attach to my head, I managed to inquire, quietly, "Excuse me…"

The nurse looked up and smiled at me. "Yes, dear?"

I flashed for a terrible dizzying moment on a memory flood of Aunt Julia. And the last time I had seen her, she was evaporating into mist. Because those soldiers had shot her. There had been so much blood. At the time I had been too much in shock to even register this, but she had been full of blood, and it had gushed out everywhere, spreading over the expensive carpets, and even the blood had dissolved into that eerie mist. I remembered that now.

Oh, Julia, I'm so sorry. So very sorry. I was having trouble breathing.

The nurse was saying, "You'll be just fine, Mrs Black. Nothing to worry about at all."

The doctor commented, out of my sight, "We've got the very latest machine here. Very expensive it was, too." That machine was humming loudly now. It sounded like malignant things whirring around with electric glee.

"But why...why do you want my soul?"

Before either the doctor or the nurse could answer, Father William, from the far corner of the room, piped up: "It's the best part of you. Source of almost limitless power, Mrs Black. A magician with a decanted soul can work the most powerful magic there is, for a while. It's a profound sensation, reaching into the heart of so much power, and bending it to your will. A humbling feeling. As if God Himself is at your beck and call."

It was odd. For a man who was telling me about the marvels of great power, he sounded sick and weak as he said it. I was reminded, for a moment, of stories I had heard of people who had succumbed to opium and cocaine, and who had given it up. They spoke of the drug the same way, with a kind of bitter longing.

"Well," I said, feeling strange in my mind, as if the rational part of me were trying to flee my head. "You're not having my soul, I can tell you that right now!" I noticed I sounded eerily like my mother, saying this.

"Mrs Black," the doctor said, leaning in so I could see her. Her perfume was delicate; her green eyes were kind. "You have no choice in the matter. I mean, this is why you were sent to us. This is your purpose."

"Purpose? I beg your pardon? I came here to find His Holiness over there. There was this rather singular man, Mr Brown, who offered me a choice, that—"

"Yes, Mrs Black," the doctor said. "Mr Brown is one of ours. He sent you here."

Father William added, even as a cold numb horror spread through my body, "You are a creative soul, my dear lady. Your...imagination enhances your soul's power. Whoever is granted access to all that raw energy..." He made a wet hissing sound that I realised, after a moment, was his idea of whistling with awe.

I started struggling. I'd struggled before, but now I did not care if I broke or tore things, and I did not mean the restraining straps.

The nurse came over and patted my hand. "Now now, Mrs Black. If you struggle like this, I'll have no choice but to sedate you." She smiled an airy little smile that looked so reassuring and so innocent.

My mind revolted. I screamed. I fought the restraints. As I convulsed, as I felt straps cut through my skin and my muscles wrenched and tore, I could also hear the doctor saying, "I think we might need a bit of an injection for the patient, Sister."

The doctor managed to attach that cold metal headset over my temples, despite my frantic efforts to throw it off. I could feel and smell the sticky substance on the contacts. *"You are not taking my soul! You are not taking it!"*

The nurse appeared, bearing a large glass syringe, needle attached, full of something that looked like viscous water. She flicked the side of the barrel to remove bubbles. "Now now, Mrs Black. I'm afraid you're only doing this to yourself. You do realise that, don't you?"

Still I struggled; still I fought. I knew I had torn muscles, ripped flesh; everything burned with pain; there was blood everywhere, horribly lubricating my struggles.

Then a strange, harsh chattering sound erupted from somewhere outside. It came in repeated bursts, with irregular popping sounds, like fireworks going off somewhere. Under the chattering sound, I heard people screaming and running. I was so busy trying to fight these monsters that for a moment I did not comprehend what I was hearing. The doctor swore, "They're here!" and then to the nurse, "Get on with it!"

The nurse, armed with her syringe full of what could have been horse tranquiliser, turned on the doctor, jammed the needle into the doctor's backside, and drove the plunger home with the heel of her hand.

The doctor, shocked out of her wits, stared at the nurse. "But..." she said, and fell, hitting her head. She hit the floor hard, her eyes open and staring in confusion, and stayed there. Outside, it sounded like the assault was coming closer.

Father William struggled up, coughing. I still could not see him. He said, "Sister, I demand an explanation!"

She was too busy cutting my restraints with a scalpel. "Are you all right under all that blood, ma'am?" Her voice and manner were different. She was all business, with the effortless efficiency of a highly trained soldier, I noticed. There was no trace of that airy innocence at all.

My head and limbs free, circulation restored, fresh pain flooded through me. I just stared at her as she helped me sit up.

"Sister!"

The door burst open. Two men stood there, their black machine-guns smoking, charcoal-grey berets perched over one side of their heads, looking like the commandos of the occult who had captured me and killed Julia. Their hollow eye-sockets managed to look full of dark purpose. I still could not speak. There was too much noise. So much screaming. The War had come to me after all. One of the soldiers said, "Everything under control in here?"

"Just about. Be right with you," the nurse said.

"Righto," he said, and they left.

I managed, "What in God's name...?" I rubbed at my wrists. The blood was shocking to see.

Father William approached, grabbing the nurse. He held her by the shoulders. I did not know how the nurse could stand it, but she did. She let him grab her, and she stood there, staring up into the depths of his hood, not intimidated or frightened at all. "Father William Dennis," she said, still with that icy, competent tone, "you are hereby under arrest, according to the terms specified in Article Four, Section Twelve of the Balance of Universal Powers Treaty of 1904." She produced a small, flat pistol from a pocket.

He muttered and blustered, pushing her away. "You're threatening me—with *that*?"

"Please be aware, sir, that everything you have so far said to Mrs Black has been taken down, and will be used against you at trial. You are entitled to legal counsel. If you cannot afford adequate counsel, counsel will be provided at nominal cost. Do you understand these rights?"

He stood there, staring, first at the nurse, then down at me. So, I thought, all I had to do was talk to him, and let him hang himself. I couldn't help imagining him talking to my father, absolving him of his own sins. At length, Father William started laughing, in so far as it was possible for him to laugh, then coughed so hard he needed to lean against my bed. Once he recovered his monstrous composure, he smiled at the nurse, nodded to me, then turned and took a step towards the door.

"Take one more step," the nurse said, "and I will shoot you."

"You wouldn't dare," he gurgled, and shuffled on.

She fired. It was so loud I could only barely hear it. Smoke filled the room.

He had stopped cold, hands raised.

"Next time," she said, "I won't shoot the floor."

"I don't...I don't understand!"

"I'll second that," I said.

Two different soldiers appeared at the door, one of them with a bloodied bandage wrapped around his upper arm. "Heard a bit of a bang, love. Everything all right?"

The nurse smiled, and pushed Father William's shambling form at them. They flinched at his odour. "Cuff him. I've given him his rights and charges."

"Section Twelve?"

"At the very least," she said. "Give me a while. I might think of more."

The soldiers cuffed Father William's wrists. I could not look. They led him away.

She turned to me. "I must apologise for all of that."

"I beg your pardon?"

"All the... carry-on outside. The guns. All of that."

"That's quite all right. Rather that than have my soul sucked out of me, frankly."

She nodded ruefully. "That was never going to happen, ma'am. I had a contingency plan, in the event the assault was late."

"You might have let me know."

"I needed Father William and the doctor to believe they were safe. I can only imagine how..." She trailed off.

"Indeed. You can only imagine."

I noticed I could no longer hear guns and screams. I supposed the winning troops were mopping up out there. "Where *are* we, then? What is this...?" I looked around the room.

"Order of Pentacles Outpost Six, Alpha Zone."

"No, I mean, where *are* we?"

"Ah," she said. "Still jolly old Thanatos. Out in what you might perceive as the countryside."

"Right. So, about Mr Brown. Was that...?"

"He works with us. Rather a complicated relationship. You were never in danger. We just needed to get Father William and his nasty mates to make a fatal mistake, come out of hiding, so we could locate this outpost. You have our gratitude. And, on a personal note, Mrs Black, I am sorry about your father, your husband, and of course your Aunt Julia. For what it's worth, there are worlds beyond this one. Millions of worlds."

I stared. "I don't quite follow..."

"You write scientific romances. You dream of travelling to other stars, and other worlds."

"It's crossed my mind." I was thinking that I must have gone mad.

"Here, when we talk about 'the deadworld,' we do not only speak of one planet, as such. It would more accurately be called 'the universe of the dead'. Because, if you think about it, about all the people throughout history who have died..."

"They could not all be squeezed into one world," I said, starting to see.

"They've spread out. They've gone to the stars. At a certain point in their time here, they learn to fly like birds through space."

"You're saying Julia is out there, somewhere?"

"Somewhere, ma'am."

I sat and said nothing for a long while, as the nurse cleaned my wounded wrists and ankles, removing the blood, bandaging them up. It was a lot to absorb at once.

"Thank you. That's...that helps." I thought of Julia out there, flying across the universe. "Will I see her again, do you think?"

"Never say never," she said.

"And what about me? Father William said my time was up, that I was stuck here."

The nurse checked her fob watch. "Um, no, actually. You still have three hours, give or take."

"Three hours!"

"Until extraction."

"You make me sound like a troublesome tooth."

She smiled sadly. "At least you get to go back."

"There's one thing," I said, nervous now.

"Yes, ma'am?"

"My husband, Antony Black. Is he here somewhere? Do you know?"

"Not me, no, sorry. Never heard of him, in any case."

"It's just, I need to know." I hated how weak my voice sounded as I said that.

"He's dead, he's one of us?"

"I don't know. That's the trouble."

"Ask at the Great Library, then. If he's here, he's there, if you..."

"I take your meaning. Thank you. That's most helpful."

One of the commandos came back into the room, tall and strapping. He had a smell of battle about him. He asked after me. I said I would be fine. "Any chance of a lift back home?" I said.

39

I woke in Ward B of Rockingham Hospital. Only a few weak lights were on. A nursing sister sat at the head of the ward, monitoring the room. All was peaceful, but for some gentle snores from other patients. Rutherford was there, looking tired, reading a book, sitting quietly next to the bed, eating grapes from a brown paper bag. It was a wet night outside. I had never been so happy to hear rain.

I went to speak, but my voice was dry. I coughed and gasped.

Rutherford looked up, stunned, blinking. "Oh...! Ah..."

He allowed me a brief smile, before striding off to get the nurse.

They kept me there for several long weeks, recovering. My voice returned. Rutherford visited every day; sometimes he brought Vicky or Sally or even Murray. Ryan, they said, was much too busy cleaning up his latest catastrophic accident. "We thought you were dead," Vicky said one day. "The police told us. It was in the paper."

Rutherford said, "I have of course saved all of the clippings about your death and obituary."

"You are too kind," I said.

He nodded minutely, and went on. "I should also mention that we organised a memorial service in your honour. There was no—" He paused here to catch his breath and resumed. "There was no body to bury, but we managed as best we could, under the circumstances."

I had not considered this. "A memorial service..."

"It was a very tasteful service. In Rockingham."

"Oh God. Did Gordon attend?"

"I'm afraid not, ma'am. He did send a thoughtful card to the house."

"I see. I—"

"Yes, ma'am. It was a shame to see the poor attendance, it must be said."

I thought about this. Who would come to the funeral of a known murderer—and the murderer of a priest, at that? I did not know if I would attend such a funeral. I also thought of my reclusive ways. Perhaps I could essay a few changes to my routines.

We sat in silence for a long moment. Rutherford looked embarrassed. He offered to fetch me a cup of tea. I said, "Do any of you know how I came to be here?"

"Two days after you... er, well, 'died', ma'am..." Vicky opened.

Sally finished, "We got a telephone call from someone. Didn't leave his name. He just said you were here, and you were going to be all right, and that."

"He didn't leave his name? No details at all?"

"Nothing." Vicky nodded at that.

Rutherford said, "I motored up here, and, as promised, here you were."

"No-one told you how I came to be here? None of the doctors, or anyone like that?"

"No-one would tell me anything at all, ma'am. Believe me, I did endeavour to find out."

"How long was I... out?"

"You were unconscious for nine days."

I thought. Nine days unconscious, plus two days at that mysterious warehouse Mr Brown had described, plus several weeks stuck here eating awful food and all the grapes a person could manage, would make today...

Sometime in early August?

"My deadline!"

Rutherford said, "I sent a telegram to your publishers, ma'am. They were greatly saddened to learn of your death. They sent a beautiful wreath for your memorial..." He looked as uncomfortable discussing it as I felt. He added, "I have not yet advised them of your revival, so to speak."

*

On another occasion, Rutherford, by himself, appeared one evening, bearing the latest edition of the *Pelican River Record*. "I thought you might find this of interest, ma'am," he said, handing me the thin paper. He remained standing in the familiar at-ease position.

"No grapes tonight, Rutherford?"

"I believed you would prefer to see the newspaper, if I may be so bold."

I unfolded it and saw the headline:

WAR DESERTER CONVICTED IN PRIEST SLAYING

Startled, I read the first few paragraphs. Cox wrote that the homicide case against me, which had looked so strong, had been abandoned. The crucial fingerprint evidence, it appeared, proved "unreliable under expert scrutiny". In fact, the article went on, the police had "stumbled" on a fresh lead in the "baffling case" when a "deranged former soldier, Mr Alfred Kinney", of no fixed address, was brought in for questioning on an unrelated matter. It had subsequently developed that Mr Kinney's fingerprints were a much closer match for those found on Father William's letter-opener and in his study. Mr Kinney, it further developed, was a deserter from military service who had been on the run in the backblocks of the countryside for quite some time. His attack on Father William was, apparently, "a desperate robbery attempt gone horribly wrong". Cox went on to lay out the police case, describing how, that fateful night, Mr Kinney had broken into Father William's cottage looking for food, money, or anything of value, and Father William had discovered the "mad-eyed killer" in his study. The bitter irony, of course, was that Father William had no money.

The article concluded with a formal apology, in large print, addressed to "the memory of Mrs Ruth Elizabeth Black, the noted local author, whose fine reputation has been unjustly tarnished by this sordid affair".

I laughed, reading this last part. I laughed a great deal. "*Local author! Local!*" When Rutherford exhibited signs of concern, I said to him, "When we get back home, Rutherford, we're inviting Bluey Cox here to dinner. He's a scholar and a gentleman!"

*

Life eased back to something resembling normal, once I came home. I was still trying to sort through everything I had learned, and everything I was still feeling. It helped that I had taken, every Friday afternoon when I visited the Commercial Hotel, to "shouting the bar", as they say here. People came up to me saying things like, "I never knew you was such a top bloody sort!" A lady knows she has arrived when the locals say such things about her.

It helped, too, when I contacted my publishers in London to advise them that reports of my death were, as a wise man once said, premature. Apparently my demise released me from the contract for *Too Many Worlds*, and their lawyers said that my "return to life" could not be used in order to make me comply with the contract's terms. So I was off the hook. I was glad. I had long decided that that book was more trouble than it was worth, and I happily abandoned it, despite the great amount of time and work I had invested in it. I had also learned over the years that failed books could be stripped for parts, so it was not a complete loss. In any case, I told my editor, I had a better idea for a book that I thought they might like.

40

Towards the end of winter, one afternoon, I sat wrapped in heavy blankets, gloves and a thick woollen cap out on the seaweed-strewn beach of Hagan's Head. Rain seemed likely. Cold south-westerlies blasted sea-spray against my face. Seagulls and terns, adults and juveniles alike, huddled nearby on the sand, their spindly legs folded beneath them, all of them angled into the wind. The roaring grey sea churned and roiled.

I was still consumed with everything that had happened and everything I had learned these past few months. Finding my equilibrium again would take time. I still did not know what to make of Antony, other than that he was a peerless actor, a proper bastard, and I could not decide whether I wanted him back because he was my husband and I loved him, or whether I wanted him back because I hated him and wanted to kill him myself. He had destroyed my father; but my father, for his own reasons, had needed to be destroyed, I could see that now. I thought about all those afternoons I spent with Father's shooting parties, out in the countryside, hunting pheasants. How many of those other men, friends of Father's, had been who I had been told they were? What schemes had my father been involved in, beyond the ones I now knew about? Would I ever know? I thought of whatever remained of my father's spirit, on the wing across the stars, along with Julia. While Julia would love it, I knew Father would absolutely hate it.

Indeed, I was so caught up in this busy world within my head that at first I did not hear the alarming new sound cutting through the bracing wind off the sea.

I first realised something was seriously amiss when all the sea birds I had been watching abruptly took to the air, squealing and squawking, and flapped further up the beach.

I said, "That's odd," and looked around.

I looked behind me, where a storm of beach sand, shell fragments, stray bits of seaweed, all whirled hither and yon in a great howling vortex.

And I heard an engine, something like a spluttering motorcar engine, coughing a little, choking perhaps on all the sand. "What on Earth?"

In the centre of the whipping vortex of noise and sand, a machine of some unearthly sort had formed, as if from the sand and grit of the beach, as if it were building itself, grain by grain, as I watched. I got up, and stood well back, holding a hand across my eyes and nose.

Soon I could smell the engine's exhaust; it reeked of kerosene.

And there, in the centre of this insane machine, was none other than Gordon Duncombe, wearing goggles, working a bank of levers and pedals inside what I now could see was a sort of gondola, as if his life depended on it. He took a fraction of a moment to wave at me as he attempted to shut the contraption down.

"Gordon...!" I was stupefied.

At length, I heard the engine splutter and die. The sandstorm lost its energy and the sand settled back to the ground. I could once again feel the cold wind from the sea at my back. What remained was listing at a slight angle on the beach, and venting clouds of thick black smoke from what I gathered was some sort of exhaust. The acrid smoke stank. It crossed my mind that something inside the machine might explode. Gordon, I could see, was trying to investigate, lifting some sort of hatch—more dense smoke billowed out and was swept away on the breeze. I yelled to him to get out of there while he could.

He heard me, nodded, looked regretful, and leapt clear, just as the machine exploded.

I dumped my blankets, raced over and managed to grab him and pull him down the beach, away from the conflagration.

As we stood there, he pulled off his gloves and lifted his goggles, revealing a clean area around his eyes. "Are you sure you're all right?" he said, checking me over.

"I seem to be quite well," I said, clutching my hat with one hand, over the roar of the sea and the burning machine. "How are you?"

He was studying his pocket watch, and muttering to himself. I noticed that his pocket watch was highly unusual: there were two extra hands, and three smaller dials embedded in the larger face, whose readings I couldn't make out. Gordon, his hands shaking, was peering at it as if it was the most important thing in the world. He said, "That was two years, three months and nineteen days! Which would make today…"

He told me what he thought should be today's date, and he was correct. I told him so. "Thank God, Ruth," he said. "Then it hasn't happened yet. We still have time."

"Gordon? I beg your pardon? You—"

Gordon was leading me up the beach away from the conflagration, talking much too fast to make any sense, rambling, talking in circles, repeating himself. "I had to warn you. I had to make sure you had time to prepare. You…" He was patting his many pockets, searching for something, very distracted. "There's a crash, a big crash. I had some newspaper clippings in a notebook, I—" He was unable to find anything in his pockets beside the usual assortment of useless bits and pieces. "My notebook—" He turned and stared back at his burning machine. "My notebook…"

"Gordon," I said. "Gordon—it's all right. Slow down. Take a few deep breaths. Yes, that's it. Whatever it is, it will be all right. So—"

"The *Navigator* works, Ruth. Time travel. It actually worked! My God—it actually worked!"

Whilst I was overjoyed to see Gordon after all the months

of silence and solitude, it was deeply troubling to see my old friend like this, so agitated, so confused. He was still rambling, still digging in his pockets, still trying to tell me about some crash that was coming, some global catastrophe. He sounded, and looked, quite mad, and that was a dreadful thing to see. Had his journey through time affected him?

He said, "I had a notebook. All the newspaper clippings I could find, I pasted them in the notebook, I wrote copious notes, don't you see? I had to show you evidence, Ruth. I knew neither you nor anyone else would believe me without evidence." Again, he was staring back at the wreck. I started to understand. "You left it in your machine?"

He started to run back to the wreck, but stopped after a few steps, his hands clutching his knees, gasping in pain, swearing under his breath. I caught up to him, and held him. "It's all right, Gordon."

"No. It's not all right. You don't understand. I saw it all. I was there. The whole world ruined. The whole world. But I don't remember the details, you see. I don't remember what caused it, how it happened. I had it all documented. But my mind—it feels scrambled, as if part of me is still there, but I can't reach it. Ruth, we have to prepare! We have to tell people."

I was not at all sure what to make of all this, but I felt the most profound sadness. My dear old Gordon Duncombe, reduced to this.

He said, "Let me just go back to the *Navigator*."

"It's too dangerous. It could go up again."

"The notebook was carefully wrapped. It might be—"

"Gordon. Look at me. I will not have it. You are not well, and now that you're back, I have no desire to lose you once more. Once... Once was enough." I nearly broke down, saying that. He looked up at me.

"I really must apologise, Ruth. When I saw you last. I was..." He shook his head, and stared for a moment at the weed-strewn sand between us.

I smiled. "I really meant it when I said you should take my arm."

He was still shaking his head, still frustrated, and trying to peer at his unusual pocket watch. He said something I could not hear. I noticed a lot of dog dander on his clothes.

I said, "I beg your pardon?"

After an anxious moment, Gordon suddenly hugged me. He hugged me like few people ever have, and like he certainly never had. In my ear, he said, his voice was not steady, "I thought I'd lost you..."

"Never, Gordon. Never." My eyes stung, and I wiped them.

When he let me go, he looked me up and down, and I could see he was embarrassed. He said, "In any case, if any limbs were to be sacrificed, it would have had to be one of mine."

"Oh," I said, but as I thought about it, I could see his point.

"And, the thing is, it was my choice to be there, with you that night. I had no-one else to blame. It was unjust of me to..." His voice faltered, and he looked away, towards the burning machine.

"Two years, you say?"

"What? Oh, yes. Quite so. I had to tell you about the crash, Ruth. You—"

"Yes, you said." I was thinking about the last time someone close to me felt they had to see me as soon as possible with urgent news, and a chill went through me that had nothing to do with the stiff wind from the sea. "You honestly can't remember what it was, this crash?"

"It's as if it were at the very tip of my mind." He slapped his leg with his leather flying cap, still staring at the wreck. It was only too easy to imagine him going straight home tonight and starting work on a new time machine.

At length, Gordon stood there staring at me, all his pockets turned out, empty, the most desolate look on his face I had ever seen. "Gordon, whatever it is, whatever this crash is, it will be all right. Do you hear me? It will be fine. We will survive, you and me. Yes? We will stand fast."

"Ruth, you don't understand—it's...dear God I've been such a fool."

"Don't worry. It doesn't matter. You're here. You made it back here, and you've warned me. We can prepare, as I say. It's all right, Gordon."

"It was important, Ruth. I had to reach you."

"Gordon, it will be all right. Come on, let's go back to the house, have a cuppa—"

"How could I have been so stupid!"

I gathered my blankets and we walked away up the beach towards the Tulip. Gordon stopped me, pale, even shocked. He said, "What do we do about the other me?"

I turned and looked at him, then the problem became clear. "The other Gordon. Yes, of course. Oh dear. Yes."

There were now two Gordon Duncombes here in Pelican River: this one with me, who had come from the future; and the other, who was already here, and no doubt at his property, possibly even now working on his time-machine project. And who still refused to speak to me. It hurt, that silence.

"Should we go and see him, do you think?" I said.

Gordon was thinking hard. "I don't remember you coming to visit with this version of me in tow."

"Maybe time isn't fixed."

"I'm not sure it's a good idea. The two of us meeting, him and me. But then—although, what if...? Damn it all, Ruth. I don't know what to do."

"Leave it to me. I'll invite him to dinner tonight. You can tell him about your time machine. The pair of you can start thinking about this crash." I was not at all sure what to make of Gordon's news. It was inconceivable enough that he had actually travelled in time, let alone returned from a world lying in ruins from some nebulous catastrophe only two years away. A new war, perhaps? So soon? It was possible, I supposed, but again, it all seemed so unlikely, so remote. Was the future set? Were we doomed to that fate? Or could we avert Gordon's catastrophe? It was the stuff of philosophic nightmares.

We'd reached the Tulip. I was exhausted from the long slog through the sand. I listened again to the roar and thump of the surf, and the cries of the seabirds. The endless sea, grey and churning, stretched as far as the eye could see, like the future.

There was a Great Library in Thanatos, that nurse had told me. If Antony were there in the deadworld—the *universe* of the dead—he would be listed there. My head was filling with plans.

We got into the Tulip. I started the engine.

Then Gordon asked something he had clearly been wanting to ask, but lacked the courage, perhaps. "What was it like, being dead?"

I smiled, thinking about running for my life from the commandos, about the explosion of raspberry-ness in my mouth, about the weird quality of the light in the city, the unbearable heat of humiliation when I fell over in the middle of Purvis's department store.

"It made me feel alive."

I looked out the window down onto the beach and the burning machine. "What should we do about the wreckage, do you think?"

Gordon said, sounding like his old self again, "I'll speak to the fire brigade in the morning."

Acknowledgements

This book, like all books, has had many friends in the course of its long life. When it came to specific research details, several people and organisations really helped me out, including the St John Ambulance service; the WA Police Historian, Peter Conole, who gave me a great deal of information about police work in 1920s Western Australia; the British Government's Ministry of Defence, who, when asked by some doofus writer in Australia about how they did certain things during the First World War, were only too happy to help, and sent two potted histories of the organisation, which answered all questions. As always, I am amazed at what people will tell you if you just ask them.

There is no real-world town of Pelican River in Western Australia, but there is the seaside town of Mandurah, one of my favourite spots in the world, and which served as a very loose model for the fictitious Pelican River. In putting together my portrayal of Pelican River I mined the heck out of a volume of local history, *Mandurah: Water Under the Bridge*, by Jill Burgess (1988, City of Mandurah), which provided many colourful and intriguing stories about the town's past (including the bit about cattle wandering loose in town from time to time). Other valuable resources were the Facebook groups Lost Perth and Lost Mandurah, which are filled with vintage photographs from the period in question, and which did a great deal by way of showing the look of the historical Mandurah. Pelican River, as shown in this book, is considerably more developed.

Speaking of Facebook: I cannot thank enough my friends and supporters, many of them also writers, for their tireless support and encouragement of me and my writing efforts and struggles over many years. You folks are a big part of why I'm still here, and still plugging away. This goes double for my Canadian and American friends (including those on Twitter), whom I hardly ever see in real life, for hanging in there with me, a constant source of enthusiasm and love.

My thanks also to Fremantle Press, who gave this book a good home, and in particular to Publisher Georgia Richter and Editor Extraordinaire Naama Amram (who did wonders not only in editing the manuscript but also as a volunteer research assistant, helping out with countless details small and large throughout the editing process). My thanks to them also for not freaking out about the idea of elves and all the supernatural woo-woo in the book. This finished volume would not look nearly so good without their peerless contributions. Any mistakes remaining are mine.

I would also like to thank my literary agent, Ineke Prochazka, for negotiating the deal with Fremantle Press; and Robert J. Sawyer for helping me fully grok the contract details.

Last, and most importantly, my wife Michelle and my parents Marie and Ken Bedford kept me pushing through. I could not have made it this far without them.

WINNER
T.A.G.
HUNGERFORD
AWARD

THE WEAVER FISH

ROBERT EDESON

'Evocative writing, in which the science is an essential
character. The ideas stimulate and mesmerise.'
Robyn Williams, ABC Radio National's The Science Show

Cambridge linguist Edvard Tøssentern, presumed dead, reappears after a balloon crash. When he staggers in from a remote swamp, gravely ill and swollen beyond recognition, his colleagues at the research station are overjoyed. But Edvard's discovery about a rare giant bird throws them all into the path of an international crime ring.

The Weaver Fish is fiendishly clever ... a novel unlike anything you've read before. Books+Publishing

Evocative writing, in which the science is an essential character. The ideas stimulate and mesmerise. Robyn Williams, ABC Radio National, The Science Show

• ISBN 9781922089526 • EISBN 9781922089533

Conway inhabits an apocalyptic future in a continent caught up in a violent struggle for control of water. On the run from the Water Board flunkies who hate him but who need his water divining skills to survive, Conway dreams his way back to the arrival of Europeans in Western Australia. Here, Captain Charles Fremantle chooses to throw off the mantle of Empire and join the Nyoongar people. History will never be the same again.

Docker isn't the first writer to imagine our founding fathers might have spilled a lot less blood and wreaked a lot more good but the scenes he conjures up on the banks of the Swan are a tantalising vision of what might have been. Sydney Morning Herald

• ISBN 9781921696947   • EISBN 9781921696954

First published 2015 by
FREMANTLE PRESS
25 Quarry Street, Fremantle 6160
(PO Box 158, North Fremantle 6159)
Western Australia
www.fremantlepress.com.au

Consultant editor Georgia Richter
Editor Naama Amram
Cover design Ally Crimp
Cover photograph '1920s Silhouette of woman standing in doorway carrying
candle holder', ClassicStock 846-02797418

 A catalogue record for this
book is available from the
National Library of Australia

ISBN 9781925161410 (paperback)
ISBN 9781925161441 (ebook)

Fremantle Press is supported by the Western Australian State Government
through the Department of Cultural Industries, Tourism and Sport.

Publication of this title was assisted by the Commonwealth Government
through Creative Australia, its arts funding and advisory body.